W9-AXQ-577
WITHDRAWN

Judah's Wife

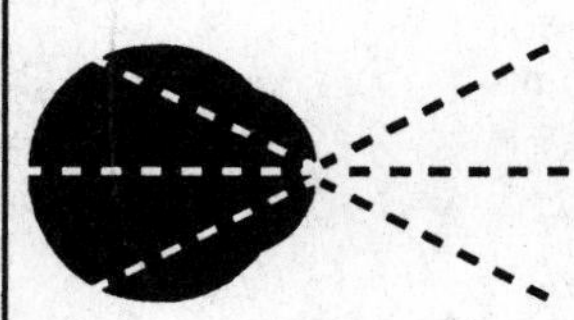

THE SILENT YEARS

Judah's Wife

A NOVEL OF THE MACCABEES

Angela Hunt

THORNDIKE PRESS
A part of Gale, a Cengage Company

Farmington Hills, Mich • San Francisco • New York • Waterville, Maine
Meriden, Conn • Mason, Ohio • Chicago

Thorndike Press, a part of Gale, a Cengage Company.

Thorndike Press® Large Print Christian Historical Fiction.
The text of this Large Print edition is unabridged.
Other aspects of the book may vary from the original edition.
Set in 16 pt. Plantin.

LIBRARY OF CONGRESS CIP DATA ON FILE.
CATALOGUING IN PUBLICATION FOR THIS BOOK
IS AVAILABLE FROM THE LIBRARY OF CONGRESS

ISBN-13: 978-1-4328-4936-8 (hardcover)

Published in 2018 by arrangement with Bethany House Publishers, a division of Baker Publishing Group

Printed in the United States of America
1 2 3 4 5 6 7 22 21 20 19 18

In the Christian Bible, one turns the page after Malachi and finds Matthew as if only a few days fell between the activities of the prophet and the arrival of Jesus Christ. In reality, however, four hundred so-called "silent years" lie between the Old Testament and New, a time when God did not speak to Israel through His prophets. Yet despite the prophets' silence, God continued to work in His people, other nations, and the supernatural realm.

He led Israel through a time of testing that developed a sense of hope and a yearning for the promised Messiah.

He brought the four nations prophesied in Daniel's vision to international prominence: the Babylonians, the Persians, the Greeks, and the Romans. These powerful kingdoms spread their cultures throughout civilization and united the world by means of paved highways and international sailing routes.

God also prepared to fulfill His promise to the serpent in Eden: "I will put animosity between you and the woman, and between your descendant and her descendant; he will bruise your head, and you will bruise his heel" (Gen. 3:15).

For God never sleeps, and though He may not communicate as we expect Him to, He can always speak to a receptive heart.

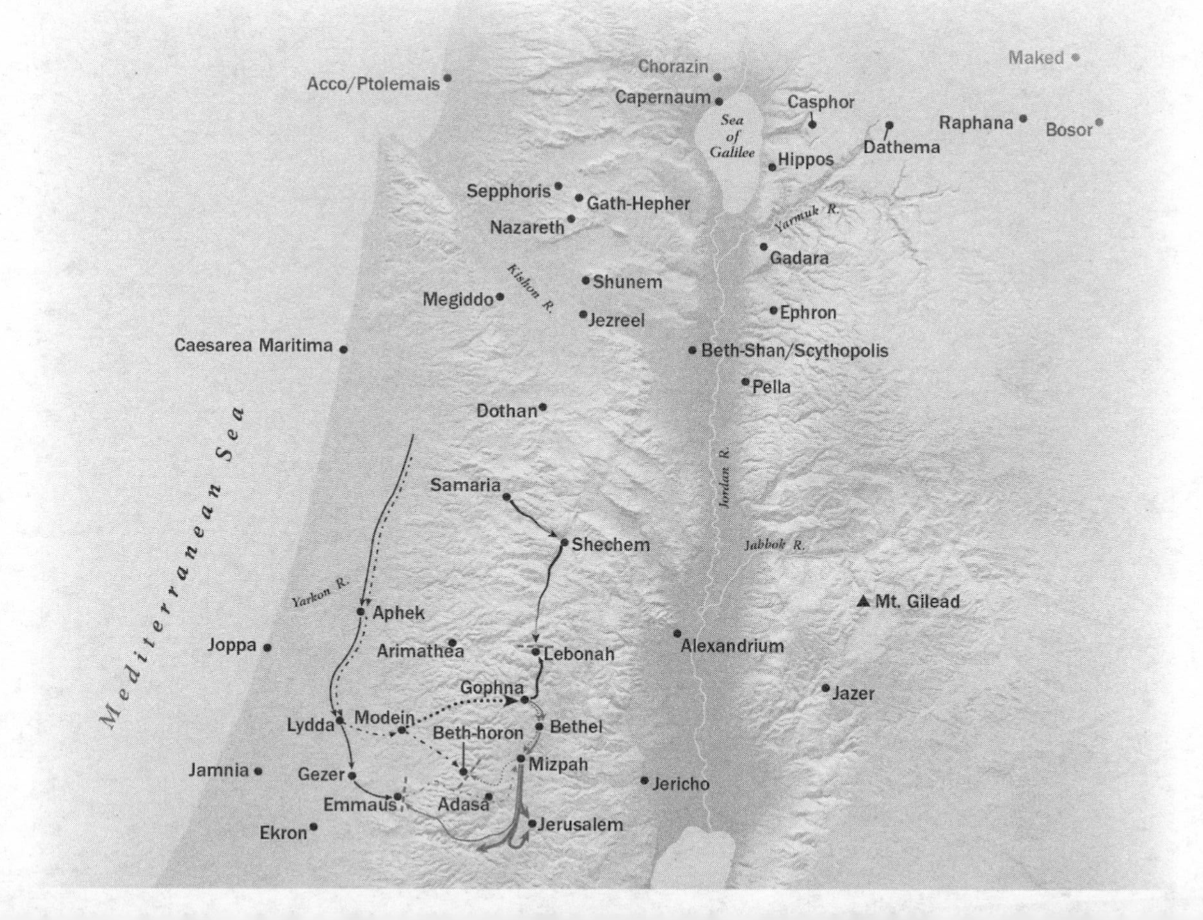

Maked
Acco/Ptolemais
Chorazin
Capernaum
Sea of Galilee
Casphor
Raphana
Bosor
Dathema
Hippos
Sepphoris
Gath-Hepher
Nazareth
Yarmuk R.
Gadara
Kishon R.
Shunem
Megiddo
Jezreel
Ephron
Caesarea Maritima
Beth-Shan/Scythopolis
Pella
Dothan
Mediterranean Sea
Samaria
Jordan R.
Shechem
Jabbok R.
Yarkon R.
Aphek
Mt. Gilead
Joppa
Arimathea
Lebonah
Alexandrium
Gophna
Jazer
Lydda
Modein
Beth-horon
Bethel
Mizpah
Jamnia
Gezer
Jericho
Emmaus
Adasa
Jerusalem
Ekron

Beth-zur
Hebron
Ziph
Dead Sea
Arnon R.
Bozrah

The Maccabean Revolt

- Battle
- Mattathias slays Modein's emissary under Antiochus and then flees to the mountains near Gophna
- Commander Apollonius of Samaria sets out to quell the Maccabean uprising but fails in the attempt
- Judah Maccabeus, along with the insurgents, leads an attack against Apollonius and kills him, taking the dead warrior's sword
- Commander Seron of Syria, a Seleucid, organizes his army to beat down the Maccabees and their uprising
- Judah Maccabeus takes Seron's army by surprise at Upper Beth-horon
- Syrian Proconsul Lysias, under the command of Nicanor, Ptolemy, and Gorgias, leads an army to Emmaus in yet another attempt to crush the uprising
- Gorgias takes 5,000 soldiers and 1,000 cavalry and moves inland with orders to capture Judah
- With the Syrian army divided, Judah and his men march to Emmaus's main camp
- Judah and men lay siege to Jerusalem until 165 BC; the Jews recover possession of the Temple

▪ ▪ ▪ ▪

PART I

▪ ▪ ▪ ▪

In those days Mattathias . . . had five sons, Johanan surnamed Gaddi, Simon called Thassi, Judas called Maccabaeus, Eleazar called Avaran, and Jonathan called Apphus.

He saw the blasphemies being committed in Judah and Jerusalem, and said, "Alas! Why was I born to see this, the ruin of my people, the ruin of the holy city, and to dwell there when it was given over to the enemy, the sanctuary given over to aliens?

Her temple has become like a man without honor; her glorious vessels have been carried into captivity. Her babes have been killed in her streets, her youths by the sword of the foe.

What nation has not inherited her palaces and has not seized her spoils? All her adornment has been taken away; no longer free, she has become a slave.

And behold, our holy place, our beauty, and our glory have been laid waste; the Gentiles have profaned it. Why should we live any longer?"

And Mattathias and his sons rent their clothes, put on sackcloth, and mourned greatly.

1 Maccabees 2:1–14

Chapter One: Leah

168 Years Before the Birth of Christ

Of the many lessons I learned in childhood, one made a permanent impression on my soul: God should be feared, and so should my father.

Experience reinforced the lesson every seventh day, when with trembling fingers my mother lit the Shabbat candles and recited the blessing. Then she sat very still while Father broke the bread and ate the meat, a luxury we enjoyed only on Shabbat. When Father had eaten his fill of the meat, vegetables, fruit, and bread, he stood and walked away, allowing me and Mother to share whatever remained.

Then we would go to the synagogue, or Father and I would go, since Mother never left the house when a bruise marked her face. I would walk behind Father through the winding alleys of Jerusalem, careful to avoid the potholes and mounds of manure in the street. I made a game of remaining in Father's shadow, for I'd be in trouble if he turned and found me missing.

When we arrived at the synagogue, I would sit with the women while Father took his place with the men. He usually sat down front, and when the men prayed I could hear his voice above the others. I would lower my head and put my fingers in my ears because I frequently heard that same voice cursing my mother, or declaring her fat, lazy, and stupid. Sometimes that voice demanded to know why he had agreed to marry such a sow, and at other times it declared her the ugliest woman in all Judea.

My mother was not fat, ugly, or lazy, so she did not cry when she heard such insults. But she seemed to draw inward, shriveling like a worm in the salt jar, until little remained of her but a pair of hands and feet destined to do Father's bidding.

While sitting in the synagogue, I would lift my gaze to the ceiling and wonder how HaShem and my father became connected. They must have been close, for Father prayed every morning with great gusto and never missed an opportunity to speak to the Torah teacher.

I would listen intently as the teacher spoke of how HaShem parted the Red Sea and massacred the pursuing Egyptians to set our ancestors free. I learned about how the Master of the universe consulted Abraham before destroying everyone in the sinful cities of Sodom and Gomorrah, and how He strengthened Joshua to rid the land of Canaanites so that we, the children of Isra'el, could live in the Promised Land. The Creator of the universe, the teacher said, had a plan and purpose for everyone.

HaShem sounded as if He were as strong as my father, and every bit as angry.

I resolved never to do anything to displease my father or HaShem. I obeyed every command and answered every call. In Father's presence my thoughts spun like a dancer as I tried to guess what he would want next, find ways to keep him calm, and think about how to prevent him from beating my mother.

I did not always succeed. When I brought him figs instead of bread, or when I put his slippers by the window instead of the door, Father would notice my mistake. "How could you have borne such a worthless child?" he would say, turning to Mother. He would strike her, and Mother would gasp and slide down the wall as I took a deep breath and stepped into the trembling space between them. If all went well, Father would go out, leaving us alone to ponder our offenses.

Later, when Mother found her voice and the marks faded from red to purple, I would curl up next to her on the pallet and whisper, "I am sorry, I am sorry, I am sorry."

She would murmur that I had nothing to be sorry for, but her voice carried no weight and her words no meaning. If I had been quicker, smarter, or more pleasant, I could have made him happy.

And a happy man had no reason to fight.

Like fronds from a palm tree, the years of my childhood fell away, one after the other. Mother and I knew our places and clung to them — she belonged at home, while I belonged in the market stall Father rented. There I sold my mother's cheeses and helped keep starvation from our door.

Father, of course, belonged everywhere, for he was a man, and men, Mother told me, were prone to wander.

One morning my friend Miriam and I were walking to the market when a young man stepped into our path. With one glance I knew he was dangerous. He wore a short linen tunic and the silly hat favored by so many Hellenes, the Jewish youths who followed the practices of the Seleucids who ruled this region. Though this young man was old enough to sprout a beard, his cheeks were bare, like those of the Gentiles who had infiltrated Jerusalem. His mouth curved in a smirk when he saw us, and his eyes snapped like a man with mischief on his mind.

"Look here," he called to a group of similarly dressed youths who loitered outside the gymnasium. "Two pretty young things out for a stroll. Where do you think they are going?"

My stomach tightened as I glanced around. Wagons and people crowded the street, but no one seemed likely to be interested in an unfolding drama involving mere girls. Miriam and I were quite alone, and if this young man convinced his friends to join him, we could easily be dragged into an alley and —

My mind slammed the door on the awful possibilities.

"Going somewhere, love?" His baritone dissolved into a breathy whisper. "Can I come along?"

Somehow I found a sliver of courage. "Leave us alone," I said, my voice thin and weak against the tumult of the street. "We want nothing to do with you."

"Really? Nothing at all?" The youth leaned

closer, and on his foul breath I detected the odor of strong drink. "I promise you, girls — I am quite fascinating. Like Zeus, I'm a lover, and I've come from the Temple where I paid my vows all night. Furthermore, I am a man who appreciates a pretty face . . . even if that face is still round with youth."

He smiled, and his gaze raked my tunic in a look that felt like a violation of several commandments. I recoiled as several of his companions approached, their faces alight with expectation.

I had heard my father speak of the despicable acts now routinely occurring at the Temple — indecent rituals dedicated to pagan gods and practiced in the sacred courts. If this young man had just come from the Temple . . .

Somehow I found my voice again. "Leave us. My father will not like this."

The young man pointedly looked around. "Is he here? Shall I call out his name?"

This drunken fool would not be dissuaded.

I grabbed Miriam's hand and squeezed it. "If he comes any closer," I whispered, "turn and *run.*"

"Sharing secrets?" The youth lifted a manicured brow. "Care to share your confidences with me?"

I retreated another step as he leaned toward us, but before I could flee, a large hand clutched the youth's shoulder and spun him around. A man stood in the street, a broad-shouldered, bearded fellow in a rough wool tunic. Clearly, he was no Hellene.

"Have you nothing better to do," the newcomer growled, "than to bother girls on the street?"

I gripped Miriam's arm as the men eyed each other. The other young men shifted, forming a semicircle around the two whose upper lips had curled like snarling dogs'. The second man had friends, too, and they formed a half circle behind him, their eyes alive with challenge.

"What sort of behemoth are you?" the Hellene asked, his voice dripping with scorn. "And what gives you the right to interrupt my conversation with those girls?"

"Those *young women,*" another young man answered, stepping up beside his bearded companion, "did not appear to be enjoying your attention. They are daughters of Abraham and deserve your respect."

The insolent youth snorted. "They are daughters of the old order," he said, flexing his fists. "Probably the whelps of farmers. Take a good look and you'll see that they have never been introduced to the wonders of the public baths."

Without warning, the big man charged the youth, and for several moments the two figures struggled against each other. In a dance of defiance they careened through the street, smashing into walls, upsetting baskets, scattering chickens, and stopping traffic. The circle of onlookers widened as the brawl continued, and Miriam teetered on the edge of full-blown panic. "Let's go," she urged, grabbing my sleeve, but I could not tear myself away.

Never in all my fourteen years had any man risen to my defense.

The atmosphere thickened with grunts and curses as the onlookers fought, bearded men pushing clean-shaven youths, the lot of them shouting and stumbling over the uneven paving stones. Miriam kept trying to drag me away, but I would not leave. Something more than our honor seemed to be at stake.

Of all the men involved in the altercation, the big one caught and held my attention. "Do you know him?" I asked Miriam, pointing.

"How would *I* know him?" Miriam shrieked, wringing her hands.

Mindful of her frayed nerves, I dragged

her into a sheltered doorway. "Calm yourself. Those youths are no longer interested in us. But since your family knows nearly everyone in Jerusalem, perhaps you know one of those men."

Miriam swallowed hard, then peeked out to study the group who had come to our aid. "The big one is Judah Maccabaeus," she said, nodding. "His family is well known in this part of the city."

I frowned. The word *maccabaeus* meant *hammerhead,* so how had he come by that name?

"Is he a carpenter?"

"No." A dimple appeared in her cheek. "My mother told me that when Judah was a child, he was so much taller than the other children that they called him *Goliath.* He didn't like the name, so he pounded on the other kids."

"He's a bully, then."

"Would a bully have stopped to help us?"

I stepped out of the doorway and peered through the crowd of onlookers to study the brawling men. Judah was the tallest of the pack, with shoulder-length hair and skin the color of raw honey. The young men who fought alongside him varied in height and build, but they shared one particular feature: each of them had remarkably large, dark eyes. They had to be brothers.

The big man and his brothers would not escape this fight without suffering some damage. A trickle of blood ran from a gouge on Judah's forehead, and a purplish bruise marked another brother's eye. Another had been pinned by one of the arrogant youths, but Judah walked over, pulled the assailant away, and then punched the Hellene in the belly.

I caught my breath as Judah lunged for the youth who had stopped us, catching the young man by the waist. The Hellene pounded on Judah's back, but Judah merely tightened his grip, straightened his legs, and lifted the other boy from the ground. The silly Greek hat flew off as Judah twirled with the boy on his shoulder, displaying his prize before an appreciative audience. Then, in one move, he dropped the arrogant youth onto the street and knelt to pin him in place. The Hellene lay limp and groaning on the stones, belligerent no more.

"It's over," I whispered, simultaneously awed and terrified by the violence that had been instigated on my behalf.

Miriam saw the look on my face and frowned. "Don't his actions please you?"

"Yes," I said. "They do. But they're so — rough."

"Violence frightens me," Miriam confessed. "Men like that are so unpredictable. My father says men should be peaceable and dignified."

"Would your brothers agree? I've seen them fight."

"True. But still . . ."

I tugged on my braid and watched the wounded warriors pick themselves up and inspect each other's cuts and bruises. None of them looked as though they would be permanently scarred.

I had seen far worse violence in my own home, but Miriam didn't need to know my secrets.

I took another look at the triumphant young man in the road, then surrendered to Miriam's insistence and let her lead me away. But I couldn't resist a glance over my shoulder. The youths from the gymnasium limped down the street while Judah and his four brothers clapped each other's shoulders and lifted their hands in victory.

I had no idea that I would soon come to know them all.

Chapter Two: Judah

"That was invigorating."

Eleazar grinned at me. "Father will be upset to hear you started a fight in the street."

"Not when he learns *why* I was fighting."

"Come on, you two," Simon called. "This is not a good day to be late."

After dusting myself off, I walked with my brothers to the Temple, then stood with them near the gates of the outer court. None of us had been inside the Temple since the horror that had occurred — Father would not allow it. But he and the other Levites still felt bound to fulfill their duties, even if it meant they did nothing but sit in a storage room and wait for the Temple's restoration.

Simon came over to whisper a private word. "Better wipe the blood off your forehead. You know how seriously he takes these things."

The feeling of accomplishment that had heartened me drained away, but Simon had always given me good advice. Though I stood a head taller than both of my older brothers, years of experience had taught me to respect them.

I spat onto my fingertips, then wiped my forehead. I licked my finger and cleaned a bloody scratch on my upper arm. I could do nothing about the dirt on my best tunic, and from where I stood I could see that Eleazar had a rip in his.

I caught my younger brother's eye, pointed to the corresponding spot on my tunic, then pointed at his. He grimaced when he saw the torn fabric at his knees.

Smiling at his awkward efforts to hide the tear, I folded my arms and looked toward the gate through which Father should soon appear.

My mother drifted through the small group of relatives and stopped next to me. "You've been fighting," she said, her gaze drifting absently over the Temple wall.

I will never understand how she knew what we had been doing.

"It couldn't be helped," I told her. "A group of upstarts threatened a couple of girls."

She looked up. "Hellenes?"

I cleared my throat; the very word brought a bad taste to my mouth. Because those who ruled over us had been influenced by a conqueror who came from a land he called *Hellas,* we called anyone who followed their precepts *Hellenes.* We expected our Seleucid rulers to be Hellenes. What we found astounding was how many Jews had become devoted advocates of all things Greek.

"They were practically wearing the uniform, complete with that ridiculous hat," I told Mother. "They must have been coming out of that cursed gymnasium when they spotted the girls."

Simon leaned into our conversation. "I've heard about what goes on in that place. Naked wrestling, for one thing. Indecency."

Mother stepped away, as a modest woman should.

"Are we talking about the Hellenes?" Eleazar came closer. "I've heard that some of our own Hebrew brothers have taken to wearing a leather strap to hide their circumcision. Others have sought out physicians to stretch the foreskin —"

"Enough." Simon held up his hand as we grimaced in unison. Hard to believe that any self-respecting Jew would undergo the pain of a medical procedure to undo the act that marked his covenant with HaShem, but we lived in a peculiar time.

Mother came closer. "What's happening in the gymnasium couldn't be worse than the obscenities taking place right in front of us," she said, proving that she had not stopped listening to our conversation. "Your father is heartbroken over the state of the Temple."

"Hard to believe he has served twenty-five years." Simon's gaze drifted over the other men lingering outside the South Gate. "I don't know how he's lasted through these troubling times."

"Harder still to believe he is fifty," Eleazar went on, giving Mother a gentle smile. "But he has the zeal of a much younger man."

"And the strength." Simon grinned. "I believe he is strong because he had to keep Judah in line. He says teaching you was often like milking a bull."

I crossed my arms and frowned. My brothers often made jokes at my expense, but what could I do about it in public? At home, I might have pounded them until they stopped laughing, but I could not do that here.

And not today. Not when so many of our friends and neighbors had come to observe a special occasion in Father's life.

The South Gate opened, a trumpet blared,

and my father's thin form appeared in the outer courtyard. I lifted my head to better see the man we all loved and respected: Mattathias the Levite, from the priestly family of Joarib. Fifty years old and ready for retirement, as the Law of Moses decreed.

When Father reached the gate, the crowd surged forward to greet him with warm embraces. "Well done, Mattathias!"

"Congratulations, Father."

"Twenty-five years! May HaShem reward you for your service."

When at last I stood before him, I couldn't find the words to express my depth of feeling. So I drew him into an embrace and released him after a moment.

"Ah, Judah." Father looked up with a wistful gleam in his eye. "Lead us home, will you? There are things I must discuss with you and your brothers."

I didn't know what occupied his thoughts, but I set off, leading my family away from a Temple that had once been the home of our God.

Chapter Three: Leah

I clung to sleep as long as I could, despite the grumbling that came from the table and the quick, light steps of my mother.

"Name of a name, can't you do anything right?" Father snapped. I opened one eye in time to see him spit out a hunk of bread. "That's not bread, it's a mouthful of desert. You've got so much sand in there it's a wonder my teeth aren't worn down to nubs."

"I am sorry," Mother whispered. With great care she slid a bowl of figs onto the table, then folded her hands and retreated to the wall. "Would you like fruit?"

"Not figs — yesterday you gave me one with teeth marks on it. How could you offer me something the rats have been at? You are a stupid, good-for-nothing creature. You bring me nothing but trouble."

Mother lowered her head, but not before shooting a quick glance toward the corner, where I pretended to sleep. Even shadowed, her eyes glowed with warning, urging me to stay abed.

Father had other ideas. "Why doesn't the girl rouse herself? I need her to get to the market."

Mother stepped forward as though she would approach me, but I saw no reason to make her cross the room and risk attracting more of Father's ire. "I am awake." I tossed off my thin blanket. "What do you want me to do, Father?"

He grunted and turned in my direction. "Set one of the finest cheeses aside for the high priest. He will stop by the stall today, so give him the cheese and take nothing for it." He lifted a finger. "Do not make a fuss, but you might mention that the usual cost for such a cheese is twenty drachmas."

"But the cost is usually ten drachmas."

A muscle clenched along his jaw, a visible warning I had learned to heed. "Forgive me, Father — I am slow to understand. You want the high priest to know how valuable the cheese is."

"Exactly." His jaw relaxed as he pushed away from the table and stepped over the long bench. "You" — his hairy finger swiveled toward Mother — "do not forget to clean my best tunic for the butcher's wedding next week. And buy bread for my dinner, so I can enjoy something good for once."

Mother tucked her chin, and we held our breath as Father walked to the door, took a last look around, and stepped outside.

Once the door closed, Mother and I both sighed.

I tied my leather belt around my waist. "Not in the best mood, is he?"

"Not the worst either, praise be to HaShem. Do not forget to set that cheese aside."

"I won't. But why would someone as important as the high priest stop by our booth?"

Mother made a noise deep in her throat. "Your father has been courting friends in high places."

I broke a generous piece of bread from the loaf on the table and dribbled honey over the torn edge. I took a bite, hoping to quiet the rumbling in my empty stomach. Mother went back to work at her bowl and pestle.

"Yesterday," I told her between bites, "a man and his brothers intervened when some of the boys from the gymnasium stopped me and Miriam."

A line appeared between my mother's

brows. "Who were these men?"

"I did not know them, but Miriam said the big man was Judah Maccabaeus. His father is a Levite. All the sons wore beards and did not cover their heads."

The faint suggestion of a smile appeared at the corner of Mother's mouth. "A fine family, then."

"Mother." I shaded the word with reproach.

"Despite what you may think, you need to leave this house," she said. "You are old enough to find a husband and go. Why not Judah Maccabaeus or one of his brothers? I hear the priest has five sons."

I ignored her comment about leaving. "I doubt the fellow will remember the incident today. But he seemed to enjoy the fight."

"They actually fought?"

"Out in the street. I don't think anyone was seriously hurt, but those young Hellenes will think twice before stopping girls again."

Mother shot me a look of concern, then shook her head. "It is good to know some are still practicing the old ways. Too many of our people have abandoned the Torah. They pay more attention to the customs of the pagans —"

"And why wouldn't they try their best to

survive? We do not live in the time of Moses, Mother. We are not struggling against those who would keep us slaves; we are trying to survive under men who learned from Alexander the Great. The Greeks nearly conquered the world, so it is only natural that Greek ideas should permeate the lands they conquered."

"Run along, Leah. You'd better get to the market before your father decides to check on you."

Frustrated because she would not discuss these ideas with me, I threw a wool scarf over my tousled hair, slipped into my sandals, and gave her an obligatory kiss on the cheek. She tied up a small cloth filled with bread and figs and put it into a basket, then added two wrapped cheeses.

I picked up the basket and went out the door. I left the house later than usual, because the sun had already crested the eastern hills. The market would begin to bustle in a few moments, and people would be eager for a fine cheese.

I lowered my head and walked faster.

The houses stood farther apart here on the outskirts of Jerusalem, and the sounds of animals mingled freely with the shouted greetings of neighbors. Our closest neighbor kept chickens, and we kept four goats in the courtyard — one buck and three does. Mother spent her mornings milking the does; during the afternoons, she made cheese.

I worked with the goats, too, but did not care about staying inside to make cheese. I much preferred to work in the marketplace, and Father agreed. He said that since I was far prettier than Mother, I would work at the market until no one wanted to look at me anymore.

On the way to work, my thoughts kept returning to Judah Maccabaeus, who had so nonchalantly stepped forward to defend me — Miriam and me, that is. I simply could not believe that a man who did not know me had willingly, even gladly, risked injury to himself. My mother paid the price for defending me often enough, but mothers were expected to defend their children. Yet I meant nothing to Judah Maccabaeus or his brothers, and they had volunteered to stop that brazen youth.

Father would not have come to my aid because he admired the Hellenes. The first time I heard him refer to himself as a Hellene, I thought he was talking about some strange tribe of Israel. Then I heard him tell Mother that a Hellene was a deep thinker who loved intellectual exploration. "The

Greeks are noble people," he said, narrowing his eyes as if he doubted she could ever understand. "They produced Alexander the Great, who changed the world. We would all do well to emulate them."

Even the High Priest Menelaus loved all things Greek and frequently traveled to Antioch to pay tribute to King Antiochus. Though Hellenes could be Jews or Seleucids or Samaritans, they agreed on one thing. If an idea or deity or fable had originated in Greece, it had to be far superior to anything else.

Mother did not consider herself a Hellene. Though she was careful to keep her face blank when Father was extolling the virtues of the Greeks, with me she felt free to release her scorn on those who tried to forget they were children of Abraham. "Did the Greeks build Solomon's Temple?" she asked one morning. "Did HaShem promise the Greeks a land flowing with milk and honey? No. Yet here they are, ruling over our Promised Land as if it belonged to them. It does not, because this land has been promised to the seed of Abraham forever."

"Father says Jews live all over the world now," I said. "He said the greatest Jewish scribes live in Alexandria, a city of Greeks in Egypt. Many of those Jews no longer speak Hebrew, but only Greek."

Mother dropped her work and came toward me, then leaned forward until her face loomed only inches above mine. "Your father is neither good nor godly. Keep that in mind when he speaks to you."

The heat in her eyes caught me by surprise. Where was that fire when Father sparked into one of his rages? When he lifted his hand to her? Without fail, the flame died just when it would have made the most difference.

While I loved my mother, I found it difficult to heed or respect a woman who habitually submitted to my father's cruelty.

Though they attempted to lower their voices, my parents could not have a private conversation in our one-room house. They rarely spoke of important things when I was awake, and their serious discussions, if Father's bluster could actually be considered speech, usually occurred when they thought I could not hear them.

I had just drifted into a hazy doze when Father's rumbling voice snapped me back to wakefulness. "I have heard stories," he said, "about the sons of Mattathias the Levite. Apparently they defended our daughter and her friend from trouble on the street."

A long silence, then my mother responded, "It is true."

"The girl is already past the age of betrothal," Father went on. "It is time she married. We would do well to unite with such a powerful family. Any of the priest's unmarried sons would make a fine son-in-law."

Somehow, Mother found the courage to offer an opinion. "I believe most of them have already taken wives. Perhaps the youngest."

"How like you to point out the problem with my plan." Father coughed, then cleared his throat. "I will make inquiries tomorrow. It is time our daughter married."

"They are not Hellenes."

"So?"

"They are devout, part of the Hasidim. Their son may not want to marry the daughter of a Hellene."

"Why would he care? The girl has no opinions. She will believe whatever her husband wants her to believe. And I am nothing but careful in my dealings with all men. I am whatever people need me to be."

I clutched at my blanket, taking care not to shift my position lest the rustle of my straw-filled mattress overpower my mother's soft response. But she said nothing, and within a few moments I heard Father snoring.

If Father had his way, my life would soon change. He wanted me married, and what Father did not want to see his daughter settled with a fine husband?

But my father would act out of selfish reasons. Not tomorrow, and perhaps not this month, but before long he would send me away, not out of love and care but in order to reap benefits from a profitable social connection.

Chapter Four: Judah

The odors of donkey manure and open sewers hung in the air as my brothers and I walked through the center of Jerusalem. When we reached the marketplace, I deliberately slowed my step and drifted away from the others. I had no particular interest in shopping, and no wife to please. I had come along only to fill my stomach, and I could usually find fresh bread and good cheese in the merchant booths.

While Eleazar searched for yarn and Johanan looked at jewelry, I followed the scent of fresh bread and stopped at a baker's booth. After purchasing a warm loaf, I wandered to the next booth where several slabs of cheese sat on a wooden counter. A slice of cheese would be wonderful with bread . . .

"Can I get you something?" The gruff voice startled me. I looked up to see a short man behind the counter, an apron tied around his ample middle.

"I would like some cheese."

"What kind?"

"What kind do you have?"

The man frowned. "These are goat cheeses. We have sweet cheese, mild cheese, and a mushroom cheese."

I stared at the row of cheeses. "Which is best?"

The man squinted up at me. "What do you like to eat?"

"Everything."

"I'll give you the sweet cheese." Shaking his head, the man took out a knife and cut a slice, then extended it toward me, the cheese riding the blade.

I took it and placed it in the center of my loaf, then pulled a few coins from the drawstring purse at my belt.

I had no sooner dropped them into his hand when a girl darted into the booth, her face flushed and her breath coming in quick gasps. "I'm sorry, Father. The errand took longer than I thought it would."

"You are too slow," the man grumbled, yanking the apron from his waist. He wadded it up and threw it at his daughter. "Get to work."

Without another word he left the booth, leaving the girl flustered.

Turning toward the counter, she knotted the apron around her waist, then looked up. "May I help you?"

A betraying flush brightened her face in the moment our eyes met, and I knew I'd seen her before. Was she friendly with one of my brothers' wives? No, I would have remembered seeing her. Perhaps she had served my mother . . . no, too young.

I lifted my bread and turned it so she could see the cheese in the loaf. "I have what I came for."

She arched a brow. "Are you sure?"

"Why would I want anything else?"

Surprising, that a woman's face could bloom in so many shades of red. Deep scarlet patches appeared on her cheeks, pink colored her forehead and chin, and a rosy flush mottled the flesh at her neck as she turned and pretended to arrange wrapped parcels on a bench.

I felt a strange lurch of recognition in her movement. I had seen her turn away before, not at home but in the street. On the day of Father's retirement, when we fought with the Hellenes who had accosted two young girls . . .

This was one of those girls, but she was not as young as I'd thought. Though she wore a modest tunic, I could trace the outline of hips and breasts, so she had to be at least thirteen or fourteen. Which meant the gruff little man who sold me the cheese would soon be offering this girl for marriage, probably to the fellow who offered the highest price.

She glanced over her shoulder at me, and after a moment she sighed. "You probably think I have no manners," she said, keeping her eyes downcast. "But I want to thank you for defending me and my friend Miriam the other day. HaShem surely sent you to keep us safe."

I nearly laughed aloud, but something in her demeanor warned that she might turn skittish if I proved too loud or unruly.

"HaShem has never sent me to do anything," I told her, hoping my smile might calm her fears. "And I did not act alone. But I will tell my brothers you are grateful."

She nodded. "Please do."

"Shall I . . . may I tell them your name?"

She hesitated, her eyes darting left and right, and then she responded in a whisper so low I nearly missed it: "Leah."

By the time I reached our home, the house had filled with friends and relatives who had come to congratulate Father on his retirement.

I stepped into the front chamber, nodded at some friends who turned to look at me, and slid into an out-of-the-way spot at the back of the room.

"My time of Temple service," Father was saying, his gaze roving over his guests, "has ended. Though many Levites of retirement age remain in Jerusalem to lend a hand in training younger men, I can no longer bear to witness the terrible things that have befallen the City of David and our holy Temple. So I have made a decision — after Sukkot, I am moving my family to Modein, where I was born and my brother still lives. The town is small, but its people still follow the old ways. There my sons can raise their families according to the Law of Moses and we can worship Adonai in peace. We can no longer do those things in Jerusalem."

I glanced around, trying to read the faces of my brothers. Johanan, who stood next to Neta, his wife, wore a thoughtful look, but did not seem distressed by the thought of leaving the only city we had ever known. Simon was busy trying to keep his little son quiet, so he had probably only half heard Father's announcement. Eleazar was whispering in his wife's ear — probably assuring her that she could sell her weaving as easily in a small town as in Jerusalem. Jonathan, my youngest brother, stared at Father as if bewildered, and I shared his astonishment.

What would we do in such a small village? We had work in the city — Johanan and Simon were scribes, Eleazar sold his wife's weaving in the marketplace, and I served as a messenger, carrying letters from the Temple to various city officials. How would we survive as farmers and shepherds?

I shifted my attention to the center of the room, where Father stood in a rectangle of light from the window, a tuft of shining silver hair on his forehead. Without warning, he smiled directly at me. "Judah, I know what you are thinking — how are you and Jonathan to find wives in a small town like Modein? Jonathan has time to wait for his bride, but you are overdue. So I will find you a wife before we leave. On the appointed day, you will leave this house to fetch your bride, then you will escort her to your new home in Modein."

As our guests cheered and clapped, I swallowed the boulder that had suddenly materialized in my throat. "How can you find me a wife . . . so quickly?"

The corner of Father's lined mouth twisted upward. "How did Abraham find a wife for Isaac? How did Isaac find a wife for

Jacob? They trusted HaShem to guide them."

"But they had help," Simon pointed out, grinning. "Abraham sent his servant, and Jacob himself went to find Rachel."

"Judah has us." Eleazar punched my shoulder. "We will help Father find your bride."

"Father doesn't need help," I argued. "And I don't need a woman."

Father held up a rebuking finger. "Look at your brothers and see how happy they are with their wives. 'Two are better than one,' wrote Solomon, 'in that their co-operative efforts yield this advantage: if one of them falls, the other will help his partner up — woe to him who is alone when he falls and has no one to help him up. Again, if two people sleep together, they keep each other warm; but how can one person be warm by himself?' "

I lowered my head as my married brothers chuckled and drew closer to their women. How could I expect them to understand my reluctance? Johanan had inherited my mother's attractive features. Half the young women in Jerusalem had been in love with him before he married Neta. Simon was not known for his looks, but for his wisdom, and others paid handsomely for his advice. His wife, Morit, had never lacked for anything.

Eleazar had bravely declared himself in love with Ona before Father arranged a betrothal, and Ona, who possessed an equal boldness, declared herself willing to marry Eleazar before witnesses. Their betrothal ceremony served as a confirmation of what everyone already knew — Eleazar and Ona had been created for each other.

That left eighteen-year-old Jonathan, and me . . . the one who hoped to remain unmarried forever.

The next afternoon I asked Mother if she needed anything from the marketplace. "I have to deliver a scroll near the square," I said. "So do you need oil? Grain?"

"You are a thoughtful son." She patted my cheek. "I suppose you could pick up some figs. And some eggs. Enough to bake the Shabbat loaves."

I nodded and set out, taking long strides through streets crowded with people and edged with rickety structures that looked as though they might collapse in a good rain. I dodged a wagon loaded with salt from the Dead Sea and cut in front of a tradesman pushing a handcart filled with jars of olive oil. I turned onto a street bordered with beautiful buildings and delivered the scroll to a high-ranking Torah teacher's house.

Finally I entered the shaded marketplace, ignoring invitations from other merchants as I searched for the cheesemaker's booth. There — beside the baker's display. I hid behind a fluttering scarf at a weaver's shop until I made certain the girl was alone. She stood at the counter, her eyes distant, her hands folded. What thoughts filled that lovely head? What did she do when she wasn't selling cheese?

I looked around to be sure no customers were heading her way, then decided to wait before approaching her. After I had bought the eggs and figs for Mother, I would visit the booth again.

I took my time searching for perfect figs, examining several fruits before finally selecting a dozen. The merchant rolled his eyes as he dropped my choices into a burlap bag. "A man of your stature should not be wasting his time at the market," he said. "Get your wife to do the shopping so you can do something useful and beat up some Greeks, eh?"

I found the egg merchant and had him place a dozen eggs in a straw-lined box. I thanked him as I paid, then stood motionless amid the bustle of the marketplace. I had no more errands to run and no other tasks to perform. Eleazar would laugh if he could see me standing helpless in the marketplace.

How could any son of Mattathias be paralyzed by the thought of speaking to a young woman? I had not been at all nervous when I defended her before those idiot Hellenes, but I had considered her a mere child, and children did not have the power to intimidate me. But women . . .

I could no longer put off my task.

I cleared my throat, steeled my unstable courage, and walked back to the cheesemaker's booth, my steps firm with determination. The young woman looked up at my approach, and her eyes widened when I stopped in front of her. "Have you any cheese?"

Her eyes softened as she smiled. "Of course."

I wanted to slap myself, but her smile held no trace of scorn. Perhaps she was not like the others.

"I — I am Judah Maccabaeus," I told her, forcing words over my unwilling tongue. "And you are Leah."

"True."

"I will have a cheese, please."

She picked up a small package and offered

it to me. "Will this suit?"

I did not bother to examine it. "It will."

I placed ten coins on the counter and blinked when she took only three. She slipped them into a purse at her belt, then pushed the cheese over the wooden surface. Our fingers touched when I picked up my purchase, and I felt my face grow hot. "Thank you."

"Good-bye, Judah Maccabaeus." She smiled again, as if she had been amused by my awkwardness. Why wouldn't she be? Women had been laughing at my clumsiness ever since I learned to walk.

"Good-bye." I took a deep, quivering breath to calm the leaping pulse beneath my chest and walked away without another word.

Chapter Five: Leah

I did not know what to think of Judah Maccabaeus. He fought in the street like a wild lion, but today he had reminded me of a large, ungainly puppy, the sort who might roll over and let you rub his belly if you approached him in the right way.

Father would approve of Judah Maccabaeus, but not on account of the man's virtues. Father would approve because Judah's father was a Levite, and the priests still wielded a measure of authority in Jerusalem. The Temple of Adonai no longer demanded respect or reverence, yet the priests had power because they had been born into the line of Aaron. Gentiles could defile the Temple, steal her treasures, and bully their way into the courtyards once reserved for Jews, but they could not change the bloodline of an authentic Levite.

Yes, Father would approve of Judah, the priest's son. Mother would approve of the ungainly puppy.

As for me? I saw no reason to approve or disapprove of him. I had encountered him only three times, and unless our fathers met and hammered out a betrothal agreement, I might never see him again.

And yet . . . my heart had danced when I looked up and saw him standing at my booth — not once, but twice. His smile seemed to wrap me in an invisible warm blanket, and those brown eyes — all the brothers had nice eyes, but Judah's seemed to hold shifting stars that shone with the most lovely light.

What was it about him that made my knees tremble? Did all girls go through this sort of thing, or had I eaten something that addled my senses?

"He is nothing to me." I said the words aloud, not caring if a passerby heard me talking to myself. Hearing the words spoken outside my head made them real, gave them context. In the world outside my market booth, Judah Maccabaeus and I had nothing to do with each other, nor were we likely to have anything to do with each other.

But he had come here . . . twice. Father had met him. And Father knew of Judah's ties to an old priestly family.

I dropped to my knees behind the half

wall, hiding myself from prying eyes. "Holy HaShem," I prayed, pressing my hands together, "if it be your will, find a way for Judah Maccabaeus to be my husband. Please, Adonai. I do not ask for many things, but this I ask with every breath, hope, and desire that is in my heart. Amein."

I stood and braced myself on the counter as I considered my prayer. I had probably wasted my breath, just as I wasted my entreaties when as a child I begged Father not to hit Mother. When Father didn't listen, I had begged HaShem to stop my father's angry fists, but my prayers had been no more effective than wishing on the moon.

But in case HaShem was listening, and if I had done something to please Him, perhaps this time He would hear and answer His neglected daughter's prayer.

Chapter Six: Judah

I strolled through the marketplace in a contented daze, Mother's basket under my arm and my purchases safe in the basket. *Leah.* Such a lovely name, and the same name as Jacob's wife, mother to six tribes of Israel. Yes, the girl seemed reserved, but her quiet composure would be a nice change from Simon's giggly Morit and Johanan's hard-to-please Neta. And she must know how to make cheese. Eleazar frequently boasted of Ona's skill with a loom; I would brag about Leah's cheeses. Goat cheese, cow cheese, camel cheese . . . surely she could make them all.

Walking with my head down, eyes intent on the uneven street, I nearly stepped on the sandaled feet that abruptly blocked my path. I adjusted by moving to the right, and the feet did the same.

I gritted my teeth, looked up, and recognized the arrogant Hellene from the gym, the young man who had accosted Leah and her friend. He stood before me now, a smirk on his unrepentant face.

Forgetting everything else, I dropped Mother's basket and lurched forward, grasping the brazen youth's cloak and holding it firmly against his neck with my right hand. While he stammered and gasped, my left hand twisted the fabric until his face went the color of a rose.

"You are a fool to deliberately cross my path again." I spat the words as he attempted to slap my arm away. "I ought to give you a beating, but I am in a good mood and do not want to spoil it. But if you ever stop a modest woman again — if you are the cause of even a maidenly flinch, I will hear of it and I will find you. I will then teach you a proper lesson about how the daughters of Isra'el are to be treated. Do you understand?"

His eyes glared into mine until I twisted the fabric again.

When he finally nodded, I released him and stepped back to watch him collapse at my feet. "Go," I said, my chest filling with sudden elation. "Go your way and do not come near this marketplace again."

Holding his throat, the belligerent youth picked himself up and hurried off. Not until he had advanced a considerable distance did he look back to see if I was still watching. With folded arms I stood and dared him to come toward me, but he did not. He continued on his way, and I did not think I would meet him in Jerusalem again.

I glanced around, half expecting to discover that someone had stolen my cheese, figs, and eggs, but the elderly woman who had picked up Mother's basket returned it to me with a broad smile. "May HaShem bless you," the woman said, a dimple winking in her lined cheek. "And may your wife be as fruitful as Rachel and Leah."

The mere mention of the latter name made my heart constrict. I thanked her with a smile and set out for home, my steps long and my heart light.

That night, I told Father that if I had to marry, I would marry the cheesemaker's daughter. Two weeks later, Father called me out to the courtyard where he and the Torah teacher had been working on the *shitre erusin,* the marriage contract we would take to my prospective bride's home. Father had already spoken to Yoel, the cheesemaker. If he accepted the agreement, my betrothal to Leah would be settled, and we would be married within a few days.

The teacher squinted up at me. "It is a brief betrothal period."

"Yes. But we are soon moving to Modein."

The teacher turned to Father. "What will your son give as the *mohar*?"

Father looked at me. "Have you considered the gift you will give your bride?"

I chewed my lower lip. Before Leah, I had never envisioned myself as a married man, so how could I have arranged for a mohar? But lately I could think of nothing but Leah. As I continually replayed the two occasions in which I had spoke with her, I kept seeing her father's cruel visage and hearing his rough voice. Would it not be an act of mercy to remove her from his house?

"Would she value a piece of Ona's weaving?" I looked from Father to the teacher. "I have no sisters, so I have no idea what women like."

The teacher made a guttural sound in his throat.

"Why don't you consider jewelry," Father suggested. "A fine necklace or pearl earrings. A silver bracelet."

I shrugged.

"The purpose of the mohar and the shitre erusin," the teacher said, uttering words he had undoubtedly recited many times before, "is to assure the bride's father that his daughter will not be left impoverished. If something happens to you, she will inherit your property. What property do you possess, Judah?"

A slow fire burned my cheeks. At twenty-four, I had not yet built a house or established a business. Father joked that I was a slow starter, but Mother called me her rock and had never made me feel ashamed for not following in the footsteps of my older brothers. After all, she often reminded me, Isaac was forty when he sought and married Rebekah.

"I will build a home in Modein," I said, "and if something happens to me, she will inherit it."

"She will always have a place at our family table," Father added. "She will be part of the Hasmon family, and we will never send her away, nor any of her children."

The teacher scrawled words on a parchment. "It is customary," he said after a moment, "that you promise not to make your bride leave the land of Isra'el, or the city of Jerusalem, or exchange a good house for a bad one without her consent. Yet you and your family are planning to leave Jerusalem, so she should be warned of this. She may not want to leave her family behind."

I frowned, alarmed by the reminder. What if Leah didn't want to go to Modein? After all, she had known nothing but her parents and her home, and though her father seemed an unloving sort, perhaps she loved him nonetheless. In offering this bridal contract, I would be asking her to leave her family, her synagogue, and the only city she had ever known.

I looked at Father. "What if . . . ?"

He arched his brow.

"What if she does not agree? Can I live in Modein without a wife?"

Father looked at the teacher, then shifted his gaze to me. "My son, it is a man's responsibility to marry and raise children in the knowledge of Adonai. HaShem commanded us to be fruitful and multiply. Marriage is your duty."

I bit my lower lip. "But before Leah, I never wanted to marry."

"Then you should pray that she accepts your offer." Father blew out a breath. "Son, Modein is a small village. There you will have few choices, but Jerusalem is filled with worthy women. Why would you limit yourself later when now you could have almost any woman you wanted?"

I tented my hands and looked at the floor, not certain I could find the words to explain my reluctance. Father might think me arrogant; the teacher might think me odd.

"My brothers talked about the sort of woman they wanted long before they married," I said. "But though I feel certain HaShem has a purpose for my life, I have never felt that marriage was part of that purpose. Until Leah. If she refuses . . ." I spread my hands and shrugged.

Father closed his eyes. "Son, not many nights ago you came to me and asked me to arrange this marriage. I spoke to the cheesemaker. He is open to our offer."

"A lot of young men go through this." The teacher grinned at Father. "The misery of second thought."

Father shook his head. "All these things work together, Judah," he said in the calm tone he used whenever something frustrated him. "The *Ruach Ha-kodesh,* the spirit of holiness, guides us into knowing what is right. He introduced you to a woman who occupies your mind like no other. He made the cheesemaker agreeable. Is this not the work of HaShem?"

With great reluctance, I nodded.

"Do you not remember the words of Solomon?" the teacher asked. " 'There is a time to be born and a time to die.' A time to pray, and a time to create a marriage contract."

The teacher wrote more words on the parchment, then passed it to my father, who read it in the glow of a torch. He smiled as he handed the parchment to me.

I looked at the words. As usual, they seemed to arrange themselves in confusing order on the page, yet I could trust the Torah teacher.

I gave the contract back to him. "It is good."

"I will prepare a formal copy," the teacher said, tucking the parchment into his robe, "and bring it to you within two days. Prepare your gift, Judah, and make sure you have a clean tunic. You wouldn't want to unnerve your bride by appearing in dusty clothes."

I stood when he did, and swallowed the words that sprang to my lips. *It is far more likely that my bride will unnerve me.*

"Go ahead, I will find you later," I told Jonathan, who was walking with me. He shot me a questioning look, then grinned when he saw I had veered toward the marketplace.

"Now I understand," he said, still grinning. "Are you sure you want to see her now? The teacher has not yet returned with your contract, so nothing is yet official."

I waved him away. "I need to see her."

"Can't stay away, eh?" Jonathan laughed and strode toward an inn, leaving me alone with my pounding heart.

In truth, it wasn't love that drew me to the marketplace — anxiety spurred me to find Leah. I had promised to present her with a marriage contract, but before the betrothal became final I needed to be sure she wanted to commit to the challenge of being my wife.

I wandered throughout the marketplace, passing the baker's booth, the sellers of olives and olive oil, the fig merchant, the man who sold sandals, and the women who sold woven fabrics. I walked past the stall where for two drachmas a man with iron pinchers would pull anything — a sore tooth, a nail, or a weapon — from a living body.

Finally I reached the cheesemaker's stall, and there, looking at me, stood Leah.

I managed a trembling smile as I drew nearer. An idea had occurred to me, a notion that might make things easier. "The day is nearly done," I said. "Will you close your booth?"

Her brow rose. "Why?"

"So I can walk with you. Escort you to your house."

She tilted her head, then offered me a distracted nod. "All right. Let me tidy up."

She took the few remaining cheeses, placed them in a handcart, and covered them with a cloth. Then she tugged on a rope that dropped a curtain between us. A moment later she came around the corner, expertly gripping the cart's handles. She wheeled it into the alley, then turned to me. "Ready?"

"Yes." We traveled a short distance before I realized she was breathing more quickly than I, probably because she was pushing the cart up a hill. "Let me do that." I took the cart from her and bent to push it through the thinning crowd. I found the thing difficult to maneuver at first — I wasn't accustomed to pushing in a stooped stance. But after a few strides I developed a rhythm and the task became easier.

Reluctantly, I drew a deep breath and shifted my attention to the girl at my side.

"I thought you should know," I said, keeping my eyes on the rutted road, "that my father and I will be visiting your home tomorrow night. With the Torah teacher."

Her eyes widened as a rush of pink stained her cheeks. "Oh!"

"I also want you to know that marriage — well, I was in no hurry to take a wife. But then I met you."

She snapped her mouth shut and looked at me with a perplexed expression, as if she had a question in mind but lacked the courage to ask it.

"My father," I went on, "wants me to marry before we leave Jerusalem. He has retired from Temple service and wishes to live in a place where we will not be pressured to give up our way of life." I lowered my voice. "In truth, Father strongly opposes the king's edicts. We will live in Modein, where we can follow the Torah and obey Adonai's laws without persecution."

A frown settled between her brows. "So . . . you are being pressured to marry."

"Yes — and no. It was Father's idea, but after speaking to you, the idea seemed good to me. Still, you may not wish to take me as a husband under these circumstances. We will have to move. You will have to leave Jerusalem. And I grew up with four brothers, so I know nothing about women."

"Did you have a mother?"

I blinked. "Of course."

"Then you know more than you realize." She looked away, her gaze fixed on some distant point I could not see. "So . . . you are not coming to my house out of love. You are coming out of necessity."

I hesitated — the truth sounded harsh when she put it into words. "I am coming . . . out of obedience. And . . . good nature."

"Good nature?" She stopped in the road and stared at me, her back stiff and straight. "I have no idea what that means."

"It means — *your* good nature — pleases me. I think we could be friends."

"Friends."

Heat scalded the back of my neck, but at least she couldn't see my flaming flesh. "Yes."

"I understand. And in the town of Modein, would your wife be required to sell cheese?"

I shrugged. "Only if she wanted to."

Leah relaxed, her lips spreading in a thin smile. "You will be welcomed at my home tomorrow night, Judah Maccabaeus. I will have the wine ready."

Chapter Seven: Leah

When Judah left me outside my house, I stood and watched until the crowd swallowed up his broad-shouldered form. Why had he bothered to seek me out? Our fathers could have arranged everything without a single word to me, yet with words from his own lips Judah Maccabaeus had wanted me to know what he was like.

That realization made my heart sing with delight. A man who cared what I thought. A man who looked into my eyes when he spoke to me, and even used my name.

No matter that he did not know women; I would teach him. No matter that he did not immediately take the heavy cart from me, at least he had taken it, which was more than Father ever did. No matter that he was marrying me only out of obedience to his father; most of my friends married for the same reason.

I wheeled my cart into the courtyard,

closed the gate, and hurried inside.

Mother sat by the fire, stirring a pot on the coals. She shifted her attention to me, and the grim line of her mouth relaxed. "I have long wondered if I would ever see that look on your face," she said. "And now I know you have found a way to escape this place."

"What look?"

She smiled. "Nothing."

I sank onto the bench near the door. "Judah Maccabaeus will come here tomorrow with his father and the teacher."

"And this pleases you?"

"Yes. But he took care to tell me that he does not know anything about women. He is marrying only because his father requires it."

Mother shrugged. "This is nothing to worry about; he will learn. Does he please you?"

I opened my hands and stared at the floor, superimposing Judah's image on the packed earth. "I see nothing unpleasant in him. He is far taller than Father, with thick hair and eyes like pools of ink. His shoulders are nearly as wide as our doorway, and he is kind — he wheeled the cart for me." I smiled. "But only after he saw me struggling."

Mother pressed her lips together. "I said nearly the same things to my mother when I first saw your father — except your father has never been tall. He has always been a small man." A grim smile flickered over her face. "About a year after we were married, I realized he was not the man I wanted. He did not care for me as a husband should care for a wife. He was harsh when I needed softness, brutal when I needed kindness. He was not cruel when we married, but in time I began to see the real man."

She turned her face to mine, her eyes softening with seriousness. "But here I am, and there you are, safe and as yet untouched by brutality. You, daughter, gave me a reason to live."

I stared wordlessly, stunned by her transparency. She had never spoken of these things before.

She shifted her gaze to the glowing coals, then held her hands over them as if testing the heat. "I pray you will not experience my fate, and from what you have said, I do not believe you will. Ask HaShem to guard the man you marry, study him well, and serve him as best you can. Then, perhaps, you will be happy and blessed."

I stood and impulsively kissed her forehead, then retreated to my bed where I could face the wall and ponder the upheaval about to enter my life.

How could one know a man before marriage? Most of my friends had been betrothed to men they'd only glimpsed across the synagogue. None of them had spent much time together, so none of my friends had really known their future husbands.

But though I had never met Judah before last week, on the afternoon he stopped to help Miriam and me I learned more about him than in a year of shy conversations. I saw him demonstrate his care for the helpless. I saw his strength. I saw his virtue in action, and I was unspeakably grateful. With Judah Maccabaeus, I told myself, I would finally feel safe. I would live in a home filled with peace.

My father came home late on the appointed night, a smile wreathing his round face. "I have spoken to Mattathias the Levite," he told Mother, "and it is agreed. His son Judah will take our girl to be his wife, and they will move to Modein. I told him we would pine for the sight of our only daughter, and he promised to send one hundred drachmas to console us. I told him that would be consolation indeed."

"I thought —" I glanced at Mother,

wondering if I should speak — "I thought they were coming here."

"Here?" Father snorted. "I would not have a priest enter this ill-kept house. No, we settled the matter at the inn. We lifted our cups and drank to the marriage, and everything is arranged. Oh." From his belt he took out a small fabric bag, opened it, and pulled out a string of pearls. "Judah Maccabaeus gave this as the mohar. Nice pearls, I say."

My fingers itched to touch the necklace, to feel the glowing orbs against my fingertips. I knew little about fine jewelry, but I knew pearls were rare and expensive, especially for those who did not live by the sea.

"They should bring a good price with Aaron the jeweler," Father said, sliding the pearls back into their fabric bag. "I will take them to his shop tomorrow."

I stood still and heard my heart break. The crisp sound echoed in my head, and in that moment I vowed that Father would never hurt me again. It would have been a small thing for him to pass on the gift Judah intended for me, especially since Father had also bargained for one hundred drachmas. But no, my father would not even allow me to enjoy a blessing from my future husband.

I crossed the room to my pallet, lay down,

and faced the wall. The pillow felt cool against my flaming cheek, and my fisted hands went pale as I squeezed the color out of them.

Father had undoubtedly behaved badly during the meeting, dangling his only daughter like some kind of rare prize. Mattathias must be a generous and loving parent, for any other man would have been repulsed by my father's naked greed. But kindness had prevailed, or perhaps Judah had spoken up for me. The betrothal was accomplished and the marriage arranged. If all went as planned, I would soon be traveling to a new home with the new man in my life. My husband.

I lifted my blanket to my shoulders and chewed on my thumbnail. Did Judah know the sort of woman he had bargained for? Despite what my father had implied, I was no great prize. I was like my mother, neither beautiful, smart, nor particularly skilled. I knew how to make cheese only because I had watched Mother make hundreds, but she had taught me no other skills. She had not been a great beauty in her youth, and she had never been clever enough to answer Father's insults with her own. But by far her worst fault was her lack of strength — she had never been able to stand up to

Father, nor had she tried.

But I was not weak. If Judah ever laid a hand on me, I would rise up with fists ready and arms curled, determined to show him how strong I was.

Judah Maccabaeus did not seem the sort of man who would beat his wife. Yet if he was, I would not be like my mother and take his violence.

I would sleep with a dagger.

Chapter Eight: Judah

The sun had begun to lower in the west by the time I entered an inn near the city gates. I knew I would find Simon inside.

He sat by himself, a bowl of porridge and a stone cup on the table. I slid into the seat across from him and breathed in the scents of boiled meat, spilled wine, and unwashed bodies. I smiled at my bleary-eyed brother. "Does your wife no longer cook for you?"

He shook his head. "Morit doesn't cook when she's expecting. Says the smells make her sick."

"So this is what you eat?" I nodded at the thin gruel in the bowl. "You could do better at Father's house."

Simon swatted away the suggestion. "Sometimes I don't want to listen to Father's complaints and Mother's questions. You and Jonathan are usually at the table, too, and sometimes a man prefers quiet."

"You call *this* quiet?" I gestured to the

dozens of men around us.

He grinned. "You'll understand soon enough, now that you're betrothed. When's the big day?"

I shrugged. "Father says the wedding can take place anytime before we leave for Modein. So I think I'll wait until the day before."

Simon blinked. "Dreading it that much?"

"I'm in no hurry."

"I will never understand you, brother. And that reminds me." Simon leaned across the table. "Tell me, why did you pick that one? Out of all the beautiful girls in Jerusalem —"

"I didn't want a girl. I wanted a woman."

Simon snorted. "What is she, thirteen? She's barely —"

"Fourteen, and she seems older. Around the eyes."

My brother blew out a breath and leaned back in his chair. "You'll learn that girls turn into women soon enough. Give them a baby and a cook fire, and the next thing you know they are shouting orders and yelling about what they need you to do. Bedding a wife is pleasurable for the first year or so, but as soon as the babies come, the wife has no time for you."

"I'll get a wet nurse," I said, remembering

what I'd once overheard Morit telling Johanan's wife. "Someone to give my wife a rest from the child."

"Women never take a rest from their children, only their husbands." Simon picked up his bowl and slurped the gruel, then looked at me over the rim. "Your girl sells cheese, right?"

I nodded.

"That trade brings a good income. Maybe you're smarter than I realized."

"She may not want to make cheese," I said. "And that would be all right."

Simon gaped, giving me a good look at his back teeth. "She may not *want* to?"

"That's what I said."

"By heaven and earth, brother, are you mad? She will do what you tell her so your family can survive. Do you think Morit *wants* to bake all day, especially with a baby at her knee? She doesn't, but she does it because we must. Just as Ona weaves and Mother makes baskets —"

"I'm sure my wife will do something," I interrupted. "But I would rather not make her do anything she doesn't want to do."

Simon pinched the bridge of his nose and closed his eyes. "You are an odd one, brother. I wish you well, but I will never understand you."

He slurped in silence while a servant brought wine. I sipped from my cup, lowered my head, and looked around.

Two strangers sat at a nearby table. Their curled beards and fancy caps marked them as Seleucids, and from their colorful robes and jeweled fingers I surmised they were government officials, perhaps even royal retainers. The tavern servant brought them a platter of venison, which they began to devour as soon as the dish hit the table.

"Hey." I caught Simon's attention, cutting a glance to the foreigners behind him. "Wouldn't it be nice to eat like that?"

Simon lowered his bowl and turned. When he looked at me again, a muscle quivered at his jaw.

Neither of us had forgotten what happened the last time Seleucid soldiers invaded Jerusalem. A year earlier, King Antiochus Epiphanes had taken his revenge on Jason, the high priest who seized his position from Menelaus, the king's choice, while Antiochus fought in Egypt. When the king learned what Jason had done, the people of Jerusalem paid the price. Supporters of Menelaus opened the gates of the city, allowing Seleucid soldiers to enter and massacre over forty thousand men, women, and children. Many of those who did not leave ahead of the king's army, as we had, were rounded up and sold into slavery. Menelaus was reinstalled as high priest while Jason fled to Egypt. To further compound his atrocities, Antiochus entered the Temple and ransacked the sacred space, stealing the golden candlestick, the altar of incense, the sacred vessels, and other priceless treasures.

Our family had been devastated by the king's actions, and those of us who survived the slaughter mourned for months after we returned to our homes. Antiochus had departed by that time, taking the sacred Temple treasures with him to Antioch, his capital city. To remind us of his displeasure and to pay for his luxuries, delegates, and expensive wars, he initiated new taxes for the Jews of Judea: a poll tax, a crown tax, and a temple tax. The king claimed up to a third of our grain harvest and half of the fruit harvest. The occupying Seleucid army frequently helped themselves to the livestock of Judea, and the poor in rural villages became even poorer beneath the king's grasping hand.

Simon lowered his bowl and stared blankly as we eavesdropped on the king's men. They spoke Aramaic, which we understood well.

"The Egyptians chased the king out," one man said, grease dripping down his fingers as he tore a piece of meat. "Their governor appealed to Rome, and that was the end of it. Rome sent an ambassador, who promised that Rome's armies would follow if Antiochus didn't leave. So he did."

"Kicked out of Egypt," the other man replied. "The royal temper will be hotter than the fire of Hephaestus. If he sends for you, better think of a reason to be indisposed."

"Like what?" the other countered. "You'd have to be on your deathbed to avoid a royal summons."

"Better to be dead, then." The second man wiped his hands on a towel and leaned back in his chair. "I can almost pity the poor Jews camped on the border. The king will have to cross their lands to get home, and they're certain to feel the sting of his temper."

I lowered my fist to the table and leaned forward, staring into my brother's eyes. Would that cursed king come to Jerusalem again?

"Father," Simon said, speaking Hebrew and carefully choosing his words, "is wise to leave Jerusalem. The lunatic king may well return."

"But why?" I opened my hand. "He has already stolen our treasures and murdered thousands. Why would he come back?"

"Because he is king," Simon said. "Because he can."

After Sukkot, we dismantled our tent shelters and began the process of moving. As we emptied our houses, we said farewell to our neighbors and gave them the furnishings we could obtain or make in Modein. Father's house was to go to a friend, and the man's wife had already slipped into our home twice, apparently trying to measure the windows and imagine her furniture against our walls.

"Only one more thing to do," Father said, slipping his arm around my shoulders. "We have to pick up your bride and have a proper wedding. Then we can be off to Modein."

When the last of our possessions had been strapped to the wagons, my brothers and I changed into festive clothing. They followed me as I went to get my wife. Freshly bathed and wearing my best tunic, I led the parade of friends and family through the valley of the cheesemakers. I stood outside Leah's house and called her name. After a minute, a lone figure appeared in the doorway — my bride, wearing a linen tunic and an embroidered veil as a head covering. Though my heart threatened to pound its way out of my chest, I took her hand and led her to my father's house. Amid cheering, jangling tambourines, and the ululation of the women, we ate a small wedding supper, then crossed the threshold of the decorated bridal bedchamber.

The door closed, muffling the noisy celebrants. With trembling fingers I lifted the veil and looked at the young woman with whom I would spend the rest of my life.

I had asked Simon, who never lacked for words, what I should say to Leah when we were alone together for the first time. He gave me a cocky grin and remarked that words would not be necessary, but in the silence of that moment, *my* moment, I yearned for something to say.

And thanks be to Adonai, words sprang to my lips.

" 'Three things are too amazing for me,' " I said, quoting from Solomon's proverbs in a voice that scarcely seemed my own, " 'four I do not understand: the way of an eagle in the sky, the way of a serpent upon a rock, the way of a ship in the heart of the sea, and the way of a man with a maiden.' "

Her eyes, which had been wide with apparent anxiety, creased slightly, turning up at the corners as she smiled.

I too smiled, thrilled by the small but satisfying victory. And now — what?

I was not completely ignorant of women — no man who had spent a lifetime living in close quarters with family members could remain ignorant of what the act of love entailed. Yet I did not know *this* woman, and she did not know how something deep within my chest trembled at the thought of being alone with her.

She stepped back and sat on the edge of the bed, her hands in her lap as her liquid eyes explored my face. I unbelted my tunic and pulled it off; she did not speak or move as I approached and dropped my hands to her slender shoulders, then tugged the veil from her hair.

I thought I should say something else, but I had no other words to give her.

Our coupling was brief, embarrassing, and awkward, and when it was over I rolled onto my side and stared at the wall, shuddering with humiliation. Had I injured her? Did she find me repulsive? She was so quiet, surely I had failed in some way.

I startled when her hand brushed my arm. "Husband," she said, and in her voice I heard a note halfway between entreaty and gratitude, "I have to thank you . . . for setting me free."

Chapter Nine: Leah

I did not sleep with my husband on the first night of our marriage — none of us slept that night. When Judah and I emerged from the bridal chamber, blushing and embarrassed, the family cheered, his brothers slapped him on the back, and my new sisters gathered around to look me over. Judah's mother, who told me to call her Rosana, introduced them quickly: Ona, married to Eleazar; Morit, married to Simon; and Neta, married to Johanan.

I smiled at each of them, and Rosana placed a wrapped parcel in my hand. "Run along outside until you find Judah, then climb in his wagon. We want to be out of Jerusalem before they close the gates."

I blinked, surprised to hear we were leaving so quickly. The gates closed at sunset, so if my parents were going to show up at my wedding, they would have to come soon.

I went outside where neighbors and

friends were embracing Mattathias and his sons. I saw Judah hitching a mule to a wagon at the end of the line. I walked to the corner and peered down the street, afraid I would see my parents approaching. I had said farewell to my mother when Judah arrived at the house, but Father had been out, only Adonai knew where.

When a quick survey revealed no sign of my family, I walked down the line of wagons, remaining close to the buildings to avoid being drawn into a conversation. After just being married, what did I have to say? I still had a thousand emotions to sort through, a hundred feelings to decipher and interpret.

"There you are." Judah's eyes lit when he saw me, and before I could respond, he had placed his hands around my waist and lifted me onto the wagon seat. I thanked him and slid over, leaving room for him to join me, but he turned and said something to his brothers.

I opened the parcel Rosana had pressed into my hands. Inside the parchment wrapper I found a honey cake that proved to be delicious. The light texture rested easily on my nervous stomach, and its sweetness brought tears to my eyes . . . or had my tears sprung from something else?

Judah reappeared, yelled instructions to one of his brothers, and climbed into the wagon with me. He gave me a quick smile, then hesitated. "Is something wrong?" he asked, concern in his eyes.

I shook my head and blinked away the tears. "I was . . . feeling grateful. Your mother is so kind."

"Oh, that she is." He gave me a curious look, then glanced down the street. "I do not see your people. Should we ride by your house on the way out?"

I shook my head. "You are my family now, so I will go where — when — you go."

"All right."

He clucked his tongue against his teeth and picked up the reins. Ahead of us, the caravan of wagons began to move. Neighbors waved and said noisy farewells. Some even threw wedding flowers and called, "Blessings to the bride!" and "May you be as fruitful as Rachel and Leah!"

I gritted my teeth as we traveled the crowded streets, for I could have walked faster than the wagon. I wanted nothing more than to be through the gate, away from Jerusalem, before —

"Daughter! Wait!"

I cringed at the sound of a familiar voice, then slowly turned my head. My father was coming down the street, wobbling on his unsteady feet as he waved at our wagon. When Judah pulled on the reins and stopped the mule, my heart stopped, too.

"S-son." Father gripped the side of the wagon and gave Judah a drunken smile. "Let me be-be the first to congratulate you, Son." He blinked up at my new husband. "If sh-she gives you any trouble, do not be afraid to take a switch to her. That will bring her right around."

I turned away, unable to look at my father or my husband. Was this some kind of punishment from HaShem? I was supposed to honor my father, but for years I had feared and dreaded him. Perhaps this was what I deserved.

"Good to see you, sir," Judah said, and I heard the chink of the reins as he lifted them. "Be well and prosper. Shalom."

Then we were moving again, though I kept my eyes averted as we pulled away.

"He is gone," Judah said after a while. "You need not be afraid."

I studied my husband's face as he guided the mule through the streets. I had never discussed my father with Judah, but apparently he understood without being told.

Perhaps this understanding was part of marriage. If so, I was grateful for it.

I finished the honey cake and wiped the sweet stickiness from my fingers with the parchment wrapper. We passed through another round of farewells as we rode out of Jerusalem's western gate, then I settled back and rested my hands in my lap.

Thus far, marriage pleased me well. Judah had proven himself kind and thoughtful, and he was attractive to my eyes. His brothers seemed pleasant enough, and their wives, while not exactly welcoming, had not been unkind. His mother was sweet and his father pious. My father had been pious in public and apathetic toward godly matters at home, so perhaps HaShem would look on me more favorably now that I had aligned myself with holier people.

One thing seemed clear — I did not believe Judah would behave like my father, but I did not plan to test him. My mother angered my father nearly every day, but I would obey Judah completely and do whatever he asked. I would not prod him to anger, and he would not beat me. Our home would be a place of peace and safety, and I would not become a withdrawn, cowardly woman like my mother.

"Leah?" Judah's voice interrupted my reverie.

"Yes?"

"Are you all right? I thought you might be tired."

I nodded. "I am . . . a little. But if you want me to stay awake, I will."

"No need for that. The sun will set soon, so if you want to climb in the back and sleep, go ahead. I put blankets in the corner, in case you wanted to rest."

My heart warmed to know he cared about such a small thing. "Thank you," I said. And then, because he seemed to *want* me to rest, I climbed into the back, found the blankets amid the bundles and chests, and lay down next to a crate of nesting hens.

I smiled as I closed my eyes. My friends and I had harbored a rosy view of marriage in our younger days. We would giggle as the Torah teacher read from the Song of Songs, and we would sigh when he said that love was better than wine. Though I had never been taught to read, I had memorized many of the words, and they seemed to echo in the darkness around the creaking wagon: *"I belong to the man I love, and he belongs to me."*

I exhaled a long sigh. Despite the uncertainty of the future, I had escaped my father's house. I did not know Judah Maccabaeus well enough to sigh over him, but if love could be built on a foundation of gratitude, I was halfway to loving him already.

Chapter Ten: Judah

At some misty hour before dawn, a sudden surge of happiness startled me from sleep. I lay motionless in the gray gloom, glorying in an odd cocoon of exhilaration, yet not remembering its origin. I blinked rapidly, batting away the cobwebs of sleep, and lifted my head. Then I saw a woman next to me in the wagon, and I remembered.

Leah. Woman. Wife. Eve to my Adam, light to my darkness, soil to my seed.

I propped my head on my hand, letting my eyes adjust to the semidarkness. She slept on her side, a bundle of fabrics for her pillow, a trunk jutting into the bend of her legs. I stroked the air over her wide forehead, high cheekbones, and pointed chin, then traced the long neck down to the flat plane of her belly.

I had never seen anything as breathtakingly beautiful. With four brothers, I had only glimpsed women from a distance. Like delicate treasures, they were carefully hidden beneath tunics and veils that disguised their lovely curves. I lifted my hand again, yearning to touch my bride, and gasped when she opened her eyes. I glimpsed a flash of alarm in those dark orbs, then something else took hold. She smiled at me, her expressive eyes assuring me of her contentment.

"Judah Maccabaeus," she whispered. "Judah Hammerhead. Do you not wish to cast off that name?"

I drew a deep breath but kept my voice low lest I disturb the others sleeping in wagons around us. "All of us have names. They call Johanan *Gaddi,* Simon *Thassi,* Eleazar *Avaran,* and Jonathan *Apphus.*"

"I can understand why the firstborn might be called *fortune,*" she said, "and I hear that Simon is wise, so perhaps he is a *good guide.* But hammerhead! You are now a married man, not a street brawler."

I shrugged. "It is only a name. And I have had it a long time, so I cannot imagine being without it. Besides, if my brothers and I encounter trouble, I am always the first in line."

"Like the day you came to my defense." I glimpsed the shimmer of white teeth as she smiled. "Or have you forgotten?"

"I will never forget." I touched the slope of her forehead and let my finger trail across her rounded cheek. "A man would have to be blind not to notice you. After that day, I kept experiencing the oddest yearnings for cheese."

I drew her close as she laughed, and before I knew it, her arms had slipped around my neck and her lips were against mine. And this time, with no waiting celebrants and only the lovely sounds of birdsong to accompany us, we experienced the fullness of what Adonai designed to create one out of two.

And, as the Torah says, it was very good.

▪ ▪ ▪ ▪

Part II

▪ ▪ ▪ ▪

In those days Mattathias the son of Johanan, son of Simeon, a priest of the sons of Joarib, moved from Jerusalem and settled in Modein.

1 Maccabees 2:1

Chapter Eleven: Judah

After Morit's rooster broke free of his crate and woke everyone with his crowing, my mother walked from wagon to wagon, giving each family a portion of bread, cheese, and fruit to break our fast. As we climbed down and stretched the stiffness from our muscles, Father called everyone to gather around. He stood in his wagon as we gathered to listen.

"My children," he said, lifting his hands once everyone had settled. "I know your hearts have been heavy over the past year. We have watched an enemy invade Jerusalem, an enemy that came not only with swords and spears but also with evil ideas, blasphemies, and bribes. The last two men who held the title of high priest have been from the line of Aaron, but their hearts were false, more focused on power and treasure than on Adonai."

A wind rose, sending flurries of dry leaves

skittering past us with a sound like the pattering of small feet.

"Like the wind" — Father waved to acknowledge the breeze — "false ideas have scattered our people, drawing their hearts and minds away from the worship of HaShem and obedience to His Law. Nowhere is this blasphemy more evident than in Jerusalem, where the holy Temple stands looted and profaned. Some of you have lamented moving away from the Temple, but that edifice is now only a building. Our holy place stands debased and ruined, and we do well to avoid entering it.

"You may have wondered if we alone worship Adonai and observe His laws. You may have feared, like me, that only a remnant of obedient Hebrews remain in the land. Like me, you may have begged HaShem to spare us, to save us from a king who seems intent on wiping us and our Law from the face of the earth."

A glow rose in Father's lined face, for Adonai had sparked a fire within him. "Do not despair, my children, for today we stand before the Lord as a family who will worship Him and honor His Law. No matter what edict the king proclaims against us, no matter what armies he sends to cut us down, we will worship the Almighty One.

We go to Modein in search of safety, but even if the forces of blasphemy come against us there, we will persevere in obedience to the Torah. Are you with me, my sons?"

With my brothers, I lifted my head and shouted, "Yes!"

"Are you with me, daughters?"

I stole a look at Leah, who stood wide-eyed by my side. I was not certain how she felt about Greek ideas, but she did not shout her agreement with my sisters-in-law. Perhaps my father's speech had confused or overwhelmed her. One thing I knew — her father had never held family meetings like this one.

Father extended his hand to Mother; she took it and gave him a confident smile.

"Let us now finish the journey to Modein," Father said, "and may the Lord prepare our way, so we can worship and obey Him in peace."

After this benediction, our entire family — Mother and Father, Johanan and Neta, Simon, Morit, and their small son, Leah and me, Eleazar and Ona, and Jonathan — took the road that led into the region of Lydda.

My new bride barely spoke as we traveled through territory she had probably never seen. The trip took us down the rocky hill called Beth-horon, and when her eyes widened, I guessed that she had never visited the barren plains.

I leaned forward and turned to better see her face. When I was convinced she did not hate me for moving her into the wilderness, I broke the silence. "Have you traveled in this part of Judea?"

A quick smile, then she shook her head. "Father did not travel outside Jerusalem. And if he had, he would not have allowed us to go with him."

I shifted my attention back to the road. "Within Jerusalem, was selling cheese his only business?"

Leah smoothed her tunic. "I don't know what he did when he was out of the house. He never told us anything about his business or his friends. He rarely spoke to us at all, except to command us or to complain about something we did or did not do."

I glanced at her, expecting to see tears or a plea for pity in her expression, but she stared impassively at the landscape.

"Interesting," I said. "My father knew something of Yoel the cheesemaker's activities. Many nights your father would go to the inn to drink with the king's officials. Father says he seemed to be quite friendly with them."

Leah shrugged. "He considers himself a Hellene when it is in his interest to agree with the authorities. He says it is better for his business if he is friendly with the people in charge. But I wouldn't know anything about his trips to the inn."

"I guess you wouldn't. A woman has no business being in a place like that. Bad enough that men drink until they become fools, but harlots linger outside —"

I fell silent, suspecting that my conversation had ventured into an area one should not discuss with a modest woman. So what did husbands and wives talk about? We had no children, so we could not talk about new teeth or scraped knees. We had no home, so I could not compliment her cooking or sewing. We had shared one night together, but I definitely did not want to talk about that, and we had taken part in a wedding.

Would she come to regret marrying a man who did not know how to talk to women?

We rode in silence for a long while, then I leaned toward her until our shoulders touched. "I want you to know," I said, keeping my eyes on the road, "that you are the most beautiful thing I have ever seen."

She did not answer, but from her quick intake of breath I assumed my words had achieved the desired effect. Later, when I finally summoned the courage to directly meet her gaze, her small smile hinted that my admission had pleased her.

That thought gave me great pleasure.

We traveled most of the day, but as the sun began to dip toward the west we finally glimpsed the mud brick walls around the village of Modein. The small, sleepy town, patriarchal home of the house of Hasmon, did not have much to recommend it. Situated on bare, rocky ground, the land offered little but abundant limestone, a rock that proved useful in building terraces that kept the soil from being washed away by the occasional rains.

When we arrived, Ehud, my father's brother, gave us a warm welcome, embracing Father and each of his nephews. After complimenting our wives, he pointed through the darkness at land on which we could plant our crops, raise livestock, and build our homes.

"Until you build your houses," he said, smiling, "you must stay with us. We will erect tents for your families. Tomorrow we will plot out the land, your women will work with our women, and you will share in all we have. Welcome to Modein."

I stood at the side of our wagon and

glanced at Leah, curious about how she would adjust to a land and family she had never met. But she slipped out of the wagon and walked directly to Rachel, my uncle's wife, and asked how she could be of service.

"Would you look at that." I turned to find Simon standing beside me, his attention focused on my new bride. "Made herself right at home, didn't she?"

I grinned. "I believe she did."

"Good." Simon placed his hands on his hips and jerked his head toward the light load in our wagon. "When you've unloaded that bit, come to my wagon, will you? Morit has packed more than three people should ever need."

"I'll be there."

I lifted the first basket out of our wagon, but before walking toward the area where Uncle Ehud's sons were erecting tents, I looked for Leah. I spotted her standing between Rachel and my mother, stirring a pot over the cook fire as the older women talked. Though she had to be exhausted, a gentle smile lit her face as she listened.

Perhaps Father was right. Marriage might be a fine thing, even for me.

Chapter Twelve: Leah

The women who traveled with me to Modein seemed to fall into a well-rehearsed routine the moment we climbed out of the wagons, but I did not know what to do or what was expected of me. I jumped out of the wagon and looked to Judah for instruction, yet he and his brothers were occupied with greeting their uncle. So I did what my father would have ordered me to do — I walked over to the uncle's wife and introduced myself, then offered to serve her in any way I could.

Rachel, Ehud's wife, embraced me in a warm welcome, then explained that she was preparing dinner. She had butchered a lamb and was boiling the meat for a stew. Had I brought any root vegetables from the city?

I had brought nothing but a small chest of clothing, but soon my sisters-in-law came over and offered to help. So I joined them in searching the wagons for fresh herbs, vegetables, anything we had brought that might enrich the stew.

At first I felt as though I was trespassing when I looked through the other couples' belongings, but apparently Mattathias's sons shared everything — the goods in the wagon, the livestock, even their bad jokes. I wasn't sure my sisters-in-law would prove as generous — women, in my experience, were generally more possessive of personal belongings — but the men still behaved as if they were boys living in the household of their parents.

Yet the women worked with a cheerfulness I had never witnessed. The happy mayhem was encouraged by Rosana, my mother-in-law, and my sisters-in-law reveled in it. They tried to include me — Morit tossed me a pomegranate, but I was so flustered I dropped it. Like a child who is given a toy and doesn't know how to play with it, I fumbled their smiles, their remarks, and their jokes.

"Give her time," I heard Rosana tell the others. "She is newly married and newly moved to a new place. The poor thing has to be overwhelmed."

Embarrassed by her pity, I settled on a bench and rested my chin in my hand, studying the women of my new family.

Rosana, Judah's mother, moved with the restless energy of a small bird. Her dark hair, veined with silver, had been pulled back and tied with leather strips to keep it out of her way. Her hands seemed in constant movement as she cooked and arranged and pounded the food we would soon eat. She carried herself with a confidence befitting the mother of five sons and commanded her daughters-in-law with genial authority.

Neta, Johanan's wife, could draw admiration from a dairy cow, so attractive were her features and figure. She exuded grace and confidence, and a close look at her face assured me that she was older, probably in her late twenties. She did not talk much, but when she did, her words were slow and melodious, almost as if she had rehearsed her speech.

Morit, married to Simon, the second son, had a wealth of brown hair that flowed like a river down her back and created a definite shadow on her upper lip. I blinked the first time I saw her, and wondered why she had not availed herself of mixed potash water and yellow flowers to bleach that mustache. Yet however odd her beauty choices, Morit possessed a merry laugh, which frequently rippled through the house.

Eleazar had married Ona, a girl only a year or two older than me. She looked familiar, and I thought I remembered her selling linen in the marketplace. Though we had never spoken, I felt certain we would get along because our backgrounds were similar.

Ever since descending from the wagon, I had dreaded one particular moment, and it finally arrived. Morit sashayed over to me and with a teasing smile asked, "So . . . how do you like your new husband?"

Every woman in the kitchen went silent and leaned forward, waiting to hear what I would say.

"I like Judah very much," I finally said, choosing discretion over details. "I look forward to our life together."

Morit giggled. "Listen to her," she called to the others. "She is tactful, this one."

Rosana shook her head. "Maybe she does not yet trust you."

"It is all right, you can say anything you like," Neta said, stepping closer to me. "We do not tell the men what we talk about when we are together."

"Sometimes a woman has to talk to another woman," Ona added. "So this is a circle of secrets."

"And sometimes a bit of trouble." Rosana

cast a reproachful look around the circle of sisters, then settled her kind brown gaze on me. "Welcome to the family, Leah. If you are having trouble, you can come to us. What is said in the kitchen usually remains in the kitchen, unless one of us wants to feel the sting of her kinswoman's tongue."

I looked up, a little overwhelmed by the outpouring of attention. "Thank you," I said. "I . . . am glad to be here."

"Good. Now." Rosana looked around the kitchen. "We need wine for the table. Leah, can you fetch a bottle from the cupboard? Thank you. Hurry, ladies, the men will be here soon, and they will be hungry."

My heart hummed in contentment as I rose to fulfill my job in the family.

Chapter Thirteen: Judah

Within a week, we had fenced areas for the goats, sheep, horses, and cattle we would buy now that we were no longer city dwellers. Within a month, my brothers and I had built the basic structures for our homes. My uncle had been making mud bricks ever since learning of Father's desire to return to Modein, so he had supplies ready for us.

Leah surprised all of us with her industriousness. I had expected her to be a good worker — after all, had she not worked every day in the marketplace? — but what I found most surprising was her willing attitude. She never complained, not even when the other women took advantage of her youth and good nature. Each night she crawled into bed beside me and smiled when I took her into my arms.

I had heard enough complaints about tired wives from Simon, Eleazar, and Johanan to know that such willingness was not the way of most women. I yearned to ask Leah if she was happy and if I pleased her, but I could not bring myself to speak of such things in her presence, or even discuss such things with my brothers.

Time, I assured myself, would bind us together. We would grow to understand each other so completely that we would not need to talk.

As I adjusted to life with a woman, the village of Modein adjusted to our family. With less than one hundred inhabitants, the people naturally looked to my father for leadership. Because he was a Levite, they asked him to be the Torah teacher at the village synagogue. Father agreed, and I was happy he had found a way to continue serving Adonai. Simon had worried that Father would be bored in such a small settlement, but as we built our homes and tended our flocks, the worry lines in Father's forehead eased. For hours he would sit outside, his eyes on the southeastern horizon, his prayers directed toward heaven . . . and Jerusalem.

We bought livestock with the money we had earned selling furnishings from our homes in Jerusalem, and in those first few months my brothers and I prepared fields for plowing. Uncle Ehud also taught us how to handle herds of livestock. Most families in Jerusalem kept a goat and a few chickens, but in Modein we planned to maintain larger herds. The sound of lowing cattle and the bleating of the sheep filled me with pleasure and sent me off to bed with a feeling of accomplishment.

In the afternoons, when I worked the fields alone, I often collected wildflowers for Leah, sneaked back to the house, and left them on her pillow when she had gone to the well.

With my brothers I cleared the soil, hauled blocks of sun-dried bricks, and built walls in the sweltering sun. I felt an unexpected surge of pride when I stepped back, looked at the finished structure, and realized that we had built our homes with our own hands. My one-room house stood between Johanan's and Simon's, and for the first time I felt a unique kinship with my married brothers.

At the end of each day, as the sun set and the air turned cool, we splashed water over our aching arms and backs and headed home. On the short walk, I often laughed aloud, for no reason other than contentment. I would soon enter my house and eat a dinner prepared by my wife. Then, in the silence of the evening, I would sit and play with the strands of her hair while she thanked me for the flowers and told me what she had done during the day. And when all our words and thoughts had been shared, I would take her to bed, where, like a rose, she unfurled beneath my loving hands and we two became one.

After eight months, we brothers had settled into specific jobs in order to relieve Father and Mother from the burden of supervising the family. Johanan became the overseer of fields where his training as a scribe proved useful when he wrote up trade agreements between our family and people from other villages. His wife, Neta, was supposed to help with the harvests, but I thought the sun more likely to melt than that vain woman to help in the fields.

Simon tended the orchards, where Uncle Ehud graciously allowed us to share in the harvest of pomegranates and figs. His sons preferred to work with cattle, so he was glad to see Simon step into the role of overseer. Simon's wife, Morit, agreed to sell baked fruit pies to assist the family.

Even in the city Eleazar had displayed a gift for calming horses, so he became the caretaker of all the carriage animals: horses, mules, and donkeys. We did not have many animals, and our only horse was a mangy, stubborn specimen, but Eleazar insisted that the quality of our animals could only increase. His wife, Ona, had long been a weaver, so she would continue to sell her work.

Since I had no gifts particularly suited for the farm, Father suggested that I care for the goats because Leah knew how to make cheese. She went pale at the suggestion but did not protest. Only later, when we were alone, did she confess that she had never made cheese; she had only watched her mother make it.

"Then do not worry," I assured her. "I will take such good care of the beasts that they will give you milk that practically turns itself into the stuff."

My remark made her laugh, and after a couple of attempts, Leah was able to produce the best cheeses in Modein. They were also the *only* cheeses in Modein.

Jonathan, my youngest brother, tended the sheep. He would live with our parents until he decided to marry, then like the rest of us he would build a home for his bride and bring her to live with him. One afternoon, after I caught him intently watching a fair and distant cousin, I suspected that Father wouldn't have to send Jonathan very far to find a wife.

By the time summer arrived, life had settled into a pleasant and peaceful rhythm . . . but I have since learned that such respites do not last.

As pleasant as life was in Modein, stories of unbelievable blasphemies in Jerusalem continued to reach us when travelers stopped at the well for water or hospitality. One man told us that even the priests of Jehovah were exercising in the gymnasium, casting off their holy robes to wrestle naked and contend for the applause of the eager crowd. My father shook his head in disgust when he heard the news and replied that those priests were engaged in activities "fit only for hired clowns — hired *pagan* clowns, as no self-respecting son of Israel would do such things."

The Hellenes had also celebrated idolatrous festivals in the holy city, including the drunken feasts of Bacchus. In Tyre, a coastal city in northern Judea, the Hellenes held athletic games in honor of the Greek god Heracles. With great dismay we noted that heathen rituals and ceremonies had not only infiltrated Jerusalem but also were spreading throughout the land of Judea.

We were preparing to plant the late crops when an old man and his grandson stopped at our well for refreshment. Obeying the commandment of hospitality, Father invited them into his house to rest.

"May Adonai bless you for your kindness," the older man said, clasping Father's hands while his eyes overflowed.

Mother set food before the guests, and Leah kept their cups full as the grandfather told a story that lifted the hair at the back of my neck. "I'm sure I will be the first of many to come your way," the old man said. "We fled with our lives when soldiers entered our neighborhood. Those who did not run were either killed or captured."

"Seleucids?" Father asked, a spasm knitting his brows.

The old man nodded. "Under the command of a general called Apollonius. I don't know what spurred the king's ire this time, but over twenty thousand soldiers entered the holy city and went on a killing spree. They captured hundreds of our people and ran the sword through anyone who resisted. They took everyone they encountered — women, children, and men. The older people — those who didn't flee the city — were murdered in cold blood."

Tears streamed down his face as he continued in a tattered voice. "I fled with my grandson, and when we reached the plains, we looked up to see Jerusalem aflame. While we rested, another man who escaped told us the city walls had been pulled down. Oh, Jerusalem! Has any city in the world seen so much bloodshed?"

When our guest had collected himself, he told us that Antiochus had sent Apollonius, the newly appointed governor of Palestine, to collect taxes and wipe out every distinguishing Jewish custom — by stringent measures, if necessary. The king's laws now forbade circumcision, observance of the Sabbath, and reverence for the Torah. Apollonius issued orders directing his soldiers to collect and burn copies of the Law as well as Torah scrolls. Furthermore, the Temple would no longer be a place to worship HaShem, but it would be dedicated to Jupiter Olympus. The king's soldiers would also enforce these edicts in Samaritan lands, at their temple in Gerizim and in the northern capital of Shechem.

A heavy sadness filled the room as Father lifted his voice in a heartrending wail. He tore his robe, and together the two old men wept over Israel while my brothers and I silently looked at each other. What did this mean for us? We left Jerusalem because Father feared the city would fall, and now it had. Mattathias had been proven right, but it brought Father no joy to know his greatest fear had been confirmed.

The old man and his grandson stayed with us until they had sufficiently rested, then we sent them on their way with a prayer and a blessing. A few days later, other travelers came through town with even more terrible news. "The king has issued a new decree," the oldest man told Father. "All Jews are to conform to Seleucid laws, customs, and religion. Not content to forbid worship of Jehovah, the king is now commanding us to sacrifice to Greek gods and goddesses. Not content to forbid us to obey our dietary laws, he is forcing us to eat unclean foods. Anyone who refuses to observe the king's laws will be put to death."

Another refugee family told us about women who were tortured and paraded through the city streets with their dead, circumcised infants hung around their necks. "People have left a naming ceremony and gone straight to the authorities to report a circumcision," we were told. "No one is safe. Neighbors are betraying neighbors, students are turning in their teachers, and young people are denouncing their parents."

One traveler leaned toward me and confessed that he had been hoping to peacefully coexist with the Gentile king. "I thought we would worship quietly, at home," he said, his eyes reddened by grief. "I thought no one would know that we were not eating pork. But you can no longer be a secret Torah-keeper in Jerusalem. You must sin, and sin openly, to be accepted by the Hellenes, and they are everywhere. When they came for my wife — because she did not buy pork at the market — I knew I had to take the children and leave the city. My wife is doomed, but I hope to save our little ones."

I glanced out the window when he had finished speaking, wondering how many of our fellow villagers would crumble beneath the ever-present pressure to conform to the king's laws. Few men were as stalwart or as stubborn as my father.

Through our visitors we learned that the governor Apollonius was building a citadel on the knoll of Millo, a strategic point that overlooked the Temple. "To make matters worse," one man told us, "the tower is being built by the king's men and a group of Jews who have gone over to the enemy. We are betrayed by many of our own people."

Simon forced his breath through his teeth in a hiss of exasperation. "Hellenes."

The visitor nodded. "They are everywhere, prospering, while righteous Jews are tortured and killed. I often wonder if any who still follow the Law remain in Jerusalem."

Father accepted this news in surprising silence, then withdrew and kept to himself for most of the next day.

But that night he called for a family meeting. When we had all assembled inside his house, he lifted his hands for our attention:

"My sons, my family, what I feared has come to pass. We weep for Jerusalem, but if the truth be known, she is reaping what she has sown. Did we not tell our people not to adopt the ways of outsiders? Did we not warn those who visited their heathen gymnasium, who wore Greek garments and imitated Greek customs, and those who set aside our native tongue in order to speak Greek? Many of our own people rejoiced to see theaters, pagan temples, racecourses, and public baths in the cities of Judea. Caught up in the ecstasy of newfound love, they offered sacrifices at pagan altars and ate swine in the homes of Gentiles. They abandoned the holy and righteous worship of Adonai, and they forgot and neglected His commandments. So it is not surprising that Jerusalem has been given over to this pagan king and his soldiers. Jerusalem has forgotten her righteous King and followed another. So HaShem has brought her to her knees."

That night, as Leah and I walked back to our house, she slid her hand into mine. "My parents are in Jerusalem," she said, her voice breaking. "How can I know if they survived the recent trouble?"

My conscience smote me. I had been so caught up in my father's words that I had not given a thought to my wife's family. The cheesemaker was not a righteous man, and Leah had not said a word about missing her parents, but after hearing about the carnage in Jerusalem, what kind of daughter would she be if she was not concerned?

"Would you like me to look for them?" I slipped my fingers under her chin and lifted her face to mine. "I will take a wagon and leave at sunrise, if you wish it. And if I find your parents in Jerusalem, I will bring them with me when I return to you."

Her forehead furrowed. "My mother would not leave without my father," she said, "and if he still lives, he would not leave out of sheer stubbornness. He will say he is too old to start over, and his business is in Jerusalem."

"But if Jerusalem lies in ruins —"

"He has long been willing to eat swine." She dropped her forehead to my chest, rubbed her arms, and shivered. "Go. Bring them back if you can. I hope you find them alive and well."

I wrapped her in my arms and promised to return without delay.

Chapter Fourteen: Leah

Did I want Judah to fetch my parents? No, no, a hundred times no. I had married him to *escape* my family, and bringing them to Modein would only thrust me back into that prison they called a home. My marriage to Judah would not solve the root problem — my father's criticisms, his faultfinding, and his violence would infiltrate this peaceful community, and soon they would all be watching me with critical eyes, especially Judah, who would begin to wonder why he married me in the first place.

But what could I do? I could not say these things aloud without seeming like an ungrateful, unrighteous daughter, and Judah would wonder what sort of evil gripped my heart. He had never known a brutish parent, so how could he understand?

I slept little that night because I kept imagining Father glaring at me from across Rosana's table, and my mother, pale and withdrawn, working with the women and being too afraid to offer a word. If they came to Modein, everyone in my new family would know how backward I was, how sordid my past.

I finally fell into a deep sleep. When I woke, Judah was gone.

With Judah away, I had little to do but pray for his safety, make cheese, and help the other women of his family. And while I helped Rosana grind grain and played with Morit's little son, I thought about the man I had married.

In Modein, I had discovered an aspect of Judah I never imagined. I desired the marriage because I was convinced he could keep me safe forever, yet a part of me had wondered about the fighter in him. I had seen his righteous anger when he went after the Hellenes who taunted me and Miriam, and despite my gratitude, the passionate heat of his anger had frightened me. I had seen no sign of that anger since, but the question remained at the back of my mind, hideous and alluring — what if Judah's kindness and gentleness were only temporary aspects? What if they faded over time and he became a man like my father?

One afternoon not long after our arrival in Modein, we were walking to his parents' home when we saw two village boys fighting by the well. Judah lengthened his stride so he reached the boys ahead of me, then he thrust a meaty arm between them and asked why they were squabbling. After hearing the story — something about one boy insulting the other's mother — I fully expected Judah to tell the offended boy to take a punch at the offender. Instead, Judah knelt until he was eye to eye with both boys and told them they should live in peace because the world already held too much strife. Then he asked the boys to shake hands. They did, a little reluctantly, grinned, and walked off together.

I smiled when Judah stood to join me. "That is not what my father would have told them."

"Really?" His brow quirked. "I suppose he would have had them slug it out?"

"He would have hit them both — one, for causing the trouble, and the other for not beating the other boy immediately."

Judah slipped his arm around my shoulder. "I am glad you were born a girl," he said. "One less bully for me to reckon with."

We walked a short distance, then I looked up at him. "Did you fight a lot as a child?"

He lifted one shoulder in a shrug. "Most times I didn't start it — but a lot of young fools tried to take me on."

"Because you were strong?"

"Because I was big. Everyone fancied themselves David, and me Goliath. They all wanted to prove themselves, even my brothers."

I digested this information and then peeked up at him again. "Do you think our sons will be urged to fight?"

His eyes widened. "Do you — are you — ?"

I felt my cheeks burn. "No, I mean, I don't know. I was only thinking about the future."

"Ah." He calmed himself with a deep breath. "If our sons are big, they will probably have to fight. But we will teach them how to be gentle."

They will probably have to fight. The words echoed in the space around us and would not leave my ears.

Why did some men love violence? Why did they become professional soldiers, killers, executioners? What was it that made little boys want to pummel each other? Was it the same quality that made some men want to beat their women?

Pondering these questions, I tried to frame an unselfish prayer that would beg HaShem to bring Judah home alone. I made several attempts, but could never find words that did not make me feel ashamed and guilty.

So I gave up and decided to wait without praying. When Judah returned, I would see what HaShem had done.

Chapter Fifteen: Judah

At daybreak I had brought a mule out of the pasture, hitched her to a wagon, and set out for the City of David. Mother reacted with joy and fear when I announced I was going back to Jerusalem — she worried I might be attacked in the war-torn city, yet she hoped I would be able to bring back a report on her friends who still lived there. I kissed her good-bye, then stopped at my house to take one last look at my sleeping bride. If I were to die on this trip, I wanted to carry Leah's image with me into the afterlife.

She did not wake when I opened the door, so I studied the shape of her young face, then backed out as quietly as I had entered. The sooner I began my journey, the sooner I could return.

The well-worn track led me down a rocky slope to the plain, where the residents of Modein had planted olive groves and vineyards. A little farther on, pastures teemed with goats and sheep. All seemed peaceful in the bright light of early morning.

Yet worry bedeviled me as I rode — what would I tell Leah if I found her parents dead? She was a quiet girl, and I still knew so little about her. She had seemed pleased to wed me and she was an obedient wife, but was she *happy*? What did she want from life, and from me? The questions felt too personal to ask aloud, and she had never offered to share her dreams.

Did she even have any?

An approaching caravan snapped my thoughts back to reality. I was not alone on the road. I met several caravans coming from the port at Joppa, wagons and camels laden with goods from Egypt, Rome, and Tyre. Several red-caped Roman soldiers rode with the caravans, undoubtedly guarding the richly dressed merchants. A tax collector, recognizable by the stylus hanging from his belt, rode atop a lanky camel, counting coins in his palm even as he rocked with the ponderous beast.

I also passed refugees coming from what remained of the holy city. Entire families traveled on the road, their feet gray with dust and their faces marked by runnels of sweat. Mothers with their infants tied to their backs or carrying toddlers in their arms. Few of them rode in wagons, and fewer still traveled with supplies. They had fled with their most precious possessions, their children, and their lives.

Finally I caught a glimpse of Jerusalem. The great wall that had rimmed the holy city lay in pieces on the hillside like blocks tossed by a giant. Two of the wall's distinctive towers had been torn down, and smoke still drifted upward from a nearby valley. As I rode closer, I recognized the unforgettable scent of burning bodies and realized that the governor's men were burning the dead.

I entered at the Joppa Gate amid a flock of bleating sheep. With the stink of death in my nostrils, I turned the mule away from the shepherd and his flock. I left the beast and wagon at a stable and made my way through burned-out buildings to the Tyropoeon Valley, home of the cheesemakers, the only home Leah had ever known. The valley lay between Mount Moriah and Mount Zion, and the buildings in that area appeared to have escaped the flames.

The marketplace was but a shadow of what it had been when we left, but a few valiant merchants had set up booths to feed the city's starving survivors. I walked past baskets of dried figs, a bakery offering hard loaves, and a merchant selling soot-covered jars of Arabian spices. Not enough to make a meal, perhaps, but something to fill the belly.

Then I reached Leah's booth . . . and found it empty. I turned, not knowing if I should keep searching the market or make my way to her house.

A sharp voice cut into my thoughts. "If you're looking for the cheesemaker, he's dead." I turned and saw a woman with brazen red hair leaning against a post.

"What happened to him?"

The woman groaned. "Didn't I say it would happen sooner or later? He dined and drank with the Seleucids, that's what happened. Apparently he got into an argument and pulled a knife on one of the king's men. He always had a temper, and now he is dead."

I considered this news, and felt relief. "What about his wife?"

The woman — surely a harlot, to have hair that unnatural — lifted a meaty shoulder and shrugged. "Haven't seen her. But nobody has been in that booth since the governor's men came through the gate."

I nodded my thanks and set out for Leah's house.

I found my wife's former home without

much trouble. The fires had not touched this part of the valley, and the little house appeared deserted — the door hung askew on its leather hinges and a jagged bit of fabric dangled from a window.

I moved closer to the rough wooden door. I heard no sound from within, but the door was closed, so someone might still be inside. I knocked and heard nothing. Leah's mother must have fled, especially if she no longer had a husband to protect her. But where would she go?

I was about to leave when a neighbor across the street thrust his head out of a window. "She's in there," he said, pointing to Leah's door. "Aren't you the big fellow who married their daughter?"

I nodded.

"Then have a care and take Sabra out of here. She'll die unless someone takes her away. The governor's men knocked her around before they killed her husband. Left her for dead, I'd wager."

Without waiting to hear more, I pushed at the unbarred door and entered the house. The small table had been overturned, the bench tipped over. A female form, covered only by a thin piece of wool, occupied a straw mattress.

I knew a man should not look at a woman

who was not his wife, so I turned my eyes away. But that quick glance assured me that the neighbor had spoken the truth — Leah's mother would not live long without proper care.

"I'm going to find some food for you," I said, hoping she could hear me. "And then I will take you to your daughter in Modein. You will live with my family from this day forward. Our home is not large, but you are welcome in it."

She did not speak, yet when I glanced her way again, I saw an uplifted hand and fluttering fingers. She was still alive.

I hurried out the door, determined that I would not have to tell my wife that *both* her parents were dead.

For three drachmas I hired a woman to remain in the house and care for Sabra until she was strong enough to travel. By sunset of the second day Leah's mother had regained her voice, and her first words to me were a question: "Is my daughter well?"

"She is."

"Is she happy?"

I knelt by the woman's side and observed the mottled bruises on her arms and face. "I believe so. I know I am happy with her. Life is good in Modein — our village is so small, the king's men do not bother with us."

A ghost of a smile flickered at the edges of Sabra's mouth, then she closed her eyes and slept.

On the morning of the fourth day, I carefully lifted my mother-in-law and carried her to the wagon where I had padded the bare boards with a few blankets and other fabrics I found in the house. Traveling with a sick woman and a stubborn mule would not grant me a speedy journey, but my bride would be happy to learn she had not been orphaned.

We were half a day's journey past the ruined city walls when I spotted a man and his horse on the side of the road. The beast, a magnificent Arabian, was refusing to lower his foreleg while the rider struggled to calm the high-strung animal.

After glancing at my passenger to make sure she slept, I stopped the mule and climbed down from the wagon. The balding man wore the colorful robes of a Seleucid diplomat, and his clean-cut face assured me he was not Jewish.

Thinking of Jerusalem, which lay in ruins and ashes because of this fellow's king, I approached cautiously. "Is your horse lame?"

The man pulled himself up in a vain attempt to look me in the eye. "I have nothing against Jews," he began, "and I had nothing to do with what happened back there."

I frowned. "Did I accuse you?"

"Well —" He blew out a breath. "I don't know horses, you see, and this creature nearly threw me before he stopped."

"He's not yours, then."

"Rented."

"Ah. Well, he's a magnificent beast. My brother would love this animal." As the stallion tossed his head, I caught the reins and held them, then rubbed my hand over the animal's jawline. The stallion's eyes were wild with pain, and his breath came fast and heavy through his wide nostrils. "Have you examined his hoof?"

The foreigner, who barely came up to my breastbone, gave me a sheepish look. "I am a man of letters, friend. I would examine his foot, but he makes me nervous. What if he were to kick all the letters out of my head?"

"He might," I admitted, suppressing a smile, "if you make *him* nervous."

I murmured soft shushing sounds and

handed the reins to the little man. "Hold them firmly, with no sudden movements." With the horse's head secure, I ran my hand down the stallion's foreleg, then bent the leg to examine the hoof. Bracing my shoulder against the stallion's side, I spotted a pebble embedded in the tender flesh inside the hard outer surface. I clucked in quiet sympathy as I tried to slip my finger into the space, but the pebble was too deeply embedded.

"I see the problem," I said, easing the leg back down, "but I will need a tool to solve it."

"If I can do anything to help —"

"Just hold his head," I said, walking toward my wagon.

I took a short knife from a leather pouch by the driver's seat. I returned to the stallion, bent the creature's foreleg again, and managed to slip the blade between the pebble and the soft interior of the foot. By pressing my finger near the pebble, a quick twist of the knife forced the pebble to pop out and rattle over the hard ground.

Before lowering the leg, I observed that the interior part of the hoof was red and swollen. The poor animal had borne the pain for as long as he could.

"This animal needs to rest," I told the

man. "Ride him gently — or better yet, lead him — and at the next town, find an inn with a stable and put him up for the night. Give him good food and let him rest. The swelling should go down during the night, and you may be able to continue your journey tomorrow. Avoid roads with small stones, and do not ride him hard on the way home."

"Thank you." The man patted the huge horse on the shoulder and smiled. "I am called Philander, and I owe you a debt."

I shrugged. "You owe me nothing. You owe the horse a gentle ride."

"Will you at least let me provide a meal at the next town? Please — my mount will be able to rest while we break bread together."

I tilted my head, considering. He had a point. Though this foreigner was completely undeserving of that magnificent horse, and though his king had desecrated our Temple and destroyed our capital city, I was hungry . . . and, if the truth be told, a little weary of hearing myself think.

When we reached Beth-horon, a small mountain town mostly inhabited by shepherds and goat herders, we went to an inn across from the village well. Philander led his horse to the nearby stable while I checked on Leah's mother. Sabra appeared to sleep soundly, but I would check on her again before returning to the road.

Philander noticed my sleeping passenger. "Is your mother ill?"

"My wife's mother." I managed a small smile. "I cannot forget to bring her something to eat when we leave."

"You are a good son-in-law — better than most, by far." Philander led the way into the inn.

Like other inns in Israel, the place was little more than a family home with an extra table for guests. I sat at the table and Philander sat across from me. The owner lifted a brow when he saw us, probably surprised to see a Jew sharing a meal with a Seleucid dignitary.

"What can I get you?" he said, coming over.

"Whatever you have." Philander folded his hands and smiled. "Anything but pork."

The innkeeper and I shared a quick look — why would this heathen object to eating swine?

When the innkeeper moved away, Philander lowered his voice and leaned across the table. "I know you have no reason to trust me," he said, glancing around, "but I am sympathetic to your cause."

"My cause?"

Philander shook his head. "Your clothing gives you away. You wear a long tunic, you still have your beard, and your head is uncovered. You are one of those who cling to the laws of your fathers — what do they call you? Hasidim?"

I hesitated. Was this some kind of trap?

"Anyway," Philander went on, "I respect your position. After all, we Greeks cling to the religion of our fathers. Yet our king feels he can impose his religion on others. Not even the Persian kings attempted that." He propped an elbow on the table. "Now I have a question for you. You were leaving your capital city, and you had to be upset by what you saw. Yet you stopped to help me, a man who is obviously affiliated with the enemy. Why did you do so? Were you planning to kill me and take the horse?"

I snorted. "I have never killed anyone, and I am not likely to start now. Truth be told, I didn't want to stop for you. But the Torah commands us to show hospitality to strangers."

"Even the enemy?"

" 'If your enemy is hungry, give him bread to eat,' " I quoted, " 'and if he is thirsty, give him water to drink.' " I smiled. "The Torah commands us to treat a foreigner as we would the native-born among us. We are to regard you as we regard ourselves, for we were once foreigners in the land of Egypt."

Philander stared at me, his fingers absently tugging at a few straggly hairs on his chin. "An altruistic god. Fascinating."

I braced my elbow on the table and rested my chin in my hand. Either this Philander was truly sympathetic or he was trying to catch me saying something that would merit a death sentence. "You say you live in Syria?"

"In Antioch — yes, the king's capital city. You might as well know the whole story: I work for Antiochus. I'm one of his scribes."

"A man of letters."

"Yes. As I said."

"What brings you to Judea?"

The little man sighed. "The king's business, of course. I brought a packet of messages to Apollonius. The king sent me because I am — how did he put it? — invisible. No one would suspect an unassuming man like me to be carrying messages from Antiochus Epiphanes. You, on the other hand — you will never be invisible."

I felt a slow grin stretch across my face. This man was so honest, so unassuming, I was tempted to believe every word out of his mouth. But how likely was it that I would encounter one of the king's scribes on the lonely road to Modein?

"If you really work for the king —"

"I do."

"I was trying to think of some way you could prove yourself. But I can think of nothing."

Philander shook his head. "You lack creativity, my friend. Ask yourself — why would a little man like this be traveling on a valuable horse and not know how to care for it? If I were a wealthy merchant, I would have goods to sell or pocketsful of money. If I were a military man, I would certainly know how to care for my mount. If I were a farmer, would I have hands as clean as these?" He held up his hands, displaying soft pink palms and manicured fingernails.

"You could be a spy."

He laughed aloud. "If I were a spy, would I identify myself as one of the king's scribes? I would pretend to be something I am not, so I am obviously who I said I am. I could be nothing else."

The host stepped over to our table, carrying a wooden platter loaded with two cups of wine, a loaf of crusty bread, and two generous hunks of goat cheese. Philander pulled a slender moneybag from his belt and paid with gold coins, then jingled the bag before my eyes. "Hear that? I have just enough to get home. No wealth here, and none hidden on my horse."

"I'm not going to rob you."

"Good." The man bit off a chunk of cheese, then made a face. "Not as good as that of the king's house, but better than starving."

I sampled the cheese, too. "My wife makes cheese, and hers is better than this."

"You have a wife — children?"

"Not yet."

"Where do you live?"

I narrowed my eyes. For one who was not a spy, he asked a lot of questions. "Why would you want to know?"

Philander shrugged. "Because I enjoy conversation. Fine, don't tell me where you live, but do tell me your name. After all, I gave you my name without hesitation."

"I am called Judah Maccabaeus."

He wrinkled his nose. "What does that mean? Something to do with your god?"

"It means *hammerhead.* Because I like to pound things."

The scribe's round eyes went wide. "Should I be more careful with my words? A diminutive man like me might not survive a good pounding."

"Mostly I pound people who blaspheme

HaShem," I answered. "And I haven't heard you do that."

"Nor will you." Philander broke the bread and selected the smallest piece. "I have learned it is not wise to come between a man and his god. The king has other ideas, but I don't subscribe to them — I only write them down. And I like you Jews."

"Why?"

"Why not? You keep to yourselves, mostly. You are a literate people, and as a man who prizes literacy, that is a great virtue. You have persevered through many persecutions — present, past, and, I daresay, future."

"Why would we face persecution in the future?"

"Why does the fox chase the hare? Because he is always hungry."

I considered his answer and decided that Philander was an honest and practical man. At least he seemed to view the world with clear eyes. "I cannot find fault with your opinions."

"Then let us be friends, finish our meal, and depart in peace." He lifted his cup and held it before my eyes. "To you, Judah Maccabaeus — a swift journey and a prosperous life."

I couldn't help myself. I lifted my cup, too. "So be it, Philander the scribe."

■ ■ ■ ■

Because his horse needed rest, I left Philander at the inn and continued on.

Sabra said very little on our journey. I thought she might be a quiet person by nature, which helped explain Leah's reserve. My wife might have inherited her mother's quiet disposition just as she inherited the woman's nose and jawline.

Though we traveled slowly, I pressed to reach Modein within a single day. I did not want to spend a night with a woman to whom I was not married, no matter who she might be. A righteous man of Israel should not do such a thing.

And, if I am honest, I was also motivated by the thought of sleeping with my wife in my own bed.

The road had emptied by sunset; most travelers had turned aside for dinner and a good night's rest. The sun dipped below the horizon and turned the sky blue-black, then the residual light disappeared and left us with a diamond-spangled sky. Fortunately, a round moon lit the countryside, coating the worn road with a silver sheen.

I was humming one of Father's favorite hymns of ascent when a voice startled me:

"That is beautiful." Startled, I turned and saw Sabra lying on her back, one arm pillowing her head, the other extended as if she could catch stars with her fingers. Was the woman losing her mind? Or was this her way of expressing admiration for Adonai's handiwork?

"It is," I answered, watching for her reaction. "Nearly as beautiful as your daughter."

I expected some sort of reply, but the woman simply smiled and lowered her hand to her belly, apparently content to ride the rest of the way in silence.

Darkness lay heavy on the horizon by the time I reached Modein. I pulled up outside my father's house, hitched the mule to a post, and woke my sleeping passenger. "This is my parents' house. I am going to wake them, then we will get you settled."

The quiet sound of steady breathing was the only reply.

Father came to the door, his eyes wide and his hair standing up around his head. He glanced beyond me and saw the wagon. "Did you find Leah's parents?"

"Her mother," I answered. "The cheesemaker is dead. The mother is not well. The governor's men beat her."

"Bring her in."

"I was going to take her to our house —"

"She'll be more comfortable with us, son. I'll wake Rosana."

By the time I brought the frail woman inside, my mother had prepared a pallet near the fire. I laid Sabra on it, then gave my mother a grateful smile. "I do not know how badly she is hurt," I said. "But I'm sure Leah will be relieved to hear her mother is safely out of Jerusalem."

"Do not worry." Mother squeezed my hand. "She will receive tender care here with us."

While Mother knelt by the woman's bed, Father took me aside. "How fares Jerusalem?" he asked, unspoken pain glowing in his eyes. "What damage did the heathen do this time?"

I took a deep breath, uncertain of how honest I should be. "The damage is severe," I finally said. "The walls are down, and the city is crowded with the king's men. Entire neighborhoods stand empty and burned out. Children wander through the ruins looking for their parents. Food is scarce. The survivors are trying to help the injured and restore order, but the task will not be easy."

Fresh misery darkened Father's face. "Is

it so truly bad?"

"The rumors we heard are all true. The enemy has established a citadel in the old City of David, and they are using stones from the destroyed walls to fortify their position. They will be close enough to the Temple to observe anything done there."

Father groaned.

"That's not the worst of it. The men doing the work are not all Gentiles. Many are Jews who have given themselves over to the king's men."

"And his gods." Father frowned, then spat on the floor as if the thought of such betrayal had left a sour taste in his mouth. "At least we are no longer there to witness the desecration. I am grateful Adonai led us away. We will stand for Him here, in Modein, and we will welcome others who join our cause."

I glanced around, wondering how my father's house was supposed to hold the others he spoke of. He and Mother would be crowded by the addition of even this refugee.

"Go home to your bride." Mother stood and slipped her arm around my waist. "Tell Leah not to worry about her mother. We will care for her, and she can remain with us for as long as she likes. But no newly married couple needs a mother hovering in the shadows of their home."

I opened my mouth to protest, but Mother pressed her fingers across my lips. "Go home, son." Gently she pushed me toward the doorway. "And tell your bride she may visit her mother in the morning."

Chapter Sixteen: Leah

Judah had been gentle and solicitous when he gave me the news about Father's death, but he had never lived in my father's house. His father was a decent, reasonable man, but my father had never been anything but a tyrant. Yet the Law of Moses commanded me to respect and obey that tyrant, and Solomon promised a blessing for those who honored their parents.

Why would HaShem command me to honor a man who constantly injured those he was supposed to love?

I bit my lip and lowered my eyes, not wanting Judah to see the extent of my relief, but he was more observant than most men. "You are . . . glad to hear this? I knew your father was harsh, but —"

"My father was not a good man." I lifted my chin and met his gaze. "Living with him was not easy . . . not for me, but especially not for my mother. Life will be better for her now that he is gone."

Judah's face went blank with shock. "But he was your *father.* The Torah commands us to —"

"And I did, as best I could, until you took me away from that terrible man. But I will not mourn him. And neither will my mother."

Judah shook his head back and forth, like an ox stunned by the slaughter's blade. He might not understand, but he had grown up in a much different home. From what I could tell, I had come from a freakish family.

"One thing, Judah." I caught my husband's hand. "Say nothing of this to your family. I would not have them think less of me or my mother because Father was a monster. We survived him, though at times I did not think we would. He routinely beat my mother and several times she almost died, but you are the only one who needs to know the full truth."

Upon hearing this, Judah had tilted his brow, given me an uncertain look, and blown out the lamp.

Now I drew a deep breath before approaching my father-in-law's house. HaShem had answered the prayers I had dared not breathe, and my father was dead.

Mother was here, and I was glad for it.

With Father gone, Mother could learn how to live her own life. She could smile without fear, she could relax, she could sit and do nothing if she wanted to. She could learn how to speak without evaluating every word beforehand; she could laugh and know she would not be scorned or silenced. She could learn how to stand erect and walk with confidence, holding her head high and knowing that she had survived the worst kind of nightmare.

What would she be like now that she did not have to weigh every attitude and action in the mercurial light of my father's cruelty? Who would she be, now that she was no longer Father's wife?

I paused outside the door and tilted my ear toward the open window, but I heard nothing from inside Mattathias's house. Then I knocked, and a moment later Rosana called and bade me come in.

I found Rosana and my mother inside. My mother-in-law stood at the table, working with her pestle to grind spices. Mother reclined on a couch, her hands in her lap, her gaze focused on Rosana's work. Her face, when it finally turned toward me, seemed vacant and lifeless. Had Father stolen her soul before he died?

"Mother." I walked forward and kissed her forehead, then sank to the floor at her feet. "I am glad you are with us."

Are you? She did not speak the words, but I heard them as she looked at me with exhausted eyes.

If we had been alone, I might have asked about what happened to Father and how she came to be injured. But Rosana was listening and might not understand what had gone on in our home. I had been part of her family long enough to know that Mattathias treated her like a friend and a partner, showing her respect and rarely acting without asking her advice.

"How are you?" Mother's brows flickered above a tentative smile. "How do you like being a wife?"

I felt my face heat. "I like it well enough. My husband is . . . nothing like Father."

Mother's smile deepened. "Good."

The sons of Mattathias and Rosana, including Judah, also treated their wives with respect, and as one of those wives I did not always know how to respond. When Judah asked for my opinion, I hesitated to give it, certain that it would be met with an insult. When he approached with his arms outstretched, I found myself bracing for a blow; when he turned abruptly to flash a smile, I flinched.

And when he reached for me at night in the early days, my inclination had been to lie like a dead woman, biding my time until his breathing became deep and regular. Then I would remove his heavy arm and roll toward the edge of the mattress, clinging to the side as if it were a log in a raging river. In those moments I felt like I was two women, one who wanted to give herself to a man who had demonstrated nothing but kindness, and another who doubted that the kindness and generosity could be real . . . or permanent.

Surely my mother understood what I was feeling. She must have been in a similar situation when she was a young bride. Father might have been like Judah, tender in the days before brutality took root and grew into a weed of bitterness.

I took Mother's hand and squeezed it. "When you are stronger, we will take a walk and I will show you around the village," I promised. "Until then, I must be about my work at home. But I will check on you every day. I want to hear all the stories you could never tell me . . . until now."

She looked at me, weariness and wisdom mingling in her eyes. *I know,* her eyes seemed to say, *and understand all the things you cannot say.*

While I took leave of my mother, Mattathias and his brother Ehud stormed into the room, their faces tight with strain.

"I tell you, it will not happen." Ehud shook his finger in his older brother's face. "I will not risk my grandson's life."

"Would you disobey HaShem?" Mattathias spun to face his brother. "Would you ignore the Torah because you fear the king? God is greater than your fears, Ehud. There is no reason for you to disobey."

"What if it was one of your sons, *your* grandchild? Would you risk their lives?"

"I expect that it will be one of my sons, perhaps soon," Mattathias replied. "If HaShem blesses my daughters-in-law."

Ehud braced both hands on his hips and looked around the room, but when his angry eyes crossed mine, I turned away and pretended to study the grain in the wooden table.

"In any case, the decision is not mine to make," Ehud finally said. "My son and daughter-in-law will have to decide. After all, they are the ones who will pay the price if they are discovered."

Mattathias grunted. "Have you always let your children make their own decisions?

Did you let your toddling son wander into the fire so he could feel its heat, or did you guide him with your wisdom? Ehud, sometimes you must speak frankly and tell your children the truth. Especially when the truth concerns the will of Adonai."

"And how do I know what that will is?" Ehud raised his arms as a thunderous scowl darkened his brow. "The Almighty has not written it in the clouds or on the stones of my house —"

"He has written it in the Torah," Mattathias countered. " 'Generation after generation, every male among you who is eight days old is to be circumcised, including slaves born within your household —' "

"I know the Law." Ehud blew out a breath and frowned at his brother. "You are right, of course. I will speak to my son and his wife. I will remind them of the Law of Moses. But if they choose not to circumcise their infant, I will say nothing more. I cannot gamble with their lives."

Mattathias closed his eyes for a moment, then reached out to clasp his brother's shoulder. "That is the right thing to do. You have decided correctly."

While we women watched, the two men embraced and kissed each other on both cheeks. Ehud left the house while Mattathias looked at us with sudden interest. "Leah," he said, smiling, "I hope you are happy to have your mother with us."

"I am," I said truthfully. "I am looking forward to knowing her better."

My mother chuckled from her bed while Mattathias frowned. "What do you mean?"

Rosana grasped his elbow and guided him toward the table. "Come eat, husband, and tell me about your day."

Three days later, Judah and I had just finished our midday meal when a woman's voice called at the door. Judah smiled at me and bade the visitor enter.

I blinked when my mother came through the doorway. She looked much stronger, no longer like a reed that could be blown over by a strong wind. I stood and hugged her, my heart filling with gratitude for a husband considerate enough to think of rescuing my mother from Jerusalem.

Judah pushed his chair away from our table, eager to be on his way. "I'll be milking the goats," he said. "I'll be back before dark."

"Do not go yet." Mother extended her hand. "I would have a word with both of you before you leave."

Judah looked at me, silently asking if I

wanted him to stay, so I dipped my chin in a barely perceptible nod. He sank back into his chair as I gestured for Mother to take my seat. Then I went to stand behind Judah.

Mother sat, then turned toward me. The hard light streaming through the window lit her face, and for the first time I saw how living with my father had aged her. Her face was like a plot of sunbaked earth, furrowed with stark lines — a map of pain and disappointment.

"I know what Mattathias is planning," Mother said, casting a nervous glance at Judah as she folded her hands on the table. "He wants to defy the king and his men. But surely he can be made to see how unwise this plan is. Judah, for the sake of my daughter and your future children, you must make him understand that his actions will spell disaster for this family. Please — if you love my daughter, you must do this."

I blinked, stunned as much by Mother's manner as by her words. To my knowledge, she had never spoken more than a few words in Judah's company, and never in my entire life had I heard her speak with such determination.

What happened to the meek woman who used to shrink when my father looked in her direction?

"I can tell you feel strongly about this," Judah said, clearly trying to be respectful. "But you must realize that my father — all of us — feel strongly about the worship of Adonai. We will never capitulate to the king's edicts. How could we give up our Law and our worship when those are the things that make us who we are?"

"Worship as much as you please in your home," Mother whispered, leaning closer. "Say your prayers, read the prophets and the writings, practice the commandments in the Torah. But do not publicly commit any act that would displease the king's men. Do nothing to draw attention to yourself. That is how you survive when you are ruled by a tyrant. It is how I survived these many years."

Judah looked at me, then shifted his gaze to Mother's tense face. "Sabra, I cannot —"

"Please." Mother clutched at his arm. "I know pain. And I would not wish it on you, my daughter, or your family."

Firmly, gently, Judah took her hand and laid it on the table. "Do not worry, Mother. We will trust in Adonai."

She flinched. "You think Adonai listens to our prayers?"

"You think He doesn't?"

Mother lifted her chin and swallowed,

then leaned back. "I do not know what the Almighty does. But I know He has never listened to my prayers." She shifted her attention to me. "Might I trouble you for a cup of water?"

While I moved to the jug, Judah stood. "I'm seeing to the goats," he said, then he threw me a look of concern and left us alone.

Mother wiped pearls of perspiration from her brow. "I have spent hours searching for the words to convince him," she said, her voice heavy and tired. "Apparently I did not succeed."

"Judah has a mind of his own in these things," I said, pouring water into a cup.

"Does he? Or does he simply follow his father's direction?" Mother took the cup and drank, then lowered it to the table. "You must make him think of you first, Leah. I have watched him carefully — he is not like your father. He is a kind man and he seems to love you. You must make him love you more than he loves his family. If he doesn't . . ." She shook her head. "His father is walking a path that will lead to destruction, and hard times can change a man. I would hate to see your gentle husband turn to violence."

I sank into a chair, my thoughts spinning.

I had always assumed that a good husband would place his wife first in all things. After all, didn't the Torah say that a man would leave his mother and father and cling to his wife? My father had not been a good husband, but Judah was.

"I believe he does love me more than his family."

"Then you have to ask him to stop listening to Mattathias and listen to you." She took my hands, gripping them so tightly that her short nails cut into my flesh. "I'm not trying to make trouble between you; I'm trying to keep you safe. You didn't see what happened in Jerusalem after you left. You didn't see the young mothers who were crucified for circumcising their children. I did."

I cringed before the fearful grimace on her face. How could I answer? I wanted to be safe, but I didn't want to upset Judah when he had shown me nothing but kindness. "And how am I supposed to convince him to listen to me?"

She relaxed her grip on my hands. "Give him a child, Leah. Giving him a son will so delight him that he will place his son's welfare above all else. Even above Mattathias."

"But Judah respects his parents. He would

never —"

"You would be surprised what some men will do for their sons." Mother sank back into her chair. "So do not delay. Give the man a child."

I glanced away. "I am trying."

"Are you sure?" Mother leaned forward again. "Do you go to his bed with resignation or joy?"

Heat seared my cheeks. "Mother!"

"When I was a child," she continued, ignoring my embarrassment, "my mother explained that the marriage bed was for pleasure and procreation, for joy and children. I know —" she swallowed hard — "you saw little joy in your father's house, but that is no reason for not experiencing joy in your own. So hear me, Leah. Welcome your husband to your bed joyfully and often." She smiled and tilted her head. "And then perhaps your husband will think first of his own house and keep his loves safe from the king's threats."

Silenced by embarrassment, I looked up and watched as she stood and folded her arms. "In many ways, I failed as a mother," she said, a dusky tide advancing up her throat. "But I will not fail you now."

With stiff, brittle dignity, she said goodbye and left me alone with my thoughts.

Chapter Seventeen: Judah

Though the naming ceremony should have been a happy occasion, an air of dread hung over the gathering, made even more obvious by the mother's wide eyes and the father's trembling voice. Even Leah had seemed anxious about the occasion, and as we prepared to leave the house, I found her looking at me as if she wanted to say something. When I asked if she had something on her mind, she shook her head and turned away.

Now she moved toward the other women, who hovered at the edge of the crowd like shadows. I squared my shoulders and joined the men — Johanan, Simon, and Eleazar were already present, as was our father. Jonathan was late, as usual.

Father caught my eye and lifted his bearded chin in a silent salute. I stood next to Simon and folded my arms, then sought our host's attention. Caleb, father to the baby fussing in his mother's arms, caught my eye and attempted a smile, then lifted his hand in a broad public welcome. "Thank you for coming," he said, addressing everyone in the gathering. "My wife and I are delighted you were willing to join us."

How many times had similar words been spoken at naming ceremonies? Thousands, if not millions, of times in Israel. But never had they been spoken with more feeling or greater significance.

To observe the event, we stepped closer, forming a tight circle around the new parents.

Caleb took a small pillow from beneath his arms and held it on his open hands. He looked at his wife, who placed their baby on the pillow and unwrapped the swaddling cloths. The infant boy startled, his arms and legs stiffening. Then he drew in his limbs and blinked at his father's face. His mother took a blade from her belt, and her hand quivered as she held it above her child.

"Blessed are you, Lord our God, King of the universe," Caleb prayed, his voice booming throughout the gathering, "who has sanctified us with His commandments and commanded us concerning circumcision."

His wife drew a deep breath and swiftly

performed the procedure, then dropped the foreskin to the ground. Silence hung over the gathering for an instant, and then the baby wailed and Caleb returned the child to his mother. He lifted his hand to recite the traditional blessing: "Blessed are you, Lord our God, King of the universe, who has sanctified us with His commandments and commanded us to enter into the Covenant of Abraham our father."

We observers responded in unison: "Just as he has entered into the Covenant, so may he enter into Torah, into marriage, and into good deeds."

With the act completed, the underlying tension broke. The women swarmed forward to congratulate the relieved mother, while Caleb came toward us, his face pale beneath his beard.

Father clapped the young man on the shoulder. "You have done well, nephew."

"I am grateful to have done it at all," Caleb said, looking at me as he replied. "I don't know how I found the courage."

"You were courageous because it is the right thing to do. God has commanded us, and who can say otherwise? You have done well. You have made your father proud."

"Indeed, he has." Ehud stepped forward and embraced his son, then took the baby from its mother and held the child aloft. "To the future!"

As everyone raised their voices in celebration, I watched my father grasp the edges of his robe and stroll through the crowd. I knew what he was doing — his sharp eyes were noting which villagers had come to support Caleb and which had stayed away.

I shouldered my way through the men and found Simon, who had a small son of his own. "Were you as nervous when you circumcised your boy?"

Simon shrugged. "The situation was different. The king had not yet issued his edict."

"But you knew the Hellenes frowned on circumcision."

"We knew a lot of things, but we didn't believe any Jew would honor the opinions of a king over the commands of HaShem."

I sighed and watched Caleb make his way through the crowd. He looked like a man who had fought a hard battle and won, but the danger had not passed. If the authorities learned what had happened here today, Caleb might yet hear a knock on his door.

And the king's punishment for circumcision meant death for both mother and child.

Chapter Eighteen: Leah

Even though I did not know her well, I slipped my arm around the distraught mother's shoulder.

"Will he ever stop crying?" she asked, her teary eyes meeting mine as she patted the screaming baby in her arms. "What if I did it wrong?"

I squeezed her shoulder. "I think you did it exactly right." I had never witnessed a circumcision at such a close distance, but I saw no reason to confess that nonessential truth. "I've been to at least a dozen naming ceremonies and every mother did exactly as you did. Your baby will be fine."

"If only he would stop crying."

"He will." I lowered my arm and studied the baby's angry scrunched-up face. "He will fall asleep soon, and when he wakes, he will have forgotten all about it."

"He won't hate me?"

"Of course not." I smiled with an assurance I had no right to feel since I had never been a mother. But I was at least a year older than this girl, and age carried its own authority.

"Leah, did you hear?" Neta sauntered toward me, narrowly dodging another woman's elbow on the way. Her perfectly oval face had gone pale, except for two red spots, one in each cheek. "About those two poor women in Jerusalem —"

"Come, let's talk inside." I wasn't sure, but I had a feeling Neta had been talking to my mother. I took her elbow and steered her away from the worried young mother. A woman who had just circumcised her baby did not need to hear about women who had been crucified for doing the same thing.

I pulled Neta into the courtyard of Mattathias's house, where Rosana had set out a tray of sweet breads. "Um, those look good," I said, taking one of the treats. "Would you like one?"

Neta's dark eyes widened. "How can you stand there and smile as if nothing is amiss? The governor ordered those women to be thrown from the tower of that citadel they're building! I heard they were forced to hold their babies as they fell, so the mothers *and* their infants were dashed on the stones below."

The bread stuck in my suddenly tight throat. *This* story I had not heard. With a terrible effort I swallowed the bread. "That is unthinkable."

"Yet Caleb *still* held a naming ceremony for his son? He could have ignored the tradition of circumcision and no one would have protested. After all, the occasion is to name the child, and surely giving a name doesn't require the shedding of blood."

"The occasion requires the circumcision," I said, gripping her arm. "Mattathias says the child's name isn't nearly as important as obedience to Adonai."

She stared at me, a frown settling between her arched brows. "Since when have you started parroting the old man?"

"What does it matter what I think? He is the head of the family, but —"

"But what?"

"What does your husband say?"

Her expression cleared. "Johanan agrees with his father, but I think we can live at peace with the king's men as long as we are quiet and don't openly flaunt the new laws. But circumcising a baby in public —"

I pinched her arm as Mattathias walked by. When he had passed, I exhaled slowly. "You should keep that opinion to yourself."

"But they are killing women," she whispered, her voice tinged with terror. "I hear they're threatening to crucify people, even women, who follow the Law of Moses. So if Johanan thinks I'm going to say the Sabbath blessing when Seleucids could be lurking about —"

"There are no Seleucids in Modein." I stepped away from her. "And you should speak of something else. It would be better for all if you did not mention such troubling matters today."

After the naming ceremony, we gathered at Ehud's home for the Shabbat meal. Since he was a widower, Rosana stepped in to arrange the celebratory dinner.

Simon's young son Johanan toddled from uncle to uncle, clinging to their hairy legs as the men folded their arms and discussed the latest distressing report from Jerusalem. Caleb and his wife sat apart, their attention on the crying baby.

We women kept busy with the meal. Rosana had butchered and roasted a lamb the day before, so I helped her pull the meat off the bone as Neta and Morit crushed dry herbs to mix with olive oil.

Rosana tossed a bone out the window for the village dogs. "How fared the naming ceremony?" she asked me, lifting a brow.

"Did Caleb manage it without fainting?"

I laughed. "He was anxious, anyone could see it. So was his wife. But the thing is done and another baby is circumcised."

"Blessed be Adonai," Rosana murmured. "And blessed be those two for their obedience. They have more courage than many priests in Jerusalem."

I made a soft sound of assent as I placed several hunks of the steaming meat in a serving bowl. I couldn't tell which spices Rosana had used to season the lamb, but I had never smelled anything so appetizing.

I saw my mother sitting on a bench across the room. She wore a blank look, but at least she had joined the family celebration.

"How is my mother?" I asked Rosana.

My mother-in-law's busy hands slowed for a moment. "She does not say much," she said, her gaze drifting to the far side of the room. "Mattathias thinks she may have been violated by the soldiers who entered her house. But she does not seem unhappy."

"Thank you for looking after her," I said. "You have shown such kindness to us."

"You are both part of our family now." The warmth of Rosana's smile echoed in her voice. "In truth, it does me good to see your mother again. I knew her as a young girl — she was quite the beauty."

The unexpected revelation stole my breath. "She was?"

Rosana lifted a brow. "Can you not see it? She is much the same, but the years have been hard on her. That man." She shook her head. "Still, I am glad she is with us."

She dropped the last handfuls of meat into the serving bowl, checked the bread, and stood back to survey the dishes on the table. Then she smiled at me. "You may ask Ehud to call the men for dinner. The sun is about to set, so tell them to hurry."

I approached the periphery of the men's circle, caught Uncle Ehud's eye, and crooked my index finger, then pointed to the table. He understood and interrupted Eleazar long enough to say that dinner was ready.

The entire family sat on couches and benches as Rosana lit the candles and welcomed the Sabbath. As she brought her hands to her face in the ritual gesture, Simon leaned over and untied the strap that held the leather curtain at the window. It rolled down, blocking what remained of the daylight, and my mother abruptly lifted her head as if confused by the darkness.

"Simon," Mattathias said, his voice firm, "tie up the curtain again."

"But that would be work on the —"

"Tie it up."

Silence hung over the gathering as Simon stood to roll the curtain again. If any Seleucid travelers happened to be in the vicinity, they would have a good view of our family's Sabbath meal.

We all knew why Simon had closed the window, yet if the dinner had been taking place in my home, I might have closed the windows beforehand. I certainly wasn't eager to be hauled off, tortured, and executed. In Jerusalem, where it was nearly impossible to hide from one's neighbor, thousands had already been killed.

But no one had been arrested in Modein. Not yet. The small village seemed to be occupied only by devout followers of Adonai, so perhaps we would not have to fear the sort of persecution that had decimated Jerusalem.

Judah and I settled onto a dining couch as Mattathias lifted a linen napkin from the herbed bread and recited the blessing: *"Barukh atah Adonai, Eloheinu, melekh ha-olam hamotzi lechem min ha'aretz."*

Blessed are you, Lord our God, King of the universe, who brings forth bread from the earth.

"Amein," a dozen voices chorused.

As we ate, I looked around the gathering

and wondered how many of these people would have the courage to observe the Sabbath if Mattathias and Rosana were not here to lead them.

Chapter Nineteen: Judah

During dinner, I couldn't stop a wry smile from lifting the corner of my mouth. Neta, Johanan's wife, kept whispering in her husband's ear, and Johanan wore the look of bored tolerance I had seen a thousand times. Johanan had insisted on marrying a beautiful but peckish woman, while I married out of obedience and had been blessed with a gentle beauty.

"Judah?" Father's voice broke into my musings. "Have you heard a word I've said?"

"Um . . . yes." I nodded. "The situation in Jerusalem grows worse."

Father grunted, barely mollified. "They say this movement springs from the great Alexander, who wanted to unite the world into one race and one people. But he failed, as all men will fail if they attempt a task only HaShem can perform. How can a man unite the world when Adonai has set people apart? We are the seed of Abraham, a chosen race and a peculiar people. The world will be blessed through us, but we are commanded to remain separate."

"I believe," Uncle Ehud said, "this latest edict is designed to promote the king's religion. Is his name not Antiochus Epiphanes, 'God manifest'? These foreign kings yearn to be worshiped as gods. They desire our worship, our allegiance, and our offerings."

"Especially our offerings." Eleazar made a face. "He would bleed Jerusalem dry if he could."

"I have a name for him," Simon announced. "We should call him Antiochus *Epimanes,* which means 'the mad one.' "

Eleazar bent over his plate, choking with laughter, and Jonathan giggled so freely that I couldn't help chuckling.

Simon stifled his urge to laugh by rubbing a finger over his lip.

"We must never give a human king what belongs to HaShem," Father said, his voice calm. "We are the people of Adonai."

"Perhaps we should go to Egypt," Uncle Ehud said. "There are thousands of Jews in the south. Antiochus is not allied with Egypt, so we could dwell there safely."

"And leave our Promised Land?" Johanan

said. “And leave the Temple, ruined as it is?”

The others raised their voices in dissent, but Father lifted his hand for quiet. “This is not a time for arguing,” he said. “It is a time for careful consideration.” He straightened, his shoulders twitching as he eased into the authority he wore like an invisible mantle. “I will not deny that HaShem has led some of our people into Egypt — Adonai has His reasons, and who am I to argue with Him? But how can we abandon the Promised Land out of fear? Shall we capitulate to the Hellenes and surrender our Temple? Shall we submit to the high priest who has betrayed his people and used his office to bribe a pagan king?”

“But what are we to do?” Simon asked Father. “We are members of a priestly family, but we can do nothing about the current high priest. He bribed his way into power, and we are not wealthy enough to bribe the king into appointing someone more appropriate.”

“He used Temple money to pay his bribe,” Johanan said, his lips thinning. “He would not be wealthy if he had not stolen money from the Temple treasury.”

“What are we to do? We are to pray.” Father lifted his gaze from our circle and looked out the dark window, beyond which lay Jerusalem in all its troubled splendor. "We are to remember that a heathen altar has been raised above our sacred stones, and we are to pray for its removal. We are to remind each other that profane animals are being sacrificed in the Holy of Holies, and that Zeus is revered in our holy place, not Adonai, the Lord of heaven and earth. And we are to teach our children that no king can ever take the place of HaShem in our hearts. The Hellenes may abolish our Temple service, they may forbid us to circumcise our children or observe the Sabbath, and they may encourage us to eat unclean animals. But they can never unseat HaShem from His throne. He still owns heaven and earth, and He still controls the fate of kings and priests."

"Amein," I said with my brothers.

And in that moment, as I looked around the circle of my family, I sensed a presence among us. I have never seen a burning bush or the glowing angel of the Lord, but as I sat and watched shadows lengthen across the room, I felt a sense, unanchored but strong, that Adonai was among us and that He would honor my father's prayer. And that everyone present had a role to play in the coming days, a purpose that would result in the salvation of Israel.

Only when I tasted the salt of tears on my lips did I realize I was weeping.

Chapter Twenty: Leah

At the conclusion of the meal, Mattathias stood and rapped his knuckles on a table. "My children," he said, his eyes sweeping over everyone in the room, "how I wish I could prepare you for the coming trouble. For it is coming to Modein, even as it came to Jerusalem."

I looked at Judah and lifted my brow in an unspoken question. I had not been taught the Torah as he and his brothers had, and though I had grown up in the synagogue, I always understood that my husband would be responsible for teaching me — or his father, as was the case that Sabbath night.

"Alas!" Mattathias closed his eyes and lifted his hands to his white head. "Why was I born to see the ruin of my people and the destruction of the holy city? Why did HaShem allow me to dwell in the City of David when the Temple had been defiled and the sanctuary given over to aliens? Our Temple is like a woman without honor, her altars desecrated by heathens who do not know Adonai. The infants of Israel have been slaughtered, her youths struck down by the sword of our enemies. What nation has not inherited Jerusalem's palaces and seized her spoils? All her adornment has been taken away. No longer free, she has become a slave. The glory of Jerusalem has been laid waste; the Gentiles have profaned it. Why would HaShem allow this to happen?"

His gaze shifted from one son to another as he waited for an answer. All five men lowered their heads, and at length, Mattathias sighed.

"HaShem is doing what He has always done — Israel has sinned, so we are being disciplined by our enemies. We have become a people who follow the Law without heeding its intention; we sacrifice on every holy day and ignore the hungry stranger at our door. But most important, we have ignored Adonai, the God who brought us out of Egypt, who brought us back from Babylon, and who gave us this land. How long has it been since we lifted our voices in honest prayer? Since we praised His majesty? Since we thanked Him for His goodness? Since we asked HaShem to send His Spirit to convict us of sin and fill us for His use?"

I lowered my head and peered around the room. I had never witnessed a family like this, and words like these had never passed my father's lips. He had spoken more about himself than about Adonai, and to my knowledge he had never given a thought to sin, starving strangers, or gratitude.

"We, the children of Israel," Mattathias went on, "have taken pains to do all that has been commanded in the Law of Moses, but we have forgotten how to be people of HaShem. We have dedicated our hands but not our hearts. So when other ideas and foreign gods entered our land, our hands kept doing, but like an unfaithful wife our hearts followed strange gods. We have sinned as a people, and Israel's sin has touched all of us — especially me."

I stared, shocked, as the old priest bowed his head and struck his breast. "Why should we live, if we are living apart from HaShem's blessing?"

Silence fell over the gathering, a quiet so thick that the only sound was the thin whistle of the old man's breathing.

My husband spoke first. "I'll tell you why we should live," he said, color rising in his face. "We should live to restore the holy

Temple and return it to Israel."

"War!" Eleazar shouted. "Joshua led the children of Israel to war when conquering this holy land, so why shouldn't we pick up weapons in order to keep it? David was a man of war, also Samson. Adonai gave them strength against their enemies and allowed them to prevail against impossible odds."

I blinked at the unexpected outburst. My husband had proven himself to be gentle and not at all violent except when he had to be. I knew he would fight if attacked, and he would use all his strength against anyone who came against his family. But go to *war*? I pressed my lips together and hoped that Mattathias would counsel against such rash action.

But Mattathias looked at Eleazar with approval in his eyes. "You have always been the boldest of your brothers," he said, a smile in his voice. "It may be that Adonai has given you the heart of a warrior for this very place and time."

Johanan leaned toward his father. "What of me, your first-born?"

"Ah, Johanan." Mattathias smiled at his eldest child. "You are the most ambitious of my sons. You will yearn for victory, but you must always remember that there can be no victory apart from HaShem. Without holiness, your efforts will fail."

"And me, Father?"

"And me?"

Jonathan and Simon pressed for their father's attention, but Mattathias had transferred his attention to Judah. "In the past," he said, "Adonai punished Israel by sending the Philistines, the Babylonians, and the Canaanites. Now He has sent Antiochus Epiphanes. If we are to restore the Temple, if we are to bring Israel back to Adonai, we must purify ourselves before we can do anything. After that, we shall see how HaShem leads us."

He spread his hands, indicating the remains of the feast on the table. "From this moment until sundown three days hence, I will eat nothing. I beg you to join me in this fast, so that we will be ready when Adonai opens the door for action. Will you fast and pray with me?"

One by one, the brothers voiced their agreement. The women remained silent, though I knew we would be expected to do whatever our husbands did. But three days without food! My father would never suggest such a thing.

"We will join you, Father." Judah spoke for all the men present. "And we will wait for your instructions."

The old man fixed his penetrating gaze on my husband. "The time is coming, Judah," he said, his eyes burning, "when you will walk away from your goat pen and pick up your sword. When that time comes, trust in no man, but in Adonai alone. Can you make that promise?"

Judah inclined his head. "I can."

"Good." Mattathias turned to me, as if he wanted to be sure I had borne witness to the exchange. "Very good indeed."

Our little house was not far from Mattathias's home, but when the door closed and the window coverings lowered, we might have been a world away. When Judah crawled onto our bed and I saw the light in his eyes, I hoped that fire burned for me — and not for his father's cause.

"What say you, wife?" Judah caught my hands and held them between his. "Have you decided to leave my family and go in search of your father's clan? Surely things are quieter there."

"I did not come to Modein in search of quiet." I lifted my head long enough to plant a quick kiss on his cheek. "I came in search of laughter — and Simon always makes me laugh."

"Simon?" Judah roared with pretend

indignation, then lowered his head until his lips grazed the side of my neck. "Are Simon's jokes as pleasing as this?"

I closed my eyes as my blood began to rush through my veins. "No."

"Or this?"

His questing lips found my palm, a sensitive spot that never failed to pebble my skin. "All right, I confess! I never laugh at Simon."

"So you laugh only at me?"

"I laugh . . . *with* you."

His lips covered mine. I returned his kiss in a surprising rush of feeling, then pointedly turned my head.

"What's this? Have I done something to displease you?"

I averted my eyes. "Your father wants us to purify ourselves and be holy, and surely it is wrong to lie with your wife on Shabbat."

"Wrong to —" He blew out a breath and grinned. "Who would teach you such a thing? Loving one's wife is not work; it is a *mitzvah.* A good deed."

"If lighting a fire is wrong because it is an act of creation, then lying with one's wife must also be wrong, for it might result in the creation of a child."

Curious, I peeked up at him and saw

thought working in his expression. "But the Torah commands us to be fruitful and multiply. It also commands a husband to provide his wife with food, clothing, and the intimacy of the marriage bed."

He had gone serious, an effect I had not intended. "Judah?"

"Hmm?"

"I was teasing." With the tip of my finger, I traced his brow, the curve of his cheek, and his lips. "And when you take me in your arms" — my voice thickened — "I care not what day it is."

His arms tightened around me as he smiled. "You are surely a wanton woman. A woman who terrified me when we first met."

My jaw dropped. "Why?"

He nodded as a rush of color stained his cheeks. "Because you were so beautiful."

I wrapped my arms around his neck and surrendered to him, reserving only a small portion of my thoughts for wondering if this night might result in the child I needed to keep Judah safe from his father's enthusiasm for war.

An abrupt sound woke me from sleep. I stiffened as a thrill of fear shot through me, then I reached out for Judah and felt only empty space.

"Judah?"

"I'm here."

Frightened by something I heard in his voice, I stumbled out of bed and hurried to the window. Not caring if it was the Sabbath, I tore down the leather blind, allowing moonlight to flood the room.

Judah remained in our bed, but he was sitting erect, his face and chest pale in the silvery light. His eyes were wide, his lips parted, and his hands . . . were shaking.

"Are you all right?" I hurried to his side and knelt on the floor, my hands seeking his. "Are you sick?"

He shook his head. "I . . . had a dream."

Relief washed over me in a flood. "Oh. It's nothing, then."

I gripped his hands, which continued to tremble, and forced a smile. "Judah, I am here. It was only a dream. Nothing of importance."

He shook his head again. "I . . . have them sometimes. I see things, sometimes horrible things, and . . . they are real."

I leaned back as my stomach clenched. Was my husband losing his mind?

"Judah, dreams are meaningless visions."

"You think so?" His wide eyes moved into mine. "I dreamed of Eleazar. He was carrying a sword and spear, and a monster appeared as he walked through a field. It walked on four legs that looked like tree trunks, and it shrieked, scattering every bird in the sky. Eleazar ran toward it, as bold as ever."

I rubbed Judah's arm, hoping my touch could bring him back to reality. "Monsters do not exist, Judah. You are thinking about the behemoth Job described. Your father mentioned that beast at dinner the other day."

Judah stared at me for a moment, then he smiled. "You must think me a mere child, to wake in such a panic."

"You are not a child." I rose and crawled into his lap and raked my fingers through his thick hair. "And you are not a coward. I have had terrifying dreams myself and know how real they can seem."

He drew in a deep breath, exhaling it slowly, as if breathing out the last lingering shadows of his disturbing nightmare.

"Sleep," I whispered, and pressed my lips to his eyelids. "Lie back and sleep until morning."

He nodded, put his arms around me, and fell backward, making me laugh as I fell on top of him.

As I pulled the blanket over us, I smiled, reassured to know that my perfect husband had at least one vulnerability. If he ever had another bad dream, he would depend on me to bring him back to reality.

Judah rose before daybreak. I heard him step outside to relieve himself, then the quiet rub of the door as he came back into the house. Opening one eye, I watched my handsome husband go about his morning routine. Standing bare-chested in the shadows of dawn, he drew water from the bucket with a ladle, then drank deeply, his throat working as he swallowed. He wiped his mouth with the back of his hand and turned to peer out the open window.

Judah was the tallest of his brothers, well formed and broad in the chest, with a slim waist and long limbs. His dark hair flowed over his shoulders, and his beard covered his jawline in a smooth shadow.

Watching him, I wished I knew what thoughts filled my husband's head. If he remembered his nightmare, he gave no sign of it. I sighed in relief and hoped that pleasant dreams had erased every trace of the vision that had awakened him.

Judah was kind to me, and gentle, but he was also ten years older and a man of the world. I kept waiting for him to display some sign of temper or cruelty, but thus far

I had seen nothing but goodness from him.

Perhaps he was gentle with me because of my youth. When I watched him talk to his brothers or cover his head for prayer, I often felt like a sheltered child. From the way he and his brothers occasionally fell silent when I approached, I knew he did not tell me everything.

But though I had attained only sixteen summers, I desired to understand my husband. I wanted to know what moved him when he prayed, and what he dreamed of when he considered our future. When his eyes clouded with dark thoughts, I wanted to know the source of the problem, yet he steadfastly refused to tell me anything that might, as he said, "trouble such a sweet face."

An unexpected sound from outside the house interrupted my reverie. I looked up to see Judah leaning against the wall and watching me with a soft smile on his face. "She wakes," he said, folding his arms. "What were you thinking? You looked pensive."

I propped my head on my hand. "You share your nightmares with me, but you do not share all your thoughts."

"I don't want to worry you." He pulled himself off the wall and came over to kiss the top of my head. "At the Shabbat service today, Father will address the community. Will you meet me there?"

"Won't we go together?"

"First I have to see my brothers." He lifted his tunic from a stool and drew it over his head. "I expect we will talk until everyone has gathered."

"Then yes, I will meet you there."

He kissed me again and left the house.

I rolled onto my back and pressed my palm over the concave landscape of my belly. Had God quickened my womb? Was today the first day in our child's existence, or had our night been fruitless?

I closed my eyes, searching for some new sensation, but my belly had not changed in appearance and my flesh had not warmed with joy.

Sighing, I threw off the blanket and prepared to dress.

Nearly everyone had taken a seat by the time I arrived. Several benches had been arranged in front of the village well; the men sat on the right and the women on the left. I smiled first at my mother and Rosana, then nodded to each of my sisters-in-law.

I sat next to Morit, then looked at Mattathias, who had stood and turned to face those who had gathered for the Shabbat service.

"Shema Yisra'el," he began. *"Adonai Eloheinu, Adonai Echad." Hear, O Israel: Adonai is our God, Adonai is One.*

He led us in prayers, and we recited a psalm of David. Everything proceeded as usual for a Shabbat service, then Mattathias halted. At the place where he would normally present a lesson from the Torah, he lifted his hands and looked at us.

"My people, my kinsmen," he began, placing one hand across his heart, "you know that a foreign king holds power over our holy land. You know Jerusalem is filled with the pious Hasidim and the Hellenes, who have adopted the ideas and laws of Gentiles rather than the laws of HaShem."

A murmur rippled through the assembly as Mattathias reminded us of matters that seemed far removed from our lives. Though we could travel to Jerusalem within the span of a single day, when we plowed our fields and tended our animals, most of us tended not to think about the Temple, the king, or the authorities who enforced the royal edicts.

"Jason, the former high priest," Mattathias said, "desired to turn Jerusalem into a Greek dominion. He built a gymnasium and encouraged the priests to train their bodies there. He wanted to establish Antiochus as the ultimate authority in Jerusalem, and not Torah, which is the government and law HaShem gave us. But that is not all."

The atmosphere surrounding us seemed to swell with silence as we braced ourselves for the latest report.

"You have heard that Antiochus Epiphanes led his army into Jerusalem on the Sabbath, when the righteous would not resist him. He ordered the destruction of the walls of the city. Next he went to the Temple and knocked down the inner wall of the sanctuary, the wall beyond which no Gentile could pass. The king declared that sacrifice at the Temple would be open to all, and he replaced the sacred altar with a Greek altar, upon which he sacrificed a pig."

We gasped, repulsed once again by horror.

"Afterward, the king ordered a statue of Zeus to be placed in the holy of holies, the sacred space that once housed the Ark of the Covenant. And he declared that every year on the king's birthday, special sacrifices are to be held throughout the empire, a way to offer obeisance to the king, the supposed son of Zeus. And when we who are pious said we could not sacrifice to or worship anyone but our God, the king proclaimed that our faith should be abolished. Pagan altars have been built in the villages and towns of Judea, and the king's overseers have been charged with forcing the people to worship the king and not Adonai."

Morit and I looked at each other with grim faces. Our little town had no heathen altar, nor would Mattathias allow one. Thus far, no one from the king's government had appeared in Modein to insist otherwise.

"I now have news you have not heard," Mattathias went on, pulling a parchment from his robe. "I have received an account from Jerusalem that I find most troubling." He swallowed hard, the veins in his throat standing out like ropes. "Johanan, Simon, Judah — do you remember our neighbor, the widow with seven sons? She was called Miriam."

I glanced up at Judah as he nodded.

Mattathias cleared his throat as a cold, congested expression settled over his face. "One of the Hellenes informed on her and her sons, apparently because she refused to buy swine at the marketplace. I received this account of what happened to them after they were arrested and taken before the king. I shall read it to you."

He unfurled the scroll, scanned the writing at the top of the parchment, and began to read:

"One by one the king's men commanded the woman's sons to taste swine's flesh. When a torturer put the eldest son under the lash, the son said, 'What would you ask or learn of us? We are ready to die rather than to transgress the laws of our father.'

"Then the king, being in a rage, commanded pans and cauldrons to be made hot. And when they were hot, he commanded his men to cut out the tongue of the eldest son, and then to cut off his fingers and toes and place them in the pans and cauldrons. This they did while his brothers and mother looked on."

A horrified hush fell over our gathering. Was this the news Judah would not share with me? I had never heard anything so reprehensible. My father always said the Greeks were great thinkers, noble, and lovers of reason, but why would any man torture a woman and her sons this way?

"Now when the eldest son had been maimed in all his members," Mattathias continued, his voice growing hoarser with the reading, "the king commanded his men to put the eldest son in the fire alive and to fry him in the pan. And while the odor of burning flesh filled the room, the remaining brothers exhorted one another to die manfully. They said, 'The Lord God looks upon us, and in truth has comfort in us, as Moses in his song said, 'And He shall be comforted in His servants.'

"During all these torments, the mother was marvelous above all and worthy of honorable memory. When she saw her sons slain within the space of a single day, she bore it with good courage because of the hope she had in the Lord. She exhorted every one of them in her own language, filled with courageous spirit, and stirring up her womanish thoughts with a manly stomach, she said to them, 'I cannot tell how you came into my womb: for I neither gave you breath nor life, neither was it I who formed the members of every one of you. But doubtless the creator of this world, who formed the generations of man, and found out the beginning of all things, will also of His own mercy give you breath and life again, as you now regard not your own selves for the sake of His laws.'

"And when all seven of Miriam's sons had been tortured for Adonai's sake," Mattathias said, "last of all, the mother died." He lowered the parchment as a silence settled over us, a dense absence of sound that threatened to choke those who could still breathe.

Then, sharp as a dagger, the sound of keening ripped the silence as Rosana tore at her veil and lifted her voice in mourning. Other women did likewise as the men began to pray, rocking back and forth on their knees as they beseeched the God of heaven to look down in mercy.

After several minutes of communal mourning, Mattathias lifted his prayer shawl and covered his head. "Adonai, we beg you," he prayed, turning his face toward the gray and foreboding sky, "look down on your people who have been trodden underfoot and have pity on our profaned Temple. Have compassion on the City of David, which has been sorely defaced, and hear the blood that cries to you from the ground. Remember the wicked slaughter of harmless infants and the blasphemies committed against your name. Show your hatred, O Lord, of the wicked, for we know you always hate what you hate even as you always love what you love."

Later it would be said that when Mattathias stood praying in the midst of righteous men and women, he could not be conquered, for his cries turned the wrath of the Lord into mercy.

But instead of weeping for my sins or for Israel on that day, my thoughts centered on thankfulness. Because the situation in Jerusalem was beyond endurance, HaShem had been good to send my mother and me to safety in Modein. If HaShem continued to shower us with His goodness, we would all remain safe and protected — me, Mother, Judah, and everyone in my precious new family.

I looked across the crowd and saw a serious, dark look on my husband's face. Like Rosana, he must have been greatly distressed by hearing about the horrible deaths of Miriam and her sons, and I could understand the depth of his compassion for them. But we no longer lived in Jerusalem, and we were safe. HaShem had blessed us.

As Mattathias closed the service by leading us to recite a passage of Scripture, I pitched my voice slightly above the others in an overflow of gratitude: "Give thanks to Adonai for He is good, for His mercy endures forever."

Chapter Twenty-One: Judah

Two weeks after that emotional Shabbat service, the mournful blast of a *shofar* interrupted my work. I left the goats in the field and hurried to the village center, where I saw three horses tied to a post at the well. The animals were too fine for this region, and for an instant I hoped that Philander had paid me a visit.

But I did not know the three men drinking water from the well. Each of them wore fine embroidered garments and the infamous Greek hats. Behind them, watching from the shadows, Johanan stood with the shofar in his hand.

Though I had been perspiring all day, I suddenly felt slick with the cold, rancid sweat of fear.

I avoided the strangers and hurried home where I found Leah peeking out the window. "Cover your head," I told her, "and come with me."

"What do those men want?" she asked, a quaver in her voice.

"I hope they're only stopping for water," I said, glancing out the window again. "But they may be here to enforce the king's edict. If so, it is our turn to face the tests so many others have endured."

"Do we have to go out there?"

"You don't. But I am going to stand with my father."

"I — I'll go, too." Leah's hands trembled as she fastened her sandals and pulled on her veil. We stepped outside and walked slowly toward the well, watching as other family members came from several directions. Simon and Morit, who carried their toddling son in her arms. Eleazar and Ona, Johanan and Neta, and Jonathan. Behind them came my mother and father, both of whom walked with stately dignity and unhurried steps. Leah's mother, I noticed, did not come outside.

Other villagers also moved toward the village square — Uncle Ehud and his family, as well as several people who were not related to us.

I led Leah to a bench, then sat beside her and held her hand. While we waited, the three strangers conferred with each other in low voices. Dread snaked down my spine when I noticed a pile of stones next to the well. The uppermost stone was flat, the perfect surface for an altar of sacrifice.

If the three men had piled those rocks, my worst fears were about to be realized.

When the benches had filled with the residents of Modein, the three men turned to address us. The man in the most extravagant robe lifted his head like a dog scenting the breeze. "Is the priest called Mattathias with us?"

I was not surprised to hear him call Father's name. Mattathias of the Hasmons was a man of some renown and still commanded respect in Jerusalem.

Father stepped forward, leaning heavily on his staff. "I am here."

The man smiled. "Mattathias," he said, his voice warm as he extended his hands. "I am Appelles, an officer of Antiochus Epiphanes, and I bring you greetings from the king. You may have heard about the king's order requiring every Jew to sacrifice to the king's gods instead of Yahweh. The king wants all the people in his dominions to lead happy, contented lives, so we have been sent to make certain all the king's subjects understand what is required of them. No more will you have to travel to Jerusalem in order to make your sacrifices

— you can perform all the necessary rituals right here in Modein."

A strangled sound came from my father's throat, but the king's envoy continued as if he had not heard. "We are aware, Mattathias," he said, "that the people of this village look to you with great respect. Therefore, if today you will be the first to offer a sacrifice to Zeus, you will be greatly rewarded and honored by the king. If you and your fine sons will set the example, the entire village will be blessed with the king's favor."

Appelles gestured to the pile of rocks, silently inviting Father to approach the makeshift altar. The second man lit a stick of incense and set it on the stone, releasing a pungent aroma into the air. The third man uncovered a crate of turtledoves and brought it forward, the birds obviously intended for sacrifice. He set a pair of blades on the edge of the well, next to the turtledoves.

"Knives?" Leah whispered.

"Tools necessary for sacrifice," I replied, my tone wooden in my own ears.

Father looked around, taking in the altar, the birds, and the blades. He turned to face the crowd. "I will not sacrifice to the king's god," he replied, calmly resting his hands atop his staff. He looked at the king's men. "You may tell Antiochus that in Modein we worship Adonai, the invisible God who does not tolerate idol worship. Why should we commit the sins for which our ancestors were judged? We will not. As for me and my family, we serve Adonai alone."

An unnatural silence prevailed. Even nature itself seemed to wait for the envoys' response.

"By all the gods, what does it matter? This priest does not speak for all of Modein." A stout farmer, a distant kinsman of Ehud, stood and waddled toward the altar, smiling at the king's men. "Let Mattathias and his sons remain at odds with the king — I and my house are willing to serve him. I will freely and happily sacrifice to his gods, and I pray the king's favor will shine on me and my family."

Appelles smiled and watched as the farmer plucked a dove from the crate and expertly twisted its neck. He placed the limp body on the stone, then took one of the blades in order to open its chest —

My heart leapt into the back of my throat when Father caught the farmer's free arm. "Jael, you do not want to do this."

Jael cursed. "Out of my way, old man."

Father shook his head. "We have been a

faithful village and faithful people. How could you betray the truths you have known from childhood?"

Jael's lip curled. "I am leaving the old ways behind. Now get out of my way, priest, or I'll —" The farmer lifted the blade as if to strike at Father's chest, a move Father must have anticipated. He released the farmer's free arm and grabbed the arm with the knife, holding it firmly and turning it toward his assailant. Jael lost his balance and toppled backward, taking our father with him. The man's falling body upset the crate, creating a jumble of flying feathers, fluttering wings, and spattered blood.

By the time the scuffle was over, Jael lay mortally wounded in the dirt, and our Father stood upright, the dagger still in his trembling hand.

The king's men spun into action. The first man came toward Father, his lips bared like a snarling dog's. "You will surely die for your obstinacy, priest." He must have thought he could easily handle a thin old man, but Father was stronger than he looked. When the first man lifted his hands to attack, Father cut his throat, then whirled and used the knife handle to knock the second man to the ground with a sharp rap to the temple. As the second man groaned and attempted to rise, Father cut his throat, spilling blood on the thirsty ground. The third emissary fumbled at his waist for a sword belt he had neglected to wear, then ran for the horses.

My brothers and I reacted in concert, for we knew the man could not leave the village alive. He would run straight to the governor, and soldiers would invade our village within hours, intent on burning our homes and slaughtering our people.

We surrounded the remaining envoy before he could mount a horse, then I took one arm and Eleazar the other. The man's panicked gaze slid over each of us. He bent forward, seeming to melt under our combined stares, and closed his eyes as Father lacerated his throat, then fell forward onto Simon, who caught the dying man and gently lowered him to the ground.

The villagers watched in stunned silence as Father backed away. Before the wide eyes of his neighbors, his bony shoulders braced and broadened as he accepted the consequences of his actions. "We will not stand and wait for the king's men to arrest us," Father said, his eyes snapping at the center of his blood-splashed visage. "If any of you wish to serve this Gentile king and his false god, you are welcome to leave Modein. This village shall remain holy to HaShem."

My pulse pounded as the people of Modein stared at the carnage and allowed Father's words to sink into their hearts. Then Uncle Ehud shouted and ran toward the well, leaving his family in his mad rush toward the makeshift altar.

For an instant I feared he would attack my father, but he threw his energy into dismantling the pile of rocks. Other men joined him, their callused hands lifting the stacked stones and hurling them into the clearing until nothing remained of the heathen altar but dust and a dead dove.

"Let the king send others," Ehud said, passion sparking in his eyes, "and we will do the same to them."

My brothers and I stood motionless, not knowing what we should do next. Should we bury the bodies? Tie them to their horses and send them away?

Father read the questions on our faces. "Leave them where they fell," he said. "Those who come searching will read the scene and understand what happened here. They will learn that the people of Modein will not sacrifice to a false god, nor will we obey a king who would force us to ignore the Law of Moses."

Simon raked his hand through his hair.

"But Father, when they find these men, they will also find us —"

Father showed his teeth in an expression that was not a smile. "They will not. Go home, all of you, pack your possessions and load the wagons."

"Where are we going?" Mother asked, appearing as surprised as everyone else.

"The wilderness." Father reached for her hand and twined his fingers through hers. "We knew this day would come. There is a time for everything, and this is the time for leaving. At sunset we will meet to discuss our departure."

As he led Mother away, Father raised his free arm and shouted in triumph. As one, my brothers and I responded in kind, and so did the other men of Modein.

Not until much later did I realize that our women had remained wide-eyed and silent.

Chapter Twenty-Two: Leah

When the unthinkable happened, I did not wonder whether Mattathias was right or wrong to kill the king's men. I did not think at all. I simply sat on my bench and stared as wave after wave of shock slapped at me.

But as the blood of four men seeped into the dirt, I knew my father-in-law's actions had forever changed our lives. When the king heard about this, he would seek revenge. He would publicly punish us to demonstrate the high cost of rebellion. We might run, but we could never be anonymous. Everyone knew Mattathias, the priest with five sons, and soon everyone would know what he had done in Modein.

We might run, but we would never be able to hide.

The king would send his men, and next time they would not come with turtledoves and wearing fancy clothes, but with swords and armor. They would not ask us to comply; they would kill us without discussion. They would execute not only the priest, but anyone affiliated with the village of Modein.

The pleasant, safe life I had enjoyed since my marriage was over.

With the other women, I walked home without speaking. Morit walked with me, her hand never leaving the mound of her pregnant belly. Even if by some miracle she survived whatever the king had in store for our family, the king's edict would forbid her to circumcise her son. But how could she refuse circumcision when she was Mattathias's daughter-in-law? She would take a knife in her hand and do it. The king's men would find her and they would kill her *and* her baby, probably in full view of everyone.

Overcome by a wave of gratitude because Judah and I had not yet conceived a child, I went weak-kneed and nearly stumbled.

Ona caught my arm. "Are you all right?"

I blinked at her. "Are *you*?"

"Perhaps . . . perhaps things are not as bad as we think they are."

I glanced at Morit, who kept her head low, then looked back at Ona. "What are your thoughts?"

"I'm thinking" — she lowered her voice — "that I will have to leave our home and my flax field, that we will wander like the

Israelites of old, and I will not be able to take my loom."

"And you think that is not so bad?"

"Alive is always better than dead."

I swallowed and looked back at the village center, empty now but for the four dead men, three horses, and Jael's wife, who wept over his body.

"I am sure we will all make sacrifices," I answered, thinking of the dusty soil I had hoed and the many buckets of milk I had carried from the goat pen. "But will we be safe? We are a small group of people, and the king has an *army* —"

"Mattathias is an old man." Neta stepped closer and cut into the conversation. "If he is captured and executed by the king's men, then he is reaping what he has sown. He has already lived a full life and sired five sons. He may choose to sacrifice his life, but we do not have to be captured with him. Our husbands do not have to fight for him."

I winced, taken aback by her attitude. "I — I am not sure I agree with what he did here today, but I would never wish him ill."

"I do not wish him dead." Neta shrugged. "But sometimes the old are inflexible and unable to change their ways. Did you hear about Eliezer of Jerusalem?"

Morit, Ona, and I shook our heads.

"The old man was a scribe," Neta said, speaking quietly. "Some of the king's officials invited him to a feast. They served meat from the sacrifice offered to the king, and Eliezer took a bite and spat it out when he learned he was eating swine's flesh. The king's men took note of it and were eager to punish him, but other Jews took Eliezer aside and begged him to get some lawful meat and eat it, pretending that he was eating from the king's sacrifice. If he would do so, the king's men could not accuse him."

"Good advice," I said, considering. "He could maintain his conscience and save his life."

"Yet some people cannot recognize good counsel." Neta frowned. "Eliezer considered their words, measured them against the Law of Moses, and then told the other Jews to send him straightway to the grave. He said it wouldn't be right for a ninety-year-old man to pretend to be eating pig because young people might think he had left the worship of Adonai in his advanced age. He said he'd be a hypocrite to pretend, and while it might keep him from being killed by the king's men, it would not allow him to escape the hand of Adonai. So he chose to leave a good example by refusing to eat, saying he would die willingly and courageously for the holy laws."

"He would not listen to them?" I asked, aghast. "When he could have saved himself so easily?"

Neta gave a taut jerk of her head. "And thus a wise old man became a fool," she said. "And those who had been his friends became his enemies. When he was ready to die, he said he was content to suffer being beaten and killed because he feared God."

"So he died for nothing," I finished, guessing the end of the tale. "Leaving his story as an example of courage and virtue to all who would throw their lives away."

Neta nodded in agreement, Morit's eyes widened in alarm, and Ona chewed on her thumbnail. We were all wondering if Mattathias would follow the example of the old scribe . . . and lead us to certain death. Would our husbands insist on following their father? Would we perish in the desert or die at the hands of a Seleucid executioner?

One thing was clear — we had no time to consider such questions. The patriarch of my husband's family had sent us to pack. I would obey, but not because I believed in his cause.

I would pack because to remain in Modein almost certainly meant death.

Chapter Twenty-Three: Judah

"We must not linger in Modein," Father told the villagers at his hastily arranged meeting. "We cannot go about our work and wait for the king's authorities to come."

"Perhaps we should send someone to Jerusalem to listen for rumors," Simon suggested. "The story will probably reach that city before nightfall tomorrow. All it will take is one traveler to stop here for water."

"We could hide the bodies," Johanan suggested. "Bury them in the sand. That would grant us time."

"Not much," I pointed out. "Those three men have friends who will wonder what happened to them. They will come here and ask questions."

"What about those who remain in the village?" Eleazar asked. "What of our wives and our livestock?"

"Our children are young," Simon said. "They cannot travel far, and they cannot travel quickly."

Mattathias lifted his hand, silencing the debate. "We will leave Modein at sunrise tomorrow," he said. "All of us. We will drive our livestock before us and travel across the watershed to the Desert of Beth-haven. There we can hide our women and children in the caves. We can hunt for meat and eat wild herbs."

I glanced at Leah, who met my gaze with a tight look around her eyes. She had been expecting this news, but the expectation had not made it easier to hear.

"How long?" Simon asked, looking at his pregnant wife. "How long must we remain in the wilderness?"

Mattathias shook his head. "As long as the Lord wills. Until the king relents."

My mind vibrated with a thousand thoughts, none of them terribly clear. "If we go to the wilderness," I said, thinking of our forefathers who spent forty years in the desert, "we must not behave like victims. We will put our women and children out of harm's way, but we men must fight for freedom. We can hasten the end of our exile by harassing the king's representatives wherever and whenever we can. We can sabotage the work of the governor's men. We can raid apostate villages and pull down heathen altars."

A smile gathered up the wrinkles by Father's lined mouth. "We will not remain a small group," he said, tenting his hands. "Others will certainly join us. Most of the Hasidim still revere Adonai's laws. They will join us in the struggle, and HaShem will give us the strength and wisdom we need. And He will provide the men."

"No matter what, we will firmly adhere to the Law of the Lord," I added. "We will not eat swine. We will circumcise our sons on the eighth day. And we will honor and observe the Sabbath."

"Wait." Father shot me a warning glance. "We cannot forget that Jerusalem was attacked on the Sabbath. Neither can we forget the other group who was pursued by the king's soldiers because they refused to sacrifice to him in their village. When the Sabbath came, they hid in a cave, and when they were discovered, they refused to come out, for that would have violated the Sabbath laws."

Emotions moved beneath the surface of Father's face, like a hidden spring struggling to break through. "Though over a thousand men, women, and children sheltered in the cavern, the king's men built a fire at the entrance and killed them all."

After a collective gasp, the debates began once more.

"How can we violate the Law?"

"How can we lie down to die?"

Protestations and angry buzzing rose from the assembly until my father lifted his hand again.

"Consider this, my brothers — HaShem did not tell us to rest on the Sabbath for *His* sake, for He does not need to rest. He created a day of rest for *our* sakes, but a man cannot rest when his family is under attack. In a time like this, we must make an exception to the Law regarding the Sabbath, or the Gentiles will take advantage of our obedience and our people will be utterly destroyed."

"So," Simon said, staring thoughtfully at Father, "we will allow for self-defense on the Sabbath. We will not attack on the seventh day, but if they come for us, we will be free to defend our people."

We fell silent, most of us recognizing the irony in the words. We were fighting for the right to observe the Law of Moses, but in order to do that we would have to make an exception where none had been granted before. We would have to bear arms on the day of rest, knowing that hundreds of our people had died rather than do what we were planning to do.

But Father was right. If we did not deviate from the Law in this situation, the Gentiles would simply attack on the seventh day, knowing we would meet them like meek and defenseless sheep.

"So be it," I said, meeting Father's gaze. "We will modify the Law in order to preserve the Law . . . and our people along with it."

Chapter Twenty-Four: Leah

I drifted between wakefulness and sleep, the hours of darkness filling with images that played on the backs of my eyelids. I saw myself hiding in the courtyard, drawn into a knot beneath the window as my father raved inside the house, his shouts punctuated by the occasional curse or crack of his hand on my mother's flesh. I saw the four dead men in the village square — the first deaths my eyes had ever witnessed. I saw my strong, resolute husband with blood spatters on his face and bloody wounds on his limbs.

I woke shivering in the night and slid over to be warmed by Judah's body. Feeling me next to him, he turned and drew me into the circle of his arms where I finally slept soundly.

The next morning I rose before sunrise, lit a lamp, and plaited my hair into a single braid. I slipped on a cool tunic and my most comfortable sandals, leaving my ornamented pair beneath the bed. Let the rats have them — I should only need one pair of shoes. I tiptoed around the house, touching objects as I considered them. Would I need my brass kettle? Probably. It was light and easy to carry. The bread pot? I would leave it behind. Clay was heavy, easily broken, and unnecessary. I could bake bread in heated sand. The resulting loaf would have a crusty skin that could be peeled away or even eaten, if one didn't mind grit between one's teeth.

I picked up a sharp blade and wrapped it and a wooden stirrer in a square cloth. I would need the blade for cutting herbs and skinning animals, and every stew needed a stir stick to prevent burning at the bottom. I would need my water jar, the wineskin, some cloth for straining cheese and, if necessary, for wrapping injuries. If the men honestly intended to fight, I'd need bandages and medicinal herbs and a bowl to hold clean water.

By sunrise we had all finished packing. Simon parked a wagon and mule outside the house, and Morit and I loaded it with necessary items. Judah insisted we would be able to get supplies from devout Hasidim in other villages, but apparently Neta did not believe him. She brought over a wooden chest stuffed with garments, sandals, and girdles, and only when Johanan caught Morit rolling her eyes did he force his wife to leave the chest of luxuries behind.

"But I can't wear the same tunic every day!" she wailed.

"You can bring one other," he told her, his voice unusually stern. "But only one. Look at the other women — are they carrying trunks? Even Morit travels with little more than the clothes she's wearing, and she has a child."

Neta thrust out her lower lip, but left the trunk in her house and secured the door on her way out. I shook my head when I saw the knot that held the door shut. "What's so funny?" she asked.

"You," I answered. "As if a simple knot would stop anyone who wanted to ransack the place."

As I loaded the last of our things into the wagon, I glanced toward Mattathias's house and saw my mother standing in the shade. I caught her eye and nodded, a gesture she acknowledged with a slight lift of her chin. She did not look happy.

I strode toward her, determined to know the cause of her unhappiness. "Mother — do you have everything you need?"

"Rosana and I have packed the necessities."

"Good. It should be a fine day for travel. The breeze will keep us cool despite the sun."

"We should not be leaving this place."

I tilted my head, not certain I had heard her correctly. "We have to go. After what happened yesterday —"

"That should not have happened, and you know it." She narrowed her eyes. "You grew up in your father's house, so surely you remember what violence is like. What did you see there — a place of joy and freedom?"

I looked toward the horizon and felt my smile fade. Our home had been anything but a place of joy. "We survived, did we not?"

"Barely. Your marriage took you away, and the Seleucids who killed your father saved me from death at his hands. But now our lives are at risk again. Mattathias may not see it, but I do. Like an obstinate wife, he will rail against a domineering king until that king is forced to deal him a fatal blow. And then, daughter, it will be too late — for all of us."

Her eyes traveled to the flat expanse of my belly. "Rejoice that you have no child, for when the enemy comes, you will be able to run. Your young legs will carry you safely away and perhaps you will survive the desert. I am old and I cannot run." She glanced at the long line of wagons and the village families who had joined Mattathias's caravan. "So I march with all of you toward death."

"Would you have Mattathias bow to a king who denies HaShem?" I asked, speaking as my husband would. "Surely . . . surely HaShem will honor those who honor Him."

"Do you truly think so?" The thin line of her mouth compressed even further. "What good does honor do a dead woman?"

I took her arm and led her to the wagon where I cleared a place for her in the back. She and Rosana would ride together while Mattathias rode next to Simon, who would drive the mules. I would walk by my husband's side.

This family was not united in belief or zeal, but we were one in purpose: we wanted to survive.

So we left Modein in the first hour of the day and traveled toward the sheltering caves of the Gophna Hills.

For a girl who had never left Jerusalem until her marriage, the next few days offered me a window to the world. I might have enjoyed seeing the wonders of the changing landscape if I were not so anxious. Mother had filled me with trepidation, and not even a look at Judah's confident face could banish my anxiety.

What would we do if a company of Seleucid soldiers appeared on the horizon? We had only a handful of weapons to defend ourselves, and at least half of our company were women and children.

We traveled through the green Jordan Valley, then crossed the watershed to enter the Desert of Beth-haven, a rocky area where neither clouds nor trees provided shade from the relentless sun. After living in Jerusalem and Modein, where a journey of a few steps could always bring you to a friendly door, the desolate landscape seemed alien and isolated.

When Mattathias lifted his hand and halted our caravan, I glanced around and saw nothing that looked like shelter — no buildings, no huts, not even a tree. "Why are we stopping here?" I asked Judah.

He gave me a grim smile as he wiped perspiration from his forehead. "We will shelter in caves tonight." He pointed to a line of hills not far away. "Once we unload a few supplies in this spot, we will take you over there. You women and children will be safe in the caves."

I frowned at the barren spot where we had stopped. "But why are you unloading supplies here? There is no shelter at all —"

"Men do not need shelter." His somber look melted into a wry grin. "My brothers and I have camped in the desert many times. We will build a fire and string up a tent if necessary. But this is where we will establish our base camp."

"Camp — for what?"

"For the army of Israel." He leaned forward, bracing his elbows on his knees. "We have taken a stand against the king, and others will join us. We will remain out here for training. But don't worry — we will send someone to check on you every day. If you need anything, you only have to ask."

He was planning to leave me . . . in a cave.

I stared at him for a moment, then gritted my teeth as he jumped down from the wagon and hailed his brothers.

That was it, then. No discussion, no debate. I would not be working alongside my husband, but would be trapped in a cave with the other women. And we would probably be trapped there for a long time.

Sighing, I climbed into the back of the wagon with Rosana, Mother, Morit, and little Johanan. Ona and Neta joined us, then Simon came over, grinning at us as he climbed into the driver's seat. Without speaking, he picked up the reins and turned the mules toward the mountains.

After another hour of riding in the blazing heat, the wagon halted. Upon closer examination, the hills of Gophna appeared to be huge slabs of stone thrown together in a string of heaps. The haphazard piling of the flat stones left fissures between them, creating dark, cool caves. After entering the first one, I had to agree that they would make decent accommodations.

"Spread out your supplies," Simon told us. "Don't keep everything in one place. Hide yourselves and explore the caves so you will know where to run in case of an attack. Make sure a passing stranger would see no sign of habitation if he looked in this direction."

Morit frowned. "Does that mean we cannot light a fire?"

"Not in daylight." Simon's face softened as he regarded his pregnant wife. "Do your cooking after dark, if you must. But do not light anything if there are strangers in the area."

"Where," Rosana asked, "do we draw water? I see no spring."

"The residents of Gophna," Simon answered, "will allow us to draw from their well. We will send a wagon for water every morning."

I swallowed hard, my throat already beginning to feel parched. Something in Simon's voice warned that the residents of Gophna were not thrilled at the thought of sharing their water. How could we be sure they would not take offense at some trifle and bar their gates to our wagons?

We could not. So we would rise each morning and pray that we would not be bitten by poisonous snakes, die of thirst, or be killed by the enemy. We were about to embark on a venture requiring courage, good fortune, and faith, yet none of us women had volunteered for it.

What can I say of the days that followed? They were difficult and so similar that I lost all track of time. Were it not for Shabbat, which we carefully observed, we would have no idea what day it was.

We women created sleeping areas deep in the caves and kept our small stores of food in various caverns. At night we lit fires for cooking and for warmth, and as the flames died down we sat in a circle and told stories. Rosana told stories about each of her sons, and my sisters-in-law talked of growing up in their distinctive families, most of whom were from Jerusalem. I listened, mostly, because I had no interesting stories to tell.

Every morning we rose, put our empty water jugs into the wagon, and waited for them to return from Gophna with water for drinking and washing. We spent most of the afternoon napping, playing with Morit's little boy, or skinning animals the men brought us. I learned to skin a deer and fox, and Ona taught me how to stretch the skins for sewing.

At dusk, after we had built our fire and prepared the clean animals for cooking, I would go to the entrance of the cave and stare into the purple plain of evening where I could sometimes see the distant glow of the men's campfires. Did Judah miss me? Did he reach for me in the night? Were they truly training an army, or was all this an excuse to go into the woods and live like unmarried nomads?

Neta had first presented that disloyal notion. One night she declared that our husbands were only exercising their right to do as they pleased, and soon they would grow tired of hunting and camping. "Then they'll come back for us," she said, pushing stray hair out of her eyes. "And we will no longer have to live like animals."

I blinked at her statement, then glanced around the circle to see if any of the others were taking her seriously. Rosana's face had paled, and Morit's lower lip had edged forward in a pout.

But my mother put Neta in her place. "You cannot be serious," she said, her voice edged with iron. "Would Mattathias have killed four people if he only wanted to play hunter for a few weeks? Only a vain and silly woman would even imagine such a thing." She looked around the circle, shaking her head. "I cannot say I agree with the man's decision to put us in this position," she said and shifted to sitting cross-legged on the dirt floor, "but he was right to bring us out here. If we had remained in Modein, we would already be dead."

"We have entered a war," Rosana added while staring at her foolish daughter-in-law. "And perhaps one day you will understand that by coming out here, my sons have surrendered their very lives to fight for Israel's freedom."

"They cannot win a war alone!" Neta glared at Rosana. "My husband will die because he has only his father and his brothers to fight with him. I am not the fool — I think *they* are foolish because they have been blinded by family loyalty. They will be slaughtered as soon as the king's men learn where they are hiding."

"They are not hiding." Ona's calm voice filled the stone chamber. "They are waiting for others to join them. Others will come soon, and Adonai will give our men the victory."

My mother looked as if she expected me to add something to the conversation, but I had nothing to say. I did not know whether the men were heroes or fools, selfish or selfless. I felt like a flower petal caught in a swift-flowing gutter, pushed one way and then another, and about to go under at any moment.

I had believed that marriage to Judah would mean peace, safety, and an end to strife. I could not have been more wrong.

Time proved Ona right. Other sons of Israel did join our men, most following hastily whispered directions from kinsmen in outlying villages and Jerusalem. From our home in the caves, we watched tents sprout like mushrooms on the plain — first there were two, then five, then twelve, then fifty, then two hundred.

On one of his visits to the caves, Jonathan explained that Mattathias and one or two of his sons went out nearly every day, visiting towns and villages to rally others in the fight for freedom. They would go to the village well, and while they refreshed their thirsty bodies they would tell the residents about their fight to preserve Israel's freedom and follow the Law of Moses. Most of the residents had already heard about the priest's action in Modein, and reactions ranged from enthusiastic approval to boisterous condemnation.

"Love us or loathe us," Mattathias would tell his listeners, "but if you wish to worship the God of our fathers, come join us."

They came — devout men and their families formed a living stream leading into the desert. The women and children joined us in the hills, often bringing their flocks and fresh supplies. The men met our warriors in the desert, where the harsh elements strengthened their endurance and military training forged nerves of steel.

Among the newcomers were large groups of Hasidim, a conservative sect that strongly opposed the Hellenes and the edicts against religious freedom. Jonathan reported that the Hasidim were more given to prayer and study than fighting, so they did not always make good soldiers. But they were eager to do what they could, even if it meant sharpening swords or fashioning shields.

In the evenings, Jonathan told us, Mattathias led the men in prayer for wisdom and strength. The newcomers found hope in Mattathias's zeal, and we women found encouragement in the camp's increasing numbers.

Every day, it seemed to me, one of the new women mentioned that we Jews should be accustomed to living in temporary quarters. "Abraham and Sarah lived in tents," some recent arrival would say, "and so did Jacob and Rachel. Moses had spent the remaining years of his life sleeping in the desert, and if he could survive the sand, sun, and scorpions, so can we."

Every time I heard that refrain, I stopped working and looked at Neta, who returned my glance with a twisted smile. She had also lived in Jerusalem before her marriage, and except for the flimsy temporary structures we erected for Sukkot, we city dwellers had rarely even *seen* tents, much less lived in them.

"If Adonai had meant for me to live outdoors," she once whispered to me, "He would have made my skin far less delicate."

When Mattathias's fledgling camp housed more than a thousand men, he decided he was ready to send out raiding parties. Under cover of darkness, small bands of his warriors crept into villages where his message had been spurned. Shouting the name of Adonai, the warriors of Israel tore down the heathen altars, smashed statues of Greek gods, and awakened the sleeping residents. When they discovered families with uncircumcised sons, Mattathias's men immediately performed the rite. When they encountered Hellenes who openly blasphemed the sacred Law of God, the army of Israel struck them down, knowing they could not allow such men to betray their cause to the enemy.

I must admit, I was horrified to hear that my father-in-law's men were killing people they pulled from their beds. That news touched something in me, a thread of fear I had tried desperately to tuck away. In my youth, violence had often awakened me in the middle of the night, and the memory of my father's ranting, mingling with the recollection of his violence against my mother, sent ghost spiders scrambling down my spine.

One day when Judah brought water to the caves, I pulled him away from the others and drew him into a shallow cavern.

"What's this?" he asked, his hands circling my waist. "I have missed you, too."

"Wait." I pressed my fingertips to his lips. "I have heard about the raids on the villages. About the killing and the circumcisions." I began to shiver. "Judah, tell me this is not true. Such violence cannot be a good thing —"

He drew me closer, his hand pressing my head against his chest. "Hush, dear one. You are too young to understand."

"I am not!" I lifted my head and met his gaze. "A woman does not have to be old to realize that violence is terrible."

"That is why you are here and not in the army." All traces of softness disappeared from Judah's face as he looked at me. "HaShem does not tolerate sin, Leah. He is holy, and Israel must be holy, too."

"But to kill so many people!"

"There is a time for mercy, but this is not that time. This is a time to purify Israel. If we tolerate heathen ideas, we are lost. These ungodly practices are like leprosy — they eat away at a man's flesh little by little until the entire body is diseased."

A tear trickled down my cheek, and gentleness returned to my husband's eyes as he wiped it away. "Do not think about these things if they bother you. But have faith in my father. He knows what must be done to ensure Israel's freedom."

I was not sure I could ever put such thoughts out of my mind, but what else could I do? I wrapped my arms around my husband and told myself to trust him.

With every victory over blasphemy, my father-in-law's followers grew more numerous. "Clearly, HaShem is with him," the newcomers remarked as we served the midday meal. "He will not let sinners gain the upper hand in Israel."

No, he would not.

In those first few months of Mattathias's crusade against the Hellenes, I do not think King Antiochus was greatly concerned about my father-in-law's private war. The local governor had undoubtedly relayed the news, but Antiochus, safe in his capital city, did not seem greatly troubled by Mattathias's refusal to follow his edicts.

But the tide was about to turn.

Chapter Twenty-Five: Judah

Living as a devout Jew in Jerusalem, a city filled with Hellenes, I frequently fought with those who were determined to prove the strength of their convictions with their fists. The Hellene youths who regularly participated in games, exercises, and wrestling matches at the gymnasium seemed especially eager to prove their superiority to those of us who followed the Law, so I came home with busted knuckles two or three times a week.

But those fights were child's play compared to our desert training. The persistent afternoon sun glared down on us like an enemy, and the dry air knifed at my starved lungs and throat. At sunset, when men gathered around campfires and ate what little food was available, I sat in my tent and stared out at the barren landscape, studying the rocky hills and searching for signs of movement. The air seemed lifeless at that hour, the light melancholy and filled with shadows of things invisible.

How was Leah faring without me?

Thoughts of her leapt into my mind like an unruly puppy, distracting me from what I should be doing and causing me to worry about her.

I also worried about my father. His strength had always been centered in his mind and soul; his slim body and thin bones had begun to weaken with age. Since leading us into the wilderness, he had begun to skip meals so that others could eat. More than once I saw him give his food to a boy who had joined our camp, or to Jonathan who was still young and growing. I gently rebuked Father, but he only smiled and replied that Adonai would supply the strength he needed.

"One day, when Adonai is finished with me," he said, grinning as he took my arm, "then, my son, you will understand what David meant when he said, 'Adonai is the strength of my life.' "

I blinked in dazed exasperation. "Father, what are you talking about?"

"Go see your wife, Judah," he said and pushed me toward the wagon. "Give me another grandson."

I did not see Leah as often as I wanted

because I did not want to spark jealousy in the other men, many of whom had left their wives and families unprotected at home. I did not want those men to worry or fret, lest their responsibilities as fathers pull them from their duties as men of Israel.

Leah seemed happy to see me when I did go to the women's settlement, but she no longer resembled the young bride who welcomed me home after a long day in the fields. Lines of anxiety marked her youthful face, and she had begun to wear her hair tied back in a severe knot. She had lost weight since leaving Modein, and ever since my explanation of the nighttime raids, something in her spirit had dimmed.

When I halted the wagon in front of the caves, the other women would call her, usually with sly smiles and affectionate teasing. Leah would come out, wiping her hands or smoothing her hair, and after giving me a quick hug, she seemed content to sit outside and look at the stars in quiet contemplation. Occasionally she would ask how we fared with the training, and I always gave the same answer: "It goes well."

After a while she stopped asking.

I would try to spark a conversation by telling her about the villages we had cleansed and the victories we had won, yet I soon learned that she did not want to hear about vanquished Hellenes and demolished altars. Once, when I showed her a deep cut on my arm, she flinched and turned away.

Most men would have realized this long before I did, but when my bride became more interested in stargazing than talking, I knew I had lost her.

Chapter Twenty-Six: Leah

Worn down by age, responsibility, and the zeal that consumed him, Mattathias finally grew so weak he could not stand. His sons brought him to the Gophna caves where we made him a comfortable bed, fed him, and watched him grow more feeble with each passing day.

Though the fire within him still created an impression of great power, as he reclined and closed his eyes on his pillow, he looked like the mere shell of a man. More than once I went into his stone chamber to seek Rosana's counsel, and the sight of Mattathias's pale countenance gave me a start.

Everyone could see the inevitable truth, although several days passed before my father-in-law would admit that his life was drawing to a close. He would die without accomplishing his goal, but he earnestly believed he had set the nation of Israel on the proper course. He would entrust the future to his children.

When the old man's breathing grew irregular and the act of filling his lungs became agony, Rosana sent for his sons. They came, and all of us gathered around the patriarch's bedside to hear his parting words:

"Arrogance and reproach . . . have now become strong," he said, gasping out each word. "This is . . . a time of ruin and furious anger." His bright eyes roved over us in the chilly cave. "Now, my children . . . show zeal for the Law . . . and give your lives for the covenant of our fathers. Remember the deeds of the fathers . . . which they did in their generations . . . and receive great honor and an everlasting name."

His voice broke in a horrible, rattling gurgle. Rosana helped him sit up and patted his back until he found the strength to clear his throat.

"My children . . . be courageous and grow strong in the Law, for by it you will gain honor." The dying man's gaze flicked to his second-born son. "Now behold . . . I know Simon your brother is wise in counsel. Always listen to him; he shall be your father."

Simon covered his face with his hands in an attempt to silence his grief.

"Judah Maccabaeus" — yellowed teeth flashed in Mattathias's gray beard — "has been a mighty warrior from his youth. He shall command the army for you and fight the battle against the peoples."

Judah bowed his head as if humbled by the statement.

"You shall rally . . . about you all who observe the Law, and avenge the wrong done to your people. Pay back the Gentiles in full and heed what the Law commands. Trust in no man, but in HaShem alone. And now . . . my task is finished."

As tears welled in my eyes, each of the old man's sons knelt by his side, received his blessing, and stood. When he had finished, Mattathias smiled at Rosana and took his last breath, his eyes focused on her face as he exhaled in one long sigh.

Then we heard nothing but a sough of wind whispering at the entrance of the cave.

Simon wiped tears from his eyes and announced that we would pack the wagons at sunrise. We would take Mattathias back to Modein and bury him in the tomb of his fathers. The men slipped out of the cave, leaving us women to ceremonially wash and wrap the body.

As we worked, I thought about how deeply Israel would mourn for Mattathias. Though not everyone agreed with him, everyone admired him for having the courage to act on his principles. I knew I ought to be proud to be related to this remarkable man, but his passing had filled me with a new and unexpected fear.

With the father gone, what sort of future remained for his sons?

Chapter Twenty-Seven: Judah

Johanan, Simon, and Jonathan rode ahead of us, leaving Eleazar and me to take a wagon with the women back to the Gophna Hills.

"Do you think anyone will be left in camp?" Eleazar shot me a sidelong glance. "After all, we've been gone a full week."

I stared at the mules' hindquarters and shifted the reins to my other hand. Did I want the camp to remain full? Or would it be better if we returned to the wilderness and found the camp deserted?

"It will be as God wills," I said, giving my younger brother a grim smile. "If He wants us to fight, we will have an army. If not . . ." I shrugged. "If we find ourselves alone, perhaps we should go to Egypt and raise our families there."

"You could never do that — not after Father appointed you commander of the army."

I shook my head. "I did not ask for that honor."

"But Father knew you would make a great commander. That's why he chose you."

"Father did not know me very well. He saw my size, and to him, *big* meant *strong.* Fierce."

"Are you not fierce? Have you not defended your brothers, including me, countless times?"

"Defending is not attacking. I am happy to defend my loved ones. But what Father asked us to do, going into villages and killing our brothers —"

"They were apostate! They were spreading blasphemies like a contagion!"

"They were sleeping peacefully when we hauled them out to be executed. I could obey Father because the Lord commands me to honor him. Now that he is gone . . ." I looked up and saw Leah's tear-streaked face in the empty air before me. "If the camp is deserted, I will not be disappointed."

"But if God commands you to fight —"

"If HaShem commands me I will obey, but have you heard Him speak of late? Have you been visited by a prophet who shared a word from Adonai?" I stared at Eleazar, my eyes probing his, then I lowered my gaze.

"Neither have I. If I lead men to fight, I will be doing it on the strength of Father's conviction."

"I think," Eleazar said, speaking in the tone of a man carefully choosing his words, "you can no longer consider the renegade Jews your brothers. They have turned their backs on Adonai, so you are acting defensively when you strike them. You are defending Adonai. You are defending your devout brothers against those who would turn their hearts away from HaShem and toward false gods."

I tilted my head, considering Eleazar's advice. His reasoning made sense, and I could almost hear Father speaking through his words.

We rounded a bend and approached the Gophna Hills. I searched the rocks, looking for signs of activity, knowing my heart would rejoice if I saw nothing but empty space. But within a few moments I saw two women who shaded their eyes as we approached, then released joyous shouts and ran into the caves.

"We have been recognized," Eleazar said.

"Yes."

I reined in the mules, then hopped down from the wagon, stretching my legs before helping the women climb down. I did not have to look across the plain to know our camp still teemed with men — they would not have gone home without their women and children.

We still had an army.

We still had a cause.

And we still had Adonai to lead us.

My heart steeled itself to the task ahead.

We were still a good distance away from the camp when I heard a shout of recognition. We had steadily stirred up dust on our approach, and now men hurried toward us, many of them with weapons in hand.

"See that, brother?" Eleazar asked. "They are eager to fight under you."

I closed my eyes, not ready to be reminded of the heavy burden Father had placed on my shoulders.

How was I supposed to lead in a time when HaShem no longer spoke to His prophets? When he taught us, Father often spoke of Adonai's silence. For generations, the Lord spoke directly to His prophets, kings, and followers. He listened when they prayed, and answered with words and signs, some of them too wondrous to be believed unless HaShem had brought them to pass. The visible Shekinah glory had led the Israelites through the wilderness and filled the Temple when Solomon prayed his prayer of dedication, but it disappeared when the people began to worship idols.

The Shekinah had not returned.

Now I was supposed to lead — without Adonai's visible presence, without a prophet to tell me what HaShem wanted, and without my father. I had only my instincts, my brothers, and a wife who seemed to abhor bloodshed . . . and me, as long as I carried a sword.

"Judah! Judah! Judah!"

My eyes opened as the men chanted my name. They had lined the path, and their eager faces shone up at me as they raised their weapons in a salute. They had already placed their trust in me, and I could not let them down.

Adonai, hear me. Lead me to do your will.

I was not as learned as my father, as pious or as zealous. But I could be faithful, so until HaShem stopped me, I would do what I had been asked to do.

Eleazar and I climbed out of the wagon and stood before the crowd. I raised my hands and told them to disperse, but they would not.

"I think," Eleazar shouted in my ear, "they want you to speak to them."

I frowned. "And say what?"

"Encourage them. They have waited a week for your return; now they are ready for action."

I blew out a breath, then climbed back into the wagon and stood on the driver's seat. I held up my hands, and this time the men quieted.

"Men of Israel," I said, looking around, "thank you for remaining true to the charge you accepted under my father. We have buried him in his family tomb, and we have hurried back here to be with you. The work is not finished, but we will continue. For the sake of Adonai and His people, we will gird on our breastplates and pick up our swords. We will search for the invaders who have turned the hearts of Israel to foreign gods, and we will strike them where they stand."

Voices erupted in a mighty roar as the men pumped their weapons in the air.

"As for the children of Israel whose hearts have hardened against Adonai," I went on, my throat tightening, "like Joshua who went before us, we will defend Adonai and purify this land so its inhabitants may remain true and holy before their God."

Another cheer rose from the crowd. With nothing further to say, I looked for Simon and gestured for him to stand beside me in the wagon. When he joined me, I saw that his eyes were wet, either with enthusiasm or sentiment.

"Speak to them," I yelled above the shouting. "Father would want you to say something."

For a moment Simon floundered, and then he lifted his hand and waited until the men grew quiet. "I am not the warrior Judah is," he began, "but I am a son of Mattathias. If you have any problems, if your wives or children have trouble in the camp, bring those concerns to me. I will administrate justly before Adonai and all Israel, and I will do my best to honor your sacrifice for this cause."

Cheers wrapped around us like water around a rock as eager hands helped me and Simon from the wagon. We were enthusiastically escorted to our tents where bread and cheese and dried meats waited. We ate our fill with Johanan, Eleazar, and Jonathan, then we stretched out, eager to refresh our bodies for the struggle ahead.

But as I drifted off to sleep, I thought of my wife and wondered what she was thinking as she lay on her pallet.

As for me, I had put my hand to the plow and there was no turning back.

Chapter Twenty-Eight: Leah

With Mattathias's other daughters-in-law, I sat by the fire and relived the moment when Judah left us at the caves. He had pulled me aside to say farewell, and his broad hand held my face as he promised struggle, trial, and victory in the days ahead. As he spoke, the hair on my arms had risen with premonition.

The man I married — the hulking, tender, protective middle son — had changed. I married a strong young man who could keep me safe, but practically overnight my husband had become a commander. He was already thinking first and foremost of his men and he was leaving me, going off to battle with his brothers-in-arms.

His first thoughts every morning would not be of me, but of his warriors. His last thoughts at night would not be of me, but of his men . . . or possibly HaShem.

An icy finger touched the base of my

spine. What had Mattathias been thinking when he singled out my husband? Had he named Judah as leader of the army simply because he was the largest of his sons, or had he done it for some other reason?

Judah was not warlike. Though I had never been part of an army, I knew war and warriors. Living in my father's house taught me how to anticipate the moves of an enemy. I understood the importance of being vigilant and why a survivor had to remain strong and alert. For years I stayed awake at night contemplating my enemy, striving to understand his motivations while bracing for the next attack. I was not beaten nearly as often as my mother, but I felt every blow he ever landed on her.

Yes, I knew war . . . and I knew Judah would spend the coming weeks, months, and years living for the struggle. His life would be spent on a new purpose: keeping his men alive until they achieved victory.

I studied the faces of the other women in our small circle. Rosana seemed content; her eyes shone with a mother's quiet pride as one of the women remarked on Judah's leadership. Ona and Morit spoke of him with open admiration. None of them seemed perturbed by the prospect of bloodshed ahead.

Then again, none of them had spent their childhood with an enemy that could not be avoided.

I looked away and considered my course. I would remain here as long as I had to, but when I had opportunity to see Judah, I would find a way to draw him back to my side. I did not want him to die and I wanted him with me.

Would HaShem think me greedy for wanting so much?

Perhaps, but surely the Almighty knew I was not like the sons of Mattathias. I was not willing to give everything to serve a God who had given nothing to me.

▪ ▪ ▪ ▪

Part III

▪ ▪ ▪ ▪

Then Judah his son, who was called Maccabaeus, took command in [Mattathias's] place. All his brothers and all who had joined his father helped him; they gladly fought for Israel. He extended the glory of his people. Like a giant he put on his breastplate; he girded on his armor of war and waged battles, protecting the host by his sword. He was like a lion in his deeds, like a lion's cub roaring for prey. He searched out and pursued the lawless; he burned those who troubled his people. Lawless men shrank back for fear of him; all the evildoers were confounded; and deliverance prospered by his hand.

He embittered many kings, but he made Jacob glad by his deeds, and his memory is blessed forever.

1 Maccabees 3:1–7

Chapter Twenty-Nine: Judah

My father had named me commander, but never had any man felt more unequal to the task. Until Father's passing, my brothers and I had simply followed him into the fray. Our attacks had always been spontaneous, specific, and effective.

Now everyone waited for me to command — and how did one learn to do that?

I considered the great military leaders of our history: Moses. Joshua. David. They were as different as chalk and cheese, yet they had one thing in common: each of them had waited on Adonai and heeded His voice. When they failed to wait and listen, they suffered defeat.

The night after we returned from Modein, I ordered our fighting men to meet me on the plain at sunrise. I rose in darkness, ate a bit of bread, and slipped out of my tent as the sun broke through the eastern horizon. Striding forward with a confidence I did not feel, I zigzagged through the tents and walked to the edge of the plain, then turned.

I stood alone. The sun had risen, the air was warming, but none of our fighters had ventured out of their tents. How were we to defeat our enemies if we could not get out of bed?

Biting back an oath, I sank to the ground and sat cross-legged, determined to wait.

For a long time I remained the only man on the field, then others began to straggle out of camp. I counted many men of my age, a few lads of fourteen or fifteen, and several who were probably born in the same year as my father. Two rode up on horseback, one sat astride a mule, and several Hasidim led donkeys loaded with water jugs, bread, and blankets.

I stifled a burst of cynical laughter. Were we such weaklings we could not survive a few hours in the sun? Joshua and Moses would laugh if they evaluated my fighting force.

When most of the men had assembled, I climbed up on a nearby boulder, crossed my arms, and stared out across a ringing silence.

"Behold!" I called, extending an arm toward the assembled group. "The army of

Adonai!"

My men looked at each other with questioning faces.

"Yes, you," I answered, pulling the words from my gut. "Adonai has called forth an army to fight those who would eradicate the Law of Moses. He has called us to crush those who would destroy and enslave our people. Adonai has called us, and we have answered. We are here, and we are ready."

The men cheered and brandished the weapons they carried — swords, shepherds' staves, whips, and pitchforks.

"Do you feel unqualified?" I asked. My words echoed in the open area as the men regarded me with grim faces. "Well, brothers, let me assure you — I feel the same way. I may be a big man, but I have never led an army. I am not the eldest of my brothers, not the smartest, and definitely not" — I grinned — "the most charming. But my father walked with HaShem, and he chose me to lead you, so I will obey. And I will promise you three things. First, when we are training, I will never ask you to do anything I am not willing to do. Second, when we go out to fight, I will always go with you. And third, we will never go out to fight unless I have begged HaShem to go with us and give us the victory."

Then, as my pulse pounded in my ears, the men roared, the noise lifting toward heaven in a deafening surge of spirit and enthusiasm.

As the cheering continued, I lowered my head and felt my stomach twist. What should I do now? These men were farmers and shepherds, skilled with livestock and hoes and spades. A few of the hunters could handle a bow and spear, but none had military experience. Generations had passed since our people took possession of the Promised Land. We fought for our kings during the time of the divided kingdom, but years of living under the rule of Babylonians, Persians, and Greeks had gelded us.

"Judah." I lifted my head when Simon called my name. My brother was striding toward me, his eyes glowing.

"Organize them," he said when he stood close enough to speak in a normal voice. "Arrange them into companies. Help them understand what you want them to do. Each man will feel needed and useful when he is given a specific task."

I nodded, grateful for the advice. Simon always knew how to cut to the heart of the matter.

Beginning with my brothers and cousins, I called men forward and awarded them the title of captain. "Go form a company of fifty," I instructed, "and see which of your men has skill with a sword, a horse, and a spear. Find the best archers. See if anyone is a metalworker or a healer. And if a man has no skills at all, set him aside, for we can always use messengers."

"And then?" Eleazar asked.

"Have them practice their skills," I answered. "Set up straw dummies for the archers to shoot and the spearmen to charge. Have the horsemen practice riding with sword in hand. Cut wooden sticks for hand-to-hand fighting. Have your skilled men teach those who lack experience. If we are to save our nation, we must train for the fight."

"What about the old and the very young?" Jonathan asked, frowning. "I have seen a few lads who are not yet shaving."

"Make runners of the young ones," I answered. "Put them in wagons and send them to the women so they can bring food and water to the camp. As to the old ones, have them pray. Not all weapons are made of wood and iron."

"Anything else?" Johanan asked, his arms crossed.

I drew a deep breath, then shook my head. "Only two things — first, when I say we are to meet at sunrise, I expect to see every man at sunrise. Second, we will honor the Sabbath in camp. Beginning at sundown tonight."

My captains nodded, then hurried off to gather their men.

After two weeks of training, I was beginning to believe the army of Adonai might be able to repel an attack of the king's forces . . . if the attacking army had been incapacitated by food poisoning.

I was pouring water at the end of a hot day when Johanan entered my tent. His hair, dripping with perspiration, hung in raveled hanks over his forehead, and his handsome face looked weary. He regarded me with bleary eyes. "Pour me a cup, brother," he said, sinking onto a fur-covered stool. "I am tired of running my men up and over the rocks."

I handed him my cup. "How goes their training?"

He drank, then wiped his mouth with the back of his hand. "It goes . . . well, especially when I consider that my men are better suited for lying on their backs and dozing in the sun. I seem to have collected a group of shepherds who know more about mating and lambing than wielding a sword."

"They'll learn soon enough," I said, pouring another cup of water. "And their training will serve them well when we are under attack. You'll see."

Johanan nodded, but his eyes had wandered to the corner where my sword lay. The old, nicked blade had been our father's. "Have you wondered why Father named you commander of his army?"

I lowered the pitcher. "I've always thought it was because I'm the biggest of the lot."

"Yet I am the oldest," Johanan answered, his tone curiously flat. "By all rights, the position should have gone to the firstborn."

I shot him a curious glance. "Do you want to command? Until lately, I have never known you to care about fighting. I had never seen you pick up a sword until last month."

"If Father needed a fighter, I would rise to the occasion — and I *did* rise to it. When he called us to war, I did not hesitate to answer."

"Then perhaps" — I spoke slowly, trying to be diplomatic — "he chose someone who did not have to rise to the role. Perhaps he remembered all the times he had to scold me for getting into trouble."

Johanan snorted. "All the more reason not to choose you as commander." His gaze moved into mine. "You've always been tough, Judah, but you are not — how should I put it? You are not sophisticated. I keep trying to imagine you before the governor or the king and . . ." He shook his head. "I simply can't see it."

I blinked, astounded by his words. "How sophisticated does a man have to be to swing a sword? Cannot a rough-mannered man kill as easily as a polished one?"

"You know what I mean. A commander must be a leader. He must be able to speak to kings, and he must understand the enemy he faces. He must be able to direct spies to gather information behind enemy lines and evaluate that information. In Jerusalem, I worked with many important people, wealthy men and even in the office of the high priest. I know how these people think."

"No man can know everything, Johanan. So I will rely on captains like you and trust Adonai to take care of the rest." I gave him a calm smile, hoping to flatter him out of his critical mood. "Trust me — I realize how heavily I will rely on you."

Johanan stared at me, his brow furrowed. "Father was not wise in his old age. You should call on me, brother, when you have to meet with emissaries from the king. I will guide you as you consider how to respond."

I sipped from my cup and nodded. "I will call on you, Johanan, because I respect you. But in the end, I will do what I think Adonai would want me to do."

"Does He whisper in your ear, then?"

I winced inwardly, for Johanan was asking the same question I had asked myself. How would I know what Adonai wanted?

"He speaks through the Torah, the writings, and the prophets," I answered. "And sometimes I think He speaks" — I patted my chest — "in here."

Johanan blew out a breath, finished his water, and dropped the cup to the ground. "I am going to bed."

"Rest well, brother. I am glad you stopped by."

"You would be." Johanan stood, his handsome face set in grim lines. "Only you."

Over the following weeks, my men and I searched out villages and towns where the king's men were tormenting Jews who chose to follow the Law of Adonai. We searched for Hellenes who had been informers and led others astray; our warriors pulled them out of taverns and inns and from the backs of swift horses. We killed them where we found them and left them on the road as a warning to other blasphemers. And though we fought with enemies in diverse places, we did not lose a single man.

Whenever I felt myself wavering in purpose or determination, I remembered what Eleazar had told me — I had been called to defend Adonai's people. Usurpers had entered the land promised to the sons and daughters of Abraham, and these Gentiles were attempting to annihilate our people and give our lands to others. This we could not allow, for Adonai, the Master of the universe, had ceded the land to us. We would not surrender our God-given heritage without a fight.

Once I reminded myself of these truths, only one individual had the power to weaken my resolve . . . and I found myself wavering every time I saw her.

Leah did not approve of my new role. Though she never upbraided me with words or actions, I felt disapproval in the chilly tone of her greeting, her refusal to meet my gaze, and her stiffness when I tried to wrap her in my arms. The woman who had been pure sweetness when we lived in Modein now drizzled gray disapproval whenever I visited the women's settlement.

None of my brothers' wives reacted with such cold hostility. Neta complained loudly and often about suffering hardship in the wilderness, but she was always thrilled to see Johanan and welcomed him to the caves with hugs and kisses. Morit was more subdued with Simon, especially since God had now blessed them with two little sons. Ona had always been quiet, yet she greeted the wagon with a smile when we visited the women and seemed delighted to welcome Eleazar.

While I desperately wanted to ask Leah why she was so unhappy with me, I could not ask such a personal question amid so many eavesdroppers. I attempted to take her to a private place, but once she realized my intention, she put up her hands and walked back to the women's camp. Frustrated with her and forlorn without her, I always left the caves feeling uneasy and unsatisfied. Somehow it did not seem right for a commander to be at peace with his men and at odds with his wife.

"I will never understand," I told Eleazar as we rode away from the Gophna Hills one afternoon, "why a woman expects her husband to read her mind."

Eleazar laughed and clapped my shoulder. "I have been called brave on occasion," he said with a grin, "but I am a complete coward when I am forced to figure out what is troubling my Ona. I might hazard a guess as to what she is thinking, but if I get it wrong" — he smashed his fist into his palm — "I would sooner take a dozen blows. She will say I don't care about her, for if I cared I would know what troubles her. How can I know when she won't speak her mind?"

For the sake of my men — and my sanity — I deliberately placed Leah at the back of my mind once we returned to camp. I could not worry about her when I was supposed to be training an army. I could not wonder what she was thinking when I had to figure out how to feed and provision thousands of Israelites who had left their families to defend our people. I could not indulge in lovesickness when my duty to Adonai demanded my best.

With each sunrise, my responsibilities chafed more urgently. Far too many of our people had willingly surrendered their heritage and identity in order to be accepted by the Gentile intruders. Adonai would have to show me what to do to deliver our people before they disappeared entirely, and He would have to grant me the strength to do it.

We were training on borrowed time. Word of our activities was certain to reach Antiochus Epiphanes, and when it did, he would send his army south. If, as I had heard, he was off waging war against the Persians and Armenians, he would send one of his generals with an army intent on wiping us from the face of the earth.

So when we were not searching for blasphemers in the villages and towns of Judea, we practiced our fighting skills and kept a wary eye on the plains. We knew the Seleucids were coming, but we did not know when.

Chapter Thirty: Judah

In a territory north of our camp, Apollonius, governor of Samaria, gathered Gentiles and a large force of Samaritans to fight against the army of Israel. When news of the approaching army reached us, we were dismayed but not surprised. The Samaritans were relatives — a people who claimed to be descended from Israelites who survived the Babylonian invasion and intermarried with native peoples — a practice forbidden by the Law of Moses. The Jews who returned to Judea after the exile never trusted the Samaritans, and nothing in our neighbors' recent behavior had improved our opinions of them.

"I can't believe he enlisted Samaritans," Simon said, his brow furrowed. "I had hoped they would stay out of this fight. After all, the Seleucids defiled their Temple, too —"

"They're on their way." A breathless scout

burst into the tent where Johanan, Simon, and I were discussing battle plans with my captains. "Hundreds of mounted men and at least a thousand foot soldiers."

An undeniable feeling of purpose rose in my chest as I looked at my brothers and my captains. Purpose . . . and eagerness. "This," I told them, a thrill shivering through my senses, "is why we have been training. This is why we have struggled, toiled, and gone hungry."

I looked at those faces — long faces, round faces, young faces, old faces, pale faces, flushed faces — and to a man, I saw the light of determination in their eyes. Today these men would stand behind me, and we would need the strength of Adonai to face the challenge approaching us.

"Have the riders mount up," I told the captains. "Archers should prepare their arrows. Tell the swordsmen to strap on their armor, and the slingers to fill their pouches."

"Will we go north to meet them?" Eleazar asked.

"We will march only as far as Lebonah," I answered, giving him a grim smile. "I know that area, and we will be able to hide ourselves on the hillside. They will ride straight into our welcoming arms."

With quickened pulses and surging blood

in our veins, we stalked out to meet the aggressors.

The night before the battle, after my men had hidden themselves among the rocks and grasses of the hills near Lebonah, I rode my horse onto a ridge and looked down at the enemy camp. Apollonius, warned either by his scouts or his false gods, had stopped short of our ambush and camped for the night.

The governor's tents were of far better quality than ours. Campfires, spaced at regular intervals, danced in the darkness, filling the plain. Several large tents glowed from the light of torches within, and even from where I stood I could see painted designs on the sprawling fabric domes. One of those tents belonged to Apollonius, whom I hoped to soon meet.

My men lay on the hillside where I had positioned them. They had no fires to keep them warm, no soft beds, no dinner, and no wives for comfort. In the darkness they might rise to stretch their limbs, but come morning they would be as still as the stones around them, waiting for the enemy to awaken and advance.

Like snakes we would lie poised to strike a lethal blow.

I let my horse pick his way down the ridge and positioned the beast out of sight behind a boulder, hobbled him, and stretched out on the hilltop. My men were obediently following orders — no one deserted his position, no one spoke. I could hear distant whinnies from the enemies' horses and the occasional burst of laughter, but nothing else.

As the wind gently scissored the grass near my ear, I drifted into a light doze in which familiar stories mingled with odd images I did not understand. I saw the faces of my people — a mother with seven sons, a copper pan large enough to fry an entire cow, a young man bleeding before his weeping mother as his brothers lay burned and broken on the floor. The scene shifted and I saw women with somber expressions, children in odd garments, bearded men with dark hats on their heads. I saw crowds shuffling forward, carrying bundles and baskets toward large boxes with wide doors. Tears streaked the women's faces and children screamed as uniformed men herded them into the boxes, then suddenly I stood in the room with them, breathing sour air, leaning against strangers as the box moved, jostling and vibrating in every corner, rattling even the floor beneath our feet . . .

Then we were walking, all of us pitifully naked and as thin as reeds. The women and children no longer had hair and the men had lost their beards. We walked toward a huge building with a chimney through which gray smoke rose to poison a pure blue sky. As we walked with mincing steps, I saw hundreds, perhaps thousands, of people piled in a ditch, men, women, and children lying atop each other like clay dolls, lifeless eyes staring at nothing, children with open mouths and pale, frozen limbs —

"Why?" I shouted, trying to wrest the others from their stupor. "Why are we walking into this place?"

The women in the slow-moving line answered with the tortured mother who had lost seven sons: *Because we did not believe anyone could be so cruel.* A murmur rose from the earth itself, trees and stones whispering words too terrible to be spoken. *Because we did not see the danger until it was too late to resist.*

We did not believe anyone could be so cruel.

We did not see the danger.

Too late.

I awakened as if slapped from sleep by an invisible hand. Gasping, I sat up and stared into the darkness, trying to make sense of where I was and what I had witnessed in the vision.

I was sitting on a hillside near Lebonah, waiting with the army of Israel. The sky above me was black, not blue. We were waiting for those who were determined to annihilate us. We might be resting with our eyes closed, but we were not blind.

I drew a deep breath, crossed my legs, and rested my arms on my bent knees, unwilling to close my eyes again.

Chapter Thirty-One: Leah

I slipped away from the other women as the sun sank below the rim of the hills. As I stood in the mouth of a cave, their careless chatter provided a stark contrast to the thick blanket of silence hovering over the men's distant camp.

Our warriors were gone, having departed the day before. They were striding forward to face their first major battle, and I knew Judah had determined to win a victory or die trying. He would not accept middle ground; no peaceful surrender would do for his army.

I wanted to be as confident as he was, but doubts swirled in my head. Up until now, he and his men had only engaged in surprise attacks. They had dragged shepherds and farmers from taverns and held swords to the throats of unarmed men. Their string of easy victories, I feared, had come to an end.

On the morrow they would face an actual

army with heavily armed men, many of them exceptionally skilled in warfare. From talking to my brothers-in-law, I learned that the Seleucids were trained mercenaries, well-fed soldiers who were paid to kill for a king. They were not fighting for freedom or justice; they fought for glory, honor, and money. If they found themselves losing a battle, they would retreat and save themselves to fight another day.

Judah, I feared, would never retreat. His ragtag group — volunteers who had been living for months on bread, goat cheese, and whatever bits of meat we could scavenge from wild animals in the wilderness — would die before surrendering.

I wrapped my arms around myself as a chilly wind swirled outside the mouth of the cave. So much for my marriage. I hated violence and had married to get away from it, yet life or fate or Adonai had brought me back to the place where I started. My gentle husband had become a warrior, and I would soon be a widow, as would most of the women behind me. And even though Judah had to know I did not approve of this war, he had not given up his command, but had plunged ahead in his reckless work.

Did he truly love me, or had he married only because his father required it? When he told me his name meant "the hammerhead," I should have known that he preferred fighting to loving. He had revealed himself to be a man's man, a creature born and bred for conflict, and he seemed to enjoy the pitched heat of a fight. He would consider it an honor to surrender his life on some blood-soaked battlefield, so why had he agreed to take a wife?

No matter what his reasons, every time I saw him straighten and prepare to ride back to the warriors' camp, I realized he was done with being a husband. To everything, apparently, there was a season . . . a time to love and, when that ended, a time to wage war.

Chapter Thirty-Two: Judah

"Three things," Solomon wrote, "are stately in their stride, four of stately gait — the lion, mightiest of beasts, which turns aside for no one; the greyhound, the billy goat, and the king when his army is with him."

Make that a governor, and I was observing a literal expression of that proverb.

I lay flat on my belly, my head resting on my fists, and watched Apollonius ride to the front line of his army. His metal armor gleamed in the morning sun, and a plume in his helmet danced to the steps of his horse. His militia, wearing similar helmets and armor, stood in a long line that seemed to stretch from east to west. He had, I noticed, placed his archers at the front, his slingers behind them, and his swordsmen at the rear. A group of chariots stood at the rear of the company, ready to fly to wherever they were needed.

The whinny of Apollonius's horse broke

the silence, and the governor barely managed to hold the animal still. He looked right and left to check his line, then he lowered his arm and pointed to the hill above our hiding place where I had stationed a line of one thousand warriors, enough to lure Apollonius forward without revealing the true strength of our force.

I smiled. Last night more than rabbits had slept on this hillside.

"Come on," I whispered, tasting grit as the wind blew dirt across my teeth. "Come meet those you have determined to destroy. Come meet the people whose God is Adonai."

On they came, striding over the barren plain. With banners waving and fine horses prancing over the sandy soil, they approached the hillside as casually as men who have set out for a walk on a pleasant day.

We had agreed that my whistle would signal the start of our attack, but I would have to time the charge carefully. I could not give the enemy archers time to nock their bows and send a wave of arrows into the hillside. I waited, patient as a spider, and felt the ground tremble beneath my limbs. I heard the chink of metal armor, the snorting of the governor's stallion, and the flapping of his bold flag.

Still I waited.

Inhaling deeply, I breathed in the odor of unbathed, hardworking men, then I whistled as I used to when signaling my brothers. My men sprang up from their hiding places, tossing aside weeds, rolling out from behind boulders, crawling out of shallow burrows. With spears and slingshots and swords they ran toward the enemies of Israel, their weapons striking legs, arms, and tender bellies. Our archers, whom I had positioned at the top of the hill, aimed low, beneath the metal helmets, striking our enemies in the throat, chest, and eyes.

I ran for the man in the shining armor and caught the reins of the governor's horse before he could turn the stallion. With my arm through the reins, I grabbed Apollonius's leg and yanked him off the beast, nimbly stepping out of the way as he tumbled into the dirt. As he rolled to avoid his nervous mount's hooves, I freed my arm, slapped the beast's hindquarters and drove it away.

Then I crouched before the man who had blasphemed the God of the Jews and the Samaritans.

"You come against the children of Israel," I said, grinning at the astounded look on the governor's face. "Let me introduce you to Adonai, your maker, and the keeper of the keys to Hades, where you will soon join your friends."

Apollonius's mouth curled as if he wanted to spit. "Are you always so stupid?" Rendered awkward by his heavy armor, he rolled onto his stomach and pushed himself up. "Or are you making a special effort today?"

I was too startled by his suggestion — and, truth be told, too slow — to come up with a witty rejoinder, so I drew my father's pitted sword from its sheath and readied myself for a blow.

Apollonius may have been a governor, but he had also trained in swordsmanship. He withdrew his sword with a flourish and swung the blade in a wide arc. He crouched in a swordsman's posture, and I knew I would be no match for his fancy footwork. Yet I possessed what he did not — skills that had been sharpened by four brothers who excelled in down-and-dirty play.

Gripping my sword with both hands, I charged him with an overhand blow, which he capably deflected. I ducked beneath his answering swing, then stepped to the side, energized by the noise of battle and the sight of sweat on his brow. My men were calling on Adonai, filling the air with cries of "For Jerusalem!" and "We have not forgotten Zion!" while our attackers did nothing but grunt and scream.

Apollonius matched my steps as we engaged in a bizarre dance to the death. "That's a nice sword you have," I told him, nodding at the intricate engraving on the hilt. "Kill many men with that?"

"Not so many men," the governor answered, lunging toward my chest, "but a great many Jews. Last year I was in Jerusalem when the streets ran with blood."

"And for that you will pay." I pulled a dagger from my belt and turned sideways, presenting a smaller target, then thrust my sword at his heart. He moved out of the way, though I did manage to slice the exposed flesh at his neck.

He winced, then set his jaw, his features hardening in a determined stare. "You have delighted me long enough. Time for you to go."

"Before you die" — I tightened my grip on my sword as I circled him — "you should know I have taken a fancy to your blade. I will use it against your king in every battle, and I will kill dozens of your countrymen with its fine edge. Those carvings on the handle will be caked with the blood of Seleucids and Samaritans and any who would come against those who uphold the Law of Almighty God."

"Enough with your bragging," Apollonius said, charging.

"Enough with your blasphemy," I answered, and as he stepped toward me, I caught his blade with my sword, turning it from my body as I sank my dagger into his chest. The edge I had honed sliced through his armor and slid between his ribs, opening a river of blood that cascaded over the fine fabrics of his tunic and left him gasping.

The governor crumpled as his knees gave way. He looked at me, astonishment on his face, and then fell forward into the dust.

I lifted my sword and shouted, "We have cut off the head of the wolf!" There were other wolves, but this one would not come against us again.

I removed the man's head from his shoulders, then picked up his sword and plunged the blade into the wound. Holding the prize high, I stepped onto the plain and lifted my bloody burden for all to see. "Hear, O Israel," I called with as much volume as my spent lungs could muster. "This day is ours!"

For the next several days, I found myself in

the center of a bewildering whirlwind. When we had finished chasing the surviving remnant of Apollonius's army back into Samaria, we celebrated, burning the enemy dead and capturing the horses that had lost their riders. We praised HaShem, we danced and sang, we went through the enemy camp and salvaged the spoils — wineskins of fine wines, gold rings from aristocratic Seleucid fingers, sets of armor from fallen mercenaries. The enemy had even abandoned their supply wagons, so we feasted on dried venison, roasted beef, and marinated fowl. We enjoyed fruits we had not seen in months and washed them down with wines fine enough to grace a king's table.

Victory made us giddy. But when the giddiness passed, I found myself feeling restless and uncertain. I knew another attack would come, but first Antiochus would have to learn about what had happened here. Then he would have to send his army. That meant we had time, a few weeks or even months, to enjoy a bit of ordinary life. We could go home to check on the livestock, tend our crops, and relieve family members who had been doing our work. Men who had left their families defenseless could go home and see that they were safe.

But what would I find at home? Leah had

been so cold and distant the last time I saw her, and I did not know how to warm her heart. I had no idea what I should say when I next saw her. Would she be expecting the husband or the commander?

I told the men they could return to their homes for two weeks. "Check on your crops," I urged them. "Repair your houses, serve your wives, and spend time with your children. Sacrifice to Adonai, for He is good. Then return to camp."

The camp emptied out the next day, but I did not go home with my brothers. Instead I took a horse and wandered through the wilderness, taking time to pray and consider what HaShem might have in store for us. He had been faithful to support us in our first battle, but I did not want to take His faithfulness for granted. I resolved to return His favor with faithfulness of my own.

After three days, I rode into Modein and dismounted, then led my stallion to the corral, now filled with uncommonly fine horses. Eleazar and Simon called a greeting, and Johanan waved from the doorway of his house. They had been home for at least two days and did not seem to have any problems with their wives.

My heart drummed in my chest as I approached my own house. I caught a glimpse of Leah through the window, and the sight of her, so small and youthful, brought a lump to my throat. I looked down at my body — dust covered me from head to foot, my limbs bore bruises and cuts, and I had not bathed in weeks. What woman would not run at the approach of such a brute?

But my appearance could not be helped. I brushed dust from my shoulders, swiped at my face with my hands, and walked into the house.

Leah froze where she stood. Her eyes widened, then she gave me a brief, distracted smile. "You surprised me," she said, moving to the table where she prepared meals. "If you are hungry —"

"Truth be told, I am tired."

I untied my sword belt, dropped it in the corner, walked to the bed and fell forward onto the mattress. I had thought to rest for only a little while, but by the time I opened my eyes again, daylight had vanished from the room.

Lit by the glow of a single lamp, Leah sat on the edge of the bed, her hair down and one shoulder bare. Her loveliness evoked my desire, and I reached for her.

She recoiled when she realized I was awake. "No."

"I'm sorry." I sat up and raked my hand

through my filthy hair. "I will clean up. Sometimes I forget how dirty a fighting man can get —"

"I don't care about that. We women get just as grimy in the caves." Her countenance had drawn inward, a pale knot of trepidation.

"Then what do you care about?"

Beneath the smooth surface of her face I saw currents of emotion, a hidden stream desperate to break through. "May I . . . speak freely?"

"I wish you would."

Her shoulders slumped in what looked like relief. "I . . . I do not think I was meant to be a warrior's wife. I cannot stand violence. I despise cruelty. And knowing that my husband is wielding a sword and beheading his victims . . ." She shuddered. "I have tried to be pleased for you, but I failed. Now I know I cannot be happy as a warrior's wife."

With numb astonishment I realized she was being completely honest. Words flowed from her like a river, faster and more freely than ever before. "What are you saying?"

"I know you want to honor your father's wishes," she said, not looking at me, "but Johanan has expressed his desire to lead the army. Why don't you let him command? He would be good at it, and you could stay in Modein and oversee the family fields. It is a good solution, I think, because I simply cannot be wife to a violent man."

I could not have been more astounded if she had announced she was an angel sent from heaven. I blinked in silence, then felt my mouth dip in a wry smile. "Did Eleazar put you up to this?"

"I have not spoken to Eleazar."

I blinked again as hope fell away. "Are you saying you don't want to be married to me?"

"I like you, Judah — I could love you because I know you have a gentle heart. But the thought of your violence . . . makes me ill. I want to be sick."

I gentled my voice. "I would worry about a woman who relished the violence of war."

"It's more than womanly reticence. I've seen you and your brothers out in the fields. You beat on each other in some kind of game, and even that makes me uncomfortable. I haven't known how to tell you this, but if we are to be happy together, I think I should be truthful. My mother never confronted my father . . . so I have to."

"What has your mother to do with this?"

She shook her head. "Will you promise to let Johanan lead the men? I understand why you fight to defend the helpless, but when you kill your own people —" She shuddered again. "I cannot bear the thought of it."

I stared at her as my thoughts spun. Did she not understand that we had to cleanse the land? I wanted to please her, but how could I refuse to do the thing HaShem had called me to do? And if I let her have her way in this, what would stop her from asking me to do some other impossible thing?

"We are not killing our people. We are, when necessary, killing those who have betrayed our people. They have converted to the ways of the Gentiles, and they have informed on those who keep and honor the Law."

"They are still Jews. They are still *men.*"

I had no answer to that.

"I cannot do what you ask." Avoiding her eyes, I lifted my arms into the light. "These are the hands of a fighter. These are the limbs of a soldier. HaShem made me for His purposes, and fighting appears to be one of them. Father knew it. Even Johanan knows it. And as my wife, you must accept it."

I expected her to nod and submit to my judgment, but fury burned in the eyes that turned toward me. "Have I not accepted enough? I did not quarrel when we moved to Modein. I did not complain when we moved to the wilderness. I have slept on the ground; I have starved when there was nothing to eat. I have shivered and gone without bathing, and I have silently witnessed murders and all sorts of violence committed in the name of Adonai. I have even come back to Modein with your family, watching every woman with her husband, but mine? He chose to stay away. And when he *did* come home, I asked for one thing, and he refused me."

Suddenly she was kneeling at my feet, her eyes intent on mine, her face lifted in supplication. "If you love me, Judah, you will understand. I left a life of violence to marry you. I rejoiced because you took me from a house where my father ruled with cruel fists. I was learning how to relax here, learning to love you, but then your father —"

"My father was a righteous man."

"He was, but Judah . . ." She clutched my hands and rested her cheek on my curled fingers. "I want to love you. I do not want to be miserable when we could be happy together. All you have to do is renounce the role your father thrust upon you."

I felt hot tears on my skin, gelding tears, and jerked my hands away. I stood and walked toward the window where I looked out at the darkness.

On the first morning I woke as a married man, my bride had opened her eyes and tried to change me. *"Judas Maccabaeus," she'd said. "Do you not wish to cast off that name?"*

How could I change who I was? Adonai had made me big and strong, and he had placed me in the middle of my father's sons. Surely these things had been ordained for a reason.

Could I remain behind while my brothers and kinsmen went off to war? Could I become a farmer-shepherd when my people needed me? I was not born a commander, but Father chose me and Adonai honored my desire to please him. If I did not lead, Johanan would. But my elder brother had always cared more for himself than anyone else, and I could not imagine him riding out to face the enemy without first having made a convenient escape plan.

On the other hand, I loved my wife and wanted to honor her. Her honest confession about her past had removed a barrier that had stood between us, and I understood why she had been so timid and silent in the early days of our marriage. But now that I truly saw her, now that I fully understood, could I place my love for her above all else? She was flesh of my flesh, heart of my heart, and I longed to sacrifice myself for her and our children.

But I could not — would not — turn my back on the task Adonai had given me. And hadn't He given me this woman as my wife? Surely the Master of the universe could find a way to reconcile my wife and my role as commander of the army.

I turned, sadness pooling in my heart as I looked at the woman crumpled at the end of our bed.

"Leah" — her name tasted bittersweet on my lips — "I cannot do this for you because I must obey Adonai. I know I am meant to command the army. I know I am meant to be your husband. So please do not ask this of me again."

Her face rippled with anguish, then she turned the focus of her gaze to some interior vision I could not imagine. She rose slowly, as if she'd been injured, and walked to her table where she removed a towel from a bowl and began to shape a ball of dough.

I drew a breath, hoping to say something that might ease the sting, but what could I tell her? I could not relent, nor could I be a part-time commander. Adonai asked for all of a man's heart, and I could not give Him less. I had given all my heart to Leah, too . . . but she didn't want the part that carried a sword.

"I can promise you one thing," I finally said, breaking the heavy silence. "When the war is over, when our enemy leaves Judea, I will lay down my sword and live in peace with you."

"You cannot promise me anything," she said, her voice soft. "Because unless you lay down your sword, you may never live with me again."

Chapter Thirty-Three: Leah

I pounded the ball, superimposing Judah's face on the wrinkled mixture beneath my hand. Not until I had beaten the loaf a dozen times did I realize the irony — there I was, beating up bread dough because my husband refused to disavow violence.

I glanced behind me and was relieved to see that Judah had slipped out of the house. I needed time to be alone, to think about other things while I figured out how to live with a man who could not fulfill my deepest need.

I covered the shaped loaf with a piece of linen, then stepped outside to study the beautiful horses that had returned with our men. Though night had fallen, they continued to stir in the corral, bobbing their heads in the moonlight and browsing the feeding trough, hoping for some leftover grain.

The Seleucids had good taste in horseflesh. Judah had ridden home on a white stallion, and the animal held himself aloof from the others as if he realized his superlative beauty. Even if no one rode him again, he would definitely improve the quality of our stock. We had not been able to afford good horses before the war, but the situation would change if Mattathias's sons kept winning battles.

I leaned on the fence railing, resting my chin on my hand. None of the other brothers was around — no doubt they were inside their homes, enjoying their wives and preparing for bed. I had hoped to do the same, after Judah promised to let Johanan command the army. I had imagined us spending the next day together, laughing and celebrating our love . . . but no chance of that remained.

How could I live with a fighter? I had finally summoned the courage to tell Judah what my family was like, yet the truth did not seem to affect him. I unrolled the nightmare of my childhood, put it on full display, and yet he remained as stubborn as ever. A man who truly loved me would have been moved to take me in his arms and comfort me, but not even heartfelt tears had swayed his resolve.

I sniffed as tears began to flow again, then swiped them from my lashes. I would not have anyone see me crying. I did not need pity. What I needed was . . . a man who would do what I asked.

I turned away from the horses and began to walk, head down, arms crossed. What could I do now? I could ask Judah to grant me a *get,* a written notice of divorce. Then Mother and I could travel to some other village. We would be like Naomi and Ruth, living on the kindness of strangers.

Yet when Judah was not covered in blood and wide-eyed with ferocity, he was a gentle man. He had ever only shown me kindness, doing more for me than most men would. He had risked his life to go into Jerusalem and find my mother. He had built me a fine house and welcomed my mother into his family.

He had placed wildflowers on my pillow.

What woman would not love such a man?

But whenever I saw him arrayed for battle, images of my wild-eyed father flooded back. I saw Mother's bruised face, Father's swollen red knuckles, his shiny fingers wet with mother's blood and tears. I heard the slap of flesh and the snap of breaking ribs.

I pressed my fist to my mouth to stifle a sob. I could not do it. I could not be a commander's wife. The anger that fueled him as a soldier would remain buried inside him, and one day, at some provocation, it would erupt against me or one of our children. He would strike out, and though he might apologize later, the violence would continue to simmer.

Judah kept insisting that Adonai had called him to be a warrior, but perhaps Adonai had called me to be another man's wife. He could not have designed me for the commander of Israel's army.

By the time I returned to our home, solid darkness had filled the spaces between the trees and the alleys between our houses. I entered quietly and allowed my eyes to adjust to the light of the lamp. Judah snored on his back, one hand pillowing his head, the other across his chest.

I knew what I had to do.

Swallowing the sob that rose in my throat, I stepped out of my tunic and lay beside him, then turned and kissed him.

Waking, he took me in his arms. He must have thought I had accepted his decision, that I had acquiesced to his will. I would allow him to think so . . . for a while.

We lay together as silence sifted down like a snowfall.

"Was it horrible?" I finally asked, looking up at him. "The battle, I mean."

Oddly enough, he smiled. "No . . . not for

me, at least. It must have been so for the enemy, for they had no chance of victory. They came at us with overweening confidence, as if we were peasants they could pick off at leisure. I doubt the Seleucids will ever make that mistake again."

I stroked the tendrils of his beard as I waited.

"That governor, though — to him, it was a game. Sport. We both knew the risks, but neither of us cared. We only wanted to win."

I rested my hand on his damp chest. "I saw the sword. Is it his?"

"Not anymore." He grinned at my shocked expression, then shifted his gaze to the sword in the corner. "Apollonius must have paid a fortune for such fine work, and I intend to enjoy it. Adonai will see that blade used for His glory."

Is that how Judah saw himself? As a tool in Adonai's hand?

"I am glad you survived." I patted his chest. "Yet I fear for you. This battle might have been easy, but surely next time the king will send more men, better men."

"I'm counting on it." He caught my hand and held it tight. "And the Lord God will strengthen and guide me just as He has in the past. I don't know how to explain it, Leah, but when I'm in the midst of the fight, I feel . . . as though I have been fashioned for it."

"So you've said." I remained silent for a moment, then tilted my face toward his. "Neta says you want to be king. That you insist on being commander so you can win a crown for yourself and our children."

His lips parted, then he filled the house with unrestrained laughter. "A king? I am not from the house of David."

"Your people are Levites —"

"The Levites are priests, not kings. No, only a man from the house of David can righteously sit on the throne of Israel, and I would never place myself in that seat. You tell Neta to mind her own business and take care of her husband. All our men have returned to their villages. We did not lose a single soul in the battle."

I drew a breath, knowing that this might be the time. If he was content and happy, he might, in a gesture of good will, give me a note of divorcement —

But in that moment he pressed a kiss to my head, pulled me closer, and locked his arms around me. Before I could summon my courage, he had fallen asleep and I could not bring myself to wake him.

Chapter Thirty-Four: Judah

Out in the harvested fields, several village youths and I were training for the coming counterattack when I saw Johanan approaching. I left the young ones and strode toward my elder brother, curious about what would bring him out in the middle of the day.

"A word with you, Judah," he said, motioning for me to come with him.

We walked down to the brook, where Johanan knelt and refilled his waterskin, then held it up to me. "Thirsty?"

"Thanks." I lifted the container and let water splash over my sweaty neck and face, then took a long, deep drink. I knelt to refill the vessel, but Johanan took it and submerged it in the stream.

"You know the Seleucids will come again," he said, not looking at me. "And this time they will not bring local recruits and a handful of Samaritans. The king will send one of his generals."

"Let them come. We will be ready."

"Will you?" Johanan stood and took a drink himself, but he kept his gaze on me until he wiped his mouth on his arm. "I would urge you to seriously consider what I am about to say. You were fortunate in the last skirmish. You overflowed with enthusiasm and your zeal influenced the others, so you won the battle easily. We came home, all of us alive and well, not because you are a great military leader, but because you are bold and brash."

His eyes narrowed as if he could peer into my mind and read a list of my capabilities. "Next time, little brother, you may begin the battle with boldness, but you will be facing war machines that fling boulders coated in burning oil. You will face men who were practically born with a bow in their hands, and slingers who can bring down a sparrow at fifty paces. When our men run forward and realize they are standing against professional soldiers . . . I'm afraid the outcome of our next battle will not be as glorious as our first."

I stared at him, unable to believe what I was hearing. "What are you saying? If you think you are the better leader, say so plainly."

Johanan looked away, then wiped dust from the breastplate of his training armor. "I am the firstborn," he said, propping his foot on a boulder. "I should lead the men. I would not run to the next battle, but I would send emissaries to meet with the king. Perhaps some sort of settlement can be arranged. Perhaps we can negotiate a peace."

I released a guffaw. "You think Antiochus Epiphanes will negotiate after only one loss? He has not yet sent his generals against us, so why should he negotiate?"

Johanan exhaled in a rush. "It is not right that the middle son should be leading the entire camp. They all look to you, even the wives and children. They wait for you to instruct them, encourage them — tell me, if they wait for you to feed them, how will you manage that? You have never been able to organize your thoughts, much less thousands of people."

I frowned, upset by Johanan's opposition but unable to argue. I was a good fighter, but I had never developed skills in managing crowds. I had never been required to keep vast numbers of people fed and clothed and content, and I did not possess a silver tongue like my older brothers.

"Perhaps that is why Father said Simon

should be the counselor," I finally mumbled, looking away. "Father knew my weaknesses as well as my strengths. I know my shortcomings and I know I am not all-powerful. So if we are to defeat the enemy, I will command the army, but I freely admit I cannot do this alone. I need you and Simon and Eleazar and Jonathan to help me."

Johanan looked at me as if he would argue further, then he squeezed my shoulder. "I was beginning to think you would exalt yourself as king before all those who have come to support us, but now I see the situation more clearly. You have never been a man of great ambition."

"I am," I insisted. "My ambition is to defeat anyone who would prevent us from worshiping as HaShem commanded."

John's thin lips spread into a wry smile. "Forgive me," he said, turning to go. "For not giving you enough credit."

Chapter Thirty-Five: Leah

Seeing no easy way out of my marriage, I decided to wait. To follow the example of countless women and hide my deepest feelings. To find another answer to my problem, a solution that would not scandalize the community or shame the family.

What, I asked myself, might convince Judah to stop commanding the army?

I had already been given one answer.

Every time I ventured outside the house, I felt my mother's eyes on me. She spent most of her time sitting in the shade with Rosana, either doing needlework or grinding grain. I knew she was waiting for me to persuade Judah to love his wife more than his war.

I found Morit down by the creek, where she was washing clothes. Young Johanan, her oldest boy, scampered over the rocks along the creek bed, and her baby, Judas, lay in a basket she had set in the shade. She kept a wary eye on the older child as she pounded wet tunics on a rock.

"There you are." I forced a smile. "I thought I'd never find you."

She shaded her eyes and smiled. "I thought I'd take the boys out for some fresh air. Rosana can bear only so much of wee Johanan's antics, then she needs to rest."

I smiled, understanding completely. Four-year-old Johanan would try the patience of Job.

Morit bent over her wet clothes, then gave me a sidelong glance. "Something on your mind, sister?"

I sat on a rock and propped my chin in my hand. "I have been married now for several months, yet my womb remains empty."

"Ah." Morit lifted a dripping tunic from the water and twisted it. "And you think I can tell you how to fill it?"

"You're the one with babies." I gave her a wry smile. "I was thinking . . . *hoping* that Judah would surrender his position with the army if he had a baby at home. Surely a man who finds himself responsible for a young child is not as willing to risk his life in battle."

Morit squinted at me. "Or maybe a man with sons and daughters is even more determined to fight the enemy who would imprison or enslave his children. Men do not go to war on a whim. They have good reasons for risking their lives or they would not do it."

I bit my lip, forced to consider another perspective. Did all men need a compelling reason to fight? Apparently not, for my father had no reason to strike my mother. Though he blamed her stupidity, slovenliness, lack of cooking skills, unattractiveness, and dozens of other qualities, even as a child I knew his accusations were only an excuse for violence. My father fought because he wanted to, therefore it seemed logical to me that good reason might persuade a man to choose peace.

"I cannot bear violence," I confessed, crossing my arms. "The sight of blood makes me sick. I would rather Judah stay home to tend to the livestock and the fields."

"Might as well tell a rooster to sleep through sunrise." Morit slapped the wet tunic over a tree branch. "You can say whatever you want, but a man has to do what HaShem created him to do."

"Is that why Simon joined the army?"

Her brow furrowed as she stopped working. "Simon fights . . . because he loves his brothers, his family, and the freedom to worship HaShem. *Not* fighting would put all three in danger."

"But he could stay here while the others went to war."

She shook her head. "Simon would never stand by while others did the hard work. He would never give them any reason to call him a coward."

"My mother said I must make Judah love me more than anything, even more than his family. She said that is the only way he will ever do what I need him to do."

Morit dropped another garment into the water, then turned to give me an incredulous look. "Your mother said *that*?"

I nodded.

"And how well did that advice work for *her*?"

I drew a breath to speak but found myself with nothing to say. My father never did anything Mother wanted him to do, and as for loving her, I had seen dogs demonstrate more love for their mates.

I sighed and wished Morit well, then left her by the creek. I had learned nothing, yet her practical answer did not dissuade me.

Though love for me could not convince Judah to surrender his fight, love for his child might.

Chapter Thirty-Six: Judah

The letter arrived on a cool day not long after the latter rains. From the window I saw Morit accept something from a man on horseback, then she came running into the house. She looked around the circle of my brothers and then handed the scroll to me.

I broke the seal, unfurled it, and stared at the unfamiliar writing. I had never been the best reader, so I gave the message to Johanan, who frowned at it for a moment, then gaped at me like a man who had just been knocked over by a charging sheep. "Do you know someone in Antioch?"

"What?"

He consulted the scroll again. "Someone called Philander?"

The name stirred vague memories of a dark night, a horse, and an inn. "Yes! He is a scribe in the king's court. I met him on the road outside Jerusalem."

Johanan chuffed. "Your friend the scribe

has sent you a letter."

"What does it say?"

Johanan read the document, then looked around the table. "In short, Antiochus has learned of Apollonius's defeat. In retaliation, he has dispatched Seron, his chief general, with a contingent of soldiers. Antiochus gave the general a single charge: 'Annihilate this party of resisters, then stamp out the Jewish religion. We will cleanse the land of Jehovah and his worshipers and put new people in their place, allowing them to colonize the land and divide it by lots.' "

I slammed my fist to the table. "Time to gather the men."

Jonathan stood. "I'll blow the shofar and light a signal fire."

I leaned toward Simon and Johanan. "Let us beg HaShem to grant us victory, so we can send our own message to the king — a living God reigns in Isra'el, and He will defend His people!"

Simon met my eyes and dipped his chin in a sober nod. "Let us hope the men have not grown soft while they were at home."

Under Seron's command, Antiochus's army marched southward through Samaria, over the plain of Sharon, and began the ascent to Jerusalem, treading where millions of my people had walked before. They took the main road from Lydda and passed by Modein, then moved toward Beth-horon, a settlement that could only be approached by a long, narrow ridge flanked by deep ravines.

By the time Seron entered Judea, the army of Israel had reassembled at the wilderness camp. Not all of our men had made it back, but we would not have time to wait for them. As soon as our lookouts spotted Seron's army, we would move out.

The women who came with us — Leah surprised me by coming along — sheltered in the caves while we men spent our time in prayer. Johanan insisted that our time would be better spent in drills, but I differed. Time spent in prayer was never wasted.

My captains and I had determined that although we could not stop Seron's army from entering Judea, we could not allow them to reach Jerusalem where our people were still trying to rebuild. We would cut them off at Beth-horon, a barren area most of us knew as well as we knew our mothers' faces. From Beth-horon's high ridge we could look out and see Modein. Behind us we could see Gibeon, and to the southwest, the small town of Aijalon.

When scouts blasted into camp with their warning, I led the army of Israel — only a handful of men, it seemed to me — to Beth-horon. Standing on the ridge, I exulted in the kinship I felt with the forefathers who had stood in the same spot. Somewhere near here, Joshua had begged Adonai to grant him a miracle: "Sun, stand motionless over Gibeon! Moon, you too, over the Ai-jalon Valley!" So the sun stood still and the moon stayed put until Israel had taken vengeance on their enemies.

Now I was asking for a similar miracle: that HaShem would look down and give a handful of His people the strength to drive the enemy away. From the ridge we could see them approaching — row after row of marching warriors, a seemingly endless spectacle that stretched from Modein to the far horizon.

"Adonai, blessed be your name," I prayed, lifting my gaze to the balmy blue sky above. "Your holy prophet Joshua wrote that there has never been a day like that before or since, when Adonai listened to the voice of a man. Like Joshua, I am fighting on Israel's behalf, and I beg you to fight for me, for us, your people. That day you sent a hailstorm to destroy the armies of the five kings who came against Israel, and today I would ask you to send whatever you like to rid the land of our enemies."

When I lowered my eyes, Simon and Jonathan stood beside me, and neither of them looked confident. "How do you expect the few of us to fight against that multitude?" Jonathan pointed to the advancing army with a trembling arm. "All day we have fasted according to your command and we have no strength. We are weak enough now; how weak will we be by the time they reach the summit?"

I noted the despair on their faces, then strode past them toward the men awaiting my orders.

"Men of Israel," I called, my voice echoing in the rocky valley, "know this — our force is considerably smaller than the one marching toward us. Yet it is not the size of the army that matters, but the strength of our God. Today we fight for the Law of HaShem, our lives, and our people. Just as Adonai gave victory to Joshua when he told the sun and moon to remain in their places, HaShem will give you the strength you need to defeat the enemy. Do not think about your weariness when the hour of victory is within reach. Do not speak of defeat when our God is willing to fight for us! He himself will crush them before us, so do not be afraid of them. We are standing where giants have stood, and we will hold the high ground until the last of our enemies is either dead or on his way back to Syria! Never doubt it!"

Instead of cheering — because the sound might have given away our position — the men waved their weapons and looked at me with confidence shining in their eyes.

"Remain in your positions until you hear the signal," I told the assembly with their spears, slingshots, swords, and arrows. "Then we will leap out of our hiding places and chase the enemy out of this holy land!"

Hundreds of weapons glittered in the sunlight as I turned and smiled at my brothers. "Return to your companies," I told them, "and encourage your men as we wait for the enemy to approach. This day will be ours."

From my crouched position behind a boulder at the top of the ridge, I eased back on my heels to relieve my cramping legs. Across the worn footpath I caught Eleazar's eye and nodded. He grinned, then gripped his sword and settled back on the rocks, as at ease as a child with a new toy. The other men of our army were hidden among the many grasses, boulders, and ledges of Beth-horon.

The sounds of the approaching army changed as they came closer. At first we heard only a sound like thunder, but now we could hear stamping feet, the occasional whinny of a horse, and the thunderous grumble of the catapult's wooden wheels. The sounds echoed in the space surrounding the narrow mountain pass, clearly announcing the enemy's advance.

Too bad they had brought their war machines over such a great distance. When Adonai strengthened us, as I knew He would, they would have to leave their machines in the dust.

When at last I heard the jangling of the horses' bridles, I stood and peered over the rocks, then I whistled. Johanan blew the shofar, and the warriors of Israel leapt from their hiding places and descended on the enemy, brandishing their weapons and attacking the hapless invaders who found themselves trapped between the steep ravines.

The surprised Seleucids scrambled away, fleeing with far more energy than they had advanced. Those closest to me sprinted down the mountain, trampling their fellows, and those at the rear released their war machines and ran as the wheeled weapons slid backward and mowed down men who could not get away from their crushing weight.

I watched from my elevated post with pleased surprise. The Seleucids in the rear were fleeing even though not a single Jew had reached them. A wave of enemy soldiers swept toward the horizon, stirring up dust as it receded. Our blockade of the narrow passage had forced the enemy army to retreat, and the terrible blast of the shofar had set off a panic I had never before seen and probably never will again. Only a few of Seron's soldiers lingered long enough to exchange blows with our men, and those who did were so terrified they did not fight well.

What had panicked them so? Had HaShem magnified the sound of the shofar until it shattered their hearing? Had He made his protective angels visible to the Gentiles who came against us? I could not tell, but clearly something had terrified the king's men.

We chased the fleeing enemy down the mountain and into the broad plains that had belonged to the Amorites when Joshua stood on this mountain and bade the sun to linger. The Seleucid general had underestimated our strength, our cunning, and our God. Indeed, we were not many, but we knew the land God had given to our people.

Our horsemen chased the surviving warriors out of Israel while the rest of us gathered weapons and armor from those who did not escape.

"They'll stay gone," one of my men remarked, but I shook my head.

"Maybe not forever," I said, "but they'll think twice before approaching Jerusalem by this route."

When Johanan and Simon approached, I withdrew Philander's scroll from my belt and held it up. "We might not be celebrating if this had not arrived." I clapped Simon on the shoulder. "We will have to write and thank him for his kindness."

A line appeared between Simon's brows. "I'll have to write in some sort of code — we can't have a letter falling into the wrong hands."

"I know you'll think of something." Then, in front of my brothers and a host of my fellow warriors, I lifted my arms to the heavens and spun in a slow circle. "All praise to you, *YHVH Tzvaot,* the Lord of Hosts, who sent angel armies to confound and chase our enemies. Glory is yours forevermore!"

■ ■ ■ ■

We celebrated in the camp that night. Sounds of music and laughter filled the air while our men devoured the meat, bread, and lentils our women had baked with hope in their hearts. A huge bonfire blazed at the center of our gathering, fueled by the enemy catapults we had dismantled. Johanan asked if we ought to keep them, but our form of fighting relied on subtlety, and those gigantic, creaking machines were anything but subtle. "And," I added as another thought occurred, "did those machines not turn on their makers? What use have we for instruments like that?"

I rejoiced because we had suffered only minor injuries, and most of those injuries had occurred when the terrified Seleucids injured our fighters in their haste to escape.

I nodded at Abner, who had his arm in a sling, and his brother Gideon, whose leg was bandaged. "What happened to you two?"

Abner flushed. "Fell on a rock and broke my arm as I gave chase. But my wife has wrapped it."

I grinned. "I hope she's given you wine for the pain."

"Enough for me and my brother here. His story is even more embarrassing than mine."

I looked at Gideon, who leaned heavily on his brother's shoulder. "Did you fall, too?"

"Horse stepped on me," he said. "One of those big stallions, in a terrible hurry to get away. Nearly broke the bone."

"But you're walking."

"Barely. Mostly the leg is black and blue."

As they hobbled away, Leah approached. She said nothing until I sank to a blanket and motioned for her to sit next to me. "Your men," she said as she sat at my side, "celebrate as enthusiastically as they train."

"True enough." I smiled. "They *eat* as enthusiastically, too. You women have done a fine job of feeding them."

She lowered her gaze, her long lashes hiding her eyes. I couldn't tell what she was thinking — not that I had ever been any good at determining what women had on their minds.

"Is this the end, then?" she finally asked, her eyes rising to meet mine. "Will I have a husband again? Are we ready to go back to Modein?"

I held up my hand. "I don't know what tomorrow holds. I think we will be able to go home, but we must always be prepared to fight. We have won a battle, but I do not think we have won the war."

She drew a quick breath and exhaled slowly as she watched the merrymakers. I couldn't read her thoughts, but I could tell she wasn't happy with my answer.

"I did not plan to be a soldier," I told her. "This is not something I would ordinarily want to do. But HaShem has called me to this task, and He has blessed my efforts. I will not — I cannot — quit until my task is finished."

I bent to examine her face, and her brown eyes came up to me wet.

"Did you want to say something else?" I asked.

She remained silent for a moment, then gave me a look that was neither angry nor loving.

"One thing," she said, her voice flat. "I was not certain, so I waited to be sure. We are going to have a baby."

Chapter Thirty-Seven: Leah

In a much-appreciated display of gentleness, Judah placed me on his white stallion and let me ride back to Modein. I had hoped he would walk beside me so we could talk, but instead he wandered from family to family, checking on his men, congratulating them on their bravery, and reminding them that the praise for the victory belonged to HaShem alone.

From my seat atop that magnificent beast I watched my husband and thought that Judah would make a very good king. The man I married was many things — stubborn, gentle, tough, and pious — but he was not ambitious. Yet his virtues were surely what a king needed. The world had too many grasping, ambitious, greedy kings, and Judah had none of those qualities.

Furthermore, he had promised he would stop fighting when the war was over, and I had decided to believe him. I was not happy being a warrior's wife, but he would not always be a warrior. He would soon be a father, and that fact alone ought to keep him home where he belonged.

In truth, I had wanted to conceive a child in the hope that it would change Judah, but the reality had changed me. I could no longer see myself without a husband, wandering from village to village with my mother. I had to think of the baby now, and a baby needed a home, a father, and an extended family.

I pressed my palm to my belly where my hope resided. Morit had told me that men often changed once their infants arrived. Her Simon, she said, had become more thoughtful and more careful, and I would be happy to see those changes in Judah. I would be thrilled if he hesitated before going out to practice archery or stone-slinging. My heart would melt if he wanted to stay home and play with his baby or spend time with his wife.

I did not worry about the coming birth. Though I knew women who had died while giving life to their babies, I came from sturdy stock and had never felt stronger. I had not experienced a single day of sickness since the child's conception and had in fact found it difficult to believe I carried a child until Morit assured me that three months without bleeding meant I was either pregnant or quite sick indeed.

I counted the remaining months on my fingers. In six months, more or less, I would bear my child, and Judah would become the husband I really wanted.

Chapter Thirty-Eight: Judah

With grateful hearts Leah and I went back to Modein and wiped the dust from the furnishings in our little house. We settled into a routine, and while Leah made cheese and prepared for the coming child, I plowed the hard ground to ready it for planting.

Yet as much as I wanted to focus on my responsibilities at home, my eyes kept drifting toward the northern horizon, where Antiochus had to be fuming at the news of Seron's defeat. He would soon respond . . . but how?

Unless Philander sent another message, I had no way of knowing. That Gentile had been Adonai's gift to us. Every night I asked HaShem to bless the scribe, and to remind him that should he ever need one, he had a friend in Israel. I did not dare write Philander for fear of risking his life, so I sent an anonymous gift with a traveling merchant — a cheese so large two men were needed to carry it.

As I tended the goats and worked the fields, I studied every rider who passed our village and met every traveler who stopped at our well. Some came only to drink or enjoy a meal at one of our homes, while others came to visit relatives and share news from Jerusalem or other settlements.

I was horrified to discover that people were coming to Modein to see me. "I never thought I'd meet the Hammerhead," one man said as he pumped my hand with enthusiasm. "The story of how you chased the Seleucids down the mountain has spread throughout Israel. And I *have* to see the silver sword you use in battle."

"It's not silver," I muttered, flushing. "It's iron."

My words did nothing to cool his eagerness.

One afternoon a stranger in fine clothing stopped by the well and proceeded to water his stallion. At first I thought he might be another Israelite in search of the Hammerhead, but the horse was too fine for a Jewish settler. While my brothers gathered around to admire the beast, the rider sought me out.

"Are you the one they call Judah Maccabaeus?"

Cautiously I nodded.

The stranger smiled. “I have something, and I was instructed to place it in your hands and no one else’s.” The man handed me a heavy parchment wrapped with cord and sealed with wax.

When I did not immediately break it open, the stranger lifted a brow. “Aren’t you going to read it?”

“Later.” I took a Greek coin from my belt and gave it to him. “That is for you — and please tell the sender, blessed be he, that we will always be in his debt.”

The man thanked me and turned away, then halted. “By the way,” he said, smiling over his shoulder, “my friend Philander says I am to thank you for the very large and most delicious cheese.”

I found Simon in his house, where he sat on a bench bouncing young Judas on his knee. Morit was grinding grain at the table, and wee Johanan, the firstborn, lay asleep beneath the bench, his head pillowed on his hands.

I gestured to the child. “Does he always sleep on the floor?”

“When he’s tired, he’ll sleep anywhere.” Simon grinned and offered me the baby. “Take a turn, will you? My knee is aching.”

Flustered, I handed him the parchment, then took the infant. "I'm sure it's news from Philander. Will you read it?"

The relaxed expression vanished from Simon's face as he accepted the scroll. "You could read it yourself, you know," he said, breaking the seal.

"I might miss something important. I'll feel better if you read it."

Simon removed the cord and unfurled a sheaf of parchments.

" 'Greetings to my friends in Judea, particularly Judah, Simon, Johanan, Eleazar, and Jonathan,' " he read. " 'May this letter find you in peace and health, and may your God continue to hold you in the palm of His hand.' "

Simon looked at me over the top of the page. "Your friend lives a dangerous life. What if someone had stolen this letter from the messenger? Our names are here."

I shrugged. "Who in the king's court knows our names? Read on."

"He certainly had a great deal of faith in his courier. Anyone would know these are Hebrew names. Surely someone might wonder why a Seleucid scribe is writing a group of Hebrews."

I shrugged. "Philander is a cautious sort. Please."

Simon lowered his head and continued. " 'News of your happy event has reached the king's court. I'm sure you can imagine how he received the report. He sorrows over the loss of glory he should have won, and he is especially sorrowful over the loss of Judean taxes. In the past few weeks, however, he has turned his attention to the temple at Parthia, which he plans to visit in the hope of refilling his treasury.' "

"He's going to rob that temple as surely as he robbed ours. I almost feel sorry for the Parthians."

Simon glared. "If you don't stop interrupting, you can read this letter yourself."

I pressed my lips together.

" 'The king,' " Simon continued, " 'is busy preparing to travel. He has appointed Lysias, one of his generals, as guardian of his son and heir, and he has charged three generals with the task of subduing Judea. I have recently written requests for the royal treasury to feed and maintain forty thousand foot soldiers and seven thousand horses, all bound for Judea. Those figures are indisputable. As they march south, they hope to pick up additional fighters from Syria and the Philistine lands.' "

My blood chilled. Would those three generals bring their huge armies from three different directions? Our army was not large enough to station defenders in three different locations. And how would we know from which direction they would come?

Simon slowed, his voice becoming more thoughtful. " 'So certain are these generals of success that they are allowing merchants to follow the military caravans,' " he read. " 'The merchants have been provided with gold and silver to feed the Hebrew slaves they hope to acquire, and wagonloads of fetters to place on the slaves' limbs.' "

Morit stopped grinding and stepped forward, her eyes huge. "They mean to make slaves of us? We will never be slaves, not again!"

"Do not worry, love," Simon told her. He jerked his head toward the baby in my arms. "As long as I live and breathe, my sons will never wear chains."

He skimmed the remaining pages. "The rest is largely ceremonial, but he does mention that he has a son who reminds him of you. Oh, and here he says the first army will march south along the plain of Sharon and camp near Emmaus. They were making preparations as he wrote."

"We have no time to waste." I tugged on my beard as my thoughts churned. So much to do! We would regroup in the wilderness, send scouts to look for the approaching armies, and plan our strategy. The Seleucids probably hoped to corral us like wild animals, and if we faced pressure from the Samaritans in the north and the Seleucids in the south, we could be trapped — but not with HaShem on our side.

"How long, do you think, until the armies arrive?" I asked.

Simon frowned. "If the rider took five days to bring this letter, and the army was about to depart . . ." The thin line of his mouth stretched tight, and his throat bobbed as he swallowed. "An army travels more slowly than a single rider, so perhaps three days. Or four. Or five, I don't know." His face went grim. "This is serious, Judah. They are bringing a huge —"

"I heard the numbers — and you must not repeat them, not to anyone. I will not allow the men to be frightened by mere numbers."

I gave him the baby and took the parchments from him, not wanting word to get out before I could prepare the army. The naysayers who lacked faith in HaShem could spread discouragement like a disease, and I would not have it.

Not this time, not ever.

Chapter Thirty-Nine: Leah

"So you are going back to your wilderness camp, even though you have chased the enemy from Judea."

My husband looked at me as though I were a strong-willed child. "I have explained this — the enemy is returning and we have no time to spare. We're not going to the wilderness camp; we're going to meet at Mizpah, which is closer."

"So you're saying good-bye to your pregnant wife, knowing that enemy soldiers will soon be in the area."

Judah's answering smile held a touch of sadness. "Trust me, wife. Better that I leave you for a little while than to be caught unaware by the Seleucids."

He picked up his bundle and went outside, striding boldly across the village square. I followed, noticing that Johanan, Simon, Eleazar, and Jonathan were also leaving their homes. Each of the married sons was saying good-bye to his wife while Jonathan said his farewells to Rosana.

I didn't care that I was the only woman shouting at her departing soldier. "What will I do if something happens to you?" I yelled, watching Judah tie his bundle to the back of his saddle. "If you leave, next year I might be raising a fatherless child."

"HaShem has promised to be a father to the fatherless," Judah called. He patted the stallion's rump, checked the girth strap, stepped back and turned to me. "You know I must go. I am sorry for leaving you, but this is the way it must be. But you will have my mother and your mother, and all your sisters-in-law for help and company."

My lower lip edged forward in a pout as I crossed my arms. Part of me felt ashamed for resorting to such theatrics, but what was I supposed to do? I had tried reasoning with my husband. I had wept, I had begged, I had conceived a child in an effort to turn him from war. None of those things had worked, so why not throw a temper tantrum?

"Leah." Judah drew me close, pinning my folded arms to his chest and leaving me helpless. "Know that I would not leave you without comfort. And know that I will be asking HaShem to keep you safe and protected by angel armies."

He kissed me on the forehead, then bent and gently pressed his lips to the growing mound at my belly. The unexpected gesture disarmed me and made me forget how angry I had made up my mind to be.

My anger cooled as the brothers mounted their horses and cantered away from Modein, Judah in the lead. The other women walked over, and Morit kept her arm around my waist until the men had disappeared from our sight.

"Come to my house," Rosana said as we prepared to go back to our homes. "Let me prepare you a cup of honey water."

I followed because I was too emotionally spent to rebel. While Rosana drew water from her pitcher, I sat on a stool and moodily watched my mother, who slept on a cot by the window.

"She naps a lot," Rosana said, following my gaze. "I think she sleeps to escape her memories."

The remark surprised me, and I said as much as I accepted the cup.

Rosana sank into a chair across from me. "Our minds are always working," she said simply. "We can think about the past, dream of the future, or worry about the present. We can work out a problem, argue with ourselves, or pray . . . I wish I had thought to pray more often. Seems to me that prayer is the best way to spend one's time."

I sipped the sweet water, then frowned. "Judah said he and his men plan to pray before the battle. But Mother once told me that she had prayed for years, and HaShem never answered her prayers."

"HaShem always answers, but not always in the way we want Him to. Perhaps your mother received an answer —"

"She didn't like?" I felt the corner of my mouth twist. "I pray for Judah to be kept safe, but I know he may die. And if that is HaShem's answer to my prayers, I won't like it. My child will need a father. I need a husband."

"And Israel needs a champion." Rosana shifted and leaned toward me. "Tell me more about your mother. She has lived with me for months now, but she never talks about her past. I still don't know much about her."

"She suffered greatly at the hands of my father." I glanced at Mother's face to make sure she was still sleeping. "When I was younger, I found it hard to respect her because sometimes she seemed to purposefully attract Father's anger."

Rosana lifted a brow. "What do you mean?"

I shrugged. "Once, when I was late from the market, Mother didn't have dinner ready when Father came home. He was furious with her, but instead of explaining that I'd been late from the marketplace, Mother smiled, which made Father even angrier. He demanded to know why she was smiling, and when she didn't answer, he struck her. Every time he hit her, she smiled again, and again, until he threw her against the wall and she passed out."

I glanced at my mother again, my heart welling with familiar sensations and old memories. "I thought she was stupid for behaving the way she did. At times I thought her the greatest coward in Jerusalem because she would never stand up to him. I promised myself that I would never let my husband treat me like that."

I shifted my gaze to Rosana, expecting her to applaud my strength of will. Instead, I saw that her face had grown pale, and tears shone on her cheeks. "My darling girl," she said softly, "I am not surprised you didn't understand, because children rarely do. But as a woman who has raised children of my own, I know what your mother was doing. Far from being a coward, she may have been the bravest woman in Jerusalem."

"I still think she was foolish."

"No, Leah. She did not tell your father that you were late from the market because he would have turned his anger on you. She smiled after each blow because she was happy to bear the pain that would have been yours. Tell me — did your father ever beat you?"

I blinked. "No. Well — once or twice. When I was a little girl. But Mother snatched me away from him."

Rosana nodded, her eyes brimming with tenderness and sympathy.

I winced as truth crashed into my awareness like a boulder thundering down a mountain. All the times I thought Mother was weak and cowardly, I was wrong. She had always been there to protect me, remaining at home to be with me, standing between me and Father, allowing Father to eat first so that we didn't give him a chance to rail at us over meals. She had sacrificed her heart and body for me, absorbing blows he would have delivered to me, breaking her bones instead of mine, scarring her flesh —

A sob rose in my throat. I tried to clamp my mouth over it, but out it came, followed by a steady flood of scalding tears.

Rosana was by my side in an instant. "Do you not see, love? This is what Judah is doing. He is bearing the blows for Israel, for you and your child. Out of love and duty he is sacrificing himself so that future generations will never find themselves bound by Seleucid chains."

Her words made me cry harder, and her arm tightened around my shoulder. When my sobs slowed, she squeezed me again, handed me a bit of linen to wipe my face, and nodded toward my mother. "Go to her," she said. "When she wakes, thank her for everything she did for you. And if she asks why you are saying this, tell her the truth — you stand at the door of motherhood, and you will soon be doing the same things for your child."

I threw my arms around Rosana and thanked her . . . for opening my eyes.

Chapter Forty: Judah

My brothers rode out at midday, visiting the villages of Judea and spreading the word about the coming attack. Our warriors, Simon and I decided, would assemble not at the wilderness camp, but at Mizpah, the spot where Samuel had gathered the children of Israel to prepare for battle with the Philistines. Samuel had the people fast and pray before the confrontation. When the Philistines arrived to attack, the voice of Adonai thundered from heaven and sent the Philistines into such panic that our forefathers easily defeated them.

Johanan had suggested that we meet in Jerusalem, but I knew we could not. The city still lay in ruins, with its walls down and its Temple desecrated and forlorn. To make matters worse, Jewish Hellenes and Gentiles held the citadel, the strong tower Apollonius had erected near the ruined Temple. We would not prepare for battle beneath their prying eyes.

So we would do what our forefathers had done. We would follow Samuel's example and strictly observe every divine ordinance HaShem had made known in the prophet's day.

Two days later, we met our kinsmen and fellow worshipers in the cool morning air outside Mizpah. By my command the men had been arranged as in the days of Moses: with captains of thousands, of hundreds, of fifties, and squads of ten. Following Moses's example, we dismissed the newly married men, the vinedressers, and the timid and unwilling.

I wanted no naysayers in our company.

When the last of the dismissed men had gone, those of us who remained put on rough sackcloth and covered our heads with ashes. Together we lamented the sins of our nation and begged HaShem for His help. We named our wrongdoings and asked for mercy and compassion. We prayed for hours, in community and in smaller groups, until strength flowed through our veins and our hearts beat in unified, bold rhythms.

Then men from my father's Levite family brought out the sacred garments of the priesthood, along with our tithes and the firstfruits of the harvest — offerings that would ordinarily have been deposited at the Temple. One of the Levites raised his hands and lifted his voice to heaven: "What shall we do with these? Where shall we take them? Your sanctuary is trampled down and profaned, and your priests mourn in humiliation. And behold, the Gentiles are assembled against us, coming to destroy us. You know what they plot against us. How will we be able to withstand them, if you do not help us?"

The hot air shivered into bits as the sound of the shofar reminded us that HaShem was Judge over all and He would grant us the victory.

A priest from my father's tribe brought out a copy of the sacred Torah, a scroll Gentiles had desecrated with ribald paintings of Greek gods. The sight of such blasphemy was enough to stir my men to action. Their faces flushed as they sprang to their feet, and I stood along with them.

"The enemy is a day's journey from us, so we must be ready. Do not listen to those who speak of numbers, of military might, and impossible odds," I called to the assembly. "Our God will go forth to fight for us. In the past, with Moses and Joshua and Samuel and David, it was Adonai our God who fought on our behalf. He allotted land between the Jordan and the Great Sea to us for an eternal inheritance. Adonai our God will thrust the enemy out ahead of us and drive them out of our sight, so we will possess the land, as Adonai our God promised."

Insects whirred from the desert trees as I paused to gather my thoughts.

"So be very firm about keeping and doing everything written in the book of the Torah of Moses and not turning aside from it, either to the right or to the left. Then we will not become like those nations around us. Do not even mention the name of their gods, let alone have people swear by them, serve them, or worship them; but cling to Adonai as you have done to this day. This is why no one has prevailed against us and why one of us has chased a thousand — it is because Adonai our God has fought on our behalf, as He said He would."

Murmurs of agreement rose around me, a ceaseless hum of cooperation.

"Therefore take great care to love Adonai our God. Prepare your heart for battle tomorrow morning, and prepare your sword for action. And do not forsake the Law of the Lord."

Our meeting ended, not with a roar but with broken whispers and heartfelt cries as thousands of men lifted their voices and begged Adonai to bless His people and heal our land.

Alerted by reports that the enemy had already camped outside Emmaus, I did not let my men settle at Mizpah, but immediately led them on the long march to Emmaus. We walked silently and steadily as the sun lowered, moving quickly as we followed a little-known southern road that was rife with opportunities to turn an ankle or fall into a ravine. The journey would have taken an average traveler a full day, yet we covered the distance in a few hours, then slowed our pace. After moving through a narrow pass, we finally reached the bare hill country around Emmaus where we could see the camp of the Seleucid army. We bedded down in the brush to sleep for a few hours, watching the glow of the enemy's campfires.

The next morning we rose under a cloak of darkness and girded ourselves with determination. My captains reported their readiness, and I offered a last word of encouragement. "Strap on your weapons and be valiant," I told them. "Be strong to fight these Gentiles who have assembled to destroy us and our sanctuary. It is better for us to die in battle than to see the continued misfortunes of our people and our Temple."

"Do you really —" Jonathan's voice wavered — "do you really think we can do this?"

"I do." I lifted my gaze to heaven. "May His will be done here today."

What Adonai did — how He preserved us — surprised even me.

I later learned what our enemy had done the day before. While my men and I prayed for HaShem's deliverance, a Gentile scout from the Jerusalem citadel spotted us and hurried to Gorgias, the Seleucid commander, with news of our gathering at Mizpah. Gorgias, hoping to attack us while we slept, took five thousand of his best men and followed the scout over the northern road to Mizpah. Though we traveled on two different roads, at some point we passed in the night, each army unaware of the other. When Gorgias entered Mizpah at sunrise and found it deserted, he laughed and told his captains we were cowards who had fled at their approach.

Yet at that same hour, I stood outside the Gentile camp with my army of three thousand. The Seleucid camp appeared strong and well fortified. I knew thousands of armored and highly trained soldiers slept within its perimeter, and most of my men were armed with javelins, pitchforks, and slingshots.

I climbed onto a boulder to address them. "My brothers" — I couldn't stop a smile from stealing over my face — "the hour has come. As you look upon the enemy, do not fear their numbers or be afraid when they charge. Remember how our fathers were saved at the Red Sea, when Pharaoh and his forces pursued them. So let us cry to heaven, to see whether He will favor us, remember His covenant with our fathers, and crush the army before us today. Then all the Gentiles will know there is One who redeems and saves Israel."

I would have laughed if I had known that we were looking at the remnant of the Gentile army, a sleepy force that was still abed. As the trumpeters blew their horns, our warriors fell on the Seleucids in their tents, attacking them exactly as the Gentiles had planned to attack us. Though the Seleucids were quick to strap on swords and grab their shields, they were no match for us.

Most of them fled as we fired their tents. My men followed, breathlessly chasing the enemy through the wilderness. Some Seleucids ran as far as the fortress of Gezer. Others fled to Jamnia and Ashdod, a day's journey from the battlefield. Those who did not run were slain by the sword.

Yet we had not struck the first blow when I realized something was missing from the scene — horses. The Seleucids always used mounted soldiers, and I spotted only a few mules in the camp. Gorgias's mounted fighters were missing.

The shock of discovery hit me like a blow. Since Gorgias and his army were somewhere in the hills, they were certain to see the smoke from burning tents and supplies. The general would realize that he had left his camp as an appetizer for our army, so he would rush back to defend the remnant.

We had to be ready for them.

I told the lookouts to blow the trumpets and recall our men. When most of them had returned, I gathered them around me.

"We are not finished," I warned. "Be not greedy of the spoils, as the real battle still looms before us. Gorgias and his five thousand are coming. When they arrive, stand against them and fight, and afterward we will seize the plunder boldly."

I ordered my captains to position their men in lines around the perimeter of the camp, to stand with weapons ready and eyes on the surrounding hills. Within an hour we saw enemy soldiers emerging from the mountain paths.

But Adonai had already won the battle for

us. At the sight of our men standing before their burning tents and fallen comrades, panic overcame the Seleucids. They ran back into the hills even more quickly than they had arrived.

When at last the hills went silent and still, we looked around the ruined camp. Philander had spoken truthfully when he mentioned that merchants would be traveling with the soldiers. At least a dozen traders had been in the camp we attacked, and they had fled at the first sign of trouble, leaving all their valuable goods behind.

"Was this an *army*?" Eleazar asked, his arms filled with bolts of blue silk and Tyrian purple. "It looks more like a marketplace."

I nodded grimly, remembering that the traders had come to add the people of Israel to their list of goods. How appropriate that Adonai should reward us with the treasures of those who wanted to sell us into slavery.

On our return to Mizpah, we sang hymns and lifted praises to heaven, for HaShem was good and His mercy endured forever.

War became our business, our daily work, and our lives. Though I granted leave to small groups so they could tend their crops and check on their families, I could not forget Philander's warning of three generals who were advancing toward us. We had defeated the first at Emmaus, but two others were on their way.

I moved our camp to a watershed near Jerusalem, an area of high ground from which all the roads to our capital were visible. The next general with his eye on the holy city might come from any direction, but we would see him before he arrived.

I did not think the next attack would come from the west — we had already defeated one army on that approach. Over the next few days, my scouts at the northern and western lookouts remained silent, but scouts from the south soon appeared in camp, their eyes wide and their reports urgent. General Lysias had entered Judea, they reported, and his army was at least sixty thousand strong — swelled, apparently, by levies raised on his march and the stragglers who fled from Seron's and Gorgias's armies. Considering the fate of those two generals, Lysias had skirted the western passes leading to Jerusalem and was advancing toward the southern ascent where travel was easier.

I was not surprised by his decision; I might have done the same thing.

I transferred my men to the high ground at the southernmost point, where we waited for signs of the dust cloud that would arise from the movements of such a large force.

As I waited, I often sat in my tent and thought of Leah. She had not been happy when my brothers and I left Modein, but I hoped she had been heartened by news of our first victory. I knew she had to be worried about giving birth, but she had both of our mothers and my sisters-in-law to help, so she would not be alone. But some things could not be foreseen, and sometimes trouble descended for no apparent reason. Would my wife be alive when I returned? And if so, would she forgive me for not being with her during her time of travail?

Most important, would she ever be happy with me again? Her sweetness had evaporated when we went to war, and her gentle and kind spirit had not returned. Whenever I spoke of the struggle she turned away; when I went out to drill with other men, she painted on an agonized expression that did not fade until the next day — and only then if no one reminded her of the army of Israel.

I couldn't understand why she so adamantly opposed our struggle. She had explained her hatred of her father's violence, but I was not her father and I had never struck her. So from where had her dislike sprung? And why had HaShem allowed me to marry a woman who hated what He had called me to do? I thought of Job's wife, who had been a thorn in his side when the Lord allowed him to suffer a grievous reversal of fortune. Hosea's wife had been a torment, not a helper, and even Eve, mother of all mankind, had dealt Adam a serious blow.

Why would the Creator of the universe give men wives who proved to be their undoing? Was life not hard enough?

I was about to put the question to Simon when a shout distracted me. I thrust my head out of my tent in time to see men pointing toward the southern horizon.

Dust. The Seleucids were on their way.

They were so far in the distance we could see nothing clearly, but I knew how quickly they advanced and how many were coming. They were marching over the plain of Epah, where the Philistines had challenged Saul and David. They would be hot and thirsty after this journey, and their scouts would tell them about the spring under the rocky escarpment near Beth-zur. That site would appeal to them, and from that settlement the Seleucids could simply continue marching northeast and within a few hours they would be in Jerusalem.

I covered my head and lifted my hands in

prayer: "Blessed art thou, O Savior of Israel, who did crush the attack of the mighty warrior by the hand of your servant David, and did give the camp of the Philistines into the hands of Jonathan, the son of Saul, and the man who carried his armor. So hem in this army by the hand of your people Israel, and let them be ashamed of their troops and their cavalry. Fill them with cowardice, melt the boldness of their strength, and let them tremble in their destruction. Strike them down with the sword of those who love you and let all who know your name praise you with hymns."

When I had finished praying, I turned and looked at the captains around me. "Brothers, gather your men. We are marching to Beth-zur, and we will be singing hymns on the way. We will meet a few thousand thirsty Gentiles at the spring, but we will not let them drink."

The captains cheered, then stalked away to alert their companies.

As we marched to Beth-zur, I realized that I no longer led a small band of warriors. Our victories at Beth-horon and Emmaus had given the people such confidence that our ranks had swelled to over ten thousand. Our people had finally begun to understand that

HaShem was the only real God, and He loved Israel. With Him as our leader, who could stand against us?

I looked at the rugged hills we had just left and thought of David, the young shepherd who had killed Goliath on the plain we were approaching. We were ten thousand and the Seleucids were sixty thousand, plus cavalry, but we had the strength of HaShem. We might appear as David to a mighty Goliath, yet we were not afraid.

Just before we reached Beth-zur, I halted the men and sent the archers to the front. "The enemy has been marching toward the spring as we marched to them," I reminded my captains. "They are tired and desperate for water. So fight with all your might and do not give ground. We are all that stands between these Gentiles and the holy city."

The army of Israel rose to the challenge. We could barely see the distant army when we reached the spring. We watered our men and animals, then we advanced and resolutely approached the invaders. When we were close enough to see individuals in the enemy vanguard, our archers released a rain of arrows, which took out the men in the Gentile's front line and terrified the remainder. They did not flee as they had in the past, but launched a desperate attack that our men quickly repelled.

When the battlefield cleared, we counted over five thousand dead Seleucids, Assyrians, and Samaritans. My own men — bloodied and bruised, but victorious, thanks be to HaShem — picked through the spoils, each man taking a fair share of horses and treasure, food and fine garments.

A feeling of deep peace and satisfaction settled over me as I watched my men reap their reward. We had defeated a governor's militia, a general's force, and a king's army. Antiochus, wherever he was, could no longer think of us as rebellious vassals. We were Isra'el, we were supported by the hand of our God, and we would defend our Law — the code that governed our nation — even at the cost of our lives.

Our people would no longer be the king's to torture and destroy.

I turned to my captains, who looked at me with expectant, sweat-stained faces. "Men," I said, a joyous tremor filling my voice, "our enemies are vanquished. Let us go up to Jerusalem and cleanse the sanctuary of our God."

Chapter Forty-One

So we went up to Jerusalem, the cold wind stinging our faces and watering our eyes, but no one minded the discomfort. We marched with light hearts and thankful spirits because we had finally eradicated the enemy who had dominated us from without and weakened us from within. Surely the time had come to reenter and restore the house of our God.

Though I had visited Jerusalem since the rampage by Apollonius and his army, I had not been to the Temple. I had heard reports and seen desecrated Torah scrolls, but I do not believe anything could have prepared me for what I saw when we approached the sacred sanctuary.

Our joyous hearts deflated as we stared at the remains of our beloved Temple. One man after another sagged as if his bones had suddenly gone soft, and I knew the sight of the desecrated sanctuary would stay forever in each warrior's memory.

We saw the sanctuary burned and broken, some of the great stones cracked and blackened, the others marked with obscene images and profane scrawling. The altar lay in pieces, with charred bones heaped around it. Thistles and wild plants crowded the Temple courtyards, tall weeds weaving their roots into cracks between the blackened flagstones. Wild olives hung on the walls of the outer court; creepers dangled from the stones like the beards of defeated old men. The beautiful gates had been chopped up or burned, and the priests' chambers lay ruined and filled with every kind of refuse.

The sight of our devastated Temple, the symbol of our people and our God, cut straight to our hearts. We tore our tunics and mourned with loud wails, sprinkling our heads with dirt and ashes.

As a nation, we had never been known for great architecture or art. Most of us were simple people who lived off the land. But our glorious Temple had been a reflection of our majestic God and the product of our most talented craftsmen. The Gentiles had vandalized our best offering and made it desolate, and we had been powerless to prevent its desecration.

We lowered our faces to the ruined stones

while the shofar sounded a mournful wail, calling us to repentance.

Eleazar interrupted my mourning by tapping my shoulder. When I looked up, he pointed to the citadel on the Millo, the stronghold that still housed the king's men and a group of renegade Jews. From their superior vantage point, the men in the stronghold looked down on us, studying our moving forms. Were they readying their weapons? One of their archers could easily strike one of our men.

"Do you think they will attack?" Eleazar asked in a low voice.

I kept my eyes on the tower where I glimpsed movement at the windows. "They are probably worried we will attack *them.* Still, I will not feel confident about working here until we are certain those men have something else to occupy their time." I nodded at Eleazar, who had never lacked courage. "Take your company and surround the citadel. Do not strike unless they strike first, but maintain your position and keep their attention." As he turned, I grabbed his sleeve. "Don't forget to stay out of range of their arrows."

He grinned. "Right."

I watched him go and wished, not for the first time, that we had kept a few of the enemy's catapults. They would have been difficult to transport through the mountains, but it would be a help to have one with us. Perhaps we could make one.

After making certain that Eleazar's men had encircled the tower, I summoned my captains and sent them to search for any priests remaining in Jerusalem. When they returned with a group of Levites, I chose godly men who were devoted to the Law of Moses and untainted by any form of heresy.

My men and I stood guard over the next several days as the priests cleansed the derelict site according to the Law of Moses. They moved the defiled altar stones from the sacred sanctuary to a location that had not been ritually purified. Then, with my men, the Levites set about the work of restoring the Temple.

As they labored, I realized that Jerusalem needed more than a rebuilt Temple. If we were to prevent another army from destroying the sanctuary, we'd have to rebuild the city's broken walls and erect watchtowers around the perimeter. I set several companies to work on those projects, and within a few weeks we saw substantial progress.

"The priests encountered a problem," Simon told me at dinner one night. "The work goes well, but the Levites did not know what to do with the old altar stones."

"They have been defiled," I said. "They cannot be reused."

"Yes, but they were once sacred. Is it right to throw them out with stones that have never been consecrated?"

I sighed, grateful I was not responsible for finding a solution to that particular problem. "Could no priest decide the matter?"

Simon shook his head. "The Levites finally agreed that only a prophet directly from God would have the proper answer. So they stored the stones in a chamber in the Beth-ha-Moked gatehouse at the corner of the altar court. The stones will remain there until a prophet arises to tell them what should be done."

"But HaShem has not sent us a prophet in over three hundred years."

"The priests insist another is coming soon." Simon lifted his cup and smiled. "They will wait."

The work continued for weeks. Laboring together, the army of Israel, the Levites, and the people of Jerusalem united to restore the Temple. We rebuilt the ruined chambers, we constructed and hung new gates, and we sent Levites to dig in the Valley of Kedron's virgin red earth for new altar stones. The priests cleaned the stones and brought them back to Jerusalem. Untouched by hammer or chisel, the stones were arranged in a wooden frame before being locked into place with mortar.

We also rebuilt the interior of the Temple. The people made new vessels of gold to replace those Antiochus had stolen. Then we brought the new lampstand, altar of incense, and table into the Temple. The priests burned incense on the altar and lit the lamps, restoring light to the sanctuary. They placed bread on the marble table and hung linen curtains of blue, scarlet, and purple over the entrance to the Holy Place.

Finally, in the month of Chislev, the priests came to me and announced that they had finished all the work they had undertaken.

Early in the morning on the twenty-fifth day of the ninth month, every man in Jerusalem offered a sacrifice on the new altar of burnt offering. As the sacrifices took place inside, we decorated the front of the Temple with golden crowns and shields, symbolizing HaShem's defense of His people and His eternal throne.

In the same season and on the same date the Gentiles had profaned the altar, the priests rededicated it, accompanied by songs and harps and lutes and cymbals.

For eight days we offered burnt offerings with gladness. Throughout the Temple we offered sacrifices of praise. With feasts and prayers, psalms and music, processions of priests bearing palm branches and every expression of festivity, we celebrated the Temple's dedication.

Then all the assembly of Israel determined that every year of the same season our people should observe a *ḥănukkâ,* or dedication ceremony, with gladness and joy for eight days, beginning on the twenty-fifth day of the month of Chislev.

Very great gladness filled all the people, because we had removed the disgrace the Gentiles had thrust upon us and our Temple.

I stood with my brothers and considered how, from that day forward, the sacred service of the Temple would resume. Each day a lamb would be examined to see if it was spotless. If it passed the Levites' inspection, it would spend the night in a stone cell to await the sacrifice. Before sunrise the next morning, the master of the Temple would summon the priests who watched in the gatehouse of Beth-ha-Moked. They would fetch the spotless lamb and bring it to the Temple as the sun broke through the horizon.

The priest appointed to conduct the sacrifice would then go into the Temple and bathe at the great laver. When he had finished washing, he would mount the stone steps of the altar and stir the ashes until he found the glowing red embers of the fire that was never extinguished. Once he added new fuel and robust flames burned, other priests would go into the sacred court and fetch the lamb, which would be sacrificed as Jerusalem woke to a new day.

Content to know that the holy city was on her way to complete healing, I bade the army complete one additional task before we departed for our homes — we had to finish strengthening the city itself. So we put off our return to our families and completed the job, fortifying Mount Zion with high walls and strong towers to keep the Gentiles from trampling Jerusalem as they had before.

Only one situation left me unsatisfied — we had not been able to come up with a feasible plan to rid Jerusalem of the Seleucids who remained in the citadel. Still, Simon encouraged me to be at peace. "Better the enemy you can see," he said, gesturing to the tall stone tower, "than the one you cannot. Keep an eye on them, and let them be."

Because enemies still remained in our capital city, I stationed a garrison in one of the watchtowers for the city's defense. I also ordered the fortification of Beth-zur, because whoever controlled that elevated city would control the southern approach from Hebron to Jerusalem.

I did not know when Antiochus would send another army, but I knew he had not finished with our capital.

Chapter Forty-Two: Leah

"Push, daughter. Hold my hand and bear down."

Rosana's voice, soft and urgent, cut through the haze of pain. I drew a deep breath and groaned, struggling to expel the child that lay like a boulder inside my belly.

No progress. The babe refused to move.

"Let me die," I whispered, turning my face to the wall. "I am too tired."

I was so weary my nerves throbbed. My mind had thickened with fatigue, and when I had clear thoughts, they were memories of Mother sliding down the wall, Father's angry face, and long nights when I pretended to sleep. I tried to remember what Rosana had told me about why Judah went to war, but the only memories that came to me were old ones, tinged with terror and dread.

Morit stepped forward, smiling at me from what seemed a great height. "Let me help," she said, lowering her fingers into a jar. When she lifted her hand, her fingertips dripped with honey. "This will ease the baby's passage. Lie still and let me see what I can do."

I closed my eyes, no longer caring what any of them did.

The first birth pangs had come two days before, when I stopped to make water in one of the fields. A sharp pain so caught me by surprise that I staggered and fell backward into the grass, an awkward collection of arms, legs, and belly. Ona giggled as she helped me to my feet. "I knew pregnant women could be clumsy, but —"

"I think the child is coming," I interrupted as a flood of water poured from between my legs. "Call Rosana. Call my mother."

"Your mother is visiting a friend in the next village." Ona took my arm. "But I will bring Rosana as soon as I get you home."

With one hand pressed to my aching back, I hobbled back to my house with Ona, then paced and breathed through my teeth as the pains came in quick succession. Rosana arrived a few moments later, and I could tell that my mother-in-law was astounded to hear that hard labor had begun so quickly.

"Squat here," she said, pointing to an empty spot on the earthen floor. "Ona, stand behind her and support her back. I will sit in front and catch the baby when it comes. When the urge is too strong to resist, push with all your might."

I did exactly as she said, obeying with a single-mindedness that rivaled Judah's passion for his army, but despite all my pushing, the infant would not be born. Rosana then asked me to lie down, and though she said she could see the baby's head, nothing she did seemed to make the baby want to leave my body.

For three days and two nights I suffered, and by the third afternoon I was past caring whether I lived or died. Weary in heart and body, I sensed an approaching darkness and an ominous numbness, and I welcomed them both.

This was my fault. I had been angry and upset when Judah left to fight again, and now HaShem was punishing me. Rosana had said that Judah was fighting for all Israel, so if I didn't want him to go, I was standing in the way of HaShem's plan.

He was a just God, and He punished evildoers. So He was going to kill me and my child.

I was about to close my eyes and surrender to defeat when a great whooshing sound filled my ears.

"Move out of the way," my mother commanded, then her iron hands manipulated my belly, pressing and pushing, shifting and squeezing. I cried out, reflexively trying to shield my weary womb. Then satisfaction filled Mother's voice. "Push again, daughter. With all your strength."

Surely pushing the child would tear my flesh apart. If so . . . let it be.

Somehow I found enough courage and strength to push Judah's son into the world.

As Mother and Rosana murmured over the baby, I waited to hear a cry . . . and realized what had happened. My baby was dead. That was why I heard no crying or happy fussing from the grandmothers. Something had happened while the child was imprisoned in my womb.

The image of a trapped soul resonated like a deep-voiced bell. I was trapped, too, in a marriage with a man who refused to be the husband I wanted. My son had died because I could not set him free, and I would die as well unless Judah came home to stay.

Wild grief ripped through me as I rolled onto my side and wept.

CHAPTER FORTY-THREE: JUDAH

Three weeks after the Dedication feast I rode home with my brothers, all of whom were anxious to rejoin their families. I was anxious, too, but for a different reason — if I had reckoned correctly, Leah should be near her time.

I might have a son or daughter.

We moved confidently through the rocky slopes, then crossed the valley that led to Modein. The sky glowed orange and red in the colors of sunset, and a group of young cousins heralded our approach with shouts and the rowdy bleat of a ram's horn. I smiled, imagining Leah's surprise at the sound of the horn, and hoped she would come out to greet me with our baby.

We entered the village a few moments later. Neta, Morit, and Ona hurried out of their houses to greet us, but I saw no sign of my wife. Fear blew down my spine as I dismounted, then I spotted my mother emerging from my house, her face tight with concern. She lifted her hand to acknowledge me and pointed to a path that led away from the village center.

A sense of trepidation crept into my mood as I dismounted and followed her. Why would Mother lead me away from my house? Nothing of importance lay out here, only fields, a pasture, and the family tomb —

I halted as Mother walked to the tomb and placed her palms against the stone. She bowed her head for a moment, then turned to look at me.

"Your son is here," she said. "Buried next to your father." Her face wore a drawn, inward look, as if she were seeing an image of the child in the air between us.

My son. The child who might have followed in my footsteps . . .

My throat was so tight I could barely draw breath to speak, but I forced the words out: "Did Leah give him a name?"

Mother shook her head. "He died without having drawn breath." She turned toward me, and the light in her eyes shone weak. "I am sorry, Judah."

Grief welled in me, dark and cold, but somehow I found the courage to meet her gaze. "Is my wife — ?"

"Leah lives," Mother said. "But she is weak. She needs to regain her health."

While I stood by the tomb, mourning my loss, Mother squeezed my shoulder, then turned and walked back to the village.

Chapter Forty-Four: Leah

From the loud greetings and commotion that spilled through the window, I knew the men had returned. I rolled onto my side and brought my arms up to cover my head, fending off imagined blows that would have come from a man like my father. Perhaps they would come from Judah, as well. I had never before cost him as much as a son. This might be the situation to reveal the depths I had dreaded, the anger and violence I would never be able to bear.

"Every man has a beast in him," Mother used to say, and Judah proved her words every time he led men into battle. I had married a fighter, through some mischief or omission I had killed his son, and now I would have to face his anger. I would try to be as stoic as Mother, but in my weakened condition I could not endure punishment for long. Better, perhaps, that I should curl up and die.

The thought of death flitted through my brain, then circled back to linger. Why not? Dying alone in the wilderness might be easier than being pummeled by the husband who once loved me. Then again, death by a warrior's hands would be quicker than slow starvation. And if I died here in Modein, at least Mother and Rosana would make certain my bones had a fitting place to rest.

I flinched as the wooden door swung on its leather hinges. For an instant I held my breath, waiting for the sound of footsteps so I could identify the trespasser, but I heard nothing.

Then the pallet beneath me shifted as someone dropped onto it and drew me toward him.

I opened my eyes, ready to face the Hammerhead's fury. But Judah lay quietly next to me, his eyes closed and his shoulders slumped, as though he had come home to a burden too heavy to carry.

Slowly, I slid away from his arms, out of striking distance.

His eyes opened. "Leah." My name came out hoarse, as if forced through a tight throat. "I do not know how to tell you how grieved I am."

Because now he would have to beat me? I rolled off the bed and took a step back.

For the first time since entering, my husband looked directly at me, his tanned face drawn with unhappiness. "I don't know what to say. I am sorry."

"For what?" I stepped backward again until I felt my shoulder touch the wall. "For killing your son?"

His face twisted as if I had slapped him. "No, no — I am sorry for not being here. Mother says you suffered greatly."

I shrugged to hide my confusion. "That does not change anything. I live. The child does not. HaShem is punishing me."

" 'Adonai gives and Adonai takes away,' " Judah whispered, staring at the wall. The corners of his mouth had gone tight, his eyes shiny. " 'Blessed be the name of the Lord.' "

I stared at him. Did he mean what he had just said? Or was he trying to lull me into a false sense of safety? Father had often tortured Mother in that way. He behaved as though nothing was wrong, then, when she relaxed, he had flown at her like a raptor.

I would not let Judah use me like that. If he wanted to beat or humiliate or kill me, better that he do it now, while we were alone. "I failed you," I said, slowly sinking to my hands and knees.

I lowered my head so I would not have to

look at him. "If you wish to punish me, go ahead. Take my life if you want it, and know this — no matter what you do to me, you cannot make me feel any worse."

I braced myself for a curse, a blow, or a kick, but nothing happened. After a moment I lifted my head, expecting to meet censure, but instead I saw a man whose eyes overflowed in what appeared to be genuine sorrow.

"What did that man *do* to you?" he asked, rising. In three long steps he stood before me. With strong hands he lifted me up, but instead of striking me, he wrapped me in his arms, held me against his chest, and pressed his lips against my forehead. "May HaShem forgive the man who taught you to expect such things," he said, his voice breaking. Then he cried, "Adonai, in your mercy, restore the things that have been stolen from this woman."

What? Did he expect to pray our baby back into my arms? Did he expect me to forgive the hurt he had caused by leaving when I begged him not to go?

Struggling against his grip, I pulled free of him and took two steps back, the better to see into his eyes. "Don't pretend," I said, throwing the words at him like stones. "I know what you are doing, but I will not keep silent."

"Leah." His jaws wobbled beneath his beard. "What are you talking about?"

"I saw it time and time again, with my father," I went on. "He would be furious about something but would act as if everything were fine. And just when my mother had begun to relax, he would pull his arm back and punch her so hard her feet left the floor."

He shook his head, his eyes screwed shut against stray beams of sunlight that fringed the window covering. "I would never do that."

"Wouldn't you? I've seen you fight."

"Leah —"

"And I know you probably want to hurt me because I killed our son. I was angry at you for leaving, and HaShem punished me by taking our baby. So it is my fault, and if you want to hit me, go ahead. I am ready to die, anyway. I still don't understand why I'm alive . . . unless HaShem wants you to have the pleasure of killing me."

I stood before him, trembling with rage and fear, breathing hard but warmed by the knowledge that I had finally been able to say everything I had wanted to say. I kept my eyes fastened to his face, ready to endure whatever would come, bracing myself for the moment when his buried anger became a scalding fury . . .

I watched, pulse pounding, as he reached down and withdrew the knife sheathed at his belt. He brought it up and held it between us, then gripped the end of the blade and presented it to me, handle first.

"If you believe I am such a man," he said, speaking with a delicate ferocity that made it clear his emotions were barely under control, "then take this and strike me. But strike well, because we will not do this again."

I took the blade, wrapped my palm around the handle, and wavered, wondering where to strike. His heart? I didn't want him dead. Judah was a hero of Israel, and I would never be forgiven for killing the man who had chased the Seleucids out of Judea.

I didn't want to kill him, but I did want to make him angry enough to grant me a divorce. If I were free, I would no longer have to worry about the anger building up inside him, his judgment on my shortcomings and failures, or his comments about how I was not worthy to be a hero's wife.

He sank to his knees and spread out his arms, then lifted his chin and closed his eyes. He was making it easy for me to strike and run, and he had placed his life in my hands. He might well kill me after I struck, so I would have to be fast.

I tightened my grip on the knife and felt a stab of memory, one as sharp as a blade. As much as I hated to admit it, I did love him. I would never forget the nights we lay in bed laughing together, the way he looked at me on our wedding day, the many times he asked about my comfort, how did I like Modein, were the other women treating me well?

I blinked the images of the past away. That was before the war, before HaShem called him to be a commander. That calling had awakened the beast within my gentle giant, and I was certain the beast yearned to kill me now. Hadn't I heard the barely restrained frustration in his voice? Hadn't my mother warned me? Hadn't I tested him beyond endurance?

I brought the blade down, slashing his face, cutting him from the corner of his eye to his beard. I stood motionless, breathing hard and waiting for some response, but for a moment Judah did not move. Then he lifted his head and looked at me, and in his eyes I saw nothing but tenderness. Compassion. Love.

If he were like my father, he would have killed me. He would not be looking at me with longing.

Comprehension swept over me in a powerful wave, one so strong it stole my breath. This man, this Hammerhead, had nothing in common with my father. He was tough, but not brutal. He was strong, but not cruel. He was my husband and master, but he had not made me his slave.

Everything I had assumed about him . . . was wrong.

"Are you finished?" he asked, his voice filled with calm entreaty. "Because you can cut me again and I will not hurt you. You can do whatever you like and I will not change toward you."

I dropped the knife and fell onto my knees as my world spun. What had I done?

In years to come, people would look at him and wonder which enemy had given him that wound. If asked, he would tell the stark truth: his wife, the foolish girl who could not believe he was a good man, the woman who could not trust him to treat her with kindness, the person who was supposed to love him best.

"Judah." Tears ran down my face, tears of shame. "Can you forgive me?"

Somehow he managed a wavering smile. "It hurts my heart," he said, his own voice breaking, "to know you do not trust my love."

I could not speak as he lowered his head into the space between my shoulder and neck. His tears, mingled with his blood, slid hot and wet over my skin.

Could Judah's love be great enough to forgive me?

I placed my hand on his thick hair, then gripped it and gently lifted his head so I could look into his eyes. The pupils were large with grief, the white areas streaked with red. I had not seen many men cry, but Judah's expression could not be false.

"Can you —" I tried to control myself, but my chin quivered and my eyes filled in spite of my resolve — "can you forgive me for killing our son?"

His eyes welled with fresh hurt. "Why should I forgive you for something that was not your fault?"

I clung to him and we rocked silently together, sharing our pain and grief.

I lowered the basket of dirty tunics to the rocks, then knelt at the water's edge to test its temperature — still cold. My fingers would be pruned and numb by the time I had finished pounding these clothes, but at least Judah would be wearing a clean tunic the next time he rode off in the defense of Israel.

I took a brown garment from the basket and immersed it in the creek. I was about to lift it out when a shadow fell over mine. In the reflection on the water I recognized my mother-in-law.

"Rosana." I looked up and smiled. "Come to wash clothes?"

"No. I've come to talk to you."

She was carrying a basket, but when she sat on a rock I saw that it contained spun wool, not fabrics. I dipped my hands into the creek again, waiting for her to speak, but for a while we sat in that pregnant silence in which words are carefully sought and sewn together.

"I have been watching you and Judah," she finally said. "How is it with you two?"

I forced a smile. "Fine. We are fine."

"Are you?" She bent toward me, her face alive with concern. "I noticed you did not join Judah at dinner last night."

"Oh." I looked away. "I knew everyone would be at your house. I did not think anyone would miss me."

"I missed you. And Judah missed you." In a voice far younger than her years, she said, "I remember when I first married Mattathias. I felt out of place whenever he insisted we visit his Levite friends. The men would talk in a corner, leaving me to speak with women I barely knew. I was always uncomfortable."

"I know the women here." I gently scrubbed Judah's tunic. "And I am at ease with everyone in the family."

"Except Judah?"

I squinted through a bright burst of sunlight that had appeared from behind a cloud. "Judah and I . . . have reached an understanding."

"A truce?"

I shrugged. "You could say that."

Rosana sighed. "I am sorry to hear you say so."

"I'm glad about it. Better a truce than two unhappy people."

"But surely it is better to have both happy."

I stopped scrubbing, and wondered if Rosana had been listening outside our window. "I don't know what you want me to say, Rosana. I cannot abide violence, and Judah is a warrior. He knows how I feel, and I know he won't change."

"Judah is a warrior because Adonai has chosen him to lead the army of Israel," Rosana said, her voice softening. "Has Adonai chosen you to oppose your husband?"

I was about to protest that I was no longer actively opposing him, but wasn't my lack of support the same thing?

"Adonai hasn't called me to anything," I answered, my tone sharper than I intended. "He doesn't speak to me."

"Perhaps you are not listening." Rosana's bright eyes sank into nets of wrinkles as she smiled. "Sometimes, after we lay ourselves down before HaShem, we simply know what is right."

I waited for another word of explanation, but when I looked at Rosana again, she was sitting with her eyes closed and an expectant expression on her face. I heard nothing but a dusty palm rattling its leaves, then Rosana stood and lifted her basket. "I should get back to work. Enjoy your washing, daughter."

I sat back and watched her walk away, a small, stately woman who had always bewildered me. Why should she care about the state of my marriage? Judah and I had reached an impasse, but at least we were no longer at odds. I was not trying to change him; he was not trying to pacify me. We slept together without touching and went about our work without arguing. And the cut on his face had nearly healed.

I went into my marriage looking for peace

and safety, and after Judah went to war, I settled for peace. No one in Israel would know safety until the struggle was over.

So what did Rosana mean by *laying ourselves down*? Was she speaking literally? Had she lain down at her husband's feet, or did she mean something else?

My thoughts whirled as I went back to scrubbing. My father had never lain down for anyone, physically or figuratively, but Mother would have gladly flattened herself on the floor if it meant keeping peace in the house. I had almost lain down in front of Judah when I confessed my guilt about losing the baby —

Was Rosana talking about an attitude? When I got on my knees before Judah, I wanted to express my regret and my sorrow. I adopted that posture because I wanted to signal my willingness to do anything, be anything . . .

I had never lain down before Adonai. Even though I had heard the stories about Daniel and David and Moses and Joshua, I never thought of Him as the sort of God who cared about individuals. Those men were exceptional, and I was only an ordinary girl. I wasn't called to be a prophetess like Miriam or a judge like Deborah. I was only me, a girl with no particular calling, while

Adonai was high, lifted up, and usually angry.

Still . . . what harm would it do?

I left my washing on the rocks and climbed the sandy bank until I reached level ground. After glancing left and right to be sure no one else was around, I sank down and stretched out on the sand, placing my cheek against the earth and extending my arms. Any passerby who saw me would think me crazy. The ground was warm and soothing. The sun kissed my ankles as the wind ruffled my hair.

"Adonai," I whispered, "if you see me . . ."

A cloud moved over the sun, covering me in a cool shade.

"I have lain myself down. Do you have something to say to me?"

Somewhere a bird wailed, lancing the silence. Then I heard something — not the bird or the wind, not the brook or the rattling palm. A voice echoed in my head but seemed to come from outside me:

Love him. As I love you.

I caught my breath, desperate to hear more, but though I waited a long time, I heard nothing but the sounds of nature.

I sat up and brushed sand from my hands, cheek, and tunic. "How silly," I announced to anyone who might be listening. "Rosana has made me look a fool."

But as I went back down to the creek, those words kept replaying in my head: *Love him. As I love you.*

As hard as the first words were to accept, the last were a balm to my wounded soul.

I knew I could not have one without the other.

Love him. As I love you.

I found myself arguing with the first point. Hadn't I married Judah? Didn't I sleep with him and wash his clothes? Didn't I allow him the use of my body when he desired it?

But even as I argued, I knew my actions were a far cry from what love demanded. Real love — the love I witnessed every day between Simon and Morit, and Eleazar and Ona, required mutual support. Morit and Ona would do anything their husbands asked, and their husbands would never do anything that might hurt their wives.

When Mattathias had embarked on his bloody mission, Rosana understood his motivation and silently supported his intentions. In the passing years, even when the war required that we uproot our lives and go into the wilderness empty-handed, I never heard her complain about Mattathias's actions or his zeal for Adonai.

Surely love existed between Rosana and her husband. What existed between my parents?

My father had certainly not loved my mother. He never supported her, cared for her, or sacrificed for her. I do not recall ever hearing him utter a tender word about her, nor did I ever see him give her anything, even something as simple as a smile, that might make her happy.

And while my mother feared my father, she did not love him. She trembled at his approach, barely tolerated his presence, and tried to avoid him whenever possible. She remained with him because she had no other options, and because he would undoubtedly track her down and kill her if she left.

Love had not existed in my home, except . . . Mother loved me. How many times had she said or done something to deflect Father's anger from me? How many times had she sent me out of the house so that I wouldn't have to deal with him? How many times had she warned me not to do something that might trigger his anger?

Mother had urged me to marry, not because she wanted to be rid of me, but because she wanted to keep me safe. And she hoped I would find love.

I closed my eyes and let my mind travel back to my wedding day. Judah had been so careful, tender, and respectful. He was not crude or rough or demanding. Even in the early days as I settled into life with his family, he deferred to me, placing my desires above those of his brothers, his sisters-in-law, and even his parents.

He had demonstrated love for me since the beginning. And, being unfamiliar with love, I didn't recognize it.

By the time I opened my eyes, my thoughts had crystallized. Mother loved me, Judah loved me, and Rosana loved me, because she had given me truth instead of chiding me for making my husband unhappy. I had not been overloved in my life, but I had been cherished.

Whom had I cherished in return?

I searched through the winding length of my memories and came up with nothing and no one.

I had feared my father. I had despised my mother for what I perceived as weakness. And I had withheld love from Judah because he would not honor me before HaShem.

I knew very little about loving, but perhaps I could learn.

Chapter Forty-Five: Judah

Leah and I were enjoying the peace of a spring afternoon when I heard Johanan's voice. I peered through the window and saw him approaching the house with Simon and several other men. I recognized Jokin, an old and esteemed Torah teacher from another village. He and his well-dressed friends were approaching with purposeful intent in their walk.

"See if we have something to offer visitors," I told Leah, stepping away from the window. "I believe we have guests."

I welcomed my brothers and their friends, then stood back to let them into the house. They sat on the carpet and filled the small space as Leah shyly offered honey water to ease their thirst.

Wasting no time with pleasantries, Jokin, the old teacher, immediately spoke his mind. "We have come to see you, Judah Maccabaeus, because you have been much on our minds."

I blinked at the unexpected announcement. "Why is that?"

The men glanced at each other, then Jokin lifted his hand and began counting off his reasons. "First, you have delivered us from the Seleucids. Second, you show true zeal for Adonai. Third, you have proven you are a leader of men. Fourth, you are a better leader than Onias, our current high priest, because he has done nothing to stop the Gentile oppression."

"Johanan told us you have sworn you will not be king," another man said. "So if you are not meant to be our king, what will your title be?"

I grinned. "Isn't Judah Maccabaeus name enough for any man?"

"If you will not be king" — the man continued as if he had not heard me — "then perhaps you would be our high priest. After all, your father belonged to the house of Joarib, so you are a descendant of Aaron."

I shook my head. "Onias is the high priest, and rightfully so. What he does or does not do for Israel — well, one day he will account for his actions."

Johanan spread his hands. "Perhaps there is another possibility."

"Such as?"

My brother sucked at the inside of his cheek for a moment, his brows working. "Jokin believes you may be the Messiah."

I barked a laugh, expecting the others to join in, but no one did. Not even Leah, who stood at the back of the room and looked at me as if she had never seen me before.

"Yes, the Messiah," Jokin said. "Consider the words of the prophet Isaiah: 'He has sent me to tell those who mourn that the time of the Lord's favor has come, and with it, the day of God's anger against their enemies. To all who mourn in Israel, He will give a crown of beauty for ashes, a joyous blessing instead of mourning, festive praise instead of despair.' "

"Have you not comforted Israel?" Simon asked, intently studying my face. "Did you not sweep away the ashes of Jerusalem and rebuild the Temple?"

I frowned because I could not argue.

"And we cannot forget the prophecies of Ezekiel," Jokin added. "He wrote of the wicked king, whom you have chased from our land, and of the humble Messiah who will come. Listen: 'This is what the Sovereign LORD says: "Take off your jeweled crown, for the old order changes. Now the lowly will be exalted, and the mighty will be brought down. Destruction! Destruction! I will surely destroy the kingdom. And it will not be restored until the one appears who has the right to judge it. Then I will hand it over to him." ' "

I gave Johanan a look of disbelief. "I have no right to judge anyone."

"But you rebuilt Jerusalem!" Johanan insisted. "You brought down the mighty king."

"Not so," I insisted. "I chased his men away, but they will be back."

My guests protested in unison.

"Do the prophets not say the Messiah is to be a son of Judah?" I asked. "I am a son of Levi, and I am not a prophet."

Johanan's brows drew into an affronted frown. "Then what are you?"

I considered a moment. "A captain?"

Johanan laughed, and after a moment Jokin tugged on his beard and nodded. "Perhaps you are right. You shall be our *Messiah Malhamah,* the Deliverer Anointed for War. You are the one Moses referred to when he said, 'When you are about to go into battle, the *cohen* is to come forward and address the people. He should tell them not to be fainthearted or afraid because Adonai is going with them to fight on their behalf.' You will be our cohen."

Johanan smiled. "That is what you have

been doing, so that is what you are. Our Deliverer Anointed for War."

I fell silent and considered all my men had accomplished over the past months. We had won at Beth-horon and Emmaus. We had defeated Apollonius and Seron and Lysias. We had restored the Temple and made good progress on rebuilding the walls of Jerusalem. We had gained no new territory, but we had reclaimed land that rightfully belonged to Israel.

Could the old man be right?

Leaning forward, I clasped my hands and looked around the circle. "I am honored by your visit, friends, but I am content with what Adonai has given me. I need no title."

Jokin smiled. "Nonetheless, you shall have one — at least when I speak of you."

I sighed, knowing it would do no good to argue.

The men drained their cups, then stood to embrace me and make their farewells.

As I lingered at the window and watched them go, Leah came to stand behind me. She leaned against me, lightly resting her hand on my arm. "How can you refuse them?" she asked. "They wanted to honor you. They would have given you any title you wanted."

I managed a choking laugh. "I am neither

a messiah nor a king. I have no right to rule over others."

She stepped around, sliding between me and the window. "How can you say that? You have been ruling over your warriors. You have been able to persuade our people to work together, while in your father's day no one would stand up to the Hellenes. What your father began, you have finished."

I slipped my hands around her waist and kissed her forehead. "Do not tempt me, wife, to be what HaShem never intended. I am going out to check on the goats. I will be back for dinner."

She did not object when I picked up my staff, but I was glad she had spoken freely and that she had offered an affectionate touch. The bond between us was yet as fragile as a daisy, and though the warrior in me burned to punish the man who had twisted her thinking, I could do nothing to a man already dead.

Chapter Forty-Six: Leah

I watched Judah go, but I did not believe him immune to the lure of power and exaltation. What man would not want to be king if offered riches and authority? My father spent his life trying to rule the Jerusalem marketplace. He thirsted for power, influence, and riches more than anything, and if he had been sitting beside Judah during the conversation with the elders, he would have urged my husband to accept their title — indeed, he would have taken a title himself if he could find a way to get one.

Why was Judah not ambitious? I had seen signs of ambition in Johanan, my brother-in-law. I had seen it in men at the marketplace and even in the village children as they played with their wooden swords. The boys yearned to be victorious, to be declared the best at their games, and to stand alone in victory.

Ambition seemed to beat in the heart of every man — the quality seemed as much a part of manhood as muscle and sinew.

But Judah, an inner voice reminded me, was not like anyone else.

I took a deep breath as realization bloomed in my chest. I had married an unusual man, and humility was only one of his rare qualities. He seemed to be content no matter where he was, in the goat pen or on the battlefield.

I moved to the window, hoping to catch a glimpse of him working, and saw Eleazar brushing a stallion he'd brought home after the latest battle. The family had prospered since the war began, and Eleazar was becoming known for his handsome horses.

And all Judea knew my husband's name.

Judah could certainly become king if he wished it. The people loved him, his enemies feared him, and his ambition, though deeply buried, might flower were his victories to continue.

Yet Judah insisted he had been born to be a warrior and nothing higher than that.

If he had been born to be a warrior, what had I been born to be? The thought that HaShem might have a purpose for my life was new to me. I knew scores of women who grew up, married, and birthed children.

I had seen old women die after accomplishing little more than these things. I had always assumed I would do the same, but what if HaShem intended me to do more?

I laughed aloud at the thought. What more could a woman do? I could not read or write. I had no money or property of my own. I was bound to a husband and part of a family. I had no great talents and few skills. A cheesemaker could only get so far, especially in a little place like Modein.

And yet . . . I was married to a hero of Israel, a man who was attempting to do what countless others had either been too afraid or too unskilled to attempt. Of all the men I could have married, HaShem had chosen me for Judah.

Why? Was it to bear Judah's children? I had already failed at that, though not intentionally. If not to bear Judah's heir, then perhaps I was meant to do something else.

I glanced around the house, looking for some clue, but nothing in our humble household evoked any feeling in my heart. If HaShem had a special task for me to perform, He would have to personally reveal it.

▪ ▪ ▪ ▪

Part IV

▪ ▪ ▪ ▪

When the Gentiles round about heard that the altar had been built and the sanctuary dedicated as it was before, they became very angry, and they determined to destroy the descendants of Jacob who lived among them. So they began to kill and destroy among the people.

But Judah made war on the sons of Esau in Idumea, at Akrabattene, because they kept lying in wait for Israel. He dealt them a heavy blow and humbled them and despoiled them.

1 Maccabees 5:1–3

Chapter Forty-Seven: Judah

"Now that you have frightened the lion away from the flock," Mother told me one afternoon, "you must tend to the rats who are stealing the grain."

I did not know what she meant until I came in from the fields one afternoon and saw a group of men waiting at the well. They looked familiar and introduced themselves as a delegation from Hebron who had fought with me during the war. To join the army of Israel, they had gone off and left their villages unprotected. When they returned home, they discovered that sons of Esau, men from Idumea, had forced their women, children, and elderly parents out of their homes and into the wilderness.

"We joined our families in the desert," one man said, "but the situation is so dire that the hills of Hebron can scarcely be said to belong to Israel anymore. We need help driving the Edomites out of our territory."

How could I refuse to help them? They had risked everything to fight for Israel, so I could not ignore their request.

"I will help you," I promised. "We will drive the sons of Esau back to their lands so they will leave you alone."

After a discussion with my brothers and a time of prayer, I sent runners to summon the army. We assembled at Mizpah and made plans to travel south. After gathering provisions, we marched over the land David had wandered when hiding from Saul. We slept in caves around Ziph and Carmel. Finally we entered the great dusty desert that runs eastward from Beersheba to the cliffs above the Dead Sea. At that point the land descends in abrupt steps toward Sinai and Petra. Above the lifeless salt marsh, the pass of Akrabbim led us to a high plateau fifty miles from Jerusalem.

From the vantage point of the plateau we looked out and saw a host of the sons of Esau. The Horites from Petra, the sons of Bean from Rehoboth, and hundreds of Bedouin had come together for their annual incursion into the cornfields and vineyards belonging to the Jews of Hebron. Before they could carry away more crops our people had planted, we swooped down from the high plateau and drove them back to

Mount Hor, where they took refuge in their desert fortress.

We did not want to conquer their land; we only wanted them to leave ours. So we withdrew, content to know that our brothers would be able to go back to their farms and villages.

Then we traveled to the highlands north of Heshbon and marched to the edge of the great oak forest of Mount Gilead. Under the leadership of Timotheus, their chief, the Ammonites had overtaken that territory and were harassing Jewish villages. After several skirmishes, we defeated Timotheus, finally attacking and overthrowing Jazer, an Ammonite city forty miles east of Jerusalem.

Grateful for the victories HaShem had granted, we returned home and were met by women, who sang and waved palm branches in recognition of our victory.

One of them, I noted with pleasant surprise, was my wife.

The lion remained silent, but rats continued to steal the grain.

We had been home no more than a month when we learned of troubles in the east, north, and west. The Jews of Mount Gilead, whom we had recently rescued from Timotheus, had been attacked again and forced to leave their villages; the Jews of Galilee were being afflicted by Phoenicians and foreigners living in Accho, Tyre, and Galilee; and the ever-troublesome Philistines kept harassing villages on the western borderlands between Israel and Philistia.

In addition to those three hot spots, I also needed to maintain a vigilant watch over Jerusalem.

I considered our needs, then asked Adonai what I should do. Each petitioner had said his situation was urgent, and I could not discern which problem was worst. I could not be everywhere.

HaShem did not speak directly to me, but in time the answer became clear: the most difficult endeavor would be the expedition back to Gilead in the east, so I would take eight thousand men and my youngest brother to handle the problem.

I dispatched Simon to Galilee with three thousand men.

For the ongoing care and protection of Jerusalem, I appointed two young captains: Joseph ben Zacharias and Azarias. I advised them to remain vigilant and on the defensive, warning them not to attempt any venture with the undermanned army reserve stationed in Jerusalem.

The Philistines, I reckoned, could wait for their well-deserved thrashing.

Chapter Forty-Eight: Leah

With great interest I listened as Judah discussed his plans with his brothers. With the army of Israel splitting up to march in different directions, a bold thought occurred to me — why not go with my husband? I could support him as well as the other women who cooked and carried wood, and wouldn't it be more loving to be near him than to wait for him at home?

I chewed on my thumbnail and paced as I considered Judah's possible objections. He would say I was too frail, but I had fully recovered from the ordeal of childbirth. Unlike Morit, I had no children to care for at home. Judah might suggest that I remain behind to look after my mother, but she and Rosana were quite capable of taking care of each other.

With my mind made up to love my husband, I pulled a veil over my hair and went in search of him. I found him in an empty field, where a group of his men had built a bonfire. I tugged on his cloak and drew him away from the men he was teaching.

"Leah?" Even in the gloom of early dusk, I saw concern shining in his eyes. "Is something amiss?"

"I have been thinking," I said, steeling my voice with as much iron as I could muster. "It is foolish for me to remain in Modein like some pampered princess, especially when your army has divided into companies. You will need help in the camp, and I am willing. Take me with you, Judah. Let me go with you."

Astonishment blossomed on his face. He turned slightly and crossed his arms, a frown puckering the skin between his brows. "Has someone in Modein threatened you?"

I pressed a finger over my lips to avoid full-throated laughter. "No one has threatened me. I only want to help you. A wife should support her husband."

He measured me with an appraising look. "You want to work in the camp. Where you will witness violence. And bloodshed."

I resisted the urge to wince. "I want to help you," I repeated. "I worked with the other women when you first became commander."

"That was different. You remained a safe

distance away."

"Still, I want to help. Isn't that what a wife is supposed to do?"

"You do not know how long the march will be," he warned. "And our enemy can be brutal."

"I know brutality, I can walk forever, and I do not faint at the sight of blood."

His expression softened. "I will not have much time for you because my attention must be focused on my men. I would not have you feeling resentful or overlooked, because a commander must concentrate on the coming battle."

"You will not even know I am present unless you seek me out. Have I been a clinging wife? When you left me before, did I cling to you and fill your ear with complaints because you chose to be the commander of Israel's army?"

"I did not choose it." His voice lowered as he looked away. "As to clinging, you only did it the one time."

"I will not do it again. Let me go with you, husband. Please. There is nothing for me to do here and I am sick of cheese."

He turned from the glowing horizon and studied my face. "Why do you want to go this time when you did not before?"

"Because . . . I want to understand. You

say HaShem called you to do this, so I want to see and know what you do. I can tell others what I have seen . . ." In my mind a door opened and the truth spilled out. Of course! I could not read or write, but I could tell a story. The women and children, the old ones at home needed to know what Judah and his men were doing for Israel. They needed a storyteller, and I could fill that role.

"I want to see it all," I told him, lifting my chin. "I will come back and tell the others what I've seen. They will tell others, and soon all Israel will know what HaShem is doing through you and your men."

Judah lifted both brows, but he did not refuse me. His dark eyes searched my face, then he took my hand and squeezed it. "So be it," he said, covering my other hand, as well. "We will leave in two days."

"I will be ready."

Chapter Forty-Nine: Judah

I left Leah in a wagon with the other women who would help support the camp, then rode to the front. I found Jonathan waiting with men from Mount Gilead. They were understandably impatient to begin their journey home, so I gave the order to set out.

Once we were under way, I asked the Mount Gilead men for details about their situation. To my chagrin I learned their trouble had been instigated by our overthrow of Jazer. Timotheus, the Amorite captain, had been stung by our victory, so in revenge he captured several Israelite towns. The women and children he kept as captives, and the men — over one thousand — he put to death. Survivors from his raids fled to a fortress at Dathema, a fortress Timotheus now held under siege.

I felt a burdensome weight of responsibility for the dead men's families. If we had not overthrown Jazer, Timotheus might have left the villages alone.

No, an inner voice assured me. *He would not have done so.*

We marched over the scorching plains of Jericho, forded the Jordan River, and climbed the rocky terrain of Mount Gilead. A sludge of anxiety slid around in my belly, for we were moving through territory we did not know. The Mount Gilead men showed us where to find food and water, and so we made quiet, slow progress toward Dathema.

We marched three days into the wilderness, where we encountered a tribe of peaceable Nabatheans who told us Bozrah was in danger of falling into enemy hands, as were the cities of Bosor, Casphor, and Maked.

"The Amorites are preparing to attack these strongholds tomorrow," the Nabatheans told us. "They will capture and destroy all these people in a single day."

Bozrah stood on the road to the Euphrates, sixty miles east of the Jordan. Though the long journey would divert us from our primary task, we could not let those people be destroyed. We turned back by the wilderness road, marched to Bozrah, and fought to free the town. Before leaving, we killed every invader.

Because the Amorites were preparing to attack the cities on the plain, we left Bozrah during the night and marched north to Dathema, the last stronghold of our people. As the rising sun brightened the area, we saw a huge company advancing toward the fortress with ladders and battering rams. I commanded the men to blow the shofar to announce our presence, then smiled when the Amorites turned to find themselves trapped between the fortress of Dathema and the army of Israel.

Though we were weary from our overnight march, HaShem gave us the strength we needed. At the sound of the shofar we charged, lifting our voices in hymns of praise. Timotheus and his army fled, but they could not escape. We killed eight thousand Amorite besiegers, relieved the captives in the fortress, and returned the surrounding area to Jewish control.

But Timotheus escaped us.

As we rested after the battle, Jonathan came over and sat beside me. "How did you know we should press on toward Dathema?" he asked. "Any other commander would have spent the night in Bozrah and marched the next morning — arriving too late."

I stretched my legs toward the crackling

fire. "I thought of Saul, who once marched all night to relieve Jabesh-gilead, which had been put under siege by Nahash the Ammonite. If HaShem gave Saul and his men the strength to march all night, why wouldn't He help us do the same?"

Jonathan grinned.

"But I tell you one thing, little brother — I am growing weary of battling Timotheus. I should have killed him at our first encounter, but I mistook mercy for wisdom."

"We will get him tomorrow," Jonathan said.

I grunted. "If not tomorrow, then soon. Because I will not make the same mistake twice."

Chapter Fifty: Leah

War, it seemed to me, consisted of riding through desolate lands while searching for food, water, and the enemy. Safe in a wagon at the end of the advance, the other women and I saw little of the actual fighting, but we did see the aftermath — which, thanks be to HaShem, was not as bloody as it could have been.

Despite the hardships of the journey, I determined that I would not complain or cause my husband distress. I had made up my mind to support him, and if supporting him required hauling water or washing wounds, I would do it without complaint. But all the while I would be watching and memorizing details of each battle, details I could relay to others once we returned home. If HaShem called Judah to be a warrior, why couldn't He call me to be a witness to the struggle?

We traveled through plains and mountains

I had never heard of; we rode by devastation I had never imagined. I had never understood the urgency of war, but as I gazed at burned villages and spotted lost children hiding in the ruins, I realized Modein could have easily been destroyed as well. If Mattathias had not led us away after killing the king's envoys, the Seleucids could have swept in from the north, killed all the men, captured the women, and left the children to fend for themselves.

When we could, we picked up homeless children, gave comfort to the dying, and buried the dead. And more than once I found myself weeping for all the innocent lives that had been callously snuffed out by the Amorites.

After relieving the siege at Dathema, we stopped to rest. I climbed out of the wagon and took my pail to the nearby spring, then carried water to the men gathered around their campfires. I saw Judah sitting next to Jonathan, but I did not want to draw attention as the commander's wife. So I silently served all the men in the circle, offering them a drink from my dipper, waiting until each had drunk before moving on to the next man.

I felt the pressure of Judah's eyes the moment he spotted me. There was no denying the heat of his gaze, and from the corner of my eye I saw a smile tug at his lips. I smiled in return, still not looking at him, and not until I worked my way around the circle did I allow my eyes to meet his.

"Water, sir?"

His smile deepened as he accepted the ladle, and the look in his eyes spurred the drops of my blood to race through my veins.

He drank, and I turned my face to the starlit heavens, pretending to be distracted. When I felt his hand on my ankle, my blood began racing again.

"Thank you, miss."

I stepped past him and offered the ladle to Jonathan. "Water?"

"Thanks, Leah." He took it and drank, but I could not deny the invisible thread that attached me to Judah. I glanced back and saw that he was still watching me.

I hoped the yearning that showed on his face was not quite as apparent on my own.

Chapter Fifty-One: Judah

Not content to leave Timotheus free to create further trouble for Israel, we pursued him. The Amorites had encamped around the city of Raphana, which lay on the far side of a stream. I sent scouts to spy out the enemy camp, and when they returned we learned that hundreds of neighboring Arabs had joined Timotheus in hope of plundering the Jews. After studying the situation, I became convinced they were waiting for us.

Clearly, the Gentiles hoped to overawe the army of Israel by their great numbers and the strength of their location. But after three years and many battles, HaShem had made us confident. We did not even bother to establish a camp but crossed the stream and attacked straightaway. The Gentiles quailed before our direct assault, and many fled. We soundly defeated those who remained.

The deserters ran to Ashtoreth Carnaim and took refuge in the famous temple of the

Queen of Heaven. Johanan wanted to leave them alone, but I suspected Timotheus had gone with them and I did not want him to slip through my grasp again.

So we followed immediately. Completely focused on the enemy, we captured Ashtoreth Carnaim and set the pagan temple aflame. Timotheus, I later learned, perished in that fire.

As we made camp and celebrated our victory, I acted on a lesson I had learned from an earlier excursion. Unwilling for the survivors at Raphana to suffer the vengeance of neighboring Arabs and Amorites, I urged them to join us on the journey home. "Come live in Jerusalem," I urged them, "where your neighbors will be brothers."

I was pleased to see that most of the city's inhabitants joined our company. We lingered two days to give the people time to gather their belongings and livestock, then we set out for the holy city.

Our journey was slow, for our caravan included not only the army of Israel, but dozens of families who would build new homes in Judea. Traveling slowly made me nervous, because we made a large and ponderous target.

We marched southwest, toward the Jordan and the fortress of Ephron. We would have to pass through that city to reach Judea, yet the people of Ephron were not willing to open their gates.

I called out with a friendly message. "Let us pass through your land to get to ours. We will not harm you; we will simply pass through on foot."

No one responded. Instead, stalwart young men with weapons appeared atop the walls. Even from where we stood, we could hear the sound of stones being stacked behind the gates. They were not only refusing to let us pass, they were also refusing to let us drink and water our livestock.

I folded my arms and considered the situation. The inhabitants of Ephron had to know that refusing hospitality in a hot and arid land was a grievous affront, for life depended on water. Without it, we would all suffer, and we could lose many lives during our trek across the desert.

"What should we do?" Jonathan shaded his eyes as he studied the men on the wall. "We don't have weapons to take down a fortress."

"We will call on Adonai," I answered, "and He will supply what we need to build them."

I instructed our company to establish a camp on the plain. I invited the families to rest in the shade of our tents while the army of Israel built catapults and cut logs that could be used for battering rams. By mid-afternoon, we moved forward to assault the gates and walls. After battering the city for several hours, the gates fell. With swords unsheathed, we entered the city and put the hardhearted men of Ephron to death.

We spent the night within the city walls. The next day we filled our pitchers and waterskins and marched through the fortress, exiting at the south side. I placed Jonathan at the rear of the procession to make sure we did not lose any of our families, and a few days later we were climbing the ascent to Jerusalem, singing the psalms of David as we advanced. When we finally arrived within the holy city, our company — families and soldiers alike — walked together toward the Temple to offer sacrifices for our deliverance and safe journey.

But before we approached the Temple, I went in search of my wife.

Within a few days of our return, Simon and his army of three thousand arrived in Jerusalem with another group of emigrating families. Simon's campaign to fight invaders from Tyre, Sidon, and Accho had been successful, the captive Jews had been released, and three thousand Gentile invaders had been slain.

Longing for security and safety, the Jewish families in the area hastened to join Simon, so we had more new arrivals to live in Jerusalem and share the work of rebuilding the city.

Both expeditions, mine and Simon's, returned without the loss of a single man. Adonai had been our sword and our shield.

But while we were away, all had not gone well in our capital. Though the young men I left in charge were warned not to attempt any offensive military action, Azarias and Joseph ben Zacharias did not heed our words. Craving fame and success, they concocted a plan to win victories of their own.

"The two of them," one of the priests explained, "said, 'Let us also get us a name and go fight the heathen that are round about us.' "

"So," another priest concluded, "they undertook an expedition you would never have endorsed, Judah. And they were not victorious."

I exhaled through tight lips. I had learned that most of my brother Jews, none of whom had been born to the sword, could wage battle against trained soldiers only if they held defensive positions on high ground or behind boulders. In my early days, I would never have dared to meet a professional army on flat, open ground.

Yet Azarias and Joseph ben Zacharias had mustered the remnant of my men and advanced against Gorgias, one of Antiochus's best generals. Gorgias had entrenched his army in Jamnia, a town at the top of a round hill above the Valley of Sorek. Gorgias held the high ground with professional warriors.

When the general looked out and saw Azarias and Joseph advancing with the Israelite army on the open plain, he ordered his men to sweep down from the mountain, swords flaring and hooves thundering. Two thousand men of Israel died that day, and Gorgias's army pursued the survivors across the plain into the Judean hills.

When word of the defeat reached Jerusalem, the city's governing council censured the young captains for acting out of disobedience and pride. "Moreover," one priest sternly noted, "these two men came not of the seed of those by whose hand deliverance was given to Israel."

A shiver ran up my spine when I heard about the priest's remark. The notion that HaShem had selected my family to deliver Israel . . . the thought left me profoundly shaken. In His sovereignty, HaShem had chosen to use the line of Hasmon for a divine purpose: He had anointed us to deliver Israel from the Seleucids and the Hellenes, who would destroy us by their laws and their idolatrous influence.

In that moment I felt the mantle of responsibility more heavily than at any time. I knew anything we brothers might do or say had the potential to influence countless others.

Never in my life have I felt so honored and so humbled. I hurried away to find Leah, certain she would understand.

A few months later, Leah and I were resting at home in Modein when a messenger brought another scroll from Antioch. Fearful that the king was about to launch another campaign against Israel, I broke the seal and recognized Philander's scrawling script. I carefully read the letter:

> My dear friend, the Hammerhead:
>
> I bring you news from far away Persia where our king has been waging war in an effort to fill his empty treasury. The king heard that Elymais in Persia was famous for its wealth, particularly its temple, where the great Alexander re-

portedly left golden shields, breastplates, and weapons.

So Antiochus attempted to plunder the city, but could not, for the men of the area had been warned and successfully withstood him. So in great grief our king departed Elymais and went to Babylon. When he had made camp, a messenger reported that the king's armies in Judea had been routed. Antiochus learned that Lysias had gone first with a strong force, but had turned and fled before the Jews, and thus the Jews had grown strong from the arms, supplies, and abundant spoils they took from the king's army. He heard that the Jews had torn down the statue of Zeus he erected on the altar in Jerusalem and that they had rebuilt the sanctuary's high walls, along with the city of Beth-zur. He also heard that Timotheus, one of his servants, had been killed by your army.

You have been busy, my friend, and your God has blessed you.

When our proud king heard this news, he became enraged. He commanded his chariot driver to prepare for a drive without ceasing, for Antiochus determined to go to Jerusalem and make it a burying ground for all the Jews.

But your God, Adonai Almighty, smote the king with an incurable and invisible plague. As soon as he had uttered those brash words, a pain of the bowels came upon him, and torments of the inward parts, and that most justly, for he had tortured other men's bowels with many strange sufferings.

Yet Antiochus did not cease from bragging, but was still filled with pride, breathing out fire in his rage against the Jews, commanding his driver to make haste on the journey. But after a while he fell down from his chariot and was much pained in all his body.

And so it was that he who thought he could command the waves of the sea and weigh the high mountains in a balance was thrown to the ground and dragged in a horse litter, displaying the manifest power of a righteous God to all who looked on him.

Worms rose out of the body of this wicked man, and as he yet lived, his flesh fell away. The stench of his body was unbearable even to his generals.

So the man who thought he could reach to the stars of heaven could not be tolerated by even his servants due to his intolerable stink.

He took to his bed and became sick from grief, because things had not turned out for him as he had planned. He lay abed many days because deep grief gripped him, and he concluded he was dying. So he called all his friends and said, "Sleep departs from my eyes and I am downhearted with worry. I said to myself, 'To what distress have I come? And into what a great flood I now am plunged! For I was kind and beloved in my power.' "

But then Antiochus remembered the evils he had done in Jerusalem — seizing all her vessels of silver and gold, and seeking to destroy the inhabitants of Judah without good reason. And he said, "I know it is because of this that these evils have come upon me; and behold, I am perishing of deep grief in a strange land."

Finally, being plagued without remedy, he began to forget his great pride and to come to a more complete knowledge of himself. Afflicted by the scourge of God, he came to the place where he could not abide his own smell. And he said, "It is fit to be subject unto God, and a man who is mortal should not think of himself as if he were God." He also vowed unto the Lord, begging Him to have mercy and saying that he would set Jerusalem at liberty.

And as touching the Jews, whom he had judged not worthy so much as to be buried, but to be cast out with their children to be devoured of the fowls and wild beasts, he would make them all equals to the citizens of Athens. And the holy Temple, which before he had spoiled, he would garnish with goodly gifts, and restore all the holy vessels with many more, and out of his own revenue defray the charges belonging to the sacrifices. Yes, and that he would become a Jew himself, and go through all the inhabited world and declare the power of God.

But even with all this, his pains did not cease, for the just judgment of God was upon him. Therefore, despairing of his health, he wrote to the Jews a letter, which you will find copied herein. I trust you will know how to deliver it to those who need to hear.

Then he called for Philip, one of his friends, and made him ruler over all his kingdom. He gave him the crown and his robe and the signet, that he might guide Antiochus the king's son and bring him up to be king.

Thus the murderer and blasphemer having suffered most grievously, so died he a miserable death in a strange country in the mountains.

May your God keep and defend you, friend.

Philander

I set aside the first parchment and found another letter, penned by a different hand:

Antiochus, king and governor, to the good Jews his citizens:

For you I wish much joy, health, and prosperity:

If you and your children fare well, and if your affairs are to your contentment, I give very great thanks to God, having my hope in heaven.

As for me, I was weak or else I would have remembered kindly your honor and good will returning out of Persia, and being taken with a grievous disease I thought it necessary to care for the common safety of all:

Not distrusting mine health, but having great hope to escape this sickness. But considering that even my father, at what time he led an army into the high countries, appointed a successor to the end that, if any things fell out contrary to expectation, or if any grievous tidings were brought, they of the land, knowing to whom the state was left, might not be troubled:

Again, considering how the princes that are borderers and neighbors unto my kingdom wait for opportunities, and expect what shall be the event, I have appointed my son Antiochus king, whom I often committed and commended unto many of you when I went up into the high provinces; to whom I have written as follows:

"Therefore I pray and request you to remember the benefits that I have done unto you generally, and in special, and that every man will be still faithful to me and my son.

For I am persuaded that he, understanding my mind, will favorably and graciously yield to your desires."

"And it is signed with the king's name."

I lowered the parchment and looked at Leah, who had been listening as she prepared dinner. "We should celebrate," I said, my voice creaking in the room. "The king had a change of heart, and his plans for evil against Israel are finished."

Leah exhaled slowly. "If his plans are finished," she said, setting a stewpot on the table, "then why are our people still under constant attack in Jerusalem? The Gentiles in the citadel seem not to know that their king is dead. Just the other day I heard that a man and his mother were attacked as they entered the courtyard for the morning sacrifice. Others have been killed as they tried to worship. What good is the king's death if his hatred still lives in Jerusalem?"

"Surely this will cease in —"

"Not unless you stop it, Judah. Besides," she continued as she stirred the ladle in her pot, "the king has a son, and the son will be brought up by men who are like the king. Our troubles are not over."

I tugged at my beard, weighing her words. My wife was certainly right about one thing — the Gentiles and renegade Jews who lived in the citadel continued to harass and harm our people, especially when they visited the Temple. We would never be free to worship until those rebels had been removed.

Well enough, then. I would remove them.

But first we would celebrate, and then I would find a way to thank Philander.

Chapter Fifty-Two: Judah

Leah and I both lost our mothers in the year after the king's death. Rosana and Sabra died a few weeks apart, and we were able to remain at their bedsides until they peacefully breathed their last. We buried them in the family tomb and mourned them both.

Aside from those losses, the first few months after the king's death were peaceful even though the Greek-loving Onias remained our high priest and many Hellenes in Jerusalem still insisted on thinking and dressing like Gentiles. The Prophet for whom we were waiting did not arrive, so we remained content to live under the Law of Moses.

But we were free to worship according to the Law, we could circumcise our children, observe the Sabbath, and study Torah. The refugees we had brought from Raphana and Galilee had strengthened Jerusalem and the surrounding towns, and persecution had awakened a new zeal in my people, evidenced by their newly enthusiastic worship of HaShem.

We were a free nation, yet none of the kings around us seemed to realize it.

My family rested during the time of peace, for it was a sabbatical year and we could not plant crops or plan offensive warfare. But several of Eleazar's mares were pregnant from the Seleucid stallions. Johanan worked as a scribe for the council of Jerusalem, and Simon was often asked to counsel the priests as they resumed Temple worship. Jonathan had yet to take a wife, but because he was the youngest, we did not pressure him.

Oddly enough, of all five brothers, HaShem blessed only Simon and Morit with children. They welcomed a daughter in that sabbatical year, giving them three boys and a girl: Johanan, Judas, Mattathias, and little Rose.

Most surprising, my wife took on a new role in the family. Soon travelers stopped in Modein not to meet the Hammer of Israel, but to listen to his wife recount stories of the battles, the struggles, and the personalities involved in the war for freedom. Leah would sit on a tall stool in the village courtyard, and when the visitors had settled, she would tell the story of brave Mattathias, of Apollonius's sword, or of Timotheus, who died in the flames at a pagan temple.

I had to admit, she had a way with a story. She never embroidered the truth, but told each tale faithfully and fairly, always giving the credit for the victory to HaShem. And when she had finished, she would look over the group of listeners and urge them to spread the word, "So all may know that Adonai lives and cares for His people."

The first time I heard her share a story, I waited until she returned home, then drew her into my arms and kissed her soundly. "What was that for?" she asked when I let her go.

"Because good work deserves a reward," I answered. "And you do good work. But when did you decide to become a keeper of our history?"

"I asked HaShem to show me my purpose."

"So you are meant to be a storyteller?"

She smiled as she looked up into my eyes. "I am meant to be your wife."

No matter what her reasons, I thanked HaShem for giving her a gift that would bless all Israel.

Because Leah looked with trepidation at the citadel whenever we went to the Temple for feasts, my brothers and I met with the Jerusalem council about how to defeat the men in the tower. The fortress held the advantage of high ground, so the occupiers could see us coming from any direction. But their proximity to the Temple made it impossible for people to worship without continually looking over their shoulders.

"We have no choice," Simon said. "We will have to put them under a siege. No one goes in, no one goes out."

"Why haven't we done this before?" I asked.

A priest on the council shook his head. "We have tried, but the attempt has always been unsuccessful. People get lazy and look away, and once the invaders are on the ground, they blend in with the crowd and we lose them."

The idea of a siege appealed to me. We would surround the fortress and prevent anyone from going in or out, ever. We would cut off their supplies, knowing that sooner or later they would have to come out for food and water. We would make certain our men were vigilant, and we would put enough men around the fortress to make sure no portion remained unguarded.

We would not win immediately, but we *would* win.

I summoned Simon's men, and together we set up a siege of the citadel. I wish I could report that the venture was successful, but not even the most attentive army can guarantee a perfect watch. Sentries fall asleep and even alert guards turn their backs at inopportune moments. And though we captured many Gentiles who attempted to slip through our line, we missed others.

Unfortunately, several of those escapees traveled to Antioch and stood before eight-year-old Antiochus Eupator and Lysias, his guardian, to complain about ill treatment by the Jews.

A few weeks after the commencement of our siege, I received another letter from my old friend in the king's court:

> Greetings, my Judean Hammerhead:
>
> My son, Eneas, sends his regards and thanks you for the fine colt. We did not know such fine horses came from Judea, but life is a learning experience, is it not? One day, Eneas tells me, he will ride down there and demonstrate how your gift has helped him become a fine rider.
>
> I am grateful for your friendship and thought you should know what is happening in Antioch.

Some men, if one can call them that, have escaped from the citadel in Jerusalem and told scalding tales to our young king. Their subject? The state of affairs in Jerusalem. "How long will you fail to do justice and avenge our brethren?" they asked him. "We were happy to serve your father, to live by what he said, and to follow his commands in Jerusalem. For this reason the sons of our people have besieged the citadel and become hostile to us; moreover, they have put to death as many of us as they have caught, and they have seized our inheritances. And not against us alone have they stretched out their hands, but also against all the lands on their borders. And behold, they have encamped against the citadel in Jerusalem to take it; they have fortified both the sanctuary and Beth-zur. Unless you quickly prevent them, they will do still greater things, and you will not be able to stop them."

Brazen men, they were, predicting loss for our king, but they achieved their desired effect. Young Antiochus became incensed, and Lysias undoubtedly feels he can no longer ignore Judea. Be on your guard, my friend, and keep your loved ones near. Lysias is preparing the army.

I am forever your friend,
Philander

The mention of Beth-zur jolted me, and with good reason. Resting on one of the highest sites in Judea, the fortified town overlooked the road that stretched between Beersheba and Jerusalem. Whoever held Beth-zur enjoyed a highly defensible position.

We had beaten Lysias once at Beth-zur, but we would have to use a different strategy if we met him again. Lysias would not allow himself to be tricked twice.

I had Simon read the letter to the army captains and saw several faces flush with determination. "We must take action," Eleazar said, "because the king definitely will."

"But he's an inexperienced child," Jonathan said.

"A child guided by Lysias, a general who bears a grudge," I pointed out. "He will not care that Epiphanes had a change of heart on his deathbed. He will be out for vengeance, so he will guide the young king to act against us."

"The army must stay ready," Simon finished. "And we must warn the border villages."

"And Beth-zur," I added. "Especially Beth-zur, because we cannot afford to lose it."

The young king and his advisor-general did not wait long to attack. After assembling a force of one hundred thousand foot soldiers and twenty thousand horsemen, they marched south along the coast, then cut through Idumea and encamped against Beth-zur. For days they maintained a siege and built engines of war, but at night the Jewish citizens of Beth-zur slipped out of the fortress and set fire to the catapults and battering rams. When the Jews encountered the enemy, they fought manfully.

When a runner finally arrived in Jerusalem with the news, my men and I left a skeleton crew to maintain the citadel siege and hurried to defend our brothers. We were unable to reach Beth-zur because of the large force surrounding it, so we camped at Beth-Zacharias, opposite the enemy army. I would have liked to remain hidden, but there was no hiding our men and horses.

Our position was the best we could hope for. We held high ground from which we could turn toward the north and see Jerusalem, where Leah waited with my sisters-in-law. To the west I could see the plains of Philistia and the Rock of Etam, where Samson had hidden himself from the Philistines. To the east were cliffs and rocks, behind them the blue mountains of Moab. And to the south, the road our enemy had chosen to reach Jerusalem.

An hour or so before dawn, one of my scouts entered my tent, his eyes wide and his brow dripping with perspiration. The young man trembled as he woke us and stammered a greeting. "They — they are coming," he said. "They have roused the beasts and are making them ready to attack."

Simon sat up. "Beasts?"

"They sounded trumpets to signal the others," the scout explained. "And they made a mix — of juices, maybe, and painted their faces red. And with their faces painted and looking like blood, they took javelins and stabbed the beasts' legs."

"What beasts?" Eleazar's eyes were wide with what looked like delight. "Lions? Tigers?"

The boy shook his head. "Larger. If you listen closely, you can hear them roaring. The animals have been angered, probably so they will be roused to fight."

I listened, then heard a shrill blast unlike anything I had ever heard before.

Simon frowned. "Could that be — ?"

"War elephants, I think. Kings in the east use them." I blew out a breath and looked back at our scout. "How many are they?"

The boy nodded. "I counted thirty-two. They are spread out over the camp, one beast for each company."

Eleazar grinned. "They are coming at us with wild animals? No matter. An animal, no matter how large, cannot outwit a man."

I lifted my hand to protest, but the scout interrupted me. "The animals do not fight alone. A thousand men wearing coats of armor and brass helmets walk with each beast. Hundreds of horsemen have been positioned in front of each one. And there are towers!"

I lifted a brow. "Explain."

"A wooden structure covered with armor; one sits atop each animal. A driver and four archers ride in the tower. They will be shooting from an elevated height."

I groaned and reached for my sword. "They have begun early, so we need to wake our men. Have your companies ready to march by sunrise. I do not think they will advance until then."

Our preparations appeared remarkably

simple compared to the formation described by our scout. By the time the sun crested the eastern hills, we had assembled — archers at the front, horsemen behind them, swordsmen at the rear.

Then the sun, rising behind us, shone on the enemy army. When the morning light struck the shields of gold and the brass helmets, the opposite horizon seemed to blaze like thousands of campfires. The elephants and their attendants were positioned along the main road, spaced as evenly as flower petals, with foot soldiers and cavalry along the sides to prevent a flanking movement from our army.

The monstrous beasts of war glistened in their armor and shattered the silence with their agitated trumpeting. I felt the skin on my arms pebble at the marvelous sight. I had never seen an elephant, and neither, I daresay, had any of my men. The racket of the beasts' trumpeting echoed among the mountains, cocooning us in bedlam.

I looked at Simon, who met my gaze with alarm in his eyes. Together we turned toward Eleazar, who had always been the boldest of us, and saw that his eyes had gone wide with anticipation.

Of course they had. The man loved a challenge.

"Men!" I yelled, my voice barely penetrating the din. "Forward!"

The army of Israel moved forward slowly, with the young king's army advancing at a more rapid pace. The fearsome noise surrounded and deafened us. The animals continued to blare above the clanking of their armor while the earth trembled with the terror of their approach.

"They are amazingly strong," I said, moving in step with my brothers. "Look how easily they carry the weight of those men."

"They are not quick," Eleazar countered. "Though the earth trembles with each step, they do not run as fast as a man."

"What are these creatures?" Simon shouted. "Can they be killed with a sword? Where should we strike?"

"Of course they can be killed." Eleazar jerked his head toward one of the approaching beasts. "Why would they be armored unless they were vulnerable? Think of the soft areas, brothers, where no armor exists."

"The skin is wrinkled," I said. "Though it is hard to see past the armor, look at that nose — it is not covered, it is flesh."

"And if it is flesh, it can be pierced," Eleazar said. "Maybe not on the nose, but perhaps through the belly? Many an armored beast has a soft underbelly."

"There are too many of them!" someone behind me shouted, and I turned to glare at the man, for nothing spread faster than cowardice.

Behind me, others were beginning to voice doubt and fear. "Perhaps they can't be killed," another man cried. "HaShem alone can strike them down."

"Never fear!" I called over my shoulder, though my tone implied more confidence than I felt. "Today Adonai goes with you into battle!"

Eleazar drew his sword from its sheath. "Are you coming with me?"

I gripped my sword. "I am."

"Then let us lead by example." He pointed toward one particular beast, more colorfully adorned than the others. "Perhaps the king himself rides there. Or his general."

I grinned at my brother. "Good thinking."

"So let us see what happens when a beast of war meets men of Adonai."

"Archers!" I called, glancing at the men behind me. "Keep the horsemen from us!"

Moving directly toward the most decorated elephant, we walked with resolute steps as our archers shot at the riders who would stop us. One of the riders came between me and Eleazar, then the Greek fell off his horse as an arrow pierced his shoulder. I stopped to dispatch him as he lay on the ground, and when I looked up again, I saw Eleazar running straight toward the elephant. The Seleucid archers aimed at him but didn't shoot for fear of harming the beast.

I stepped over the warrior who had detained me, then ran to support my brother. Another man attacked from my left, so I struck him quickly, so eager was I to reach Eleazar. Then a blow struck the nape of my neck, dropping me to my knees, and I barely had time to duck a blade. A quick upthrust of my sword ended that encounter, and from my position on the chalky ground I saw Eleazar dart between the treelike legs of the most decorated war elephant. "For Adonai and Isra'el!" he cried, then with both hands he thrust his sword into the belly of the beast.

Time seemed to stand still as I breathed in the scents of dust and earth and saw blood rush out like a waterfall, coating my exultant brother. The beast roared and shuddered and collapsed to his front legs, sending the tower forward as the men in it screamed and horses fled, and then I remembered Eleazar in a dream, O Adonai, not that nightmare . . . When I looked back at the hind legs, the gigantic creature sighed and collapsed and exhaled in a shuddering gasp as the light went out of its eyes, covering the place where Eleazar had stood.

Behind me, the men of Israel shouted with dismay, and while I lay on the ground, stunned and confused, I looked back and saw that the army of Israel, the army of Adonai, was doing something it had never done — fleeing.

I looked again for Eleazar, wondering if he had somehow made progress against the enemy's advancing line, and then I saw a sandaled foot and realized that the war beast had fallen hard upon my brother.

"Eleazar!" I rose up and would have run toward the downed beast, but someone jerked the back of my tunic and yanked me away from the line advancing as inexorably as death. I turned in fury and saw Simon, who wore a look of grim determination as he drew me away from the battle and turned me toward Jerusalem.

"We cannot lose you, too," he shouted, and we took flight like the others.

Running after my men on legs that felt as insubstantial as air, I left the battlefield in grief and disgrace.

Chapter Fifty-Three: Leah

Leaving the other women to load a wagon with supplies, I watched in dazed horror as our men streamed into Jerusalem, sweat covering their faces and arms, blood trickling from noses, mouths, and open wounds. The most badly injured remained on the road — we would not be able to retrieve them until the enemy had left the scene . . . if the Seleucids let them live.

I ran over to meet the returning men but could not find my husband.

"Have you seen Judah?" I grabbed one warrior's arm and forced him to stop. "Judah, your commander. Have you seen him?"

He shook his head and trudged away.

I ran to the wall and hurried up the stairs, slipping past two guards who would have stopped me if I had not been the wife of Judah Maccabaeus. When I reached the top, I walked out onto the rampart, shaded my eyes, and gasped at the scene before me. The road in front of the gate was still filled with our soldiers, but in the distance I saw utter carnage — the bodies of fallen men, writhing horses, and . . . monsters. The unfamiliar creatures appeared to have tails on their faces, tails that swung from side to side, lifting, trumpeting, picking up men and tossing them aside, creating the most unimaginable havoc.

One of the beasts, thanks be to HaShem, lay dead in the distance, while the others stirred up dust as they ambled toward Jerusalem, accompanied by horsemen and soldiers.

I backed away from the sight, my mind reeling.

What sort of devils had come against us today? No wonder the men had returned in such confusion.

I hurried back down the stairs and began to examine the wounded who had dropped near the southern gate. Most of them sat with heads lowered, but one group stood silently, their tunics ripped and their heads covered in ashes and dirt. No wonder they were mourning — Judah's army had never lost a battle until today.

"Leah?"

"Judah!" I whirled around and saw him

striding toward me, his face streaked with sweat and dust. Because he was limping, I slipped under his arm and supported him as I helped him find a place to sit. "You need to rest."

"I cannot." He looked at me, despair on his face. "The enemy is advancing, so we must bar the gates and get the men to safety."

"Where?"

"The Temple fortress is the safest place. We will grab whatever supplies we can and move everyone there."

I knew the place — the tower known as the Temple fortress stood in the northwest corner of the wall around the Temple Mount. I'd never been inside, but it looked large enough to shelter all those who had fought with my husband.

Judah squeezed my hand and limped away, shouting at the men who wandered about as if lost. "We are moving into the Temple fortress. Leave the tents; grab the food and water from the animals. Go at once. The enemy is coming."

As my thoughts spun in a frenzy of dismay, I ran from group to group, shouting at any man who was sitting still. "You cannot rest now. Gather your provisions and go to the Temple fortress. They are coming!"

The dazed men stared at me and reacted only when my words hit home. They had to know their enemy would not stop until those trumpeting beasts were trampling the earth beneath our feet.

"Bar the gate!" Judah's strong voice rang out over the crowd. "Send a watch to secure every gate, but bar that one at once. And obey my wife, for the enemy is coming!"

"You!" I pointed to two men who stood beside a mule, then pointed to another who had collapsed on the ground. "See to him. Put him over the mule if you must! We must get to the Temple tower at once. Hurry!"

Leaving Judah to motivate the remaining stragglers, I ran to a pen that held five donkeys. I pulled heavy saddlebags from an improvised railing, draped one over each donkey's back, and tied the animals to one another in a train.

When the ground trembled beneath my feet, I did not need to look up to know that the monstrous beasts were near the gate. They were coming, but they would not get our supplies.

As I scrambled to gather all the food I could find, a random thought occurred to me: a safe and sheltered life . . . was a boring life.

I grabbed the reins on the first donkey and tugged him toward the Temple Mount.

Chapter Fifty-Four: Judah

We lost the battle of Beth-Zacharias. Perhaps it was my fault, for I freely admit that I approached the encounter with the confidence of a man who had never known defeat. I relied on the strength of my army and took the support of our God for granted.

In any case, we lost the battle, and more important, I lost a brother.

We fled the field in disarray, and not until later did I realize that none of us had been able to secure Eleazar's body. The Seleucids would not bury our dead. I would be surprised if they did anything beyond tossing the bodies in a heap and setting fire to the lot. This realization brought me a great deal of grief, but it was nothing compared to what I would feel when I had to stand before Ona and inform her that her husband was gone.

Confusion reigned in the aftermath. Once

we were all inside the walls of Jerusalem, our men ran in a hundred different directions despite my pleas for them to get to the Temple fortress. Those who lived in Jerusalem went home to protect their families. Others asked for shelter from people on the street. Some simply scattered, preferring to hide in the rubble that still remained from the last time a Seleucid king visited the holy city.

Because they scattered rather than following my orders, I knew they no longer trusted me. They would rather fend for themselves than take a chance with Judah Maccabaeus. After all, once Lysias entered the city, his first action would be to arrest Israel's leaders.

I plodded toward the Temple Mount, grateful that Leah and the members of my family had obeyed my instructions. The walls of Jerusalem were not completely finished, so Antiochus would be inside the city in a matter of days. But the Temple fortress had been standing for years, so it should be secure.

I waited until Jonathan, always the straggler, entered the tower, then we barred the gates and sent my family and the members of the Jerusalem council up the stairs. After stationing men at the windows to serve as lookouts, I joined my brothers and their wives in an upstairs room where together we mourned Eleazar. The women comforted Ona, and we brothers comforted each other. "HaShem was merciful to take Father and Mother before this day," Simon said. "They would be beside themselves with grief."

By sunset, tense shouts from the street below informed me that the Seleucids had reached the city walls. At midnight, one of our scouts slipped a message beneath the tower door.

Antiochus Eupator, he wrote, had set up his camp at Mount Zion, the old City of David southeast of Jerusalem. Guided by his general, Lysias, the king had sent an emissary to Beth-zur with terms for surrender. The Jewish citizens inside the walls had no choice but to accept the king's terms because they could not survive a siege — due to the sabbatical year, they had no food in storage. The Jews of Beth-zur left the city peacefully, and the Seleucid warriors entered and claimed the fortress in the name of the king.

Before the battle of Beth-Zacharias, we had worried about a citadel outside the Temple. Now we had to worry about a citadel *and* an occupied fortress outside Jerusalem.

Over the next few days my brothers and I frequently slipped out of the Temple tower and observed the enemy from the ramparts of the city walls. From all directions we watched Antiochus's men set up siege towers and build war machines designed to hurl fire, stones, and boiling oil. I considered commanding my men to build the same sort of weapons, but what would be the point? Like the people of Beth-zur, we had no food stored, so we could not endure a protracted siege no matter what weapons we used.

Neither could we guard our restored Temple forever. The Levites served as Temple guards, and Jonathan informed me that the number of guards grew smaller every day. In the face of such daunting odds, the men kept slipping away, going home to safeguard their families.

I could not blame them.

Faced with a siege, looming starvation, and impossible odds, one night I walked out into the Temple courtyard to pray. As men slept fitfully around me, I fell to my knees and begged HaShem for an answer to what seemed an impossible situation. God had granted us glorious victories in the beginning, so what had changed? Why had we lost Eleazar, the bravest and best of us? Why had HaShem allowed us to lose Beth-zur? Why had we never been able to rid the city of the Seleucids and renegades in the citadel?

"And now the enemy king is camped outside your holy city," I told HaShem. "He walks in the old City of David. Tell me, Adonai, is this the end for us? Have you brought us so far only to abandon us in your Temple? Or will you save us for your name's sake?"

I waited, but I heard no answer save the snores and moans of sleeping men. Above me, the moon hid its face in the clouds, as if it, too, were dismayed by the hopelessness of our situation.

I sank to the ground and swallowed hard. I could see no way to escape. The enemy would wait until we were on the verge of starvation, then they would offer terms. They would demand that the leaders of the revolt — my brothers and I — be turned over for execution. They would insist that all worship of Jehovah cease. Then, if the young king was merciful, the women, children, and the elderly would be allowed to leave the city while the king's men set to work. They would topple the city walls, they would tear down the sanctuary and destroy the sacred altar, and they would abolish all worship of the God who had given us so many victories.

"What have I done?" I cried, my voice echoing in the Temple. "Did I disobey one of your commands? Has Israel sinned in some way? Speak to me, Adonai, as you spoke to Moses and Joshua and Samuel. Let me know what you would have me do."

But the Lord remained silent, so I could only listen . . . and wait for His plan to unfold.

CHAPTER FIFTY-FIVE: LEAH

As a faint wind exhaled through the courtyard, I stood in one of the tower windows and watched my husband agonize in a thin sheen of moonlight. When we married, I had gone to him looking for peace and safety, and he had sought the same things for Israel. And what had happened? In Judah I found the safety I sought, but he and his men had endured a crushing defeat. Worst of all, we had lost Eleazar.

When Judah lifted his voice in that heart-rending cry, I swallowed hard and blinked back tears. I had never seen my husband so devastated, not even when we lost our son. He had always managed to accept whatever HaShem sent his way, but this — this loss must have felt like abandonment.

Judah didn't have to tell me what lay ahead for us. I read the inevitable in the haggard expression on his face and in the frightened eyes of the mothers of Jerusalem.

They had begun to ration their children's food, and several nights they had sent their children to bed hungry. I saw the hard truth in the gestures of the wide-eyed priests who walked slowly through the Temple, touching the walls as if storing up impressions to share with future generations.

And I saw our reality in the army of Antiochus. Judah did not like women on the ramparts, but I climbed the stairs in search of him and saw the Seleucid army encircling Jerusalem like a wreath. I beheld the fires, the war machines, and the armored soldiers who lounged around and laughed when they looked up and spotted us. They were biding time until their attack, relaxing before the hard work of destruction would begin.

The possibility of death did not disturb me overmuch. I had heard stories of women who endured far more suffering than I had, so I would not complain. I would not exchange my life, as bleak as it seemed in that moment, for that of a peaceful country wife.

But when I looked at Judah, who had poured his heart, soul, and strength into the fight for Israel's freedom, the heaviness in my chest felt like a millstone.

I lifted my gaze to the silent sky above us.

"Where are you, HaShem? How can you abandon the lion of Israel?"

Chapter Fifty-Six: Judah

We gathered in the fortress tower to share a meager meal and determine our next move.

"Don't fret, brother." Simon dropped into the empty chair at my side and grinned. "Have you forgotten the story of the widow's stores of oil and flour? She fed Elisha every day, and her supplies did not diminish until the famine was over."

I blew out a breath, not willing to argue with my brother. He had a point, but this was not a famine, and we had no prophet with us. What we *did* have were hundreds of hungry people, including children, wounded men, more than a dozen priests, and the residents of Beth-zur who had come to us for protection.

Our scant stores would not last the day. Though we had been rationing the bread, oil, and dried meat carefully, the women informed me that we were down to the last handfuls of grain. Tomorrow we would have nothing left but water and whatever we could obtain from the families who kept goats and chickens within the city walls.

I sat in Father's place at the head of the table and glumly considered the family members who were not with us. Johanan and Neta were present, and for once Johanan's wife did not complain about the skimpy ration before her. Simon sat at my right hand, as well he should, while Morit hovered over him, refilling his cup and reassuring him with occasional caresses of his shoulder. Jonathan sat at the opposite end of the table, occasionally reaching out to tousle the hair of Morit's little boys.

Try though I might, I couldn't help staring at the space we had left empty — the spot Eleazar should have filled. Ona worked with Leah, refilling our cups with water and making small talk to lift our spirits. Eleazar's widow worked with her usual energy, but her eyes were red and her chin had a tendency to quiver. From the corner of my eye I saw Leah slip her arm around Ona's waist, then she gave the woman a piece of bread, quietly suggesting that she eat something.

I caught Simon's gaze and saw understanding in his eyes. He missed Eleazar, too, but he didn't have to feel responsible for our brother's death. I had encouraged Eleazar to attack that beast, and the burning rock of guilt in my gut wasn't going anywhere.

I closed my eyes, my heart aching. I had imagined myself HaShem's choice to lead Israel, but what good had I done Israel lately? We were hours away from losing our Temple, our holy city, and our freedom to worship HaShem. My efforts this time had accomplished nothing of lasting value.

Our morning conversation had not been encouraging. Jonathan asked about chickens — did we know how to increase egg production? — and Johanan reported on the number of men guarding the sanctuary. The number was even smaller than it had been yesterday, but I was not surprised.

"He was the first of us to die," Simon said suddenly, looking at the place where Eleazar should have been sitting. "And yet he was the bravest."

"He was trying to kill the king," I added.

"He was attempting to show our men that elephants are not indestructible," Simon said. "He accomplished that. Now we know where to strike — and we know to get out of the way before they fall."

Jonathan stared into the candle flame. "He won a perpetual name for himself. He will always be remembered."

"But he should be here. And it's my fault he's not." I looked away and pressed my lips together. Thinking about Eleazar always brought a boulder to my throat, and I didn't want my brothers to see weakness in me.

Simon shook his head. "Our lives are in HaShem's hands. This struggle may require all our lives before it is done."

I lifted my head. "Then I will pray I am the next to die. Because I cannot stand the thought of losing another brother."

I turned at the sound of scuffling outside. The guard at the door spoke sharply to someone, then thrust his head into the room. "He says it's urgent."

A young man stepped in, his eyes wide.

"What is it?" I asked.

"Emissaries from the enemy are approaching the Fish Gate," he said, his voice quaking. "What shall we do?"

I looked at Simon and lifted a brow. "Do you think they'll offer to surrender?"

Simon's smile deepened into laughter. "One can always hope, but I have to say it's not likely. But we should at least go down and see what they want."

"I know what they want," I answered. "If Lysias wants to avenge his former king, he wants us dead. If not everyone in Jerusalem, then at least the sons of Mattathias."

Simon shrugged. "He showed mercy to the people at Bethzur. Perhaps he will show the same mercy to the people of Jerusalem."

I glanced at Leah, who had halted in place with a basket in her arms. She was staring at the messenger and probably sharing my thoughts. The sons of Mattathias had reached the end. Perhaps we all had.

If this was to be our last day on earth, I prayed silently, then let it be only the men who must die.

"Leah." I steeled my voice. "Take the other women and the children to one of the rooms upstairs. Go now, please."

A ripple of despair moved across her face, but she did not argue. "Come," she told the other women, setting her basket on the table as she reached for the children. "I think we will go to the very highest room. Would you like to count all the stairs? Perhaps we can look out the window while we are up there."

When the women and children had gone, I stood and turned toward the doorway. "Brothers, we have guests. Let us greet them as warriors of Israel."

Chapter Fifty-Seven: Leah

Though I kept my voice light and casual, my kneecaps trembled beneath my tunic, and more than once I felt faint as I led the children up the stairs. When we were all safe in the highest room, I released young Johanan's hand and hurried to the northwest window. Looking out, I could see the north-facing stone wall that snaked around Solomon's quarries, and the large gate in the wall. The gate had been raised, and two groups of men stood outside it — Judah and his brothers, along with a few of their best captains, and a group of soldiers from the Seleucid camp. The Seleucids flew their king's banner and rode on fine horses; Judah and his men stood alone.

I could hear nothing from my window, nor could I see any man's face. But from the way the men gestured I could tell when each one spoke. Simon said something, moving his hands, then one of the king's men replied. Then Judah said something, then the king's man, then Judah turned and looked up and my heart nearly stopped. Was he looking at me? Before I could wave or signal him, he returned his gaze to the enemy.

"What are they doing?" Morit leaned over my shoulder. "Can you tell?"

I shook my head.

"Where's Johanan?" Neta leaned over my other shoulder. "I can't tell which one is —"

"Shhh!" I leaned closer to the window. "I can't think."

"What is there to think about?" Neta asked, her tone cross. "They're only talking."

But then several of the king's guards stepped forward and our husbands thrust out their arms. While I watched in horror, the king's men put chains around Judah's and the others' wrists —

"What are they doing?" Morit cried, her hand going to her throat.

She didn't require an answer; the truth was obvious to anyone. While we stared, the air around us heavy with foreboding, our husbands followed the king's men to a wagon, where they climbed in and were taken away.

"What is happening?" Neta shrieked, pushing me away from the window so she could have a better view. "Where are they taking them?"

I drew a shuddering breath. "To the king, most likely."

Morit shook her head. "That can't be right. Simon would never meekly submit like that, and neither would Judah. They are fighters, but did you see them struggle at all? Perhaps they are only going to talk to him."

"Judah looked back," I whispered, the image focusing in my memory. "He looked back because he was thinking of us, so maybe that's why they went meekly."

Neta sank to the ground beside me. "Explain yourself."

I gulped a breath. "How do you bind a strong man without a fight? You threaten his loved ones. Judah, Simon, Johanan, and Jonathan went quietly because the Seleucids must have promised not to hurt us. Or the people inside the wall."

Morit sat, too, as thought worked in her eyes. "That makes sense. Simon would have agreed to go without a struggle if they promised not to attack the city. He remembers what the Seleucids did the last time they came to Jerusalem. He'd agree to almost anything to prevent that from happening again."

We pondered this as the tower remained absolutely silent, as if it, too, were waiting to learn what had happened.

Morit lifted her head. "There were other men with our husbands, men who didn't get into that wagon. They'll know what happened."

"I'll go." Neta rose and hurried toward the stairs. "While I'm gone, you all remain here and keep the children safe. I will return as soon as I can."

She unbolted the door and slipped away, leaving Ona to replace the bar. And while Morit, Ona, and I pasted on smiles for the children's sake, I slid back to the window and rose to my knees so I could scan the landscape. I could not search the enemy camp because it was located to the south, but at least I could memorize the last place I had seen my husband alive.

The sun had moved only a slight distance when Ona returned with a full report. "It is as you said," she told us. "The king's men said Antiochus wanted Judah and the leaders of his army, and Judah said they would surrender only if the king promised not to harm anyone else in his family, the army of

Israel, or the city of Jerusalem. When the king's delegate agreed, our husbands were bound and taken to the king."

Grief struck me like a punch to the stomach. I had to close my eyes and swallow several times to choke down the sour taste that had risen at the back of my throat.

"I am sorry," Ona said, her lovely eyes filling with fresh tears. "To lose all of our men within a few days — it is too much."

Morit went immediately to her children, drawing them close while her tears dampened their hair. Neta stood in a corner with her face to the wall, probably contemplating whatever future she could imagine without Johanan.

Ona had already lost her husband, but her wound was still fresh. How would she face her empty house, which had been so enlivened by Eleazar's colorful personality?

As for me, it was easier to speculate about my sisters-in-law than to imagine a life without Judah. When I told the story of the army of Israel, how could I bear to end on such a note of defeat?

As the three women wept, I slipped through the doorway and walked slowly down the steps, stopping in a private chamber along the way. The small room had probably been intended for storage, but it made a perfect place for me to sink to my knees. I thought I should be crying like the others, but my eyes remained dry as my thoughts whirled.

"HaShem?" I looked out a high window, through which I could see only a sliver of sky. "My husband says you have ordained every day of our lives even before they come to pass, so is this what you had planned for Judah?" I felt a lopsided smile twist my face. "This does not feel right. That you should ask his giant spirit to submit to a boy king is . . . beyond unexpected. This is not the death he would want."

I lowered my gaze to the wall, where so many stones had remained fitted together for so many years. I ran my finger over the rough surface and felt where the mortar had worn thin in some spots. But though the mortar was no longer doing its work, the stones continued to hold because they had become attached to one another, shaping themselves for duty, cooperating to protect and shelter. . . .

Feeling light-headed, I lay back on the floor and stared up at the wooden ceiling. Isn't that what my marriage had done? When Adonai called Judah to be a warrior, when I feared that war would unleash the violence I had known in my father, Judah demonstrated his love for me. And though he bore a scar from my unwillingness to trust him, he remained faithful. And so we held together, learning how to fit with each other, how to protect and shelter one another.

Even now, as Judah stood before the boy king and his general, I knew my husband's final thoughts would be of me, his family, and his people.

I felt a tear run toward my temple. I wiped it away, only to discover that two more had welled up and overflowed. I swiped at them as well, but others followed, a veritable flood, spilling full and round over my lashes and into my hair.

Chapter Fifty-Eight: Judah

When my brothers and I were led into the ornate tent belonging to King Antiochus Eupator, I was taken aback to find myself standing before a pale, thin child on a golden throne. Next to the throne, dressed in robes as ornate as the king's, stood Lysias, the general we had met — and defeated — at Beth-zur a year before. Lysias, I noticed, had not dressed for war, but for court, and he bowed deeply before the child as we entered the tent.

"My king," he said, bending until his face was only inches from the floor, "these are the Hebrew brothers I told you about. The leader is called Judah Maccabaeus."

The child lifted his head. "Which of you is this Judah?"

I stepped forward, oddly embarrassed by the chains on my wrists. "I am."

"Oh." The child pursed his lips, his eyes lighting with pleasure. "I have heard you are a mighty fighter."

I bowed my head. "Not by choice, king. When I am home with my wife, I am happy to mind the goats and help my brothers with the crops. Ours is a simple life."

The boy tilted his head as his eyes widened. "Did you say *goats*?"

"I did."

The boy clapped both hands over his mouth and giggled. I glanced at Simon, whose brows had drawn together in a display of befuddlement.

I had not come to entertain a child. "My king," I said, bowing my head, "my brothers and I have come here because your delegate said you would not attack the people in the city or take your revenge on our families. That is the reason we stand here in your custody."

The boy's eyes narrowed. "I do not take revenge. I enact justice."

I lifted my hands. "I apologize for my inappropriate words."

"What is a king to do, Judah Maccabaeus, when a man insists on attacking other people in the kingdom? When that same man attacks and kills hundreds of the king's men?"

Unwilling to argue with a child, I bit my lip. His tutor had taught him well.

I glanced over my shoulder at Johanan, Simon, and Jonathan. I would at least try to obtain their freedom.

"My king," I said, clearing my throat, "I would like to offer myself to you in exchange for my brothers. If you would —"

"Silence, Judah Maccabaeus. I am the one who offers terms. I have had my scribe prepare a treaty that will allow peace between our people. If you sign it, my army and I will depart this land and return to Antioch. We will leave behind one squadron of my army and they will be stationed in your citadel. Agreed?"

I frowned as a scribe walked over and placed a parchment on a table, where a sharpened twig and ink waited. "My brother Simon always acts as my counselor — may he read this with me?"

The boy king nodded.

Simon stepped forward, picked up the parchment, and read the Aramaic text aloud. " 'The king, Antiochus Eupator, desires peace with you and all the Jews. He seeks no prisoners and will allow Judah Maccabaeus a full pardon if —' "

"A full pardon?" I stared at Simon. "Did you read that right?"

"Yes, yes, here it is — a full pardon. Now, if you will stop interrupting —"

"Go on, please."

" 'The king will agree to let the Jews live by their laws as they did before, for it was on account of their laws being abolished that they became angry and committed acts against the king. In return for the king's kindness, the Jews will allow a squadron of the king's soldiers to occupy the citadel in Jerusalem.' "

Behind me, Jonathan muttered an oath.

" 'They will also remember that they are still under the king's authority. Furthermore, the current high priest will be replaced by one called Jakim, more commonly known by his Greek name, Alcimus.' "

"I know of him," Simon whispered. "He is an ungodly Hellene, a renegade."

The thought of a Greek-loving high priest did not cheer me, but we had not been fighting for the high priest. We had been fighting for the right to live and worship as we pleased.

But the king and his general had trapped us. This boy and Lysias had to know our supplies were low, because the people at Beth-zur would have told them about the sabbatical year. Even at this moment, the king could command his men to execute us, and we would have no chance to resist. He had come all the way from Antioch with one hundred and twenty thousand men, we were firmly in his custody, and he was offering to let us go?

I studied the young ruler. "Let me understand — you desire peace with the army of Israel?"

The boy looked at Lysias and nodded. "I do."

"May I ask *why* you desire peace?"

The boy's mouth shifted awkwardly, then Lysias came forward. "The king does not have to explain his reasons to you. He has written up this treaty, which you may accept or reject. Will you sign it?"

Astonishment threatened to drain the blood from my head. I turned to my brothers. "Will we accept?"

"I think we should accept," Simon said calmly, as if we all were not stupefied by the treaty. "As long as the men in the citadel do not harass our people as they worship at the Temple."

"Right," Johanan agreed. "Our people must feel safe in the holy city."

The king looked at me now, but I was still weighing the matter. "I am inclined to accept," I finally said, "but I will always be curious about what caused the king's change of heart."

The child gave me no answer as his mouth

curled in a lopsided smile.

I nodded at Lysias and picked up the sharpened stick. "We are willing to accept the terms. We will live in peace with the king if the men in the citadel do not harass our people at the Temple."

"Excellent." Lysias pressed his hands together. "This treaty will take effect the day you and your army evacuate the Temple fortress. When you have done so, our army will return to Antioch straightaway."

I glanced at Simon, who cleared his throat. "We will return to our homes and villages if you agree not to harm the innocent citizens of Jerusalem or leave the city defenseless," he said. "We have worked long and hard to repair the damage done by the former king."

Lysias bobbed his head. "Agreed."

"Very well," I said. "We will begin to leave Jerusalem on the morrow."

"As soon as possible, please," the boy king said. "I am certain neither of us wishes to prolong this situation." He gestured to a soldier at the side of the tent. "Remove the chains from these men. They are free to go."

I pressed my hand to my chest and bowed my head. "As soon as possible, then. Farewell, my king."

To a man, the army of Israel marveled at

HaShem's surprising provision for our safety.

Though our overjoyed women wanted to celebrate, I was inclined to obey the king's suggestion and leave Jerusalem as soon as possible. We needed food, and the city's inhabitants needed to recover from the invasion of so many unexpected refugees. After days of being confined within the city walls, everyone would enjoy walking in open country, even if the Seleucids watched as we departed.

As for my family, we were happy to depart for Modein. I found it difficult to believe that I might be able to hang up my sword and shield, but the enemy gave us no trouble as we began to leave. They did not molest or question us, and my heart was encouraged when I saw them breaking camp, too.

The last of our refugee families walked through the gates of Jerusalem just before sunset, leaving only my family, the priests, and the permanent residents inside the walls. Johanan and I stood by the road that led to Beth-zur and watched as the Gentiles ascended the heights of Jerusalem. When the Seleucid officials met us, we stepped aside so they could enter the city. A company of warriors followed them, and I reluctantly accepted the knowledge that they would be an occupying force stationed at the citadel, the tower we had tried so long to empty.

"Go in peace." The captain of the Seleucid squad lifted his chin as I passed him. "The city is ours."

I wanted to argue that point, but the sharp jab of Simon's elbow convinced me to move out with my brothers and join our waiting families. We walked for several minutes, each of us struggling to deal with a host of mixed feelings, and then we heard the unexpected sound of thunder. Simon glanced over his shoulder at the city we had just vacated.

I turned in time to see a section of the Temple fortress crumble and fall. The thunder had been the sound of a battering ram.

"They've already broken their word," Simon said, an edge to his voice.

"Do we keep walking?" Jonathan peered at me, then looked back at the dust rising from the demolition. "Or do we sound the shofar?"

I pressed my lips together and debated the question. "The king can't afford to let us have a fortress," I said, "and he wants to be sure he can enter whenever he likes. After all, he sees the city as his."

Ona began to weep, and Morit moved to comfort her. I knew what they were thinking — Eleazar had given his life in the defense of Jerusalem, and now the city was being laid helpless . . . again.

But HaShem had granted us a temporary respite.

"We go home," I finally said. "And we enjoy the peace . . . for as long as it lasts."

"Good of Adonai to save us at the last minute," Simon quipped as we walked home in the dark. "I was already wondering who would be plowing my fields next year, since I'd be in my grave."

Johanan laughed. "I was wondering who would marry my wife."

Instinctively, I waited for Eleazar to contribute to the conversation, then winced at the sudden pang of loss.

"I miss him, too," Jonathan said. "Modein won't be the same without him."

Simon shot a pointed look at the women, who walked in front of us. "We will have to take care of Ona. I'll have Morit check on her every morning. We can share our harvests with her, and I know the other women will make sure she has everything she needs."

"She might marry again," Jonathan said,

staring into the darkness.

I chuckled at his suggestion. "That is a good idea. She is still a young woman, and you need a wife. How old are you now, anyway?"

Jonathan glared at me. "Twenty-three."

"Perfect. She can't be a day over nineteen, so why don't you consider it a match?"

Jonathan gaped at me as Johanan elbowed him. "It is the Law. You should take her as your wife and have children for Eleazar."

"Brilliant plan." Simon nodded with finality. "Ona is a lovely woman. You will be very happy with her."

Jonathan pretended to ignore our suggestions, but the matter remained on his mind because he kept sneaking glances at the women as we walked.

Once we had properly mourned Eleazar, I was certain we would be celebrating a wedding.

Chapter Fifty-Nine: Leah

Not long after HaShem spared my husband, Judah received a letter from Philander, who revealed the reason for the king's sudden capitulation during the siege. The impetus had come from Lysias, who had just learned that Philip, the late king's choice to be his son's guardian, was en route from Persia to Antioch with papers guaranteeing his place as regent until the young king came of age. Since Lysias had no wish to surrender his power and authority as acting regent, he was obligated to return to the Seleucid capital before Philip took the kingdom into his hands.

We did not care who reigned in Antioch, as long as the ruler left us in peace.

Two years passed. Life returned to what passed for normal in the Hasmon family, and I reveled in the joy of having my husband at home. Judah, the mighty warrior, took care of the goats while I made cheese to sell in the market. Johanan oversaw excellent grain harvests because HaShem blessed the earth after the sabbatical year. Simon's orchard produced juicy figs and abundant grapes, and Morit baked delicious breads and cakes. Eleazar's horses, now supervised by Judah and Johanan, received praise from all over Judea, and men came to study the brood mares and stallions. And Jonathan, the young man who had always enjoyed an idyllic unmarried life, married Ona and took care of the sheep so she would have plenty of wool for her weaving.

While the men were out in the fields one afternoon, a caravan stopped in Modein. We women had been talking at the well, so when the caravan arrived we reached for buckets to water the horses and camels. A richly dressed man on the second camel called down to us in Aramaic. "Peace to you, ladies! We have come seeking Judah Maccabaeus. I have something for him."

Another message from the scribe? I walked over to the camel and extended my hand, expecting to receive a parchment or scroll. "I am Judah's wife. I will take whatever you have brought."

The swarthy rider's cheek curved in a grin. " 'Tis not the sort of thing you can hold," he said, jerking his thumb toward the rear of the caravan.

I lowered my arm and looked back in time to see a young man, probably no more than fifteen or sixteen, slide off a mule. He walked toward me, head down, and looked up only when the man on the camel spoke again. "I leave him with you," he said, pulling on the reins of his beast. "We must keep moving."

Before the other women could offer water, the caravan pulled away and headed south, away from Jerusalem.

Who was *this*?

I studied the youth standing before me. Gray dust covered his skin, matted his hair, and caked his sandaled feet. His clothing appeared to be expensive, but it, too, had suffered on the journey.

"He's too old to be a son of Judah," Morit said. "But if he claims Simon as his father, my husband will never hear the last of it."

The boy lifted his head. "Philander of Antioch is my father," he said, defiance flashing in his eyes. "I am not a Jew."

Shock ran through me as my eyes met his. His eyes were as blue as the sea, tinted with green. No, he had not been sired by one of the Hasmon brothers.

"I understand," I said, not understanding anything. "Have you — have you run away?"

His face seemed to collapse as his shoulders slumped. "My father is dead," he said, his voice scraping as though it hurt to speak the words. "I would be dead, too, if a friend had not saved me."

"You must be Eneas." The name came back on a tide of memory. "Your father mentioned you often in his letters. He wrote . . . that you liked the colt Judah sent."

The youth brought his hand to his face as his body shook, but he did not weep. "They took the horse. They took everything."

I placed my hand on the boy's shoulder, hoping to bring some comfort, then looked to my sisters-in-law. "Can one of you fetch Judah? He should be here."

"I will go." Ona whirled away and ran toward the fields while I attended to our guest.

"Here is water," I said, picking up a bucket. "You'll feel better after you've washed the dust from your face and feet. Let me help make you comfortable, and then you can tell Judah what happened. I know he will want to hear everything."

Eneas nodded silently, then walked with me to our house.

After helping the boy wash his hands, feet, and head, I gave him bread, cheese, and honey water. I had no experience with young Seleucid men, and I wasn't certain how much more I should do for him. Though he ate silently, he seemed grateful for the food.

When the door finally opened, Judah and Simon strode into the house. Judah glanced at me first, lifting his brows to silently ask if all was well. I nodded and gestured to the boy. "Philander's son," I explained in Hebrew. "He has come with sorrowful news."

While Simon tugged on his beard and watched, Judah sank to the bench next to the boy. "I am happy to meet you, Eneas," he said, the lines around his eyes crinkling as he smiled. "I have heard many fine things about you. Your father loved you very much."

The boy stopped eating, swallowed hard, and threw his arms around Judah's neck, going quietly and thoroughly to pieces.

▪ ▪ ▪ ▪

PART V

▪ ▪ ▪ ▪

In the one hundred and fifty-first year, Demetrius, the son of Seleucus, set forth from Rome, sailed with a few men to a city by the sea, and there began to reign.

As he was entering the royal palace of his fathers, the army seized Antiochus and Lysias to bring them to [Demetrius].

But when this act became known to him, he said, "Do not let me see their faces!"

So the army killed them, and Demetrius took his seat upon the throne of the kingdom. Then there came to him all the lawless and ungodly men of Israel; they were led by Alcimus, who wanted to be high priest.

1 Maccabees 7:1–5

Chapter Sixty: Judah

When the boy could finally speak, Simon and I sat across from him and let him tell his story. Leah stood against the wall, and I was glad she would know the boy's history, too. He needed comfort at this time in his life, and women always seemed to know how to console the distressed.

"A lot has happened since my father last wrote you," Eneas said, glancing up through tear-clotted lashes. "The last Antiochus, the boy king, is dead, and so is Lysias, killed by the army of Demetrius."

"Who is Demetrius?" Simon asked, scowling. "Do these kings reproduce like rabbits?"

The boy shook his head. "Ask me not who these men are or where they came from; I do not know. I only know that kings rise and fall, and good men die along with them. Dead also is Onias, the Jewish priest who served Antiochus."

"The last of Zadok's line," Simon whispered.

"Why were these men killed?" I asked. "But most important, what happened to your father? Surely any king can use a scribe. He could have served the new king as well as he served the other —"

"All the other scribes are well," Eneas said, angrily swiping a tear from his cheek. "But the new king's man — I forget his name — was going through the desks of certain scribes, and he found a letter Father had written to you. When they called Father before the king, he would not lie, but told them he had been a friend to Judah Maccabaeus for a long time. And that he would *always* be a friend to you. And then —" he turned the catch in his voice into a cough and went on — "for his loyalty they killed my father, my mother, and my sister. They would have killed me, but one of Father's friends slipped away from court, came to the house, and took me away through a back door. My mother and sister were in the front of the house or they might have been saved, too."

I clapped my hand to the boy's shoulder and bowed my head. I felt my face twist as tears rolled over my face and into my beard. I wept for my friend, for his goodness and bravery, and for the loss of his family. And for this fatherless boy who would never know how many lives his father's letters had saved.

"Your father was a friend, indeed," I said after clearing my throat. "My people owe him a great debt, and you are welcome to stay with us for as long as you like. You may live in my house and be part of my family, for I can never repay the debt I owe Philander."

The trembling boy looked up and met my gaze. "You should know the things Father was writing to you about. There are Jews in the king's court who bear no love for your Law, nor for Israel, and especially not for any who call themselves Maccabees. They are lawless men led by one called Alcimus, who was named high priest in Jerusalem. He came to Antioch with an accusation — he said you and your brothers have destroyed all the king's friends and driven them off their land. He said you tell the people not to respect his authority. He invited the king to send a trustworthy witness to Judea, someone who will see the ruin you have brought on the land. He wants the king to punish you and anyone who helps you."

I listened to the boy's report not with

alarm, but with an odd sense of weariness. I thought we had finally achieved a sort of peace, but apparently HaShem had not finished testing us.

I lifted my face toward heaven. "We have purged the land and still you judge us?"

The boy looked confused, but Simon ignored me and leaned toward the lad. "What more can you tell us?"

Eneas pressed his lips into a thin line. "The new king has already chosen one called Bacchides — I believe he is a governor of the province beyond the river, but I know he is a loyal friend to the king. He and this Alcimus are coming to Judea with a large force to take vengeance on you." A wry smile crossed the youth's face. "Beware. That's how Father signed the letter. 'Beware, friend.' "

I squeezed the lad's shoulder again, then looked at Simon. "The time of peace is over. Another king in the north sends yet another army against us. And this one comes with a Jewish traitor."

Simon narrowed his eyes. "Shall we sound the shofar?"

I considered a moment, then smiled. "Let us send riders instead. Surprise has always worked to our advantage."

■ ■ ■ ■

Bacchides, our newly appointed governor, and Alcimus the high priest entered the land of Judea with such a large force that no one could ignore them. They sent letters filled with peaceful words to me and my brothers, but we paid them no mind — no man intent on peace arrives with a vast company of soldiers.

But not everyone in Israel could discern the truth. When the Hasidim, our allies and known for their strict observance of the Law, heard that an envoy from the new king had arrived, they protested our decision to assemble the army of Israel.

"We should not fight them," their leader told me and Simon. "Alcimus is a priest of the line of Aaron. He would not harm us."

"Why would a godly high priest bring a Seleucid army to Judea?" I countered. "Why does a man of peace need so many swords at his side?"

The leader shook his head. "If you will not meet with these men, we will."

"Go ahead, then, do what you must. I hope you are right about his intentions. But be careful."

A messenger from Alcimus promised the

Hasidim safe passage to a meeting with the priest. More than a hundred of the pious men traveled to the Seleucid camp where Alcimus met them with friendly and agreeable words. He swore that neither he nor Bacchides would seek to injure them or their friends.

Spurning my advice, the Hasidim agreed to support Alcimus. But after the meeting, during a meal meant to commemorate their agreement, Alcimus ordered soldiers to seize and execute sixty of his guests. He then sent the remaining forty away without allowing them to bury the bodies of their executed companions.

Word of the devious betrayal spread like a conflagration. When my brothers and I heard about the executions of the godly Hasidim, most of whom had fought with us in earlier battles, Simon tore his garment and wept.

"The psalmist prophesied this," he said, his voice in tatters. " 'They have given the bodies of thy servants to the birds of the air for food, the flesh of thy saints to the beasts of the earth,' " he quoted. " 'They have poured out their blood like water round about Jerusalem, and there was none to bury them.' "

Though Alcimus rightly claimed the dead

Hasidim had fought against the Seleucid kings, I suspected that he killed them only to demonstrate his authority to the survivors.

Over the next several days my brothers and I heard about hundreds of ungodly Jews who were flocking to Alcimus, for in him they found a leader who was outwardly a legitimate priest, but inwardly a raving wolf.

"He is the perfect priest for the Hellenes," I told my brothers. "He is popular without piety. Style without substance."

Alcimus and his soldier escorts advanced to Jerusalem, where Bacchides oversaw Alcimus's installation as high priest. Once the priest achieved a firm grip on his power, he and his Seleucid soldiers began to scour the countryside, searching for Hasidim and Maccabees to put to death.

Once again, my family left Modein and headed into the wilderness. Warriors from the army of Israel joined us, and again we lived like Bedouin as we attempted to stay ahead of Alcimus and his Seleucid henchmen.

As before, we heard stories of people who were tortured and killed, but Alcimus tended to use words as weapons. Desiring to strengthen his authority and popularity among the people, he led them on with kind words, speaking to everyone in a gracious and pleasant manner. Within weeks he had acquired a large group of supporters, most of whom were irreligious Hellenes. These men served as his attendants and soldiers whenever Alcimus ventured into the country. He visited cities and villages, wooing people with gentle speech, but whenever he found anyone who sympathized with the pious Hasidim or the Maccabees, he had them executed.

When my brothers and I heard about all Alcimus and the renegade Jews were doing in the heart of Judea, we realized they had done far more damage than the Gentiles.

Once again we summoned the army of Israel, picked up our swords, and retreated to our camp in the wilderness. Under the cover of night, we ventured into the cities and villages of Israel and sought the men who had aligned themselves with the treacherous priest. Then we took vengeance on them, for they were committing great evil in the sight of HaShem.

When Alcimus saw that my brothers and I had grown strong, and that righteous men joined us every day, he returned to the king in Antioch . . . to lie about us again.

After Alcimus went to Antioch and complained about us a second time, King Demetrius sent Nicanor, another Seleucid general, to Judea with orders to completely suppress "the seditious party of the Hasidim." Though the Hasidim had amicably parted ways with me when I did not agree to support Alcimus, apparently the king believed a Hasid was anyone who believed in living by the Law of Moses.

But Nicanor did not come breathing fire and waving a sword. Like Alcimus, he came with pleasant words and even sent me a cordial invitation to meet with him. I was discussing the opportunity with Johanan and Simon when Leah stepped into the tent.

Her eyes darted to the scroll in my hand. "What is that?" she asked, her eyes narrowing. "Does Philander have a friend willing to take up our cause?"

I shook my head. "It is a message from Nicanor, a general under King Demetrius. He wants to meet me by the Gihon Spring."

She laughed. "To discuss what, the weather? He cannot have anything good to say."

" 'Let there be no fighting between you and me,' " I read. " 'I shall come with a few men to see you face-to-face in peace.' "

"Don't trust him," Leah said.

Simon grinned and jerked his thumb

toward my wife. "Who would have dreamed she'd be giving you advice about generals?"

Leah blushed as I leaned back in my chair. "It is good advice. I'm tempted to follow it."

"You *could* meet with him," Johanan said, idly stroking his beard. "We could go with you —"

"It is most likely a trap," Leah interrupted, dropping a large cheese onto the table. "What can he say in a meeting that he cannot say in a message? He is probably hoping your brothers will come, then he can capture all of you in one afternoon. Do not go to this meeting, Judah. Please."

I crossed my arms and studied the woman. How long had it been since she told me she would have nothing to do with a warrior? She had changed over the years, but so had I. The war I undertook as a single task had become a full-time concern . . . and perhaps my life's work.

I dropped Nicanor's message onto the table and shoved it away. "So be it, then. I will listen to my wife and not meet with this general. If he wishes to show favor toward the sons of Mattathias, he can call off his armies and stop raiding villages where people worship Adonai and follow the Law of Moses."

At that moment Jonathan stepped into the tent, his cheeks flushed and his eyes wide. "Everything is ready," he said, "at Caphar Salma. Nicanor should receive the news soon."

I grinned at Simon and Johanan. "About time we made the enemy come to us, don't you think? Are you ready to make a little noise?"

Johanan reached for his sword belt and strapped it on. "I am always ready."

I stood and turned to Leah, who had my sword belt in her hands. "Thank you." I took it and kissed her cheek. "We must take a little journey, so you and Eneas must stay in camp," I told her. "But if Adonai is willing, we will return soon."

She nodded and did not protest as we went out to gather our horses.

Chapter Sixty-One

My brothers and I joined the army of Israel at the city of Caphar Salma before Nicanor and his forces could arrive. As I met with the local teacher to assure the residents of their safety, my men established a perimeter outside the city, hiding themselves in trees and behind the rocks of the surrounding plain. These were familiar tactics, to be sure, but they had always brought us success.

Nicanor had established his camp at Jerusalem and billeted his army in the citadel — of course. That cursed tower had been a thorn in my side ever since its construction.

Caphar Salma was located halfway between the holy city and the Beth-horon pass. Earlier in the day, the city's Torah teacher sent a group of men to Jerusalem with news that Judas Maccabaeus's men were in the town — as indeed they were — and if Nicanor wanted to capture them, he should come at once.

Now we waited, hoping the bait would prove irresistible.

We did not have to wait long. We spotted the telltale dust cloud at midday and waited in our concealed positions until the first squadron passed through the city gate.

From where I lay on the top of the gatehouse, I spotted the infamous Nicanor on a gleaming black stallion. A swarthy man with a close-trimmed beard, this friend of the king seemed like the type to be more at home in velvet and furs than in the desert. But he was now our chief foe. If we were going to defeat him, I needed to understand him.

Before the Seleucids could knock at the first house, Jonathan blew the shofar and my archers let their arrows fly. From their hiding places in the trees, on rooftops, and behind rock formations, the army of Israel killed more than five hundred of the enemy.

Caught unprepared and unable to pin down our locations, the enemy army turned and ran back the way they had come. Visibly fuming, Nicanor turned his horse and followed them, presumably regrouping his men on the way back to Jerusalem.

When they had gone, my men stacked the dead outside the city walls and barricaded the gate. Then we accepted the residents' hospitality, enjoying a hearty meal before we returned to our camp.

Leah, Morit, and Ona met us with pale faces.

"What happened?" I asked.

Leah's eyes brimmed with tears. "Jerusalem," she said. "A scout has just arrived with news."

"Send him to me."

The scout, a young man from Bethlehem, came to my tent and shared his story with my brothers and me.

"That high and mighty Nicanor acts like a conquering king," the man said, his eyes as round as one of Leah's cheeses. "But he wasn't happy when he returned to Jerusalem today. The priests went out to greet him and told him about the sacrifices offered every day for King Demetrius. They were hoping to impress the man, but he didn't care even a little for their bowing and genuflecting. He twisted up his face and yelled that unless someone delivered Judas Maccabaeus into his hands, he would burn the Temple to the ground."

The man paused to gulp water from a cup Leah offered, then wiped his mouth with the back of his hand. "After that Nicanor stalked off toward the citadel, and even the Hellenes who had honored him had a change of heart. The priests began to weep, terrified that the Temple might be burned, and I could hear them praying from where I stood. 'Be avenged,' they kept saying, 'O Lord, of this man and his army, and let them fall by the sword. Remember their blasphemies and don't allow them to live.' "

Simon and I exchanged grim smiles. Could the Hellenes finally be realizing what these Greek Seleucids were really like?

"What is Nicanor planning?" Simon asked, leaning toward our visitor. "Any rumors?"

"No rumors, facts. An army is on its way to Judea to reinforce the soldiers who came down with Alcimus. They're going to hunt you down, Judah, and they plan to kill you. That is why the priests are so worried — they're afraid Adonai will help you escape and Nicanor will carry out his threat to burn the Temple."

Johanan released a bitter laugh. "Sounds like the priests would rather see you hanged, brother."

"That it does — but I don't plan on giving them that pleasure. Anyone know where Nicanor is now?"

The scout nodded. "I talked to a servant

who waits on the general. He is moving his camp to Beth-horon where he will meet the new reinforcements."

I leaned back and looked at my two older brothers. "What do you say, then? If Nicanor and his new army are coming for us, where should he find us?"

"The area outside Adasa is nice and flat," Simon said. "It's the perfect battlefield."

"True, but we have never done well on perfect battlefields." I pressed my hands together. "On the other hand, we've never engaged Nicanor in open battle — our meeting at Caphar Salma was only a skirmish. Why don't we let him *think* we'll meet on the plain outside Adasa? Then we'll show him how the army of Israel prefers to fight."

My brothers grinned, and I turned to the scout. "My wife will get your dinner, so sit and relax, friend."

"I couldn't —"

"Feeding you is the least we can offer. You can fight with us, if you wish. Tomorrow morning we ride out to scout the area around Adasa."

"How many men should we have?" Johanan asked. "We are not yet at full strength —"

"When has that ever mattered?" I said. "We will have as many as Adonai sends us."

■ ■ ■ ■

After a quick survey of the area around Adasa, we brothers agreed — we would ride out to the plain before dark, pitch our tents, and then hide our men in the scrub and low places of the chalky ground. We would do exactly what we had done at Lebonah when we had hidden ourselves and waited for Apollonius. After sunrise, Adonai willing, we would rise up and defeat Nicanor and his men, driving yet another evil from the land of Judea.

That afternoon, as I lay down to catch a quick nap, I drifted into a dream. In my vision I saw righteous Onias the First watching us fight at Adasa and holding up his hands like Moses at Rephidim. As long as Onias held up his hands, we were victorious over our enemies.

Then I saw an aged man, majestic in appearance, who held a sword of gold. The voice of Onias surrounded me, proclaiming that the second figure was Jeremiah the prophet. Then the prophet said, "Take this holy sword, a gift from God, with which you shall wound your adversaries."

I accepted the sword, but when I woke, I found myself clinging to the sword of Apollonius, the blade I had used in every battle since the first.

I sat up and stared at the sword in my hand. I was still studying it when Leah came into the tent. Something in my expression must have alarmed her, for she stopped and gave me a curious look.

"Are you all right?" She dropped the basket she was carrying and sat on my pallet, placing her hand on my arm. "You look as though you have seen something disturbing."

"I had a dream." I lifted my eyes to meet hers. "Another one of *those* dreams."

A faint flicker of unease glimmered in her dark eyes. "What — what did you dream?"

I smiled. "It was not bad, I don't think. I saw Onias the First and Jeremiah, who gave me a golden sword. He said I would use it to wound my adversaries."

She smiled and rubbed my arm. "That is a good dream."

"Indeed it is." Then, obeying an impulse, I took advantage of our solitude and drew her into my arms, kissing her like a man who has not seen the woman he loves in many, many days.

"Oh," she whispered when I finally released her. "If you fight with half as much passion, you will do very well indeed."

Chapter Sixty-Two: Leah

On the twelfth of Adar, I stood in the chilly afternoon shadows with my sisters-in-law as Judah and his brothers gathered the men and had them sit down. Judah stood, and in the ordinary voice he would use when speaking to his brothers, he told them of his dream. He added that he had awakened holding his own sword, though he had not lain down with it.

"I do not claim to interpret dreams," he said, managing a humble smile, "but I believe Adonai wants us to know we can proceed in the confidence of His good pleasure. Our holy city, our worship, and our Temple are in danger, and we cannot let the Gentiles destroy us. We will not waste time, but will draw the enemy to us, facing them man-to-man and hand-to-hand."

"Tomorrow," one of the men said, "is the Sabbath. How can we lift our weapons and fight on a day that is sacred to HaShem?"

A slow smile spread across Judah's face. "You are a newcomer?"

The man nodded.

"Then consider this," Judah said. "This Gentile Nicanor is coming to attack us on the Sabbath, and he brings renegade Jews with him. They do not respect the day HaShem set apart as holy. They are coming to destroy their brothers, and we cannot let them succeed."

A murmur of assent rippled through the group until Judah held up his hand. "As for us, we will travel to Adasa and be hidden by sunset. We will sleep on the earth, and in the morning we will stand and defend our people. And Adonai will give us the victory."

"I heard," another man called out, "that Nicanor has boasted that he will set up a monument in Jerusalem to commemorate his victory over you."

Judah crossed his arms and chuckled. "I am fully confident that Adonai will not allow that to happen. Do not fear the enemy, brothers. Remember how the Almighty has helped us in times past. He will give us the victory this time as well."

Judah continued, speaking of the battles they had already won, of the miraculous deliverance they had witnessed, and how many times they had returned without losing a single man. He lifted his hands to heaven and prayed, "Lord, when Hezekiah was king of Judah, you sent your angel who killed one hundred and eighty-five thousand of King Sennacherib's men. Once again, Lord of heaven, send your good angel to make our enemies tremble with fear. With your great power, destroy these people who have slandered you and come down to attack your chosen people."

By the time Judah had finished praying, every man present was on his feet, and even the youngest were walking as confidently as their older brothers and fathers.

Then Judah had the men form companies with their captains, and together they set out for Adasa as the sun lowered. With other women who had come to support the army, Ona, Morit, and I watched them go. Though we smiled at one another and pretended to be confident, I could not help but feel grave concern about the upcoming battle on open ground.

Chapter Sixty-Three: Judah

Once again I told my men to hide themselves in shrubs, tall grasses, and behind boulders. Only one thousand volunteers would fight with us today, but since they were what Adonai had provided, I would be content.

Sitting in the chilly air before sunrise, I remembered that the twelfth of Adar was the anniversary of Esther's fast. She and her people had been condemned to death under the proclamation of wicked Haman and all had seemed hopeless. But because she fasted, prayed, and demonstrated remarkable courage in the face of a ruthless enemy, Adonai worked through her and saved His people.

Would we be as successful as Esther?

I rolled onto my back and gazed up at the spangled heavens as I waited for morning. Dawn was already fading the night shadows, and a faint glow on the horizon revealed where the sun would soon rise.

Where were Nicanor and his men? I had heard rumors that more than nine thousand foot soldiers had arrived to reinforce his army, and for all I knew they might be only yards away from the empty tents we had set up as decoys.

I turned onto my belly when the sun spread a layer of gold on the horizon. From the hill where I lay I could see shapes stirring in the distant shadows, monstrous shapes that might be war elephants. I strained my ears and thought I heard the grumble of the huge beasts beneath the muffled tread of men shuffling into position.

I did not whistle. I had no need to alert my army because, like me, they were lying in wait, their attention focused on the plain below. The enemy was surrounding our empty camp, approaching as silently as possible on a Sabbath morning, weapons at the ready and war elephants evenly spaced among the companies.

I smiled as the shadows faded and color crept into the landscape. There they were, a splendid military array, their backs to us and their attention focused on a flat plain where no one slept.

Silently, I slid my arm through the strap

on the back of my shield and rose to a standing position, feeling the pressure of my men's eyes. I lifted the sword I won in my first battle and drew a deep breath. "For Jerusalem, the Temple, and Adonai!"

I ran forward, my shield lifted and my sword pointed at the unprotected rear of the enemy line. Behind me, my men sprang from their hiding places, all of them charging down the hill and attacking the vulnerable backs of men and horses and elephants. They had no idea what had happened. Fighting for Adonai and the lives of our people, we chased the Gentile army over the plain and scattered them like feathers in the wind.

Then I found myself face-to-face with Nicanor — I recognized him by his golden breastplate and helmet. Lifting my sword, I announced my name and told him I was about to kill him.

His upper lip curled in a snarl. "Do your worst, Hebrew dog."

With both hands I brought my sword down and cut off his right arm. He turned to look for his blade, now lying useless on the ground, and as he shifted his position in bewilderment, I swung the sword again, lopping off his head.

The men around me cheered. One pulled

the golden helmet away and lifted Nicanor's head by its long hair. "Victory for Jerusalem!" he cried, and with that phrase on our lips we chased the remainder of the army until they had all abandoned the plain.

The next day we returned to Jerusalem. The priests, who had been fearing our defeat and the burning of the Temple, were ecstatic. Now the entire city could celebrate Purim with light hearts. They offered sacrifices and waved palm branches while singing songs of praise. Wine flowed freely, and the people declared that the fourteenth of Adar would henceforth be known as the anniversary of *two* great deliverances — the repeal of Haman's murderous edict and the saving of the Temple from Nicanor.

Someone mounted Nicanor's head on a post opposite the Temple, along with his right hand, which he had raised as he uttered a blasphemous oath against the Temple of Adonai.

With the visible evidence of HaShem's victory on full display, my family and the people of Jerusalem celebrated long into the night. After wishing my men well, I went in search of Leah and found her sitting with a group of children and their mothers, holding them spellbound with her story: "And on that day, on a hillside in Lebonah, Judah and his men defeated the mighty warrior Apollonius. . . ."

I was not the only one created for a purpose.

Chapter Sixty-Four: Leah

I danced as freely as anyone when Judah and his men returned to Jerusalem. Nicanor's mounted head and hand were not merely tokens from a slain enemy, but proof of HaShem's miraculous care and protection. Judah had declared his faith in Adonai's strength, and the Lord had used one thousand men to rout nine thousand, even sending elephants into a panicked trot over the plain.

My heart had never felt so light. My husband was a warrior, a fierce protector of Adonai's people. I saw him with new eyes, and in my view he had never appeared more handsome, more manly, or more perfect.

Oh, how I loved him. With everything I had in me, with all the ardor and devotion I had yearned to feel as a girl. I asked HaShem for a man who would keep me safe, and I received a husband who would fight for me and everything he loved. Oh, how much Adonai had given me, and oh, how blind I had been in the beginning.

We returned to Modein after Adasa, though I understood it would be for only a little while. Alcimus and Bacchides were still in Judea and still fomenting unrest, so I knew we would soon be camping again with the army. But for a few days, or even a few weeks, Judah and I wanted to sleep in our little house, feed our goats, and ignore the world outside our walls.

While we were in Modein, two young men came to meet with Judah and Simon. Jason and Eupolemus seemed like good men, respectful and pious, and they made a great fuss over meeting Judah Maccabaeus. But when pressed for their real reason for seeking him, they glanced at each other before speaking.

A cold breath of foreboding shriveled my skin in the instant of that hesitation.

"We have heard talk of a people," Jason said, glancing from Judah to Simon, "who live across the Great Sea. They are not Greek — in fact, most of them seem to disdain Greeks. They are fierce and have defeated every army they faced."

"Yet they have no king," Eupolemus added. "They rule themselves because they are enlightened, tolerant, and highly civilized."

"They are governed by a group of leaders they call a *senate,*" Jason said. "They vote on important matters, and the opinion with the most votes carries the day."

Eupolemus leaned forward in eagerness. "They have conquered many nations, yet in their gracious tolerance they allow nations to worship their own gods. These people — the Romans — do not force their beliefs on other people."

Judah and Simon did not speak as the two newcomers described the Romans, but when they had finished, Simon looked at Judah. "I have heard of these people," he said. "They are indeed fierce, and were once intimidating enough to force Antiochus Epiphanes out of Egypt. Egypt had a treaty with the Romans, and a single threat from a Roman ambassador was enough to make Antiochus return to his own capital."

"Intimidating, you say." Judah fingered his beard. "These Romans . . . what do they demand of the countries who make treaties with them?"

Eupolemus pressed his hands together. "Egypt, of course, produces grain, so Rome wanted preferential access to it. Rome pays for the grain, and handsomely, but they will not let anyone attack Egypt and threaten the grain supply."

Judah's brow furrowed. "If we made a treaty with these Romans, what might they ask of us?"

Jason cleared his throat. "I do not know," he admitted. "But usually a treaty states that each nation will help the other if it is attacked by an enemy. Each side makes beneficial promises to the other, and then representatives from each sign the document."

Eupolemus smiled. "Many nations have treaties with Rome. And Israel has signed treaties in the past — remember how the people of Gibeon established a treaty with Joshua when our people entered the Promised Land?"

"The Gibeonites were liars," Simon said, smirking. "Not the best example you could give."

"We will not be deceived." Eupolemus lifted his chin. "We would like to present you with this proposal: If you agree, and if you think it a good idea, send the two of us to Rome. We will address the Senate and explain how King Demetrius has sent soldiers against us without cause. We will tell them about how our people have been threatened, tortured, and killed."

"We will make certain any proposed treaty is fair," Jason added. "And when it is signed, Israel will have access to the forces of Rome for her defense. If Demetrius sends another army against us, he will pay the price."

"He wouldn't dare send an army to Jerusalem." Eupolemus laughed. "Demetrius knows better than to interfere with a nation supported by the Roman Senate."

Judah nodded slowly, then stood. "Thank you for coming," he said. "My brother and I will discuss what you have said. And sometime tomorrow we will give you an answer."

"Do not wait too long," Jason said. "Nicanor's forces have fled to Gazara, but Demetrius could easily send a commander to lead them back to Jerusalem."

Judah nodded again. "Thank you."

When the two men had gone, Judah and Simon sat opposite each other at our table. For a long while they said nothing, and I knew they were pondering everything they had heard.

I set a cup of honey water before each man, then cleared my throat. "May I speak, husband?"

"Of course."

I shifted my weight, not certain how to phrase what I needed to say. "You have won many victories without the help of Rome. You won because you called on Adonai. So why do you need help from a foreign nation?"

The corner of Judah's mouth twisted. "The situation is not so simple, Leah. The world is changing, and every year we seem to face a new king. We keep fighting the same battles."

"On the same territory," Simon added. "The faces change, but the battles . . ."

"How many times have we fought near Beth-horon?" Judah chuckled. "We ought to build houses there."

"But," I said, "on his deathbed, your father told you to trust in no man, but in HaShem alone."

Judah's brow furrowed, yet he did not speak.

"Rome could be a great help to us." Simon rested his chin on his hand. "They have skilled soldiers, equipment, massive weapons, and great ships."

"We could allow one of their ships to anchor off the coast at Joppa." Judah crossed his arms. "Men could disembark and travel to Jerusalem in days."

"Their system of government might even work for us. We could create a senate of leaders from the priesthood and experts in religious law. Like the judges of old, they could provide judgments when a man is accused of some crime or sin. Establishing a senate or council might prevent the sort of corruption and blasphemy we've seen with the Hellenes."

I retreated into the shadows as Judah and Simon shared their ideas. Enthusiasm filled their voices while they talked of things that might be possible, and I knew they had already made their decision. Jason and Eupolemus had dangled a new toy before their eyes, and they had been distracted by it.

But nothing had been decided yet. Even if those young men left for Rome within a week, surely it would take a great deal of time for things to change.

Chapter Sixty-Five: Judah

The years of struggle taught us a lesson we should never have learned. We had seen the Gentiles' ruthlessness and the destruction of our Temple. Every time we rebuilt the walls of Jerusalem, the enemy arrived to knock them down again. We learned that as long as a pagan king ruled our land, our cities might not stand and our families might not survive.

As the commander of the army of Israel, I had to weigh our present victories against future threats. I began to think we might need human help to vanquish the Gentiles permanently. When I heard about the military might of the Romans, I wondered if Israel might benefit from having an ally. The Romans had no king, so their king would not rule over us, and they permitted their allies to worship their own gods. What harm could possibly come from an alliance with such a nation?

With every passing day I saw that the world had greatly changed since Joshua took possession of the Promised Land. He had been charged with ridding the land of the Gentiles, and though he achieved many victories and conquered many pagan cities, he had never been able to completely clear the land. Judea was still occupied by groups of Gentiles, and our world had grown smaller, making us keenly aware of the strong nations outside our borders. These empires were not content to remain in their places, but kept trying to subjugate and tax us. If we could not chase all the Gentiles from our land, how could we possibly subdue the nations who sought our land, revenue, and people?

If we did not find a friend among the nations, one day we might be completely overrun.

Simon and I agreed — we would send Eupolemus and Jason across the Great Sea. They would go to Rome to procure a treaty to bind the people of Rome to Israel as friends and allies.

With that matter settled, I turned to the enemy at hand. Bacchides and Alcimus had returned from Antioch and attacked settlers living in caves around the Sea of Galilee. The traitorous priest was now on his way to

Jerusalem with a large number of soldiers and was expected to arrive in time for Passover.

I sent Jonathan to blow the shofar and gather our army. Three thousand men joined me at a place called Eleasa. By the time we were ready to move out, we had learned that Bacchides was traveling with twenty thousand foot soldiers and two thousand horsemen. We determined to intercept them.

As we marched over the rough terrain, I realized we would not enjoy the benefit of surprise. Bacchides had to know we were coming, just as we knew he was traveling through the valley at Berzetho. Our smaller force would travel more quickly, so Bacchides would probably find a sheltered area and camp there while he waited for us.

We reached the valley at the end of the day where we built fires and hobbled our animals. Before lying down to sleep, I walked the perimeter of our camp and prayed over the three thousand men of Israel who had joined me for yet another battle.

I woke in the early hours of morning and shivered with a chill that did not come from the air. I sat up, looked at Johanan and Simon, who slept beside me, then stood to survey the camp. The sight stole my breath. Last night, three thousand men had crowded the slopes and curves of this spot. At dawn, less than one-third remained. Entire companies had vanished in the night.

I heard footsteps and knew Simon stood behind me. "Well, then," he said, his voice dry. "We are not what we were."

I tucked my hands into my armpits to warm them. "No."

"Remember what you told the men at Beth-horon? That what mattered was not the size of the army but the strength of our God?"

Shivering, I nodded.

"Don't forget that, brother."

Simon walked away, whistling, and I stood alone to face the men, who were waking in a vastly depleted army.

I walked back to wake Johanan and Jonathan, then pulled a small loaf from a leather pouch Leah had sent with me. The women had remained behind on this trip, and I was glad my wife did not have to see that so many in the army of Israel had lost their faith . . . in me.

Why? We had been outnumbered before. We had faced far worse generals than Bacchides. We had always depended on Adonai for our victory. What had changed? The question troubled me as I climbed a pile of rocks and looked over the valley. In the foreground, my men were stirring; many looked around with astonished faces.

"Gather round, men," I called as more of them awoke. I tried to sound confident, but I couldn't escape a sense of despair.

They came toward me, and the same thought seemed to be uppermost in every soldier's mind. "Judah," one man called, "we can't fight today."

His voice was the forerunner of many more to come.

"Not like this — we are too small a number."

"We can easily retreat into the mountains. Travel farther south and attack Bacchides closer to Jerusalem."

"Where's the enemy going to go? He won't reach Jerusalem for days. We can go back and gain the high ground."

"We should retreat."

"Not today, Judah. We are only a few hundred."

"Eight hundred." Jonathan's authoritative voice silenced the others. "I count eight hundred men."

I drew a deep breath. "Brothers," I began, "far be it from us to do such a thing as to flee from the enemy. We came here to fight the Gentiles, and that is what we will do. And if our time has come, let us die manfully for our brethren, and let us not stain our honor. We will not retreat. We will not shrink back from the task before us. We have never given up, so how could we begin now?"

We had never given up, and we had never asked for outside help. Despite this fact, I sent two men to Rome looking for help, *trusting in* the Romans, a pagan people who neither knew nor worshiped HaShem, the Creator of all.

Leah had tried to point out my folly and I had not listened.

I sank to my knees, my head bowed beneath the crushing weight of guilt. "Adonai, forgive me for looking to anyone but you. I confess that I am guilty of placing my trust in the armies of Rome when you are all we have ever needed. Forgive me, Adonai, and do not judge these faithful men for my sin."

Rising to face the morning sun, with resignation I drew my sword and pointed to the hills where the enemy waited on the high ground.

The army of Bacchides marched out from their camp and took its stand for the encounter. The general had divided his cavalry into two companies, one on the east and one on the west. His slingers and archers stood at the front of the line, as did his chief warriors.

My men and I studied the opposing formation as we had many times before. My swordsmen knelt as our archers — only about seventy-five men, by my count — nocked their arrows and raised their bows. Behind them, our horsemen studied the field, alert to any movements at the flanks. Bacchides had enough riders to send an entire company to our rear, if he chose to do so. If they managed to get behind us, we would be trapped between two opposing lines, leaving us no way of escape.

I sat astride my favorite stallion. The horse pawed the ground and nickered. "Easy, boy," I murmured, patting his flank. "We'll move soon enough."

From his position on his right wing, Bacchides sat astride a handsome horse. He wore heavy black armor and a helmet on which purple plumes fluttered with every movement.

"I'd wager he's coming straight for you," Johanan said, nodding toward Bacchides.

"And Alcimus?"

"He's in his tent praying, of course." Johanan's mouth twisted in a wry grin. "I don't expect him to spend much time in the actual fight. He's all glory and no guts, right?"

I snorted. "Right."

The morning quiet shattered as the trumpeters sounded the charge. Flanked by two companies, Bacchides's phalanx began to advance. The general drew his sword and pointed it at us.

"That's it!" I yelled, looking down the line. "Move out!"

My stallion leapt forward at the touch of my heels. I remained steady on his back, my eyes focused on the armored general. Hundreds of riders thundered toward us, churning the dusty earth, and I knew we were at a distinct disadvantage. But our spearmen knew how to unseat a rider by aiming at his mount, so we ought to have those riders on the ground within a few moments.

Since Bacchides and his best warriors were on the right, I rode in that direction, bringing my stouthearted men with me. Fighting with all we had in us, we crushed the right wing and pursued them as far as Mount Azotus of the Great Sea. When those on Bacchides's left wing realized that the right wing had been decimated, they changed directions and followed me and my men.

The battle became desperate, and many on both sides were wounded and fell.

I remained focused on Bacchides, but he had surrounded himself with skilled men. Clutching my reins with my left hand, I wielded my sword with my right, thrusting and blocking, slicing and blocking. I had to eliminate many before I could reach the general.

I was fighting a one-eyed warrior with a long blade when I felt a rope around my neck. I released the reins and struggled to keep pressure off my throat, but someone at the other end jerked me backward, neatly unseating me. I found myself on the ground as my stallion galloped away. I threw the rope off almost immediately, then whirled around to see who had taken me by surprise.

A small man stood a few steps away, his face crinkled in a wide grin. He seemed to have no concerns as he reeled in his rope and wound it in a circle. I lifted my sword, expecting him to fight. Instead he shrugged and stepped aside for one of his brothers-in-arms.

That had been the point — to get me on the ground. I found myself at the center of a knot of warriors, each of them armored and armed. One of them put his fingers in his mouth and whistled, and before I knew it the knot had enlarged to eight men, all of whom had their attention set on me.

The last man to arrive wore splendid black armor and a plumed helmet, which he removed so that I could see his face.

Bacchides.

"Tell me if I'm wrong," said the general, "but aren't you Judah Maccabaeus?"

I raised the point of my sword to the level of his eyes. "I am."

"Ah, boys, we have won," Bacchides said with a smile. "We end it all by ending this one."

While I circled carefully, keeping my eye on the general, someone sliced the back of my knee. I felt warm blood dripping over my skin, though I did not turn.

"That's one," Bacchides said. "For Apollonius, the first general you killed."

I grunted. "He would still be alive if he hadn't come against Israel."

The general took another step to the right. I turned and felt a matching slice across the back of the other knee — but this one went deeper, for something in my leg gave way.

"Two," he said. "That was for Gorgias."

I gritted my teeth against the pain. "That blind fool? Gorgias marched past us in the dead of night, and our God would not let him see us."

I raised my left arm to balance the weight of my sword, then I heard a blade sing as it cleaved the air. I felt pressure at my uplifted arm, and when I turned to look, it was gone. "Ahhh!" I couldn't stop a scream as the sight of a spurting stump sent a tremor down my spine.

"Three." My tormenter smiled. "For Nicanor."

"That blasphemer?" Breathing through clenched teeth, I forbade myself to falter. This would be over soon enough.

The general slipped to the left, moving as lightly as a dancer. "You have fought well, Judah Maccabaeus, but your time is over. You and your people must realize Judea is about to change."

One of the men behind me stepped forward and severed my sword hand with a hatchet. I stared numbly at my hand — lying on the ground a few inches from the sword I had used for HaShem's glory.

"Four," Bacchides said more softly. "For Lysias. And this" — he brought his heavy sword up to my eyes and then shifted it until the blade was at my neck — "is for me."

I lowered my head. Oddly enough I felt no fear or sorrow, only a single regret — that I would die looking at this pagan and not at Leah.

He drew back his arm, gathered his strength, and swung.

Chapter Sixty-Six: Leah

I knew the truth before they told me. I could hear it in the sound of the wind blowing low and forlorn over the plain, and feel it in the way my heart slowed when I stepped outside and faced the rising sun. I saw it in the raven circling endlessly overhead, and in the deer that stopped and stared at me with wide, compassionate eyes.

My Judah no longer lived.

The villagers who returned from the battle avoided my gaze as they trudged back to their homes. Ona, Morit, and Neta looked at me with sympathy, for they had also intuited the truth.

I straightened my spine, pulled my cloak tight against a sudden chill, and went to the well to wait. As I watched our battered men returning, I wondered how I would tell this story. Most of my stories about the heroic Maccabees ended in victory.

Finally, Simon, Johanan, and Jonathan

came through the village gate. They huddled for a moment, then Jonathan and Johanan went to their wives. Simon came toward me, Morit hurrying after him.

My knees turned to water, and only the solid stones beneath me kept me from collapsing. Simon must have seen something in my eyes, for he caught my arm and turned to Morit. She stepped up and put her arms around my shoulders, holding tight as Simon gave me the news I dreaded: "Judah was killed today."

Those four little words seemed to hang on the air, then they vanished, leaving a trail of grief in their wake. I shook my head, not wanting to believe them. What small words they were! They were nothing compared to the power Judah had wielded, and they meant nothing compared to the man he had been: champion, commander, chief encourager. He motivated, inspired, and led by example. He taught his people to believe in the impossible, and he challenged them to do more than they ever dreamed they could. His name shone so brightly, even in the halls of his enemies, that those four little words could not possibly dim his luster.

"Leah, are you all right?" Simon studied me as Morit continued to hold me. "Would you like to lie down?"

I gave Simon a blank look, wondering why he was so concerned about whether I stood or reclined. Why did such things matter now? Judah was gone.

My husband had been everything my father was not: truth and loyalty and love. My lover, protector, and friend. My priest and king.

I met Simon's gaze and saw the gleam of tears in his eyes. "Thank you for telling me," I said, attempting a smile. "I think I will go inside now."

By sunset, Judah's body had been returned to his family. We women stitched him back together, washed and anointed him, and prepared his shroud. But before we wrapped his body, I stroked the scar I had put on his face and felt tears burn my fingers like hot wax. This was not Judah. It was only a vessel that had once housed one of the brightest lights in all Israel.

I leaned closer, though I knew he was not listening from this empty husk. "You once told me that HaShem had never sent you to do anything. But He sent you to save me, Judah. In so many ways."

I ran my fingers through his damp hair, then unfolded the linen cloth that would cover his face. When I stepped back, the other women lifted the shroud and respectfully wrapped his body.

We buried Judah next to his unnamed son in the family tomb.

Then all Israel mourned him, saying, "How is the mighty fallen, the savior of Israel!"

Morit and Ona did not want to leave me alone, but I insisted. Their husbands needed tending after the day's defeat, and I had never been afraid of solitude.

As the members of my family promised to come at once if I should need anything, I bade them good-night and stepped out into the gathering darkness. I unlatched the door and dropped my cloak on the bed, then felt my way to the table in the corner of the room. I lit the lamp and sat on the edge of the bed. "Adonai, what am I to do now?"

My voice echoed in the emptiness as my eyes traveled over so many ordinary sights, made ghostly in the lamp's flickering light. Judah's sandals in the corner. His cloak on a peg in the wall. Dark hairs on his pillow.

The resolve that had held me upright all day snapped and I fell over onto the bed as grief erupted within me. "My God, my God," I cried, "why did you forsake him?"

But even as I said the words, I knew

Adonai had never left my husband. HaShem created him to be a warrior and gave him a warrior's death. How could He have done anything else?

I sat up, wiped my face, and stared at the practice shield Judah had hung on the wall. Eneas had been using it, trying his best to emulate his father's friend.

"A little Judah," I whispered. "But no one can ever take his place."

I lifted my face toward heaven. "What are we to do, Adonai? I do not understand why you have taken Judah when we need him most —"

A reluctant smile twisted my mouth, for when had we not needed the Hammerhead?

In the silence I heard the answer:

He is not gone . . . as long as his story lives.

This time I knew Who put the words in my mind.

I tilted my head, listening for more, and heard nothing but the murmur of voices outside the house. Friends, family, and warriors who had come for the burial were saying their farewells. They would mourn Judah's loss, and his men, even his brothers, would for a while be like sheep without a shepherd.

But Judah would continue to live through

his story, and I would faithfully tell it. He could continue to lead his men through his example. And as long as his story lived, the people of Israel could take courage and know that Adonai had not neglected them.

I knew I would mourn deeply and for a long time, but Judah had not left me alone. He had introduced me to HaShem, who had never been more than an angry figurehead to me until Judah showed me that Adonai listened, cared, and acted on behalf of His people. Judah also taught me that a single person, when inspired by HaShem and committed to the task for which Adonai had formed him, could change the world.

So I would tell his story. "With my dying breath, Adonai, I will tell them everything."

Then I stretched out on Judah's side of the bed, because I could not bear to lie across from that empty space.

Epilogue

Leah kept her promise to the Lord Adonai. She became a source of strength for the remaining brothers and often traveled with the army, doing whatever had to be done in the fight for freedom. When the battle was not raging, she told the people of Israel everything she and Judah had learned. Eneas, who became her surrogate son, traveled with her and grew to become an outstanding advocate for Israel's freedom.

From 161 BC, the year of Judah's death, to 155 BC, Bacchides continued his campaign of persecution, but his target shifted from pious Jews to Judah's family. The Hasmonean name had become so identified with the cause of national and religious freedom that the Seleucids sought to stamp it out.

One by one, Judah's brothers gave their lives for Israel: after Eleazar and Judah, then Johanan, Jonathan, and Simon.

The year after Judah's death, Jonathan was chosen as Israel's high priest and leader. He led the nation for eighteen years, and only after he was murdered in 142 BC did Simon assume that position. He served as high priest for seven years, until he and two of his sons were murdered by his treacherous son-in-law. Simon's wife was also brutally murdered.

All five of Mattathias's sons gave their lives while working and fighting for the nation of Israel. Judah and Eleazar died on the battlefield. Johanan, Jonathan, and Simon were murdered by treacherous foes. But because of their sacrifice, the tiny nation of Israel united in fidelity and faith, clearing its Temple of all pagan abominations. Because Judah Maccabaeus and his courageous brothers sacrificed their lives, Israel was finally able to enjoy religious liberty and, for a brief period, political independence.

AUTHOR'S NOTE

I sent a proposal about the so-called "silent years" to my publisher because I didn't know much about the four hundred years between the Old and New Testaments. For me, half the fun of writing a book is learning new things. I was thrilled to discover Judah (or Judas) Maccabees, whose name had only stirred a vague memory before I began writing. What a hero!

Readers always want to know how much of a historical novel is fact, so here's the scoop. The battles described in this book are factual. The male figures in Mattathias's family are historic. The women, however, are shadows, unmentioned in the history books.

But Mattathias certainly had a wife, and his five sons probably had wives, so I fleshed out and named those forgotten women, including Leah, Judah's wife.

Many of the battles and events have been

condensed, and other events have been omitted in order to write a novel of readable length. As the author of 1 Maccabees tells us, "Now the rest of the acts of Judas, and his wars and the brave deeds that he did, and his greatness, have not been recorded, for they were very many" (1 Maccabees 9:22).

The first paragraph of the Epilogue is fiction, but all the other paragraphs are historical facts.

Those horrible accounts of torture by Antiochus Epiphanes? Historic and recorded in the First and Second books of the Maccabees. These books are part of the Apocrypha, which are not part of the canon of Scripture. But though they are not considered *inspired,* they are historic and should not be summarily discounted.

Philander, the sympathetic scribe who worked in the court of Antiochus Epiphanes, is fictional. I added him because I needed the viewpoint of a character who knew what was happening in the royal court. But many of his letters contain information found in 1 Maccabees, including the king's deathbed letter to the Jews.

Below are a few odds and ends you might find interesting:

Q: What happened to those old stones from the profaned altar?

A: "So we placed the stones in a chamber at the northwest corner of the altar court, in the great gatehouse called Moked, there to remain until a prophet should arise."

The stones of the desecrated altar remained in that gatehouse through the time of Christ until AD 70 when the Romans destroyed Jerusalem and the Temple. The prophet with the necessary authority (Yeshua/Jesus) came but was not recognized, so the stones of the original altar were scattered with the other stones of the Temple. They are now lost to us.

Q: Who were the Hasidim?

A: The Hasidim (aka Hasideans or Chasidism) were Jews who were loyal to the Law of Moses and the Torah. The name derives from the Hebrew word *hasi dim,* usually translated "saints" or "faithful ones." They were active during the time of the Maccabean Revolt, but then disappeared from the historical record, probably because they were absorbed into either the Pharisees or Essenes, later groups that existed along with the Sadducees.

What sort of Judaism did Judah and his family practice? I believe it was similar to that practiced by the Karaites, Jews who believe that the original religion of ancient Israel is prescribed by God in the Bible or *Tanakh.* Unlike most contemporary Jews, Karaites do not accept the *Mishnah* or *Talmud* as the basis for religious law and theology because those works were derived from various rabbis and oral tradition. The Karaites cite Deut. 4:2 and Joshua 8:34–35 as part of the basis for their belief. Karaism (or Qaraism) began in the first or second century before Christ, the time of the Maccabees, and still exists today.

Q: Did Judah really have prophetic dreams?

A: I doubt it. I included three in the story because supernatural elements need to be established as part of the story world if they are going to be credible. The last vision — the one about Onias and Jeremiah — has been recorded in some versions of the battle at Adasa, but it is not mentioned in 1 Maccabees, so it is probably an apocryphal addition.

Q: I'm confused by the Levites and priests, as well as the high priests from the line of Zadok and Aaron.

A: The priestly lineage can be confusing! The Levites were men from the tribe of Levi. They were considered lower in status than the priests, and they were not permitted to offer sacrifices. Four senior Levites served in the Temple: the director of music, the director of singers, the chief doorkeeper, and the director of Temple assistants. The Temple police (a group of them arrested Jesus in the Garden of Gethsemane) were also Levites.[1] Every priest was a Levite, but not every Levite was a priest.

The high priests were descendants of Aaron, the brother of Moses. In 1 Chronicles 24, we read that the two surviving sons of Aaron produced the *kohanim* priests. Jehoiarib (or Joarib) was one of those priests, and Mat-

1. Du Rand, J. A. "Groups in Jewish National Life in the New Testament Period." *The New Testament Milieu.* Ed. A. B. du Toit. Vol. 2. Halfway House: Orion Publishers, 1998.

tathias and his sons were among his descendants.

Under the Seleucid kings (who cared nothing about following the hereditary line), the office of high priest went to the highest bidder. During the time of the Romans, the high priest was appointed by the Roman prefect or governor. The powerful high priest was very nearly, but not quite, a king.

Q: Are any events of the "silent years" foretold in the Old Testament?

A: Yes. Antiochus Epiphanes and the suffering he caused in Israel are described in Daniel 11:29–35. I won't quote it all here, but I will quote one of my favorite snippets: ". . . but the people who know their God will stand strong and prevail" (Daniel 11:32b). That verse could apply to any believer anywhere.

Q: Why didn't you mention the miracle of oil at Hanukkah?

A: Because it *probably* did not occur. It is not mentioned in the books of 1 or 2 Maccabees, nor is it mentioned in Josephus's history of the Maccabean Revolt. The story does not appear anywhere until the Talmudic period, which occurred about six hundred years later.

The traditional story is based on this Talmudic commentary:

> For when the Greeks entered the Temple, they defiled all the oils therein, and when the Hasmonean dynasty prevailed against and defeated them, they made search and found only one cruse of oil which lay with the seal of the High Priest, but which contained sufficient for one day's lighting only; yet a miracle was wrought therein and they lit [the lamp] therewith for eight days. The following year these [days] were appointed a Festival with [the recital of] Hallel and thanksgiving.[2]

The first mention of the "miracle of oil" is found in a single gemara, a rabbinical commentary on the *Mishna,* forming the second part of the Talmud.

2. http://dafaleph.com/home/2015/12/8/the-historicity-of-the-miracle-of-oil, accessed January 31, 2017.

It is not found in the Jewish Bible, the *Tanakh.*

The following opinion may be valid:

"Whatever the reason, the so-called miracle of oil was invented long after the first Hanukkah, probably as a children's story, by rabbis who needed to find a way to make the existing commemoration of Hanukkah into something that meshed with their own theology . . .

"With that they downplayed the forced conversions, the brutal attacks against Hellenized Jews by the Maccabees, and the war itself.

"And now Hanukkah is the 'Festival of Lights,' even though no miracle of oil ever really happened."[3]

I include this information not to attack a much-loved Jewish tradition, but simply to be faithful to the historical record. After all, many Christians

3. http://failedmessiah.typepad.com/failed_messiahcom/2012/12/blinded-by-the-lights-you-could-easily-miss-the-true-meaning-of-hanukkah-789.html, accessed January 31, 2017.

believe that the angels sang at Christ's birth (Scripture says they spoke, not sang), that Mary rode to Bethlehem on a donkey (she probably didn't, as the donkey would have been carrying water and supplies), and that the wise men arrived the night of the child's birth (they probably came much later, as Scripture says the child was no longer in the stable, but in a house). Apocryphal stories tend to attach themselves to history, but my job as a historical novelist is to adhere to the facts as closely as I can.

The *real* miracle of Hanukkah has nothing to do with oil and everything to do with how a ragtag group led by Judah Maccabaeus defeated one of the finest armies in the world and reclaimed the holy Temple.

Q: Who actually wrote 1 and 2 Maccabees?

A: No one knows. No original text, which was written in Hebrew, survives, but scholars believe the book was first written in 100 BC. In this story I do not intend to seriously suggest that Judah's wife was the original storyteller, but since we have no way of knowing how the story came to be recorded, perhaps she could have been.

I hope you have enjoyed the story of Judah Maccabaeus as much as I did.

DISCUSSION QUESTIONS

1. As Leah contemplates marriage, her mother says: "But here I am, and there you are, safe and untouched by brutality."

   Was Leah really "untouched" by her father's brutality? How does harshness and abuse affect children? How can this problem affect generations to come?

2. Hunt says that she created Judah as a Christ-figure. He gives his life not only for his bride, but for his people, and he takes a brave stand against evil. He bears scars from his sufferings, and he loves unconditionally. He wants to lead his people, his wife, and his family, but his wife does not always want to be led.

   In what ways do you see Judah as a Christ-figure? Do you see weaknesses in the metaphor?

3. Leah wants a husband who will do what

she wants him to do — in other words, obey her and stop being a warrior. Should she have asked this of him? Why or why not?

4. How much did you know about the Maccabees before reading *Judah's Wife*?

5. What did you think about Judah's visions? The Jewish people have been persecuted through the ages, and Israel is still under constant threat. Have the Jews always defended themselves? Will they defend themselves in the future?

6. Have you read the other novels in THE SILENT YEARS series? How did this book compare to the others?

7. Do you prefer contemporary or historical fiction? What do you like most about historical fiction? Would you rather read about a period you know well (for example, the Civil War) or one you know little about?

8. Did Leah have a right to feel neglected in her marriage? What could Judah have done to ease her feelings?

9. Who was your favorite character and why?

10. Judah took steps that ultimately resulted in Rome's involvement in Jewish politics and government. How did the people of Israel benefit from the treaty with Rome? How did they suffer for it? Why do you think God allowed this affiliation?

11. What lessons or memories will you take away from this story? Would you recommend the book to a friend?

REFERENCES

——. *The Researchers Library of Ancient Texts, Volume I: The Apocrypha.* Crane, MO: Defender, 2011.

Brisco, Thomas V. *Holman Bible Atlas.* Nashville, TN: Broadman & Holman Publishers, 1998.

Conder, Claude Reignier. *Judah Maccabaeus and the Jewish War of Independence.* A.P. Watt and Son, 1894.

Easton, M. G. *Easton's Bible Dictionary,* 1893.

Edersheim, Alfred. *The Life and Times of Jesus the Messiah.* Vol. 2. New York: Longmans, Green, and Co., 1896.

Edersheim, Alfred. *The Temple, Its Ministry and Services as They Were at the Time of Jesus Christ.* London: James Clarke & Co., 1959.

Elwell, Walter A., and Philip Wesley Comfort. *Tyndale Bible Dictionary,* 2001, 440.

Fischer, Thomas. "Maccabees, Books of: First and Second Maccabees." Ed. David Noel Freedman. Trans. Frederick Cryer. *The Anchor Yale Bible Dictionary,* 1992, 440–450.

Fruchtenbaum, Arnold G. *The Messianic Bible Study Collection.* Vol. 24. Tustin, CA: Ariel Ministries, 1983.

Hall, Robert G. "Circumcision." Ed. David Noel Freedman. *The Anchor Yale Bible Dictionary,* 1992, 1025–1031.

Harrington, Daniel J. *The Maccabean Revolt: Anatomy of a Biblical Revolution.* Eugene, OR: Wipe and Stock Publishers, 2009.

Harrop, Clayton. "Intertestamental History and Literature." Ed. Chad Brand et al. *Holman Illustrated Bible Dictionary,* 2003, 831–832.

Josephus, Flavius, and William Whiston. *The Works of Josephus: Complete and Unabridged.* Peabody: Hendrickson, 1987.

Myers, Allen C. *The Eerdmans Bible Dictionary,* 1987, 674–676.

Pfeiffer, Charles F. *The Wycliffe Bible Commentary: Old Testament.* Chicago: Moody Press, 1962.

Redditt, Paul L., Professor of OT, Georgetown College, Georgetown, KY, and Fischer, Thomas. "Maccabees, Books of:

First and Second Maccabees." Ed. David Noel Freedman. Trans. Frederick Cryer. *The Anchor Yale Bible Dictionary,* 1992, 439–454.

Surburg, Raymond F. *Introduction to the Intertestamental Period.* St. Louis: Concordia Publishing House, 1975.

Toews, Wesley I. "Beth-Zur." Ed. David Noel Freedman. *The Anchor Yale Bible Dictionary,* 1992, 701–702.

VanderKam, James C. *From Joshua to Caiaphas: High Priests After the Exile.* Augsburg Fortress Press, 2004.

Walls, A. F. "Maccabees." Ed. D. R. W. Wood, et al. *New Bible Dictionary,* 1996, 709–711.

Youngblood, Ronald F., F. F. Bruce, and R. K. Harrison, eds. *Nelson's New Illustrated Bible Dictionary.* Nelson, 1995.

ABOUT THE AUTHOR

Angela Hunt has published more than one hundred books, with sales nearing five million copies worldwide. She's the *New York Times* bestselling author of *The Tale of Three Trees, The Note,* and *The Nativity Story.* Angela's novels have won or been nominated for several prestigious industry awards, such as the RITA Award, the Christy Award, the ECPA Christian Book Award, and the HOLT Medallion Award. Romantic Times Book Club presented her with a Lifetime Achievement Award in 2006. She holds both a doctorate in Biblical Studies and a Th.D. degree. Angela and her husband live in Florida, along with their mastiffs. For a complete list of the author's books, visit angelahuntbooks.com.

The employees of Thorndike Press hope you have enjoyed this Large Print book. All our Thorndike, Wheeler, and Kennebec Large Print titles are designed for easy reading, and all our books are made to last. Other Thorndike Press Large Print books are available at your library, through selected bookstores, or directly from us.

For information about titles, please call:
(800) 223-1244

or visit our website at:
gale.com/thorndike

To share your comments, please write:
Publisher
Thorndike Press
10 Water St., Suite 310
Waterville, ME 04901